Maggie Mason is a pseudonym of author Mary Wood. Mary began her career by self-publishing on Kindle, where many of her sagas reached number one in genre. She was spotted by Pan Macmillan and to date has written many books for them under her own name, with more to come.

Mary continues to be proud to write for Pan Macmillan, but is now equally proud and thrilled to take up a second career with Sphere under the name of Maggie Mason.

Born the thirteenth child of fifteen children, Mary describes her childhood as poor, but rich in love. She was educated at St Peter's RC School in Hinckley and at Hinckley College for Further Education, where she was taught shorthand and typing.

Mary retired from working for the National Probation Service in 2009, when she took up full-time writing, something she'd always dreamed of doing. She follows in the footsteps of her great-grandmother, Dora Langlois, who was an acclaimed author, playwright and actress in the late nineteenth–early twentieth century.

It was her work with the Probation Service that gives Mary's writing its grittiness, her need to tell it how it is, which takes her readers on an emotional journey to the heart of issues.

A
Mother's
Hope

MAGGIE MASON

SPHERE

SPHERE

First published in Great Britain in 2025 by Sphere

1 3 5 7 9 10 8 6 4 2

A CIP catalogue record for this book is available from the British Library.

ISBN 978-1-4087-3212-0

Typeset in Bembo by Hewer Text UK Ltd, Edinburgh
Printed and bound in Great Britain by Clays Ltd, Elcograf S.p.A.

Papers used by Sphere are from well-managed forests
and other responsible sources.

Sphere
An imprint of
Little, Brown Book Group
Carmelite House
50 Victoria Embankment
London
EC4Y 0DZ

The authorised representative
in the EEA is
Hachette Ireland
8 Castlecourt Centre
Dublin 15, D15 XTP3, Ireland
(email: info@hbgi.ie)

An Hachette UK Company
www.hachette.co.uk

www.littlebrown.co.uk

For Idris Jones, whose name was given to one of my characters by his daughter, Glendys Parker, a lovely and valued reader.

Thank you. I honour your dad with this dedication to his memory, with my love.

PART ONE

Deception
1914–1915

CHAPTER ONE

Beads of sweat stood out on Maddie's forehead as she bent over the sink full of steaming hot, soapy water.

Brushing away a stray curl, her brow creased with worry as she prayed that Reggie wouldn't be accepted for the army. She'd pleaded with him not to volunteer, but he'd joined his pals swaggering through the streets to the recruitment office, to the cheers of the crowds that had gathered, and the tears of loved ones begging them not to go.

Wiping her face on her pinny, she sighed.

Washing endless pots was her least favourite job of all those she had to do as she helped her widowed ma run their six-bed boarding house, Fosters House, which stood on Albert Road in Blackpool.

But each morning during the tense wait to hear if Reggie had been accepted, this chore had been a help. Pots and pans could be banged about without others being alerted to your stress. And the sound of the knives and forks being dropped into the jug of boiling water somehow soothed her.

Seventeen-year-old Maddie, who looked so like her ma with her dark hair rolled back and held in combs off her face, her hazel eyes and delicate features, loved Reggie and had done all her life, as they'd lived next door to each other from birth.

As children, that had been in the small town of Preesall, just a few miles from Blackpool. Their homes were in a row of cottages built for the men working in the salt mine – until that fateful day, five years ago, when the mine had caved in, burying both their das under a mound of shifting salt.

Their devastated mas had eked out a living on parish relief money, often pooling what they had, until compensation was awarded and they'd taken the huge step of buying adjourning boarding houses.

To Maddie, Reggie's ma was Aunt Jean, as her ma was Aunt Sal – short for Sally – to Reggie. They were a family, only lately her and Reggie's relationship had deepened to more than the sisterly–brotherly friendship they'd always had.

It had started a few weeks back. They'd been to the pictures and had walked to the prom. As the tide was out, they'd gone onto the sand and messed around. She'd tripped and Reggie had caught her. He'd held her longer than was necessary and then had kissed her. She'd liked the sensation, but it had unsettled her. Now she was confused. Everything was moving very fast, and she couldn't stop it without causing hurt.

Ma and Aunt Jean had picked up on everything being different between her and Reggie, and were thrilled.

4

'Eeh, Maddie, me little lass,' Ma had said, 'you and Reggie are made for one another. Me and Aunt Jean have allus said so.'

Another sigh caught in Maddie's throat as strong arms came around her. She hadn't heard the kitchen door opening. Her heart sank as she leant back into Reggie and heard the crackle of paper.

Turning in his arms, she saw the brown envelope sticking out of his shirt pocket. His grin couldn't have been wider – it lit his blue-green eyes as his handsome face shone with happiness and excitement. 'I've been accepted, Maddie!'

Tears ran down her face, and anger knotted her breast. She wanted to shout at him, *You're breaking my heart, and all you can do is grin!* But she yielded to him pulling her closer and laid her head where she could hear his beating heart.

'Aw, Maddie, love, I've got to do this. Them Germans must be beaten, and we're the boys to do it … Like the sergeant told us, "You men will turn into soldiers. You'll fight for your country, your families, and for your own futures too."' Reggie's body straightened. Pride shone from him. 'I'm doing it for you, Maddie, and me ma and Aunt Sal, and aye, for me da an' all.' His eyes filled with tears as he finished with, 'By, he'd be proud of me, you knaw.'

With this, Maddie clung to him, wanting now to give comfort, and to do as she'd read in the newspapers not long after the declaration of war in August: *The women left behind will be called upon to support their men, and to help keep this great country of ours going.*

'Eeh, Reggie, I'm proud of you an' all. We can't help but win with the Blackpudlians fighting!'

'Let's marry before I go, Maddie. I want to truly make you mine, lass.'

'But . . . Reggie! We've only just—'

'You love me, don't you? Eeh, Maddie, lass, you're me girl and allus have been. We don't have to wait . . . I don't want to wait . . . I love you, Maddie . . . And you love me.'

Confused, Maddie sought an answer that wouldn't sound as if she was unsure of her love for Reggie. 'Will we have time?'

'Aye, we will. We can have our wedding afore I leave. We've been told that we'll go next week to Aldershot – that's somewhere down south – and then be home in six weeks and will be given three weeks and two days' leave before going overseas . . . Eeh, I can't imagine what it's going to be like. I've only ever seen the Blackpool area!'

'But—'

'Aw, lass, no buts. I love you with all me heart, and I want you as me bride when I go. It'll be grand. I've got it all planned. As soon as I get home, we post the banns, and then we marry the day before I go back to barracks . . . For one night, you'll be me bride, but that memory will keep me going, as will knowing that you're me own little lass.'

All doubts left Maddie as his lips came onto hers and she lost herself in the lovely feeling of this different Reggie. He was everything to her and always had been. She loved him.

When they came out of the kiss, Reggie said, 'I've to go and tell me ma. She'll be thrilled. She's allus said me and

6

you would end up together. Though I ain't sure how she'll be about me letter. She'll be upset, I reckon, but she's allus stood by me decisions.'

'Shall I come with you?'

'Naw. It's best I tell her on me own, but then when you've got your break later, shall we go into town and get your ring? . . . A wedding ring, I mean. I knaw it should be an engagement ring first, but that'll come later as I've only enough money for one.'

Nodding her head, Maddie's face stretched into a wide grin as she said, 'Yes, oh, yes, and by, me lad, I can't believe it. Me and you getting wed!'

A shyness came over her then, as the implications of them being married hit her.

Since that first kiss, Reggie had gone further, touching and caressing her in places he shouldn't, but she hadn't stopped him. Not straight away. She'd enjoyed it and had discovered feelings she'd had no idea she could feel – she had longed for more even. But along with all of that, she'd had a niggly feeling of being unsure . . . *Oh, God, that will happen now. I'll be Reggie's wife and* . . . Her thoughts set up mixed feelings – fear, embarrassment – but she couldn't deny the longing deep inside her.

Reggie's eyes clouded. In a low and husky voice, he said, 'I'm not sure I can wait till we're married to . . . well, you knaw, lass.'

His kiss told her what he meant. It flamed the feelings she had, but then a now familiar doubt crept in, and she eased herself away from the feel of his desire.

'We – we must, Reggie. It ain't right. You knaw that.'

7

And yet as she said the words, it puzzled her as to why she always had this need to hold back. She loved Reggie, she did. So why? Why did something niggle at her when they became as close as they were now?

Feeling his disappointment, she made a joke as she turned and picked up the tea towel and wafted it at him. 'Eeh, lad, this ain't getting the dishes done. Go and tell your ma that you're going, and then see if she's got time to come round so we can tell me ma and her together what our plans are, eh?'

'Ha! Cooling me off again! Eeh, Maddie, it'll be good when you don't have to do that, lass. I want that day so much.'

He moved towards her.

Ducking her hands in the now much cooler water, Maddie splashed him. 'There, that should help!'

They both burst out laughing as a blob of soap suds landed on the end of Reggie's nose.

Then Reggie shocked her as he grabbed her from behind and his hand came onto her breast. Suddenly, he seemed to have changed from the caring Reggie who respected her to someone wanting to get a cheap thrill, every time he was with her.

Twisting in his arms and displacing his hand, she said, 'Reggie! No!'

His look was that of a hurt child. 'But you like that, lass. We've been doing it a lot lately.'

'I – I . . . Look, it's different when I'm not working, and we've been out together.' She didn't say that even then she had doubts and that they held her back. 'Anyroad, me ma

8

might come in at any moment, and I'm in me pinny ... Oh, I don't knaw ... I just don't want to spoil things.'

Reggie hung his head. 'Sorry, lass. I were out of order. It's just ... well, the excitement and everything.'

Softening, Maddie told him. 'Later, eh? We'll go for a walk tonight and ... well, you knaw.'

'Eeh, me little lass.'

As he turned, Reggie opened the door to the hallway and called out to her ma, 'See you in a mo, Aunt Sal. I'm just going to fetch me ma round.'

Maddie clung on to the edge of the sink, trying to get her thoughts to calm, but almost immediately Ma opened the kitchen door. 'What was all that about, lass? Why's Reggie fetching Aunt Jean? Mornings are a busy time for us all, we've naw time for chatting. We've the beds to make and ... Eeh, love, what's that grin about?'

'I'm just happy, Ma ... Well, not altogether happy.' It wasn't her doubts that made her hesitate. Her grin had been because they had suddenly gone. But now mixed feelings entered her as the thought came to her that Reggie was going to war!

Shaking this from her, she said, 'Anyroad, Reggie will tell you later. But aw, you needn't worry, Ma, Aunt Jean won't drop everything even if Reggie begs her. Anyway, I've just finished the dishes, I'll leave them to drain and nip upstairs. I'll soon have the beds done, while you do the sinks and the bathroom, how's that?'

'I've one more table in the dining room to set up for the evening meal and then I'll be up, lass. But eeh, I expected more tears than smiles, as Reggie told me the other day

9

that he'd passed his medical. You do knaw what that means, don't you, lass?'

Maddie straightened from where she'd bent to retrieve the basket that contained all they'd need for getting the upstairs spick and span – dusters, scouring powder for the sinks and their mainstay, bleach tablets. Once more her eyes filled with tears and as she nodded, one escaped and trickled down her cheek.

'Aw, lass, come here.'

Enclosed in her ma's arms, Maddie's emotions broke. Sobs racked her body.

'There, there, lass. I'll help you through it . . . Anyroad, it might not be for long. Our boys'll soon sort that Kaiser's lot out . . . And, well, absence makes the heart grow fonder. Come on, let's busy ourselves, eh?'

Feeling better, Maddie thought to give a hint as to why there was something pressing to tell so that her ma wouldn't have too much of a shock. 'It ain't all bad news, Ma. Me and Reggie have something to tell you, but we'll wait for Aunt Jean to be here, eh?'

Ma pulled her lips in, but showed with her glinting eyes that she was excited. As she closed the door, she said, 'Mmm, that sounds intriguing.'

Maddie laughed, and her usual happy self came to the fore as she took the stairs two at a time and began to feel the joy of her wedding day coming much sooner than she had ever imagined.

But there was the fear too, as questions came to her: what would it be like? And now her wedding was so close, should she give in to Reggie's demands?

But no. She'd always wanted to honour what her ma had taught her, that a man and woman coming together was for marriage only. Reggie would have to be patient.

Trying not to think of saying goodbye to him, Maddie got on with making the beds in the rooms occupied by two families who had originally booked for the switch-on of the illuminations – a spectacular light show that had sadly been cancelled this year – but who, now that the early September storms had passed, were enjoying the late summer sunshine despite the doom and gloom hanging over the country.

Maybe, she thought, it was a way of forgetting for a few days, as one family's chat over breakfast had been about the father having joined up.

She wished with all her heart that this war hadn't happened. And yet, she didn't really understand the implications. She wouldn't let herself think of them, as the fear was too much to bear.

A little later, Reggie stood with an arm around her shoulder in the guests' dining and sitting room – a long room that had tables and chairs in neat rows at one end and beige-coloured armchairs around the walls at the other, and in the bay window, a huge red and beige rug on which stood a small occasional table.

When Reggie finished telling Ma and Aunt Jean their plan it seemed they were shocked into silence. It took a long minute for them to absorb the news.

Aunt Jean, smaller than Maddie and her ma, spoke first.

'But how will we get ready for it?' Her head, clad in a bright red scarf to hide her rarely removed curlers, bobbed from side to side. Her bright, dark brown eyes dimmed with worry and sadness, when Maddie had expected to see joy.

Feeling for a chair, Aunt Jean sat down and burst into tears.

Rushing to her side, Maddie took her hand and patted it as she crouched down beside her.

'Eeh, I'm sorry, Maddie, me lovely lass. I'm overjoyed, but I can't take everything in. Me lad's going to war, and now he says he wants to get married first!'

Ma saved the day. 'Aw, Jean, love, it'll all work out. It's a shock, I'll give you that, but I can understand the hurry.'

'You mean . . . Eeh, Reggie, you haven't made Maddie—'

'Naw, Ma! It's not like that. I'm going away for I don't knaw how long and I want to go knowing Maddie's me wife. It'll sort of settle me.'

At this, Ma looked at Maddie. For a moment, it seemed that she had her doubts. But then she smiled. 'Well, I think it wonderful news and we should all concentrate on it, rather than the sad news of Reggie going to war.' She turned to Reggie. 'Though I say sad as I'm sorry to see you go, but eeh, lad, I'm right proud of you an' all.'

Reggie grinned as Ma hugged him and this seemed to give Aunt Jean a way of coping, as she stood up. 'Your ma's a daft old biddy, Reggie, me lad. Come here and let me congratulate you an' all. I were just taken aback by it all when I hadn't had time to take in that you were really going to war. But I'm proud of you too, and proud of the both of you for coping with it like you have . . . Let's have the best wedding we can put together, eh?'

The talk then turned to wedding preparations – where they would hold the reception, and what they should do about her wedding dress.

'Maddie, lass, I've still got my wedding gown, you knaw, and it were made of silk, and is still in good condition. I could alter that to fit you.'

Maddie laughed. 'Aw, Aunt Jean, that would be lovely, but you're so much smaller than me!'

'Eeh, but I can add a frill around the bottom and extend it into a short train. That way it will look like part of the frock.'

Unsure, but not wanting to hurt her lovely aunt's feelings, Maddie said, 'Well, I can have a try on and see what I think, eh?'

Ma chipped in, 'I remember it, Jean, love. It's a lovely gown. I was so envious of you as all my ma could afford for me was a calf-length white frock that we bought from the market!'

'Aw, you looked lovely, Sally, lass. Barry was so proud of you.'

Both swallowed hard. Always when talking of their lost husbands they became emotional. Ma put her arms out to Aunt Jean, who willingly went into them. The two women hugged, their pain lining their faces, and yet their love for each other shining from them.

Reggie stepped closer and his arm came around Maddie's waist. He whispered, 'I can't believe I'm going to make you mine.' This sent a shiver down her back. Never had she known a feeling of things not being right between her and Reggie, always they'd had an easy-going relationship, but suddenly, he seemed possessive of her and for some reason this frightened her.

Turning towards him, the feeling left her. She loved him and, yes, she wanted to be his wife. It was natural for him to feel the urgency he was showing. He loved her and faced going away from all he knew and to goodness knows what!

She was to look forward to being his wife, she told herself. Everything would be fine. She loved the feelings he gave her and on more than one occasion had nearly given in to him as his caresses of her had driven her to a point of yearning for more. When it happened, it would be wonderful and not something to be afraid of.

With this, she kissed his cheek – the only sign of their love they were allowed to show in front of their mas, but one that said she loved him. She was rewarded with a beautiful smile from Reggie and a secret squeeze that thrilled her.

Standing on the station a week later, Reggie held on to her as if he'd never let go. Clinging to him, the pain of parting wrenched at her heart. His lips on hers felt like a desperate plea. And this was in his words as he lifted his head from hers.

'You do love me, don't you, Maddie, lass? Everything will be all right, won't it?'

'Of course. And you knaw I love you.'

These uncertainties Reggie displayed had marred some of the time they'd been together in the last few days. Maddie supposed it was because he was going away. Though she didn't like it.

'Eeh, Reggie, you do trust me, don't you? I've never looked at anyone else, and nor would I! Like you say, it's allus been me and you.'

Reggie looked shamefaced. 'By, I don't knaw what's got into me. It's a feeling like I've never had before.'

Trying to understand, Maddie told him, 'You've naw need to have it. You're me lovely lad. We've allus been close, but now we've found sommat deeper ... But, oh, I wish you hadn't got to go.'

'I do an' all now. It just seemed the right thing to do ... but ...'

His body suddenly jerked forward as a huge slap on his back made him laugh. Tommy Arkwright stood there looking down on them. A giant of a lad, Tommy was always a scary figure with his mass of curly red hair, broad shoulders and a look that said no one messed with him.

'Today's the day, lad. Come on, I've got some fags, we'll light up in the carriage – that'll soothe your love lust.'

His laugh echoed around the station, until a loud voice commanded that the lads, 'Fall in.'

What that meant, Maddie wasn't sure, but the lads seemed to know as they all lined up in an orderly fashion.

'Eeh, Maddie, love, I've got to go. I'll write. I love you.'

And then he was gone. Into the crowd of faces that all looked the same now they had donned their regimented brown caps.

Maddie had thought she would cry at this point, but she didn't. She somehow felt a strange sense of relief.

CHAPTER TWO

Late October 1914

The usual quiet period as they anticipated the winter months had been turned into a frenzy of work, as Ma and Aunt Jean had received letters a week ago telling them their boarding houses had been requisitioned as billets for soldiers coming to train in Blackpool.

They were to provide bed, breakfast and evening meal and accommodate as many soldiers as possible.

Maddie's back ached from moving beds to make room for at least four lads in the family rooms, three in the doubles and two in the singles – this would mean eighteen young men in the house. Maddie dreaded the thought but felt better for telling Daisy, only to find she had a different perspective.

'Aw, it won't be that bad, Maddie, lass. I'd love it meself. It's just a pity that you'll be a married woman by the time they come ... Eeh, Maddie, I still reckon you're too young to marry – I mean, you won't be eighteen till Christmas Day! – engaged, aye, but that's different. Why can't Reggie be happy with that, eh?'

Maddie knew why, and still felt cross about it – there was one thing and one thing only that Reggie wanted. Her anger at this made her snap. 'Shut up, Daisy! If you say that once more about me being too young, you won't be my bridesmaid, and I'll go home now!'

Daisy giggled. 'Ha, to more drudgery!'

'It ain't drudgery, I love me work, and helping me ma. I want to help her to make it a success. She's put everything into the Fosters.'

'Aw, I knaw, love. I'm only teasing. But you're all on edge. What's wrong with you?'

Maddie gazed out of the window of The Copper Kettle Café, owned by Daisy's ma. It stood on the north promenade, and though usually busy, she and Daisy were the only ones in there today. Daisy's ma had taken an hour off and left Daisy to look after everything.

As she watched the sea Maddie thought it looked as disturbed as she felt, and as angry, as it crashed its waves onto the sand, throwing spray onto the road and the window.

'You should be happy marrying the man you love, and having all those other men around you while he's away!'

'Daisy!'

'Well, I'm looking forward to them landing here, I can tell you. Eeh, Maddie, I wish you wouldn't marry—'

'Daisy, please stop. I came to you for support, not a lecture.'

'And that's what I'm giving you. I'm your best mate, love, and I don't like to see you get yourself tied to one

17

man so young. Most folk don't marry till they're in their twenties! What's your ma thinking of, allowing this?'

A tear ran down Maddie's cheek. Ma had only supported her marrying, not tried to prevent it. Her wedding dress was ready, and Ma and Aunt Jean had been hoarding all the food they could for the party afterwards, which had been planned to be held in Ma's boarding house, though that may change now with the soldiers coming. Reggie's aunts and uncles had been invited. And friends too. *But why can't I be happy about it all?*

Daisy was by her side in seconds and holding her. 'Aw, lass, I'm sorry. I didn't mean to upset you.'

Leaning into her, Maddie told her, 'I do love Reggie, Daisy. I just don't feel ready for marriage, but I want him to be happy and settled while he's away.'

'Eeh, Maddie, it sounds like you're sacrificing yourself to make Reggie's war better. But you can't. Marrying him ain't going to change anything … And what if … well, what if owt happens on the wedding night, and you're left having a babby?'

At last, someone had expressed one of her fears.

'Can it happen the first time, Daisy?'

'By, you're not telling me it'll be your first time, are you?'

Maddie was shocked by this. 'Have you done it then?'

'Aye, a few months ago. I went to the Tower Ballroom one night and met this chap. He did it to me in a doorway. I didn't really want to, but I was curious. But it was nowt to shout about and was over as soon as it started. I lived in fear for months after that, though.'

18

Aghast, but not showing it, Maddie asked, 'Did it hurt?'

'A little. But, well, I did it again with Mickey Stanton, and it didn't hurt and was all right, though I felt there was sommat missing. I really liked Mickey, but he seemed to only want me for that, and didn't call round again once it had happened.'

Daisy plopped down on the chair next to Maddie. 'I wish I hadn't now. I feel sort of dirty . . . But that won't happen to you, love. I knaw you only have one night of being married before he goes, but you'll be all right after the first time . . . Where will that be, by the way?'

A little taken aback, and still thinking about what Daisy had said, Maddie hesitated.

'You're not going to be in your bedroom, are you? Eeh, Maddie, that would be embarrassing with your ma the other side of the wall.'

'Naw, you dafty, we're going to book into somewhere. Reggie said the Imperial, but that's too posh and would cost too much, so I'm not sure. Reggie'll sort it when he gets home.'

'Eeh, I'm envious now. But one thing, I'm glad it's winter and I'll see more of you, Maddie. I don't seem to yearn for more in me life when I have you.'

Daisy took hold of Maddie's hand. The same age as Maddie, they'd been friends since school days and next to Ma and Reggie, and Aunt Jean, she was the one person Maddie loved the most.

Daisy was what you would call pretty, with her mop of mousy-coloured hair, and freckles dotted over the bridge of her nose. The curls were like her, bubbly, as she always found something to smile about. And yet, if she was hurt, it really showed, like now.

Squeezing her hand, Maddie said, 'Well, it won't be like other winters, when I'm free in the daytime, but we can meet in the evenings once I've done the pots after dinner, as I won't be seeing Reggie.'

It hurt to say that, and Maddie was glad of the emotion. She'd let her worries over marrying Reggie overshadow her love for him and had suppressed her feelings so as not to suffer too much in his absence. Suddenly she longed to see him.

'Maddie, you've gone all wistful.'

'Well, I am soon to be a blushing bride.'

'By, you can change like the wind. You look happy about it now.'

Maddie laughed.

'Aye, well, I can't say I agree with it,' Daisy continued, 'but I'm glad about one thing. I've been longing for a chance to wear that bridesmaid frock that I had for me Aunt Mildred's wedding again, and now I'll have one.'

'Aw, it's perfect, Daisy. I'd have chosen pale blue silk anyway, but you already having one helps with the expense of it all. It's been a bad season with all the problems of the world hanging over everyone.'

'I knaw. Ma's takings are down to normal, but she's hoping with the news of the soldiers coming that will change, as it will for your ma and Aunt Jean.'

They hugged and, to Maddie, it seemed that her doubts really had left her, for all at once she felt excited about her wedding.

*　　*　　*

20

A week later, Maddie stood on the station. Her heart bulged with happiness. Reggie was coming home. Tomorrow they would post the banns – though Father John had already agreed the date: Saturday, the twenty-first of November at eleven a.m.

It was going to be a rush and they hoped that the few soldiers they had boarding now were all they would have by the time the day arrived. Though it should all work out if there were more, it would just be a tighter schedule.

As it was, the soldiers had to leave early each morning, so breakfast was over and cleared by nine-thirty.

Ticking all this off in her mind while she waited, the sudden activity around her, as others who were here to greet the soldiers began to mill around the edge of the platform, brought Maddie to the present. Her heart thudded against her chest. Reggie would be here any moment!

Just as she thought this, she heard the sound of the approaching train, and saw the billows of smoke, puffed from its chimneys. Then the air filled with the screeching of its brakes, and he was here, standing not feet from her.

Neither of them moved for a moment, but then, Maddie didn't know how, they were in each other's arms, clinging on as if they would never let go ... Only, there wasn't joy coming from Reggie, more a sense of desolation.

'Reggie, love ... Eeh, Reggie, I can't believe you're here. Everything's ready ... you knaw, for our wedding ...'

'It ain't happening, Maddie ...'

His body jerked in a sob.

'What? Why? Reggie, have you changed your mind? You ain't found someone?'

21

'Naw, naw, Maddie, there's naw one but you for me. But we've only got two days' leave and that's counting today!'

He guided her through to the waiting room and sat down, pulling her down beside him.

'We're losing the war, Maddie . . . The Germans are beating us . . . There's a desperate need for reinforcements and we're to be shipped out on Thursday.'

He held her shoulders and stared into her eyes, his face pale and drawn. 'Me heart's breaking, Maddie, and I – I'm scared . . . I don't want to die . . .'

Maddie's stomach turned over. She couldn't speak or react. They sat there just looking at one another, and then, suddenly, they were holding one another, each one clawing at the back of the other's coat in a desperate attempt to get closer. There were no words.

When at last they parted, they still didn't speak. Reggie lifted his haversack onto his back and took her hand. It was then that Maddie tried to alleviate his fear and her own. 'You will come home, Reggie, you will, love. And we'll marry then, eh?'

Reggie kicked a stone. 'I want to marry now! I don't want to wait!'

Turning to her, his eyes held a plea. 'You won't make me wait for us to come together, will you, Maddie? Please. All the men are doing it with their girlfriends and telling me it's the best thing ever. I want us to have that, Maddie.'

This shocked her. She looked up into his eyes and could see his need. But her anger came to the fore as she thought of what Daisy had told her about being taken advantage of then left high and dry.

'Is that all I am to you, Reggie? Is taking me to bed and doing that thing all that you want? Well, I ain't doing it. I told you all along, I ain't a girl like that.'

Reggie stormed off. Maddie stared after him but then her cheeks reddened as she became conscious of others around her. One said, 'He's just back and been unfaithful to you, lass? Aye, well, that's men for you!'

Almost running away from them, Maddie tried to stop her tears falling, but she tasted the salt of them as they trickled into her open mouth. How could this have happened? Were all men the same? Mickey Stanton had shown that that was all he'd wanted from Daisy. And now Reggie was behaving in the same way after being away for six weeks!

Suddenly, she was glad they weren't marrying as the doubts that had niggled at her hit her with a bang. Reggie did only want her for one thing!

He was waiting around the corner of Talbot Road. Grabbing her, he pulled her to him. 'I'm sorry ... Eeh, Maddie, whatever came over me? Please don't be mad at me. I love you, me little lass, with all me heart.'

'Love ain't doing that thing, Reggie. It's part of marriage and the joining of body and soul of a man and woman, not having your pleasure and that's it.'

Reggie's mouth dropped open. 'How do you knaw that then?'

'Daisy told me. She gave in and the bloke just left her – he'd only chased her till he got that. He'd said he were mad for her, then once he'd done it, he were gone!'

'I won't do that, lass ... we were to be married! You're me girl, me only reason for living! I've thought about you every minute and I've longed for our wedding. Aw, Maddie. I can't bear that I ain't going to have you completely as mine before I go away to war.'

'Well, you'll have to as it ain't happening . . . And I can't bear that being the one thing you're bothered about when you ain't seen me for six weeks! You never asked how me ma was or owt!'

'By, I'm sorry, Maddie . . . I . . . it's the only thing the others talk about. It just got me all riled up, that's all. I promise I won't mention it again. Look, let's change the wedding ring for an engagement one and you'll be me fiancée then as you can't be me bride.'

Maddie softened. If all Reggie had heard of was the others' conquest of something he'd longed for, then his behaviour was understandable, if unforgiveable. But they had so little time to be together that she wouldn't spoil it with recriminations.

'Aw, I'd love that, Reggie. Let's get home and tell our mas first. And then we'll go down to the town, eh?'

'Are you glad it turned out like this, Maddie?'

Maddie sighed. She wasn't sure how to answer this. She couldn't tell him that her feelings had been in turmoil. That yes, she'd longed for him to come home and had counted the minutes until that happened but had been battling with whether she was ready to marry him. That at the same time she had helped to make sure the arrangements for their wedding were in place, and had found peace with it all as she did, only to have it snatched away, and then have an argument within seconds of Reggie arriving!

In truth, her emotions were drained.

'Maddie?'

Without warning, tears flooded her face. 'Naw, it's unbearable.'

'Aw, me little lass. I – I behaved badly, I'm sorry. I am … I'm scared, Maddie. It's like me life's being snatched away from me. Men are dying in their thousands … I feel like running and not stopping.' They'd reached the promenade. 'Let's sit a while on a bench, Maddie. I can't go home in this state, and I want to hold you, me little lass.'

Despite the bitter cold, Maddie felt warm in Reggie's arms, though his army coat was rough on her cheeks. Her tears had dried, but her heart was heavy with sadness and fear for Reggie and fear of what the future held.

For a moment, they watched the soldiers on the beach, some running up and down, training for fitness, some digging what looked like trenches.

Reggie spoke first. 'How did it get to this, eh? Some Austrian bloke gets assassinated and it's as if Germany's gone mad, taking others' land, killing people, and then them who sit in offices in London decide we – not them, us; them soldiers out there on the beach and those I've been with, and me – need to be made to feel we should go and kill or be killed!'

Maddie couldn't answer him. Suddenly, the hard-working but carefree life they'd lived was threatened. Loved ones and friends were facing danger. Her Reggie may die, and she'd never see him again, when all he'd ever wanted was to be a painter and decorator, working for his uncle, and to marry her. It was so unfair.

*   *   *

Once home, Maddie ran through the hall, past the guests' sitting room and into the kitchen. Not finding her ma there, she turned towards the door on her left that led down to the basement flat she and her ma shared – a three-roomed cosy space they could call their own, which had all they needed: a bedroom each, and a small sitting room that led into a yard. Their lav was in the yard, and a tin bath hung on the wall for bath nights, a time that was a chore as water had to be hauled from the kitchen, but one they both loved as it was when they chatted and washed each other's backs – mother and daughter time without the worries of the boarding house.

She found her ma nodding by the fire in their lovely living room – a small square room with a brown comfy chair for Ma and a two-seater sofa to match, standing on a pink and brown rug. And on the back wall there was a china cabinet displaying Ma's 'best' china.

'Ma?'

Ma opened her eyes and grinned. 'Reggie's home then.' She looked towards the door, probably remembering that the plan had been for them to go and see Aunt Jean first and then come here.

Ma rose out of her chair. 'Where is he, lass? Aw, lass, what's wrong?'

Maddie rushed towards her ma and into her arms. Sobs racked her body as she told of how Reggie only had one night. 'The wedding's off, Ma . . .'

'Oh dear . . . Off? What, for ever?'

'Naw . . . Look, I need you to come to Aunt Jean's. Reggie has terrible news . . . Oh, Ma . . .'

Her ma patting her back usually soothed her, but not today. Today she wanted to scream against the injustice of it, and against the thing Reggie wanted her to do, and she couldn't.

There were tears from them all, and Aunt Jean was distraught over the situation that Reggie was going into, as she pointed towards the daily newspaper.

Reggie made Maddie proud then as he went down on his haunches next to his ma and held her hand. 'Aw, Ma, I'll be all right, you'll see. I'll be back here before you knaw it, and Maddie will be putting that frock on as you've made for her. She'll look as bonny as owt and we'll walk down that aisle.'

Aunt Jean managed a smile as she looked up at them all. 'Eeh, look at me. I'm a wreck, when I should be comforting Reggie and Maddie.'

Maddie wiped her eyes and blew her nose as she went over to her Aunt Jean. Putting her arms around her, she felt the love she'd always had for this lovely woman overwhelm her. 'We'll look after each other, eh? We'll be all right.'

Reggie's arm came around her. 'I feel better now, me little lass. Let's wash our faces and go into town, eh? Will that be all right with you, Ma?'

'Aye. There'll be time enough to get sorted for evening dinner when you get back. So off you go and enjoy yourselves.'

As they walked into Sam Lyon's jewellers on Church Street, Maddie and Reggie were giggling like children – the kind of hysterical giggles that follow desperate tears.

The little man behind the counter looked up as he took a small magnifying glass from his squinted eye.

On seeing Reggie's uniform, he extended his hand. 'Ah, one of our brave soldiers. What can I do for you?'

After hearing their story, he told them, 'I see. You must have been served by my assistant, but of course I can make the swap for you.'

Taking the wedding ring, he reached for a velvet tray of rings which had lain under the glass counter. 'There, you choose from these and there's no need to worry about the difference in price. That's my gift to you both to thank you for all you have to face to ensure our country is kept safe.'

Maddie had never dreamt she would be choosing from such beautiful rings. Her eyes rested on one as its two diamonds glinted in the light of the single electric bulb dangling from the ceiling. The diamonds were set so that they looked like they were curled around each other in a hug.

'Aw, I love that one, Reggie. One stone can be you and one me. We'll be holding each other, even though we are apart.'

The jeweller wiped a tear from his eye. 'I think that is what the designer may have had in mind, my dear. It's a beautiful ring. Now, let's see if it fits as it is a small size.'

He handed the ring to Reggie.

Maddie hadn't thought they could cry any more than they had done, but as Reggie slipped the ring on her finger and whispered, 'I love you', they both had tears running down their cheeks.

Once it was in place, Maddie said, 'May I keep it on, sir?'

'You may, my dear.'

As they walked along the prom, staying close to keep each other warm, Maddie steered Reggie towards Daisy's place. 'We have to tell Daisy; she thinks she's being a bridesmaid in a couple of weeks or so!'

The café smelt of chips and had its usual warm and welcoming feel. One or two tables were occupied, one by two soldiers drinking mugs of tea. This seemed to remind Reggie of what he'd only just found out about the billeting of soldiers.

'So, they take our place. Well, they'd better behave themselves. You won't have owt to do with them, will you, Maddie?'

There it was again, that insinuation that he didn't trust her. If he did, why should he ask such a thing?

She decided not to answer and walked up to the counter. Daisy looked up.

'Eeh, lass, I didn't expect to see you two today. I thought you'd have a million things to do to get ready for ... Aw, Maddie, what's wrong? I can tell there's sommat, love.'

Maddie told her what had happened.

'But that's so unfair. I don't knaw what to say.'

To stop this getting into another crying session, Maddie said, 'But we got engaged, Daisy, look.'

Daisy gasped. 'It's beautiful.'

And before the tears that glistened in Daisy's eyes could fall, Maddie added, 'And I'm starving! Throw a basket of chips in for us, love, and bring us a couple of mugs of tea to warm us.'

She turned to Reggie. His expression had changed. He looked angry and yet also afraid.

'I've ordered chips, love, let's sit down. Eeh, me stomach's rumbling.'

Reggie looked around. One of the two soldiers greeted him. He didn't answer.

The other one asked, 'Are you new around here?'

'Naw, I live here, mate. I go tomorrow to France.'

'Good luck. We'll leave you with your girl. Lucky you, she's a looker.'

Reggie crossed the room in two strides. 'You keep your eyes off the lasses around here or there'll be trouble!'

The soldier put his hands up. 'Sorry, mate, just saying. Anyway, we're not here long enough, we're being shipped out next week, so you've no worries.'

Maddie tugged at Reggie's arm. 'Reggie, come and sit down!'

When they found a seat, Maddie looked into his eyes. 'Eeh, Reggie, this is our engagement day. The day I promised to be yours and you placed a ring on me finger to seal that promise. Don't spoil it by imagining me going with others. I love you, Reggie.'

But as she said the words, the doubt that had niggled at her and that she'd put to bed crept back into her. Him worrying about going to war had changed her Reggie. He used to be happy-go-lucky and safe in their love. Now, he was possessive and quick to anger. A part of her was glad that things had turned out how they had, though she hoped with all her heart that Reggie kept safe and returned to her.

Visibly softening, Reggie nodded at the soldiers. 'Sorry, I was out of order. I go tomorrow and I'm a bit on edge.'

They all shook hands and wished each other luck. Relieved, Maddie allowed Reggie to take her hand as they went towards an empty table and sat back down. 'I'm sorry, me lass. Don't be cross at me. I'm not meself. Me disappointment and me fear are making me behave out of character.'

'And making me have me doubts, Reggie. We've to make the best of this day. Other men mean nowt to me, but you not trusting me hurts.'

There was a pause as Daisy put the chips in front of them. Almost immediately, Reggie shoved a huge forkful of chips into his mouth. Maddie knew he was trying to stop himself from crying. She tried to understand, but it was difficult when his fears meant he was almost accusing her. She sighed but thought it best to leave things at that. Reggie had such a short time before he had to leave. She wanted those hours to be happy, not filled with arguments.

CHAPTER THREE

Once home, there was no time to dwell on anything that had happened this afternoon, with potatoes to peel and veg to chop, besides keeping an eye on the large pot of stew bubbling away while her ma rolled the pastry she'd mixed ready for the apple pie topping.

'By, lass, it's hard work with just nine of them. What's it going to be like when we're full, eh?'

'Aw, Ma, it won't be any different to high season. Though we have a number of kids as well as adults then, so don't have as much food to prep.'

'Aye, and we can both start earlier, as you won't be gadding off out with Reggie ... Eeh, I'm sorry, lass. I said that as though it will be a good thing, but it won't be.'

'I knaw what you meant, Ma. And it's right an' all. We'll get into a routine, you'll see.'

As she said this, Maddie noticed her ma holding on to the table and bending over. 'Are you all right, Ma?'

'Aye. It's just this pain in me side bothering me again. It'll pass.'

'You should mention it to the doctor. It's gone on a while now.'

'I will. But it was manageable, once all the guests had left.'

Feeling concerned, Maddie looked intently at her ma and saw how pale and drawn she was. Her worry deepened. Was there something really wrong? But then, she thought, Ma had had this pain for a long time now, so if it was serious, it would have shown itself, surely?

The doorbell ringing stopped these thoughts as Maddie whipped off the pinny she'd only just put on. 'I'll get that, Ma. You sit down for a mo, eh?'

Opening the door, Maddie found two soldiers standing on the step.

'Good evening to you, miss. It is that we've been billeted here and it's sorry I am that we're for being late, but didn't the train leave us behind? It did so, didn't it, Tom?'

As the second soldier shuffled his feet, and giggled, Maddie noticed the distinct smell of beer on their breath. She looked at the one who had spoken. She loved his Irish accent, and he had the bluest eyes she'd ever seen. He was good-looking in a rakish way as his smile was charming, and yet he had the look of someone who was mischievous. Even his apology had sounded cheeky.

A shyness came over her. It was as if she'd known this man all her life, and yet she wasn't feeling that 'at home' feeling you do when you know someone.

'Will you be letting us come in, miss?'

'Oh . . . Aye, of course. Eeh, I'm sorry, it's a busy time and we weren't notified of you coming. I was taken aback, that's all.'

As he stepped in, he said, 'Mmm, there's a powerful good smell. And here it is that we are starving. Are you thinking there'll be enough food to feed us as well?'

'There is, I'm sure. But I'll need to take your details to book you in and then I'll show you your room and the . . . the facilities first. By the time you come down there'll be a tray of tea for you in the sitting room, through that door there. Just give me a moment.'

Turning, Maddie went to hurry back to the kitchen but caught her foot under the corner of the carpet runner.

There was a thud of a haversack being dropped and, in an instant, a hand grabbed her arm, and then an arm came around her waist to steady her.

The beer breath became stronger as his face came near to hers. Their eyes met and Maddie had the feeling that she never wanted him to let her go. He stared at her before seeming to shake himself out of some kind of stupor and saying, 'You're needing to take more water with it, so you are.'

Maddie wanted to laugh, but something compelled her to hold his gaze. Her heartbeat quickened. Her lungs didn't seem to want to release the breath she held.

Then he winked at her. His hand on her waist squeezed her a little tighter, and his eyes showed her something she didn't want to acknowledge.

Moving away from his body, but not wanting to, Maddie thanked him for saving her, not able to believe how deep her own voice sounded.

He held her gaze for another second that felt like eternity, then grinned, let her go, and picked up his haversack.

Making her way back to the kitchen, Maddie called back in a more normal voice, 'I won't be long with the tea. Make yourselves at home.'

But as she left them, she asked herself, *Whatever is the matter with me? It's like an unknown force has hit me and knocked me off me axle!*

Once in the kitchen, normality took over as her concern for her ma made the incident seem silly, and she told herself it was the shock of the fall that had caused the powerful sensations zinging through her, not the touch of a stranger.

Ma was still sitting where she'd left her. 'Are you all right, Ma? I mean, really all right?'

'Aye, it's going off now. Put them spuds on to boil, lass, and the water for the veg. Who was that at the door?'

Maddie put her ma in the picture as she did the jobs asked of her and shoved the kettle on the heat. 'But don't worry, it's all taken care of, Ma, and we've plenty of time as none of the other lads are home yet.'

Back in the hall, Maddie stood behind the tall desk in the corner and took details from the lad called Tom. As she did, she was mystified as to why her nerves were on edge as the chatty, cheeky one stood next to her.

But despite trying to tell herself she was being ridiculous, her heart fluttered as she turned towards him. He'd removed his cap, showing that what hair hadn't been cut off was curly and jet black. One or two stray curls fell onto his forehead, and his eyes seemed to be even bluer than when she'd first seen them.

'Me name's Arnold, but I'm for being called Arnie for short, and that's the only name I answer to, so it is. Though I jump to it when the sergeant is for bawling out me surname – Brown.'

Before Maddie could react to this being a strange name for an Irishman, Tom playfully punched Arnie's shoulder. 'And that's the colour of yer pants too, when it happens. He's scary, our sarge.'

Arnie and Tom burst out laughing and Maddie couldn't help but join them.

The laughter made her relax so that she was able to fill in the registration for them both. 'This way. I'll take you to your room . . . Well, it ain't a room of your own as you have to share with two others. It's how we were instructed to do things to get as many of you in as possible.'

'I hope we're not a great inconvenience to you, miss.'

'Naw, Arnie. If owt, you've saved our bacon as the season was poor and left us short of money. And the extra rations we're now entitled to mean we get fed well an' all.'

'That's good, so it is.'

They'd reached the top of the stairs when Maddie turned to indicate the room she'd allocated to them. Arnie was so close. Their eyes met once more and his registered surprise as if he was seeing her for the first time. He cleared his throat and looked away. Maddie was left feeling shaken. She couldn't understand what was happening to her.

An hour later, as she served dinner to much teasing from the lads, she was conscious of only one of them, though she joked with them all.

Back in the kitchen, where Ma was hurriedly filling plates, Maddie took a deep breath. Letting it go made her ma look up.

Misunderstanding Maddie's turmoil, she said, 'Eeh, lass. I'll help with the dishes, so you can spend as much time as possible with Reggie.'

Shame reddened Maddie's face. She hadn't thought of Reggie all evening. But telling herself she had to stop these silly and unwanted feelings affecting her didn't help.

Nor did reminding herself that she was engaged to her Reggie and that Arnie was just a soldier passing through their boarding house. She still knew that something strange was happening to her and that somehow Arnie was special.

With the washing-up finally finished and the kitchen all sparkling again Maddie took off her pinny and looked up at the clock, shocked to see it was already gone seven.

The kitchen door opening had her swivelling around. Reggie stood there in his greatcoat, a smile making his eyes twinkle. 'Ma's all done so I figured you were an' all, lass. I thought we'd go for a walk to the pub, what d'yer think, eh?'

Suddenly, with him standing there and talking to her how he always used to, her daft notions left her. She smiled widely as she said, 'Aye, that'd be grand. I could enjoy a glass of ale.'

An hour later, with two glasses drunk and the laughter of the packed pub cheering them up, Maddie had a bubbly feeling inside. She giggled at anything and everything, and as Reggie helped her on with her coat she missed the arms a couple of times, which seemed the funniest thing ever to them both.

This feeling continued as they walked towards home, finding the smallest things to laugh over and holding on to each other as if they would never let go. They stopped walking every now and again to kiss – light, fun kisses at first, but getting more passionate as they stood a while under a streetlight. Then, Reggie gently pulled her into an alleyway.

The darkness after the glow of the gas light clawed at Maddie and the tunnelled wind whistled around her, but none of that mattered to her. It was as if she was transported into another world as Reggie kissed her more deeply, his tongue touching hers, giving her a strange tingling feeling.

When he caressed her breast and his hand found its way down her leg to lift her skirt, it all seemed natural to her and so what she wanted and needed that she gasped deeply. The release of her breath brought with it a moan of pleasure at the sensations rippling through her.

Swept away with these new feelings urging her on, she was accepting of everything, even Reggie lifting her high against the wall and guiding her legs around him. Him pulling her knickers to one side still didn't alarm her – she wanted what was happening.

When Reggie pushed against her, her anticipation rose, but before he entered her, he let out a long, drawn-out moan of pleasure, mixed with disappointment. Gasping, he told her, 'Eeh, lass, me lass . . . I'm sorry . . . It happened too soon!'

This brought her to her senses – she had so nearly done the thing she'd wanted to save herself for until they were married.

'What happened?'

'I – I . . . it just came. The anticipation of our first time was too much . . . I'm sorry, lass, so sorry.'

Hugging him to her and telling him it was all right was heartfelt, as what upset him had saved her. What had she been thinking of?

But then, she was even more bewildered by the thought, *I don't even want it to be Reggie who does that to me!*

Once more, shame washed over her as she took his already damp hanky and wiped whatever it was that had come from Reggie off the inside of her leg.

Reggie held her all the way home, his love for her spoken over and over, as was his promise that it would be different next time. He told her that he'd got overexcited, but that it was lovely and something he would take with him to remember.

Maddie was glad for him.

For herself, she was just grateful that it had ended how it had.

The next morning, nursing a headache, and with a deep-seated feeling of relief over the incident, Maddie had no time to dwell on it. Breakfast for the lads was at seven, and she was to leave at eight-thirty to see Reggie off.

39

By the time she and Reggie were on the pavement outside, with Reggie saying his goodbyes to Ma and Aunt Jean, Maddie felt exhausted.

Aunt Jean greeted her with a hug. Her tears flowed freely. 'Pray to God me Reggie comes back safely . . . How am I to stand it – the not knowing whether he's all right or not and the fear when the doorbell rings? . . . Oh, Maddie, Maddie, love.'

'We'll get through it together, Aunt Jean. We've to send Reggie off with a smile. His fear is greater than ours.'

'Aw, Maddie, you're a special lass. We'll look after each other as you say.'

With this she cheered a little and clung on to her son, looking almost like a child in his arms. 'Be good, Ma. I'll be home afore you knaw it.'

Then they were in the cab that awaited them. Even though the station was only minutes away, Arnold Good-acre, who owned several cabs, had insisted he took those soldiers he knew to catch their trains.

With a blanket around them to keep them warm as the icy wind whipped inside the pram-type roof that was extended to shield them, but did nothing to help as it was open in the front, Maddie thought Arnold, being fully exposed, must be frozen stiff. This didn't seem to bother him as he drove with great pride, sitting up straight and staring ahead.

Reggie's arm came around her and she snuggled into him.

With his voice almost a whisper, he said, 'Eeh, me little lass, I slept well. I were dreaming of what we did.'

Keeping her own voice low, Maddie, irritated that Reggie should bring this up, snapped, 'We went a lot further than we should have, Reggie.' But then, thinking this harsh in the circumstances, softened. 'But, aye, it were grand.'

'A taste of what we have to look forward to, eh?'

'Aye.' Still wanting to appease him and to feel better about the thoughts she shouldn't be having about the Irish soldier, Maddie, hardly able to see Reggie in the dim gas lighting of the side streets, answered, 'I can't wait.'

'Aw, me Maddie.'

They didn't speak again, just sat being jiggled about by the noisy, rocking car, sitting as close as they could together and with their own thoughts and feelings.

For Maddie, these were a mixture of relief that they hadn't gone all the way, and sadness that Reggie was going. But there was a constant intrusion into these thoughts, of Arnie. It was as if he was taking her over. Her thoughts, her dreams and, yes, her longings.

This all left her as she and Reggie stood on the platform and hugged as if they'd never let go. The wind whipped around them, but they felt the warmth of each other as they clung together in desperation.

The time for parting had come. And Maddie felt her heart would break. She hadn't felt this when Reggie had gone for the six weeks, but now, it was like she was losing him for ever.

He'd always been by her side. Always it was Reggie and Maddie. When they were toddlers, then at school, and as they matured and he went on to be an apprenticed painter and decorator, making them laugh when he'd returned after his first day covered in paint of all colours – something the men at work had done to him as a sort of initiation. And then their love had got stronger. Reggie was everything. The best big brother ever!

This last shocked Maddie. She pulled away and looked up into Reggie's face, wet with tears, and the truth finally hit her. Her feelings for him were as if he was a big brother, the best. Suddenly, she understood why she'd never wanted to let him make love to her and now felt repulsed by what they'd done and the kissing and petting that had been part of their lives.

But how was she to get out of the commitment she'd made to him? She couldn't do it now. Not as he was leaving and going into untold danger.

'What's wrong, Maddie?'

'Nowt, only . . .' Digging deep and hating herself for her deceit, she continued, 'I – I don't want you to go! You're me lad, and I love you. I can't bear to be away from you.'

'Aw, me little lass.'

As he held her even closer, her tears joined his. But hers were tears that came from now suddenly knowing that it was all going wrong. And though she begged God to keep him safe, a little part of her welcomed their separation. This wasn't how it should be, but she could see the truth now. They'd drifted along, mistaking their feelings. Thinking themselves in love. And Ma and Aunt Jean had encouraged that. For a moment, she felt anger at them both, but then, how were they to know? She hadn't known herself until Arnie had knocked on the door.

As she waved Reggie off amidst many sobbing women, her own tears had died. The revelation had freed her from them. Turning away when he finally went out of sight into plumes of smoke belching from the train, Maddie looked towards a different future. One where she had to untangle herself from the commitment that she'd made to a man she now knew she adored but wasn't in love with.

Ma calling out to her when she stepped into the hall, 'Is that you, Maddie?' made her want to scream, *Yes, it's me! Silly little duped me! The idiotic fool who went along with everyone and the dreams they had for her and Reggie!* She wanted to ask her ma why. Why had she and Aunt Jean encouraged it? But then, it would have completed their family, wouldn't it? Best friends, who only had each other, seeing their children wed to each other.

A bitterness came into her. It was as if she'd been a lamb driven to the slaughter.

'Maddie?'

'Aye, it's me, Ma.' Knowing her ma would be sitting in the guests' sitting room having a cuppa, Maddie added, 'I'll just go and put me coat away.'

Once downstairs, Maddie flung her coat and bonnet on the floor, threw herself onto her bed and beat her pillow in frustration.

After a long moment, a tap on the door hailed her ma coming in.

'Aw, me lass. I knaw you're hurt. Saying goodbye to the man you love is heartbreaking. But Reggie will be home, I promise. Nowt can take our Reggie from us. Not a dozen

Kaisers. You'll see, he'll come through that door upstairs as big and lovely as ever and sweep you up the aisle. And, aye, we'll make it a proper wedding, not a hurried affair. One where I buy a big hat and a fancy frock—'

'Stop it, Ma!'

'Eeh, lass. I'm sorry. Aw, come here and let me give you a hug.'

There was comfort in her ma's arms. But Maddie needed more. How she longed to open her heart to Ma, to have her say everything would be all right, and to make things all better with a kiss and a cuddle, just as she did in the days when she was a toddler.

But Maddie knew that this hurt she was suffering couldn't be fixed as easily. And that filled her with despair.

CHAPTER FOUR

Maddie walked along the prom later that day.

The wind bit her cheeks and reddened her nose. Her long plaid skirt gave her little protection. She folded her arms around her to keep warmer, but nothing helped.

Not really wanting to go and see Daisy, but seeking solitude, Maddie was driven towards the café with its promise of warmth.

As soon as she opened the door, Daisy greeted her with, 'Eeh, lass, what are you doing out in this? It'll freeze your lugholes.'

Maddie didn't answer. She couldn't. Being with Daisy always cheered her, but she feared today that the hopelessness of her situation wouldn't be helped by laughter.

'Hot cocoa coming up, love. And a warm scone an' all. Ma's just baked them. Sit down near to the fire and I'll bring it over.'

The hot drink was welcome, but Maddie didn't think she could eat anything.

With no one in the café, Daisy sat down in the chair next to her. 'Reggie'll be all right, you knaw, love. We only read of them as cop it, but millions don't.'

Before she could stop herself, Maddie blurted out, 'I'm not in love with him, Daisy!'

For once, Daisy seemed lost for words. She just stared and uttered, 'Aw, love . . .'

'I love him, but I ain't in love with him.'

But then Daisy surprised her. 'I could've told you that a long time ago, lass, but hearing you say it took the wind out of me sails. But me and me ma have said for a good while that you and Reggie have just drifted into tying yourselves together.'

'You knew?'

'Aye. I'm your best pal, Maddie. I knaw you inside out. Didn't I beg you not to marry him? I was over the moon when you said you couldn't because of him having to go back – I mean, well, I wasn't pleased that he had to go back, but . . .'

'I knaw. Eeh, Daisy, I've been saved from making a huge mistake, but how am I to get out of it all now?'

'You don't have to. Reggie's gone, for we don't knaw how long, anything can happen before then. But don't break it off with him by letter as that'd be cruel in the situation that he is in.'

Maddie blew the steam from her cocoa. With her mind in turmoil and her heart heavy in her chest, she felt trapped by her own stupidity. It had all happened how Daisy had said, and she may never have known different, but then Arnie came into her life . . . *Oh, God, what am I thinking?*

The café doorbell clanging had Daisy jumping up. 'Come on in, lads. There's allus a warm welcome in here for you.'

'I'll be taking a drop of hot tea, please. Isn't it enough to freeze the sun today?'

'You're Irish!'

'Ha, how was it you were guessing that?'

Daisy laughed. 'Two mugs of tea coming up! What's your names then? We like first names in here.'

Maddie sat still. The voice alone was enough to send her heart fluttering. She waited for his reply, when she knew she'd have to turn and acknowledge them. But she didn't want to. She was dealing with so much as it was.

'To be sure, I'm Arnie and this is Tom. And is it that yours is a copper kettle then?'

Daisy's laughter was infectious. Giggling at the comment and Daisy's reaction helped Maddie to turn and greet the lads.

'Eeh, I thought you two were hard at work marching up and down or sommat. Not hopping into cafés for a pot of tea!'

'I was for knowing that was you, Maddie, but was thinking you didn't want to know us. Sure, we'll come and join you, won't we, Tom?'

Tom was looking at Daisy. 'Only if Daisy joins us.'

Daisy blushed with pleasure and nodded. 'Aye, I'll be over in a mo. Maddie's me best pal. We've been friends since we were nippers in school.'

Tom crossed to the counter, saying he would help deliver the teas, but Maddie could see he just wanted to flirt with Daisy. Judging by Daisy's giggles, she didn't mind at all.

'So, it is here that you escape to, is it?'

Taking a deep breath to steady herself, Maddie joked, 'Aye, I have an exciting life, lad.'

Arnie laughed. She loved his laugh.

'It wasn't you seeking comfort from your pal then as I understand your man shipped out today?'

'Aye, a bit of that.' Maddie wished she could say it was all of it. And wished with all her heart she hadn't lost that feeling of being in love with Reggie.

'You're not sounding like a girl who's just seen her man off to war. Is it that there's hope for others?'

His eyes held hers. She wanted to shout, *Yes!* But the disloyalty of the revelation brought back her feeling of shame. Reggie was at this moment on a train mourning having left her and them not being married. He didn't deserve her to immediately turn to another man. And yet, she felt as though Arnie was more than just another man.

'If it is so, I'd like to be in the running, so I would.'

Deciding to treat this as a joke and so lighten the heavy feeling inside her, Maddie laughed. 'You and the whole British army, lad. You're all the same! Thinking you're God's gift to women! You'll have a lass in every port, no doubt.'

Arnie laughed but his answer stung. 'So, you're for thinking yourself attractive to all men and it is that you can have your pick? I wasn't for having you down as that kind of girl.'

Maddie filled with rage at this. How dare he?

'Naw, I wasn't thinking that. I was thinking to put you down, as you obviously think it's right to make a pass at me. Like you say, I've seen me man off to war today, so I'd like to be left alone to get over that, ta very much!'

48

Standing, she grabbed her coat. 'See you another time, Daisy, love. I've to get back home to help Ma.'

Daisy stopped pouring the tea into the mugs. Her astonished look made her appear almost comical. 'But . . .'

'See you later, lass.'

Maddie was through the door and battling with the wind before Daisy could say any more.

The strong gusts won against the fragile hold she had on her bonnet and whipped it into the air whilst she fought to get her arm into a coat that seemed to have come alive. It danced around her and blew up into a balloon shape at the back until it was like fighting with a person!

The sound she didn't want to hear – the café bell clanging – made her swivel round. Arnie stood there laughing his head off. For two pence she could have lifted her leg and kicked him where it hurt. She didn't need him right now. She didn't need this feeling she had for him and she wished she'd never met him, and that this bloody war had never happened. Life had been so simple for her – happy and carefree, mapped out and orderly – but now it had been turned upside down and she felt lost.

She hadn't meant to cry.

Arnie sobered immediately. 'It's sorry I am, I was for being an insensitive pig. Forgive me and let me be helping you, Maddie.'

He grabbed her coat and had it wrapped around her in seconds, his arms enclosing her. She didn't want them to ever be removed. But then he said, 'Be holding on to that while I run after your bonnet.' And then he was chasing the hat she hated, while it innocently danced along the pavement as if on an outing.

That innocence soon turned into mischievousness. It seemed the wind was determined to make fun of Arnie, as each time he got within reach of the bonnet and bent down to retrieve it, it was whipped into the air and played with before being dropped a few yards ahead of him.

When this happened a few times, and other passers-by joined in the race, Maddie became a giggling wreck. The cries of, 'I've got it!' and then, 'Bugger! I missed it,' filled the air with a laughter that seemed to give back to the world the joy it had lost.

Daisy came out at that moment, and Tom pushed past them both to join in the race.

It was all too much for Maddie and Daisy. They collapsed onto each other laughing so much they had to hold on to their sides, and their faces became wet with a different kind of tears – happy tears that made Maddie's sad ones just a memory.

Suddenly there was a cry of victory. 'I'm for beating you all, for don't I have the bonnet tamed already!'

Arnie stood triumphant holding the now dusty, sorry-looking hat in his hand.

Cheers went up before everyone dispersed, saying they hadn't had so much fun in ages. For Maddie, the silly incident had, for a short time at least, lifted the cloud of doom from her shoulders.

Shaking the woolly bonnet and tapping the dust from it, Arnie bowed deeply in front of Maddie. ''Tis that I am at your service, madam!' As he straightened, he plonked the bonnet on her head and pulled it down securely.

But the simple gesture seemed to bond them in some way as his warm breath wafted across her face and their eyes locked.

Arnie turned abruptly then and made as if to go back into the café. Maddie caught hold of his arm. 'I'm sorry for what I said . . . I'm . . . well, I'm upset at the moment.'

'And I was for being insensitive. Will you walk a ways with me? Maybe it is that we can clear the air and start afresh?'

'I – I've to get back home now. Haven't you got to be back somewhere?'

Disappointment crossed his face, but though Maddie wanted to walk with him – wanted to be by his side always – she couldn't let herself be drawn into unburdening herself. She didn't know him well enough.

Arnie shivering and rubbing his hands together gave her the excuse to escape. 'Eeh, get yourself back inside and drink that hot tea, lad. I'll be fine.' With this she turned and almost ran away from him.

Once around the corner in Bonny Street, Maddie slowed her pace. She had no need to be back in a hurry and no inclination to be, all she wanted was to be with Daisy. Especially now that Daisy understood, and it seemed she had known for a long time the truth of it all . . . *If only I had listened to her!*

This thought shocked Maddie as she realised that Daisy had tried for a long time to make her see what her feelings really were, but she hadn't taken notice. She'd had no real time to herself to find who she really was. Growing up had all been done with Reggie, messing around on the beach, then sitting with an ice cream, riding on the big wheel . . . All fun times, but now she felt suffocated by them, as if she'd never had a life of her own.

'Maddie! Maddie!' Daisy's voice lifted Maddie's spirits.

Out of breath when she caught up with her, Daisy gasped, 'Ma came down and took over from me. I've got an hour off, love, and we need to have a chat. Let's go into the Brunswick pub. We'll be allowed to sit in the snug with a lemonade.'

'Have the lads gone?'

'Aye, they were getting ready to. But I have sommat to tell you. Arnie told me that he can't get you out of his mind and now thinks he's upset you so much you'll not have anything to do with him . . . Anyway, let's get inside, I'm frozen to the bone!'

Despite how emotional she felt, this message cheered Maddie so much she wanted to skip into the pub.

Once inside, the smell of ale and stale tobacco smoke almost had her turning around and going out again, but the roaring fire in the snug was too tempting.

They found two wooden armchairs free right next to the warming flames. 'You sit there and keep that one for me, love. I'll get our lemonades and make sure we're all right to sit in here.'

'Well, we go to other pubs, and we never get turned away.'

'I knaw, but we're allus with Reggie when we do and that makes it acceptable. Women and girls shouldn't really go in pubs alone, it ain't done.'

With this bit of knowledge, Maddie began to feel uncomfortable, but the two old gentlemen in the corner didn't seem to take any notice of them as they smoked their pipes and read their newspapers.

She looked around her. This bar was like others she'd been in, exposed beams, yellowing, rough-plaster walls, with brown leather bench seating, scattered wooden stools and the odd chair. Pictures of old Blackpool hung around the bar, giving Maddie the thought of how little had changed as she took in the scenes of horse-driven coaches and women wearing long frocks and jackets, not too dissimilar to what she was wearing today.

'Here you go, lass. The landlord's missus makes it herself, it's lovely. I asked for the recipe once and she said she'd have to kill me after if she gave it to me.'

They both laughed at this and it once more broke the ice.

'Maddie ... about what you were saying before, love. I want you to knaw that though I said I was glad, I didn't mean to seem unfeeling. I do feel for you and want to help you.'

Daisy's hand took hold of Maddie's.

'You're a good friend to me, Daisy. I knaw you'll allus help me. And I knaw that you were right all along ... It all just happened.'

'I knaw, and it weren't easy to watch. I just hoped that the love you had for Reggie was strong enough to get you through. But what did worry me was that Mr Right might have come along and you wouldn't have been free for him.'

'And I'm still not free! How can I be? I can't get out of it. I must marry Reggie. It would break his ma's and my ma's heart if I pulled out of it.'

'Eeh, naw, naw, love, please don't. It's not your ma, or Reggie's ma, who has to live with any decisions you make, but you. Listen to me, Maddie, you knaw I love you and would only want to help you . . . But I think you should get out more, meet more people. I knaw you meet a lot at the guest house, but they are different, they come and go. You've only got me and your family. Why don't me and you go out for the evening, eh?'

'Aw, Daisy, I don't knaw what I'd do without you, love, but—'

'Naw buts. You're coming out and that's that. What would Reggie do if he were the one left here? He'd go to the pub and have a pint. That's all you'll be doing, only it won't be a pint, but a glass of lemonade, and it'll be in the Tower Ballroom an' all.'

Maddie felt a tingle of excitement. She hadn't done anything like that for a long time and never without Reggie – she hadn't wanted to. But now she did want to. 'Aye, all right, we will. I'll wear that blue frock that I wore last Christmas when you and your ma came around for tea.'

'By, that's a lovely frock and just right. I loved how it showed a little bit of your ankle.'

'Eeh, Daisy, you make me sound like a hussy! I had me white silk stockings on.'

'Aye, and a little bit of your lace petticoat showed, and looked so appealing. I've tried hitching me green striped frock up a little, but I can't get the same effect. You'll knock

54

'em dead if you wear the frock just how you did, and if you have your hair brushed back off your face. It looks lovely like that.'

Despite her misgivings, Maddie knew an excitement to ripple through her with the thought that Arnie might be there. Then it turned into a longing for him to be.

'Aw, that's better. You look ready to take life on again, lass. I'm so glad.'

'I am ready, so ready.'

When she arrived home, Maddie was met with an unsure ma, and a warning when she told her how she planned to go out for the evening.

'Eeh, me lass, it'll do you good. But I ain't sure about your reputation, you gadding off out the moment your man gets on the train.'

'I won't be gadding, Ma, just going out with Daisy to help cheer me up, that's all.'

'Eeh, I don't knaw, lass.'

Maddie began to feel ashamed of wanting to go, as she saw through her ma's voice and look how others might perceive her doing so, but suddenly, Ma seemed to change her mind. 'Well, if you're going, you're going to have to bathe those eyes. They're very swollen from all the crying you've done. But then, it was a big thing you went through this morning, seeing Reggie off.'

'It was, Ma, a much bigger thing than you'll ever knaw.'

'You're wrong there, Maddie. I knaw the true meaning of saying goodbye.'

'Aw, Ma, I didn't mean . . . I – I . . . Oh, Ma.'

'Now, now, we're not going to start blubbing again. Let's get busy. We've the evening meal to sort out.'

Taking her cue from her ma, Maddie reached for her pinny on the back of the pantry door. 'So, what are we cooking tonight?'

'Shepherd's pie. I've minced and cooked the meat, onions and carrots, so you need to do a load of spuds for mashing. I've a suet pudding on the boil for afters, so we need the custard making.'

'Eeh, Ma, you've about done it all! How're you feeling? Has that pain gone?'

'Aye, I haven't had it today at all. And anyways, I knew it was a bad day for you, so thought I'd better get the food done. Aunt Jean helped me. She ain't got as many in as us and had her beds all done by her staff. It was good for us to be together for a while following Reggie's departure.'

'Maybe I should pop around to see her, Ma.'

'Aye, that'd be a good idea. You've half an hour before you need start on the spuds.'

Not relishing the thought of seeing Aunt Jean with her conscience still prickling her, Maddie steeled herself to go, calling out as she did, 'And don't you dare do me chores for me while I'm gone, Ma! You go and have a rest and take the weight off your feet.'

The hinges of the tall wooden gate across the yard from the kitchen door, which led through the dividing wall into Aunt Jean's yard, moaned their usual creaks as Maddie slid the bolt and opened it. Having a view now of Aunt Jean's kitchen window, she saw Aunt Jean look up from where

she'd been bent over her kitchen sink. In a darting movement she was at her back door and almost fell on Maddie.
They clung together.

Maddie, drained of tears, just held Aunt Jean and patted
her back while she softly sobbed.

'Will he come back safe, Maddie?'

'Aye, you knaw Reggie. He'll look out for himself and
others.'

After a moment, Aunt Jean loosened her clinging hold
and stood looking into Maddie's eyes. Her lace-edged
hanky seemed to just appear from her sleeve and she wiped
her eyes. 'But what about you, lass? It's going to be a long,
lonely wait for you.'

'Well, Daisy's going to do her best to help me through it.
We're going out together after dinner's all cleared up.'

Maddie cast her eyes to the ground. Her love for her
aunt made it difficult to deceive her. But she couldn't shat-
ter her and Ma's dreams for her and Reggie at a time when
they were suffering so much from his leaving to go to war.

'Out? You mean, out to a pub or sommat?'

'Maybe, or the Tower. Daisy thought it would help me.'

'But it ain't seemly, lass. Not for an engaged-to-be-
married girl. I mean, the town's full of soldiers looking for
a good time.'

'Not you as well, Aunt Jean. Why doesn't anyone trust
me any more?'

'I – I'm sorry, lass . . . I didn't mean . . . I was thinking of
you being safe.'

Once more, Maddie found herself being held, but a cold
place in her heart, where her secret feelings lay, wasn't

touched by the love offered to her, and the stark reality of who she was hit her – she wasn't an open, honest person any more and couldn't be for fear of hurting others.

Lifting her eyes heavenward, she thanked God for Daisy being in her life. Someone who knew, and who understood. Without her, Maddie thought she would go mad in a world where all those she loved expected something of her that she couldn't give.

CHAPTER FIVE

'By, you look a smasher, lass. Where are you and Daisy planning on going then?'

Maddie twirled around. Always she'd loved this blue frock, but now she had her doubts.

'I'm not too dressed up, am I, Ma? Only Daisy said about going to the Tower.'

'Naw, you look lovely. Go and have a good time, but be careful of starting any gossip that might get to Aunt Jean's ears. We don't want her more upset than she is.'

'Ma! What all of you think of me, I just don't knaw! Aunt Jean said she didn't think it seemly that I should even go out! It sounded like she thought the minute I'd said goodbye to Reggie, I'd be off eyeing the soldiers up!'

'Eeh, lass. You'll learn. It's the legacy we womenfolk live with – we go out to be with our girlfriend to help mend our broken heart, and in everyone's eyes, we're out for a good time. Me and Aunt Jean suffered from it when we lost yours and Reggie's das. We couldn't walk up the street without being accused of being after someone else's man!

We stayed in each other's houses most of the time and that's when we came up with our plan for our future.'

Maddie plonked herself down on the sofa next to her ma. 'So, you both think that's what I should do – stay at home?'

'Aye. Well, it seems the decent thing. I mean, you only said goodbye to Reggie this morning, lass.'

Exasperated, Maddie stood back up and glared at her ma, but then reason came to her. If she hadn't been hit by the revelation that she wasn't in love with Reggie, that's exactly what she would have done – stayed home and cried and been comforted by Ma and Aunt Jean. She was being unfair, as they had no idea of the real turmoil she was suffering and were rightly shocked at her dressing up to the nines to go out with Daisy.

For a moment she was torn. Should she confide in her ma?

Going down on her haunches, she took her ma's hand, ready to tell her, but though the words were there, she couldn't voice them. Instead, she said, 'Ma, I knaw what you're saying, and living in a small community as you did at the time, that would happen. But not here, not now. A few of the biddies on the street'll see me leave, but I'll have me coat on and they won't knaw as I have me best frock on underneath. What Daisy is offering is just what I need. Sommat to take me mind off the pain in me heart. We'll have a giggle together and watch them as get up to dance and that'll be that. Only, there ain't many places two girls can go out together.'

'But you should be chaperoned. It ain't no more right

today than it was in my day. I just don't want you getting a name for yourself, lass.'

Maddie knew she was beaten. 'You're right, Ma. I'll go and get changed and tell Daisy it's her place or mine, and no gadding about. I don't knaw what I was thinking when I agreed. Daisy were just trying to cheer me up – give me sommat to look forward to. But it ain't done and I shouldn't do it. I've to stop in and think of poor Reggie on his way to God knaws what.'

'Eeh, lass, I'm glad. I couldn't bear you being called a floozy or sommat worse. Life ain't easy for us women. We have a lot more restrictions than the men have, and we must live within them to keep our good reputation.'

Half an hour later, the arms and soft back of the nursing chair in Daisy's bedroom seemed to hug Maddie as she sat down in it – though why it had been made so low, she couldn't fathom.

Maddie always envied Daisy's space and her view, with Barrow-in-Furness visible across the water on clear days. She found the changing tides and moods of the Irish Sea fascinating to watch from the window of the large top floor of the two-storey flat above the café.

'So, your ma persuaded you not to go to the Tower 'cos you'd be doing wrong!' Daisy stood from where she'd been sitting on her bed. 'Eeh, Maddie, how can folk be so narrow-minded? It ain't right, your ma and Aunt Jean are running your life for you.'

'It ain't like that, Daisy. They just want the best for me. Me mistakes are mine, not theirs.'

'Well, you should tell them what you've realised then. I'm sure they'd help you.'

'I – I can't. If there wasn't this war, and Reggie hadn't gone into the awful danger he has, then I could have, but how can I add to the anguish they are already feeling? Especially Aunt Jean. She don't deserve me to hurt her like that. She's given me nothing but love.'

'There ain't nowt I can say, is there, lass?'

Maddie shook her head. Inside she was pent up and angry with life. She wanted to cry and scream against her predicament, but all her tears had been exhausted and she was drained of emotion and the will to fight the injustice of it all.

But most of all she didn't want to hurt her ma and Aunt Jean. Neither must have felt like carrying on when they were left widowed, but they did. And they built a decent life for them all. She couldn't throw that in their faces now. She must be as brave as they were.

Looking up, she saw Daisy staring out of the window. There was nothing but the blackness of the night to see. No twinkling, magical lights turning the prom into a glittering wonderland. No sounds of laughing families, wrapped up warm against the cold and enjoying the spectacle. Instead, the world had become a black hole of worry for loved ones, and fear of the changes that may be inflicted on the world.

'Aw, Maddie, this shouldn't be happening to two young women. What have we done to deserve it, eh?'

'Nowt, love. But it's our lot now and we've to make the best of it. We'll be eighteen within weeks. We should be enjoying life. Having fun and being carefree. Well, we can't be the last, but we could still have fun.'

'How? There's only the Tower and its ballroom, and the circus in the winter months. Surely you wouldn't be a floozy if we went to the circus? And of course, there's the big wheel. It was going around all day, so we could ride on that, I suppose.'

'By, I've allus wanted to do that. But Reggie never trusted it. I reckon he was nervous of it, but couldn't say so ... Let's have a go on it one day, eh?'

'Aye, I've allus wanted to an' all. And there's nowt stopping us doing as the holidaymakers do, walking the prom and the piers and playing the penny slot machines. Then in summer, when its ladies' bathing day, we can go into the sea and have a swim! Aw, Maddie, remember when we were nippers? We spent hours on the beach, splashing in the sea, and we both became good swimmers.'

'Ha, Daisy, you daft ha'peth, we'll not be allowed on the beach. That's to be a training ground for the soldiers. They're already changing it.'

'Well, Cocker Street baths are open and with ladies having their own pool, no one can say we aren't behaving in a proper manner by going there.'

Maddie could feel herself cheered by all these suggestions, though she still had a longing to go to the Tower Ballroom to watch the dancers. She'd always danced around to the music her and Ma played on the gramophone, especially 'When it's Apple Blossom Time in Normandy', 'Roamin' in the Gloamin'' and 'When Irish Eyes are Smiling' ... Suddenly, with this last thought, Arnie came into her mind. His Irish eyes smiled.

Her heart flipped over. *How could he have such an effect on me after knowing him such a short time?*

But he had. He'd taken her world – her safe world where everything was mapped out for her – and turned it inside out. She no longer accepted what had become her destiny. She was unsettled and wanted more from life than working in Ma's boarding house and walking out with Reggie.

'You've gone quiet, lass. What are you thinking about?'

Glancing over at Daisy, Maddie had an urge to tell of her thoughts.

'Arnie.'

'What?'

'Arnie Brown. He's changed everything.'

'By, Maddie. I never expected that . . . Is it meeting him that's made you realise your true feelings for Reggie?'

'Aye. But how, I don't knaw. It's silly really. I mean, we ain't said owt, just a look, and, well, I feel all funny when he's nearby. I've never felt that way with Reggie. Reggie's just Reggie. I love him . . . but oh, Daisy, I ain't in love with him.'

'Well, that sigh says it all, and while we're on this subject, it's happening to me an' all . . . Tom! The moment he walked in me café, I knew he were for me, and to confirm it, I'm having the same feelings, like me legs are all wobbly when he looks at me, and like I want to just be in his arms.'

For Maddie, it was a lovely moment as they both giggled like the young girls the world considered them to be, and yet, she thought, the feelings in their hearts had turned them into young women, ready for a future of love with the men of their choice – or was that to be ruined by the choices of others?

'But I can't have Arnie, Daisy, even if it did turn out that he wanted me.'

'Yes, you can. You've made a mistake and it ain't your fault ... They were going to be at the Tower tonight, Maddie – Arnie and Tom. They came back into the café this afternoon and I told them that you were coming tonight, and that we were thinking of going to the Tower. Arnie asked about you being engaged ... I – I told him you didn't want to be and—'

'Naw, Daisy! You shouldn't have! I told you not to tell anyone!'

'I'm sorry, Maddie. I did tell him that naw one was to knaw, and that if they did, it would break your ma's and Reggie's ma's heart. Well, after he said ...'

'What? What did he say?'

'His face lit up, and he asked, "So there's a chance for me then?" Only in his Irish way.'

Despite her misgivings, Maddie had the sensation of tingling all over – Arnie had been asking after her ... He knew she didn't want to be engaged! And most of all, he wanted there to be a chance for him and her to ... 'Oh, Daisy. Was he serious?'

'Aye. As Tom then said, "He's been lovesick for Maddie since he clapped eyes on her. You've made his day, Daisy."'

'Eeh, Daisy ...'

'But that ain't all! Tom then said, "And it would make mine, if you'd think of me like Arnie thinks of Maddie." All I could do was to nod me head. Tom burst out laughing and caught hold of me hand. It was like I'd been transported to a new world. Like me life had changed somehow, it'd been made better and brighter . . . I just knaw that I'm in love with Tom, Maddie.'

'But that's wonderful. Tom's lovely. He's always so polite. Ma likes him a lot, and she does Arnie an' all. She says the pair of them are like a breath of fresh air.'

'They could be our breath of fresh air, Maddie, love . . . Look, let's go to the Tower, eh? You look lovely, as you do in whatever you wear.'

Maddie looked down at her long grey woollen skirt and black ankle boots, which she'd teamed with the cream jumper that her ma had knitted for her. 'I can't go like this! And anyway, I promised me ma that I wouldn't.'

Daisy shocked her then. In an angry gesture, she knocked a book off the little round table next to her bed. 'They can't rule your life, Maddie! You ain't a kid any more!'

'Daisy! Calm down. It ain't as bad as you paint it. I've not given them any reason to think I wasn't happy, because I was until these last weeks when doubts set in. Look, you go, love. I'll make me way home. I don't want to spoil your life.'

'But you are. You're me best friend and it hurts me to see this happening to you and you letting it!'

Daisy had tears in her eyes.

Maddie rose and went to her with her arms open. They clung to each other in a hug that told of their love but did nothing to dispel for Maddie the unfairness of it all. But then, one of her granny's sayings came to her: *You've made your bed, now you've to lie in it.*

She so missed her granny, who'd died five years ago.

Putting Daisy at arm's length, Maddie told her, 'I mean it, love, you go. I'll walk with you to the Tower and then go on home.'

'Really? You don't mind?'

'Naw, I don't mind. I want this for you, lass.'

As they neared the Tower, the promenade became busier and busier with folk milling around, their breath like steam in the air but most still laughing, as they hugged their bodies and shivered from the effects of the bitter wind that propelled them along. And then, as the crowd parted to let her and Daisy pass, there he was leaning against the wall, lit by the lamps above him and grinning at her.

The flutter in her heart tightened her throat. He looked beautiful.

Forcing herself to look away, she let go of Daisy's arm. 'You go on from here, lass, the lads are over there. I'll get home now.'

'Are you sure you won't come, Maddie?'

'I'm sure. You go, go on. I'll see you tomorrow. In the afternoon I'll come to the café for an hour.'

With this Maddie turned and almost ran towards Bonny Street where she would turn off the prom and out of sight. But the five hundred or so yards seemed much further than they were, and she thought she would never get there.

Just as she did and turned the corner, a familiar voice came to her. 'Maddie, Maddie, will you wait up, there?'

She stood still, not daring to turn around. He came up to her side.

'I thought it was that you were coming to the Tower to meet us?'

'I can't, it ain't seemly.'

'Ha! But isn't it that you would only be coming with your friend for an evening of dancing, what is it that isn't seemly about that?'

The nearness of him was having a strange effect on her senses, something she'd never felt with Reggie. Yes, she'd always been pleased to see him and often hadn't been able to wait till she did, but this – her breathing feeling shallow, her tummy tingling and her heart fluttering – had never happened. It was a sensation she liked. It brought her alive to the world's sounds and smells, and to Arnie.

It was as if he was the part of her that was missing.

'Maddie, will you turn and look at me?'

Her movement was slow as she tried to stop herself from doing this, but there were forces stronger than her that compelled her to turn and look into his eyes.

'So, your engagement is for being a sham? Something your mammy wants for you?'

'I – I . . . Daisy shouldn't have told you that. I trusted her with me confidence, and she broke it . . . It has to be that I stay engaged to Reggie, Arnie. He's gone to war, his ma and mine are distraught. How can I let them all down? How can I make Reggie suffer any more than he is?'

'Don't be for upsetting yourself now. I'll walk with you, and you can be telling me all about it.'

Maddie hadn't thought she would open her heart to anyone but Daisy, but it all poured out – the drifting along, the doubts, the recent accusations and the intense pressure Reggie had put on her to let him go all the way.

''Tis only you who can right these wrongs, Maddie. You should be being honest with others as you are now with yourself.'

'I know, but how?'

'Sure, it is that it sounds like what you had as a child – a good friendship – has carried on so that all around you had expectations of you, and you went along and mistook your feelings for love. But remember, it is as the Bible says: "When I was a child, I talked like a child, I thought like a child, I reasoned like a child. When I became a man, I set aside childish ways." You must be doing that if it is that you are to have peace and the life that is meant for you.'

Maddie stared at him. His words were exactly how it was for her. She wanted to set aside all that she'd promised as a child. She wanted different things now she was a young woman. Wasn't it her right to have them?

'Maddie, you are for being the most beautiful girl I have ever set me eyes on. I . . .'

'Naw, you mustn't say stuff like that! Please don't. You're confusing me. I just want to go home, Arnie.'

As they walked on in silence, Maddie's insides churned. How could she have told all of that to a stranger? But then Arnie wasn't that, he had never been that and never could be – he was the other half of herself.

They hadn't gone far when Arnie said, 'Maddie, will you stop a while?'

Compelled to obey, she stopped and turned towards him. His hands held her arms just below her shoulders, and his nearness to her gave her feelings she couldn't control. Without her bidding, her body swayed towards him and moulded into his. His lips came down onto hers, completing her world, and yet lifting her out of it to a place where there was no fear, no doubts, just a happy, beautiful sensation.

When they came out of the kiss, Arnie's whispered 'I love you, Maddie' thrilled her and yet deepened her despair. For this was a love she had to deny.

Pulling out of his arms, she turned and went to run towards her home, but Arnie caught hold of her. 'Don't be leaving me, Maddie. 'Tis that everyone I love does that.'

The plea halted Maddie's flight.

'Is there somewhere we can go, Maddie? Surely it is that there's someplace in this town where it is as you're not known? Only the cold is biting, and I have this greatcoat on. You must be freezing, so you must.'

'I have to go home, Arnie. I – I shouldn't have let you kiss me . . . You knaw why . . . I . . .'

'Maddie, please. I just want to be talking to you. I promise that it is I won't touch you again.'

'Let's both go back to the boarding house, and I'll make you a hot cocoa to warm you. Ma wouldn't think that wrong as you're a guest.'

Not ten minutes later, Maddie felt safe from the longings she was experiencing as they sat in the guests' sitting room sipping their hot drinks. The silence between them was companiable rather than strained.

Arnie broke the silence. He leant forward and rested his elbows on his knees, looked into the steaming mug he held

70

with both hands and said, 'For sure it is, I feel at home here and I haven't been for feeling that since I was a nipper, before ...'

Maddie allowed his hesitation. She sensed he'd been through something bad.

His head shook. 'I've only ever been for telling one person this – a friend. Mostly, I just got on with me lot, but now, I want to be telling you, Maddie. You see, I was for losing all me family in a fire back home in Ireland. Me mammy and pappy and me two younger brothers. I was ten and was rescued by a neighbour. It appears me pappy had supped a drop too much whiskey and fell asleep in his armchair. They were for saying in the papers ... I wasn't for knowing at the time, mind, but I took meself back to Ireland and found folk who told me that the reports were that me pappy had a lighted fag between his fingers when he nodded off. It seems he dropped it in his slumber and never woke to save his family.'

'Aw, Arnie. I'm sorry. So, you were the only one left? What happened to you? Did someone take care of you?'

'Me mammy had no family, and there was only an uncle on me pappy's side, who lived in Liverpool. You see, me grandpappy was an Englishman and that's how I got me English name. He settled in Ireland when he married me grandmammy, an Irish colleen. Me mammy was always telling me that he was for being the only Englishman the neighbours ever accepted.'

Arnie hesitated. Maddie waited. She could see Arnie wanted to tell her everything.

'My uncle, who'd long made his life back in England, arrived after the fire and brought me over here to his home, but his wife wasn't for taking on a youngster and so I was for ending up in an orphanage in Liverpool and never clapped me eyes on him again.'

'Aw, I don't knaw what to say . . . Were you happy and well cared for?'

''Tis that I'm not ready to talk about that part of me life. I wouldn't want you knowing such things. It's for being in the past. What about you? What was happening to your pappy?'

Maddie told him what she knew of her and Reggie's dads' death and the few memories she had of her own father.

'Family is a powerful thing,' Arnie told her, and then reminisced: 'What it is that I remember most is being loved and the happy feeling we had when it was that me pappy came in on a Friday night with his pay. Always he was for having a bag of sweets for me, Adrian and Sean, me brothers. We'd be waiting on the doorstep so we would, and he'd pretend he'd forgotten and make us search his pockets. Then wouldn't he suddenly find them tucked into his sock!'

They both giggled at this. An easy giggle that came from those who knew each other well, as Maddie felt they did, and for her, that had been a feeling she'd known from the moment she first set eyes on Arnie.

CHAPTER SIX

With only a week to go before Christmas the lads billeted with them were all getting excited to be going home in time to celebrate with their families. They'd been given a week's leave before they would be posted.

The last weeks had been strange for Maddie. Sneaking out in the evenings, saying she was going to Daisy's, when really she was going for a walk with Arnie, and Daisy was out with Tom. Some evenings they all walked together to have a sing-song and a giggle in a pub where the girls weren't known. Arnie always made them laugh when he stood and sang his Irish ditties. With some of them, he had the whole pub laughing and clapping, and with others, he brought tears to many an eye. Maddie had to stop herself from breaking down when he sang the last lines of 'Goodbye, Sweetheart, Goodbye':

> *The tear is hiding in mine eye,*
> *For time doth thrust me from thine arms;*
> *Goodbye, sweetheart, goodbye!*
> *Goodbye, sweetheart, goodbye!*

For time doth thrust me from thine arms,
Goodbye sweetheart, goodbye.

Maddie didn't ever want to say goodbye to Arnie and was shocked to realise that although it had been such a short time since Reggie had left, she'd hardly thought of him and had to force herself to talk of missing him when with her ma or Aunt Jean. And when she did think of him, the feeling of relief that he was no longer around stayed with her.

But she felt ashamed, too, to think Reggie was probably arriving to what had been termed 'hell on earth' while she was the happiest she'd ever been.

Every night she went on her knees before getting into bed and prayed that Reggie would be kept safe, and then would add, 'And please help me to get out of the tangle I'm in with him.'

Soon Maddie knew she would be praying for the safe return of Arnie and this she knew would be a desperate plea.

Today, Arnie was going to ask to be allowed to stay in their boarding house over Christmas as he had nowhere else to go. Maddie's heart went out to him, but she dared not give him permission to stay for fear of accidently disclosing her feelings, and so they had agreed that he would ask Ma directly and make it look as though it was nothing to do with her.

'Maddie!' Ma's exasperated voice stopped these thoughts. 'The lads ain't all gone yet, and need their breakfast before they go, lass. Come on, jump to.'

74

'Sorry, Ma. I want two plates of toast and that's it . . . I'll start to clear the tables that have been vacated while I wait.'

'And no chatting to Arnie! You do too much of that, Maddie, lass.'

Maddie stood and stared at her ma. 'But—'

'No buts! Eeh, love, I knaw you talk to them all, but you do take a lot more time with Arnie.'

Thinking quickly, Maddie retorted, 'Have you tried to get away from him, Ma? He's got the Irish blarney and can talk the hind leg off a donkey that one!'

'Aye, you're right there. He's asked to have a word with me – that usually means a thank you, but with him, it'll not be a few seconds and that's it. Mind, you can't help but like him. He's a charmer, and a right nice lad . . . If he asks, tell him I'll see him once breakfast is done, eh?'

'I will, Ma, but you knaw that a simple message like that can turn into ten minutes with him!'

They both laughed and Maddie felt better for it. She hoped her ma believed her story of not being able to get away from Arnie, and she seemed to.

It was later that afternoon that the men all left to go to the station. It was a strange feeling seeing them off, knowing they were going home for Christmas and wouldn't be coming back here, but going off to France.

Maddie felt her eyes prickling with tears. She'd got to know and like all the lads over the last six weeks or so, and it was breaking her heart saying goodbye.

When they waved to them as they marched down the street, Ma said, 'Eeh, lass. I pray they all come back.'

Maddie swallowed hard. She wanted to ask about Arnie, but then found she didn't have to.

'By the way, Arnie's stopping with us for Christmas. Poor lad has no one to go to. He was telling me he's an orphan and has spent the last few years volunteering in a hospital over Christmas. He made me laugh as he said, "Now, don't you be thinking me an angel! Ha, it was me cunning ways that prompted me, so they did. For I was for being well fed."'

'Eeh, Ma, you do a good Irish accent! But where did he live when it wasn't Christmas?'

Maddie knew the answer – Arnie had told her that he boarded in a guest house in Liverpool. 'It's not for being a patch on this one, but I had a bed, and a breakfast, so at least was fed once a day.'

Her heart had gone out to him.

Listening to her ma telling her this exact same tale, Maddie smiled to herself. Yes, Arnie was full of the blarney, but she loved to listen to him. She was still denying her true feelings, but their coming parting was already slicing a pain through her.

On Christmas Eve, Arnie asked, 'Would you be coming to midnight mass with me, the pair of you?'

'By, lad, midnight mass? I ain't been inside a church since God took me man. And if I did, I'd stand and swear and curse at Him!'

'I'd like to go, and maybe Aunt Jean would?' Maddie said this in an offhand way.

'Naw, lass, Aunt Jean would be worse than me. We both fell out with God when the salt mine collapsed.' Her arm came around Maddie. 'But you can go if you like, Maddie. I'm sure Arnie would look after you.'

Maddie looked away, afraid of showing her true feelings.

'Sure, it is that I will.'

The busy evening helped the time to go by. Although the shops didn't have everything they needed, Ma had her store cupboard full. The pud had been stirred within an inch of its life, and now went into the steamer on the edge of the stove to cook overnight. They peeled spuds and chopped the brussels sprouts off the stalk they'd come on.

And laughter got to almost hysterical proportions as Arnie set about plucking the goose. He had no idea how to do it, but they let him suffer for a while before they showed him the direction in which to pull the feathers out.

He got them back by scooping a handful up and throwing them at them. A bit of fun that almost turned to disaster as Ma got one in her mouth and began to choke! But it shifted and she clouted Arnie's ear for him with the oven cloth.

The goose was the last job and so once it was plucked, Ma singed the remaining little feathers off it, leaving Maddie to stuff it with homemade chestnut, apple and pork stuffing.

'Right, we'll put that in a very low oven, and it will be done nicely by the morning ... Well, that's it. You two go and get ready, you don't want to turn up smelling of dead goose!'

*   *   *

Maddie was surprised how much she enjoyed the service, singing out as loud as Arnie and praying fervently to baby Jesus.

It was when they were walking home that Arnie said, 'Sure, that was grand having you with me, Maddie. I felt for the first time that I was there with family.'

'Aw, that's a nice thing to say.'

'It's how it was for being meant, Maddie.'

Arnie had stopped walking and held her hand, pulling her towards him. The crisp air tingled her cheeks, but his words fluttered her heart. 'I'm wanting to make you me family when I get back.'

Maddie looked up at him. Above them the stars twinkled like a million diamonds, seeming to imitate the sparkling happiness that tingled through her – Arnie was saying he wanted to marry her! She wanted that more than anything, but how could she say so? Her eyes filled with tears. With his thumb, he gently wiped them away. 'I prayed to God to be sorting this out, Maddie. He'll find a way. All I need is for you to be saying you want it too and that you love me.'

'I do, Arnie, I love you with all me heart.'

He held her then as if he would never let her go. His body shook with sobs. Maddie knew they were a mixture of happiness at their love, and sadness at having to leave her soon.

This Christmas Day had been one Maddie would never forget. Aunt Jean had eaten dinner with them, and then in the evening, Daisy and her ma, and Tom, who had chosen not to go home but to stay with Daisy, came too.

Ma had baked a huge birthday cake for Maddie – something she did every year, instead of a Christmas cake. Everyone sang happy birthday to her, and all kissed her when the song was over. Arnie's kiss, though on her cheek, held his love for her, making this the best birthday ever.

After that, the games they played were hilarious, the funniest being pass the parcel. Ma had wrapped up various items of clothing, including underwear, and the one landed with the parcel had to wear what they unwrapped! Tom had them splitting their sides with laughter as he ended up in a huge bra one of the guests had left behind, some long-legged ladies' knickers and a felt hat!

Arnie touched them all when he said it was his first ever family Christmas since he'd lost his family, and then told of a touching tradition whereby he lit a candle every Christmas Day for those he'd loved and lost. Ma found one for him and they ended the evening with them doing this and all remembering a member lost from their own family units. And then with the lights out, and just the glow of the candle and the flicker of the roaring fire, they sang carols.

It had been a perfect day.

Boxing Day night changed everything.

Maddie had no resistance from her ma when she told her that she was going for a walk with Arnie to meet Tom and Daisy at the pub.

She left the house full of joy, but they hadn't gone far when Arnie said, 'I have something to tell you, Maddie … 'Tis tomorrow that I must leave.'

'What? But I thought it was next week?'

'It is that I am deployed then, but me orders are to report to barracks by midnight tomorrow. And me falling in love with you is making it powerfully difficult to go, when it was that I was excited about it before I met you.'

'Oh, Arnie ... I – I don't want you to go ... How am I to live without you?'

'You will be for writing to me, won't you?'

'Every day!'

With this, the shame she had become used to hit Maddie afresh. She hadn't written to Reggie for over a week!

'Let us be having the best of nights tonight. Sure, it will give us something to remember.'

His arm came around her, but the gesture didn't dispel the dread in the pit of her stomach, a feeling that dampened the fun they'd said they would have.

Arnie was subdued, when he was usually the life and soul of the party. But when the others in the pub who'd come to know and love him called for him to sing, he took a deep breath. 'Didn't I say we were to have the best night, Maddie?'

'You did. And that's always so when you get up and sing, lad.'

From then on it was impossible to have a conversation as the chap who played honky-tonk piano had learnt the tunes to all the Irish songs Arnie sang and the pub became a riot of clapping, singing along, and some of the folk making a hilarious attempt to dance an Irish jig!

At the end of the evening, Arnie told them, 'Tomorrow it is that Tom and me are to begin our journey to war. I'll be taking the memories of this place with me, so I will. God bless you all.'

For a moment there was silence, and then, as if one, the crowd stood and clapped. Women, fuelled by a pint or two of ale, sobbed. Men shook Arnie and Tom by the hand. All wished them luck. One gentleman said, 'Go with me love going with you. Save us all from the evil Kaiser.'

Then there were hugs all round before they stepped out onto the pavement outside and shivered with the cold.

'Eeh, Maddie, why don't you and Arnie come to mine for a hot drink on your way home, eh?'

'Ta, Daisy. We will, lass. By, it's freezing.'

'I'll be for keeping you warm, me wee darlin'.'

With this, Arnie took off his greatcoat and wrapped it around her.

It felt to Maddie as if she was being encased in a love that warmed not just her body, but her soul.

As they sipped a mug of hot tea, sitting in the darkened café, they didn't talk much. The thought of the awful plight they faced tomorrow hung over them.

Suddenly, Daisy stood. 'Me and Tom are going up now, Maddie. You and Arnie stay as long as you like. I'll get the spare key off the hook, and you can let your-selves out.'

As she came over with the key, Maddie stood. They clung on to each other. Daisy whispered, 'This is your real goodbye, love, you can't make that at your ma's tomorrow. Make the most of it. And of the love you have for one another ... Eeh, Maddie, I wish things were different.'

As she and Tom went through the door to the upstairs, Tom turned. 'See you when we get back, Maddie. Take care.'

'I will, Tom.'

As soon as the door closed on them, Arnie stood and switched off the lights.

Lit now by the dim streetlight, the café took on a romantic glow. Maddie's senses heightened her anticipation. Her throat tightened. Her body quivered as the shadowy figure of Arnie walked back towards her.

Him sliding back into the bench next to her filled her with longing. His kiss sealed her love for him and made her swim to a place where she was lost to everything but what Arnie was doing to her – caressing her, kissing her, whispering his love.

She didn't resist when he gently lay her across the bench, nor when his hand found its way into her knickers.

Her moan at his touch didn't say 'No', but gave in to her need.

When he entered her, there was the slight discomfort Daisy had told of, but it was masked very quickly by the sensations of his gentle movements.

Soon their bodies were in rhythm, their cries were of love and deep pleasure, their promises were of lifetime commitment, until an exquisite feeling took Maddie's senses, and she clung to Arnie, begging him to be still, crying out as her body yielded to his with all the love and desire that had taken her from herself and given everything to him.

When they lay still, spent, they held each other gently. They spoke of their love, and then they cried – tears of desperation as the hours they had together ticked away.

The next morning, Ma greeted her as she came into the kitchen. 'You were out late, lass. What were you up to?'

There was a silence.

Ma broke it. 'Eeh, Maddie, lass, naw.'

'I love him, Ma. I – I'm sorry. I didn't mean to. It just happened.'

'But Reggie ...'

'Ma, Reggie is like a beloved brother to me. I feel nothing of what I feel for Arnie. Me heart's breaking at him going today.'

'Today?'

'Aye. Him and Tom have to leave today.'

'Eeh, lass ... I just don't knaw what to say ... Aunt Jean ... I – I ... By, this bloody pain!'

Ma leant over the table.

Maddie was by her side in an instant. 'Ma, you must go to the doctor's. We can afford it now with the soldiers billeted with us. Another lot will be arriving soon, and the army is paying us well ... Please, Ma.'

'But I want to put by all I can for your future, lass.'

'Me future'll be nowt without you, Ma. This could be something serious.'

'Aye, you're right. I'll contact Doctor Midgley.'

'You pay into the penny fund he runs, so it might not cost you owt, only if you have to have treatment. But if it's needed, we'll find the money.'

'I've said I'll go. Now, get the kettle on, lass, and let's get Arnie served his breakfast, eh?'

'Why not invite him in here with us instead of him sitting in the dining room on his own? After all, he's spent Christmas with us, and ... well, me and Arnie plan on marrying when he comes home, Ma.'

'Good Lord, Maddie! What on earth?'

'Ma, think back to you and Da. You knew he was right for you, and you were only my age. You wouldn't have married someone else, would you?'

'Naw, I wouldn't, lass. But this is going to cause a big upset ... Anyway, with this pain gnawing at me, I can't deal with it now. Arnie's a lovely bloke and I knaw he'll make you happy, but it ain't going to be easy. Give me a hug, me little lass, and let's get done what we have to. We'll unravel everything in time.'

With this from her ma, Maddie skipped into the dining room and straight into Arnie's arms. There she received his kiss and held him tightly.

When he released her, she told him, 'Ma knaws, Arnie, and she's all right with it. She just can't sort things yet, but she's said she will.'

Arnie's grin gave her him at his most handsome.

'I love you, me Arnie. With all me heart.'

When Arnie left, Maddie didn't go to the station with him. Ma had asked them to say goodbye at home. 'I don't want this getting back to Aunt Jean. Not the way it would if you went to the station, and everyone saw you saying your goodbyes. We'll handle it our way. But just to say, Arnie, I've fallen in love with you meself. And you take care and come home safely.'

Arnie put out his arms to her and she went into them. There was a wince from her as she did.

'Ma, it is that you're to get that pain sorted. Wasn't Maddie for telling me you've had it this good while?'

He'd called her 'Ma'. Maddie's heart soared.

'I will, lad. Now, I'll leave you to say your goodbyes.'

The kisses and hugs Maddie and Arnie shared after being left alone were full of sorrow. And yet, they held a promise of their future – although when that would be, Maddie didn't know. But she would wait. And when the war was over, she would know a deep happiness.

CHAPTER SEVEN

The new intake of soldiers seemed a different breed to what Maddie had been used to. They were younger and full of bravado and cheek. At times she found them funny, but they didn't have a line when they would stop their silly antics and behave like grown men.

She knew she wasn't as tolerant of them as she should be and often treated them like schoolboys when, in her heart, she had a sinking feeling for their safety and wanted to tell them to go home, not to volunteer for a man's job.

After one prank where a lad had stuck his foot out to trip her and sent her flying across the room, and she was only just able to catch hold of the mantelpiece to save her fall, she turned on them. 'You stupid, stupid idiots! By, for two pennies, I'd knock all your blocks off!'

Their laughter humiliated her.

Rushing out of the dining room and back to the kitchen, she burst through the door.

'Eeh, Ma, how are we to get through the next six weeks? They're schoolboys! How could the government accept them and send them to fight?' She told of what had happened. 'I could have cracked me head!'

'Eeh, I'll tame that lot. You do the kitchen work, lass. I'll serve the lads.'

Glad of the respite from dealing with the young soldiers, Maddie set about toasting a mound of bread.

They had two long-handled forks for this job and held the bread to the open grate of the huge range containing four ovens, and four warming shelves where they kept the plates.

Toasting was an art as with the door to the grate open the heat was intense. It took just the right amount of time, and distance from the flames, to achieve the perfect toast that didn't taste of smoke.

Just as soon as she had two slices ready, Ma buttered them and whipped them out.

There was no riotous noise coming from the dining room now, only a silence broken by the clatter of knives and forks and mugs being put on saucers.

'What did you do to achieve that, Ma?'

'I threatened them with me rolling pin! I said, "Any more antics and the lad responsible would have his pants pulled down and a good whacking on his bare arse."' Ma laughed. 'Ha, stunned them into silence, I did!'

Maddie burst out laughing. Ma held on to the back of a chair and laughed with her until her face creased with pain.

Dropping the toasting fork onto the grate plate, Maddie ran to her side. 'Aw, Ma, Ma!'

'It's all right, lass. It's as the doctor said, griping pains. I'm to take a dose of me syrup of figs, but you'll have . . . t – to

see to the lads now. Just be firm with them, tell them ...
Ooh ...'

Sweat beads stood out on Ma's forehead and her knuckles turned white as she gripped the back of the chair.

Maddie held her as best as she could, her heart heavy with worry. 'Let me help you to sit down, Ma.'

'But there's ... the rest of the toast to get done, lass ... Put – put one of the chairs near to the range, I'll sit there. I can stick the bread on the fork and hold it to the fire that way.'

Somehow, they got the lads served and hurrying upstairs to collect their kit.

Maddie stood by the door to see them out. One of them, a small cockney lad called Jimmy, stopped beside her. 'I'm sorry you were treated how you were, miss.'

His freckled, fresh face made Maddie want to hold him and protect him.

'How old are you Jimmy, lad?'

'Ha, me mum says I'm as old as me hair but a bit older than me teeth, mate.'

Maddie laughed but then became serious. 'I'd say you were no more than sixteen. You don't have to go to war, lad.'

'Me country needs me, miss, that Kitchener bloke said so. And that's good enough for me.'

Maddie sighed. The lad had a brave heart and thought himself a man, but it was so unfair of them in charge to accept them without checking their age.

'Eeh, lad, take care of yourself, eh?'

Jimmy grinned, but she saw his lip quiver as he said, 'Yer

sound just like me mum!' before turning and running to catch up with the others.

Going back to the kitchen, Maddie found her ma bent over. 'Aw, Ma, Ma . . .' By her side in seconds, she put her arm around her ma's shoulders and held her gently. 'Go and lie down, Ma. Take your medicine and see if you can get off to sleep. I'll soon have this lot sorted and the bedrooms done. I've got all day and I want to keep busy. I need to stop meself thinking of Arnie.'

Though she said this, Maddie knew it wouldn't happen. Arnie was on her mind and in her heart. She wept for him when she put her head on her pillow and dreamt about him, waking to think he was there by her side, or making love to her as he had at the café.

Every time she thought of that, her stomach muscles clenched, giving her a longing for it to happen again. But it couldn't. Her lovely Arnie was miles and miles away from her.

'Aw, lass. You've got yourself in a mess. Maybe it's best to forget Arnie, eh? It's been you and Reggie all your life. Arnie was just a fling . . . He – he didn't do owt to you, did he? . . . I mean, other than kissing and cuddling . . .'

This shocked Maddie. She'd thought her ma had come to terms with her being in love with Arnie and not Reggie, but it seemed now she hadn't, and her question threw Maddie. She wanted to deny it, but there was nothing she could do about her face blushing bright red.

'Maddie? Eeh, Maddie, lass, you didn't . . .'

Maddie's cheeks burnt. The act of loving Arnie suddenly became wrong. But she didn't want it to be. They loved one another and had expressed that love . . . but then to do so out of wedlock was a sin. Her heart sank with guilt.

Staring at her ma's anxious, pale face made her tell a lie. 'We . . . we only . . . well . . . touched and that.'

'Thank God. Though it's not sommat you should do, Maddie, I understand. I loved your da so much that it led to all of that. At the end of the day, we're only human. But try to put it behind you, lass. Try to think of Reggie and the promise you made to him . . . Where's your ring?'

'I – I don't wear it for work, Ma.'

'You should never take it off. It's a sign that you're taken and stops men thinking they have a chance with you.'

Maddie wanted to scream that she didn't want to be taken, not by Reggie. She wanted to marry Arnie and only Arnie and would always feel like that, but her ma's face, drawn with pain, made it difficult to say. 'I – I told you, Ma, Reggie's more like a beloved brother to me. It just took a little time, and meeting the real love of me life to make me realise it.'

Ma caught hold of her hand; her face held an appeal. 'He ain't, love. You've had a fling, that's all Arnie was. He's one of life's charmers and had even me falling in love with him. He'll go through life loving and leaving the girls. You start to think of Reggie and all the memories you have together. Bring him back to the forefront of your life, lass, as you promised to marry him, and he'll be counting the days till he can come home.'

It shocked Maddie that Ma thought Arnie such a person when he was a loving, kind man who hadn't had much in life. But she decided to give her ma some peace. 'All right,

Ma, don't worry yourself. Come on, I've to get on with things, so it'd be better if you went and rested and left me to it.'

'Eeh, lass, they say the daughters become the mas, but you're starting early! You're right, though, I could do with a lie down. You get on with everything and I'll be back helping you in an hour or so.'

Throwing herself into the chores didn't help Maddie. She just wanted to sit and cry and cry. Nothing had changed! Ma still wanted her to marry Reggie and was convinced that Arnie was just a passing phase, but he wasn't, he was her life, her love, her everything.

With her anger at the unfairness of the world propelling her, Maddie had everything done by dinner time, when it usually took her and her ma till around two o'clock in the afternoon. But then, they did natter a lot and stop for umpteen cups of tea.

Thinking of cups of tea, Maddie put the kettle on. She'd take one to her ma and she'd do as she'd been willing herself to: she'd say Ma was right. That she would forget Arnie and concentrate on Reggie. But only to give her ma peace of mind. She didn't want her to worry about anything.

Thinking over what the doctor had said – that the condition Ma had was an inflammation of the bowel, and that she needed to keep herself purged – Maddie picked up the bottle of syrup of figs that her ma hadn't taken and put it on the tray with the tea.

Ma opened her eyes as Maddie entered her bedroom. Her smile showed that the pain had settled down.

'Eeh, lass, I thought you would bring a sandwich, I'm starving.'

Maddie laughed with relief. 'Ha! I've had naw time to turn around, let alone make you a sandwich!' Then, thinking of her resolve, she added, 'And I've a letter to write to Reggie yet. Though if he's getting them, he'll be bored with me keeping on about me ma making a slave of me.'

Ma laughed, and it was a lovely sound. 'Don't, lass, it hurts when I laugh, but by, it's good to hear you talking of Reggie. I told you it was just a passing phase with Arnie. Now he's not here with his smooth talking, you'll soon forget him.'

All Maddie could say was, 'Aye, happen I will. Anyroad, I've done the spuds and minced the stewing steak. I'm going to put that on to cook with the onions I've chopped, and I'll make a shepherd's pie for supper. That's the beauty of the soldiers coming and going, we don't have to vary the menu often. Anyroad, you feel you could eat a sandwich now then?'

'Aye, I'm right hungry, lass.'

By four o'clock, Maddie had the huge shepherd's pie in the oven, and had made a jam roly-poly for pudding. She'd make the custard nearer the time, or it would form a skin and thicken up too much.

At last, with Ma still resting, she could sit and write her two letters, one to Reggie, but most importantly, one to Arnie. Both went to the army HQ even though they were in different regiments and would be shipped over to them.

It was a difficult task to write Reggie's. To avoid lying about their future, and about her feelings, she wrote more about daily life, her worries over her ma and told him that his ma was all right. But that they were all missing him.

With having just put her pen down the back door opened and Aunt Jean stood there. 'Hello, lass. I'm just going to nip out to post a letter to me Reggie, and I wondered if you had one to post.'

Reacting swiftly, Maddie stood and as she went to go towards Aunt Jean to hug her, picked up the letter for Arnie and shoved it under the rolled-back tablecloth.

'By, Maddie, that were a hug and a half! You nearly knocked me off me pins, lass!'

Maddie laughed to cover the embarrassment of her overenthusiastic action. 'I'm just pleased to see you, Aunt Jean. Ma's not well again and I've been hectic, I've only had time to write a short letter to Reggie. I've got it here.'

'Well, we write most weeks, so it's hard to think of things to say when our lives are as humdrum as they are. But I don't like to think of the other lads receiving bundles of mail and him not, bless him . . . Eeh, Maddie, I miss him.'

Maddie put her arms around her Aunt Jean once more and cuddled her to her. It broke her heart to think that one day she was going to have to hurt this lovely lady who'd given her nothing but love.

'I miss him an' all. It's like there's a hole in our lives,' Maddie lied.

'Aw, I shouldn't be like this when you're suffering. I should be brave for you, love, I'm sorry. Come on, let's cheer up . . . You say as your ma's not well again? By, it's a rum condition that she has, and she's been told there's no cure for it, poor lass.'

'What? Ma didn't tell me that. She said it would pass, that it was an inflammation that would get better.'

'Eeh, lass, she'd want to save you worrying, but they said it was ulcerative colitis. I knaw, a funny word, but it means her bowels have sores in them.'

'Is that why she keeps having diarrhoea and sickness?'

'Aye. It's awful for her.'

'Will — will she die?'

'Naw. Eeh, love, don't think that, but she will need more and more care. You should persuade her to take on a staff member. Me life's been so much better since I've had Ada. I've had a few, as you knaw, but Ada's me rock.'

Maddie didn't know what she thought of this. She'd always imagined it would be just her and her ma running their boarding house and the thought of a third person felt like an intrusion.

'Just have a maid, lass. It'll make all the difference. She can have the bedrooms done while you and your ma are in the kitchen, and then clean the downstairs and do all the laundry. I tell you, it'd change your life and your ma's.'

The idea began to appeal as it would mean she would still be with Ma in the kitchen, which was their time together. The other jobs they did separately, halving the chores between them.

'Ta, Aunt Jean, I'll make sure Ma agrees. Will you ask Ada if she knaws of anyone?'

'I will. Now, give your Ma me love and tell her I'll call in later. I've to catch the post with these. And you straighten that tablecloth, or you'll have that to iron next! See you later.'

94

A quick peck on the cheek and she was gone, leaving Maddie in a daze. *Me ma's really ill. It isn't sommat that will pass. I can't bear it. I want her well. And what about the boarding house? How will I cope?*

But she soon realised these were selfish thoughts and it was her ma, facing a lifetime of feeling how she did, who was the one to feel sorry for.

Straightening the cloth and shoving the letter to Arnie – much fatter than the one to Reggie – into the pocket of her pinny, Maddie pushed a stray strand of hair from her forehead. For a moment, she stared at the wall as if it would give her answers, but the panic remained. She didn't want her ma ill, she didn't want her to be in pain, and she didn't want the responsibility to fall on her shoulders. Always she'd been a helper to Ma.

Squaring her shoulders, Maddie spoke crossly to herself. *If I have it to do, then it's how it will be. I'll look after Ma, and see she has nowt to fret over. It's the least I can do.*

But then a heavy feeling took her as she thought about her break times with Daisy and how much she needed them. She hadn't yet been able to see Daisy after Tom leaving, or have Daisy comfort her. And she needed to be able to talk freely about her feelings too. She could only do that with Daisy.

Now, the times they had together would be few and far between. Unless Daisy came here. Yes, she could do that. The café closed at six in the evening. Whereas here, there was always someone about and asking for something. Ma had coped with that till now, but she couldn't leave anything to Ma, not to do on her own. It would be too much.

Looking up at the clock on the wall, Maddie began to panic. The lads would begin to come in soon with their demands for this and that and traipsing their muddy boots all over the place. She'd have to look lively. But first she needed a word with her ma.

Ma lay back on her pillow. Her face had a yellow tinge.

Fear gripped Maddie. 'Ma, Ma!'

Opening her eyes as if it was an extreme effort to do so, Ma smiled. 'Sorry, lass, I dropped off again. What time is it?'

'Almost a quarter to four.'

'Eeh, naw. I've to get up and get sommat done.'

'Naw, Ma, you stay there. I'll manage. I'll get some of the lads to help. There's a couple of sensible ones amongst them.'

'But . . .'

Maddie went around the bed and sat on it next to her ma. Taking her hand, she realised how thin it was, with the knuckles protruding, making it look almost skeletal. 'Aw, Ma, why didn't you tell me how ill you really are?'

She hadn't meant for a tear to fall, but suddenly life seemed so complicated with her love life in turmoil, missing Arnie to the point she felt that half of her was severed, and now finding out just how poorly her ma really was. Not to mention having the huge responsibility of running the boarding house on her shoulders.

'I've let you down, lass.'

'Naw. Don't be daft. We'll be all right. Aunt Jean is asking Ada if she knaws someone who might do bedrooms and clean for us . . . I think it's time, Ma. We'll have to have help. We can still work the kitchen together, then if you're feeling off one day, I can manage that. But I couldn't do many days like today. It's too much for one person.'

'Good idea, love.'

Maddie hadn't expected that. She'd thought Ma would argue. It made a truth of her feeling as ill as she looked – and this deepened Maddie's worry.

When the lads began to trickle back from their day of training, Jimmy was one of the first. He greeted her with, 'You look like me mum after a day of scrubbing, washing our clothes in the dolly tub, and not having a minute to herself.'

'You've hit the nail on the head, Jimmy, as that's how it's been. I'm chasing me tail as me ma calls it when we get into a panic. I could do with a hand.'

She explained to him how her ma couldn't work this evening.

Jimmy pitched in to help her without giving it a second thought. He ignored the others poking fun at him, saying he'd always wanted to be a chef.

Maddie couldn't believe the massive help he was, and laughed as he quietened those rigging him by telling them they'd get nothing to eat at all if they didn't shut their cake 'oles.

There was something about cockneys, Maddie had found. They seemed to earn the respect and love of everyone, or if they didn't, they could shut them up without causing offence as they did it in a comical way.

Jimmy was an example of this as he had all the lads laughing. Even when he donned a pinny and gave a hand with the washing-up.

'So, Jimmy,' Maddie said, as she gave him another steaming plate to dry, 'how many are there in your family, as you seem used to doing household chores?'

'Ha! If I was to tell yer that, you'd faint! Me mum has six kids!'

'Eeh, that's on the way to being a football team!'

Jimmy laughed. 'Not with most of them being girls. I've four sisters and one brother. Bleedin' nuisance me sisters are, and you asked me why I joined up!'

Maddie didn't like the word he used. She'd never heard it before but was sure it must be a swear word.

'You shouldn't use that language in front of ladies, Jimmy!'

'What language?'

'That "b" word.'

Jimmy doubled over. When he sobered, he said, 'It's not a "b" word like bugger! It's a word to express yourself, it don't mean anything . . . You weren't offended, were yer?'

'Well, let's just say we up north aren't used to using expressions like it, but I ain't offended. Anyroad, what does your dad do to keep you all fed and such?'

'I ain't got a dad. Only me twin sisters who are soon to be eighteen, Lizzie and Jenny, know who their dad was. Me mum were married to him, and loved him, but he was killed in an accident on the docks. Mum tried to cope, but the parish relief was only given every so often . . . and Mum . . . Well, don't take this wrong, she did what she had

98

to do to feed us, and keep us together, but trouble is, it led to more bleedin' mouths to feed!'

Shocked, and embarrassed by Jimmy's openness, Maddie busied herself wiping down the draining board as Jimmy carried on with his tale – the like of which she'd never heard.

'I was the first she had from going with men, and Mum told me she looked on me as a blessing, and not the shame of her actions which she'd been forced into. And then there's Betsy, fifteen, and Ruth, thirteen, and me youngest brother, Alf. He's five.'

'Eeh, lad, does your ma still . . . ?'

'No. The twins work at the biscuit factory, and give her their wages, and I used to get work at the docks, but not every day. And that's another reason I joined the army. You see, me pay'll be regular from the army, and having regular money is helping me mum.'

'By, that's good. So, things are improving for her?'

'Well, she don't have to go with men now, but what we bring in ain't enough to get her and me family out of the hovel they live in.'

Maddie's heart went out to Jimmy's ma. It seemed that all she'd done was to keep her family going, and yet, it had led to her getting into deeper trouble.

She listened and Jimmy went on.

'You see, Mum's in debt from the past and the money lender demands more and more, as he knows she's money coming in. He keeps adding interest on top for the times that she missed paying. We're all scared of him . . . It was him that forced Mum to go on the streets in the first place.'

'Eeh, lad, it sounds a tough life. Your poor mum.'

'Ha! It ain't like that, you could never pity me mum in that way. She's a strong character, and feisty with it. She'd clock yer one rather than look at yer.'

'That's probably because she has to fight for everything she's got, and she's been taken advantage of.'

Jimmy turned and looked at Maddie. His look held astonishment and, yes, she could see he was near to tears too.

'Yer a kind lady, Maddie. You've an 'eart of gold. I've never known anyone understand me mum like that. But that's how it is. She gets no respect from anyone. No one sees her struggles and how she hates what she has to do. They just see a dirty prossie and call her names.'

His sniff was to hide a sob. Maddie could almost touch the love he had for his ma. And she wanted to help in some way. She didn't know how but asked anyway.

'Is there owt I can do for your ma, Jimmy, lad?'

Without having to think, he said, 'I wish you could get her up here. Yer don't know what a paradise you live in to London's East End. We have muck on every street. The houses are hovels, they're damp and cold. We only have an outside lav that we share with the neighbour. It stinks and freezes over in the winter.' Again, he sniffed. 'And many don't bother going out to it, but pee in a pot and chuck it out of the window.' He laughed then. 'I tell yer, if yer out walking, yer have to keep your eyes peeled and yer ears pinned back so as not to be soaked in someone's pee!'

Maddie burst out laughing.

Jimmy grinned, but then became serious again.

'I ain't seen any conditions up here like we live in, and there's plenty of work for me sisters, as nearly every shop has cards up telling of vacant positions. I tell yer, Maddie, it's 'eaven up here and the bleedin' money lender would never find me mum.'

This told Maddie that Jimmy was serious. He really did want her to try to get his ma up to Blackpool to live.

Though she didn't know how she'd go about achieving that for him, on an impulse she said, 'You give me your mum's address and I'll have a think. I ain't promising, mind, as I'd have to find somewhere that had enough bedrooms.'

'More than one would be bleedin' marvellous as that's all we have at 'ome.'

Maddie was too taken aback to answer this. The picture Jimmy was painting was alien to what northerners had always believed – that all London folk were rich and didn't suffer the hardships they did. But it seemed that was the wrong impression.

'What's your ma's name, Jimmy?'

'Hattie. She's lovely, really. Funny and, like I say, with a quick temper, but she'd never hurt anyone who were good to her. She only sticks up for herself . . . I miss her. I miss her a lot.'

With this a tear plopped onto his cheek. And although not much younger than her, at this moment, he seemed like a child. On an impulse, Maddie opened her arms. 'Let me give you a hug, Jimmy, lad. If for nowt else, for helping me out.'

She hadn't thought he'd accept but he did.

His body racked with sobs.

Patting his back, she told him, 'I promise, I'll help your ma in some way. It ain't going to be easy to get her up here, but I'll try – that's if she'll come. But in any case, I'll send stuff to her. Clothes, and food, and I could send a bit of money by postal order now and again, but it wouldn't be much.'

'Ta, Maddie. Ta ever so much. Anything would help Mum.'

Maddie felt that she could have thanked him rather than he her, as it seemed he'd given her a purpose in life when she didn't know she needed one. But suddenly she realised that she was always well fed and clothed and loved, and she hadn't thought that others might not be. Well, from now on, she'd do her bit to help the less fortunate.

With this thought, Maddie knew she would cope a little better through the months or maybe years ahead, and she'd do so by helping others.

CHAPTER EIGHT

'By, Maddie, you've taken on sommat there, lass. How do you plan on doing it?'

Daisy's response on hearing Maddie's plan a couple of days later touched on Maddie's own misgivings.

'I've started by writing to Jimmy's mum saying how I'll try to help her all I can. Jimmy put a note in with me letter telling his mum all about Blackpool and how he wanted her up here.'

'Eeh, love, I understand how you feel, but it's a commitment that'll be difficult to fulfil. Blackpool's teeming and every spare accommodation is taken. If there's anywhere in the world that's benefitting from this stinking war, it's here. Ma says she's never been so well off! We're working flat out at breakfast, dinner and supper.'

'There you go then, you could do with a helping hand. Like us, your ma could employ someone.'

'Aye, she has said a couple of times that we need someone who'd take the food to the tables and wash pots. But where's such a large family going to live?'

'I knaw, but there must be somewhere! I mean,

everyone's wanting staff and Blackpudlians can't fill all the vacancies, so maybe a live-in job.'

'For six folk!'

'Naw, not all in the same place. Those over the age of fourteen – and there's three of them, one fifteen, and twins of seventeen – could have live-in jobs in one of the bigger hotels. I mean, they'd still be near to their ma. And that would only leave three to find a house for.'

'Well, put like that there's more of a chance . . . Anyroad, what does a girl have to do to get a cuppa round here? I visit you 'cos you can't visit me, and I'm not offered owt!'

'Sorry, love, me mind's all over the place.'

'I'm not surprised. You already had enough on your plate with your ma ailing. You stay sat down, love, and I'll make the tea.'

As she shifted the kettle onto the hob, Daisy asked, 'How is your ma, lass?

'She's up and down. I worry how she's losing weight, when she didn't seem to have any to lose. And she's so tired. I'm wondering if the medication the doctor gave her is suiting her.'

'Maybe it'll take time to work. But I'm glad you're getting someone in to help.'

As Daisy put the two steaming mugs of tea down on the kitchen table and sat on the chair opposite Maddie, she sighed. 'It seems ages since me Tom went. It's like someone's sliced me in two. I never thought falling in love felt like this. But on top of missing him, I feel afraid he'll never come back!'

Maddie put out her hand and placed it over Daisy's. 'I knaw. I didn't think it could happen so fast that one man could mean your whole life … I was with Reggie from birth, and he never had this impact on me. Now he's like a worry that won't go away.'

'I just don't knaw what you can do to resolve it, love. I feel sorry for you … Maybe … Eeh, naw, I'm not saying that – how could I even think it!'

Maddie instinctively knew what Daisy had been about to say – that everything would resolve if Reggie didn't come back. But Maddie didn't want that. Never that.

'Don't worry, love, these things pop into your head without you wanting them to. I knaw you wouldn't mean it. But oh, I wish things were different.'

They sat a moment in silence before Daisy said, 'Well, it's no good moping about it all. Ma says we have to take each day as it comes, and that's what I'm going to do. I knaw they'll all bring me sadness as I'll miss Tom, but that don't mean I can't be cheerful for the lads that still face having to go to war.'

'Aye, I'm the same. I just like to make sure those staying with us are comfy, well fed, and feel this is a home from home for them. But by, it's going to be hard to see this lot off. They're so young and cheeky, and I've become attached to Jimmy. He's a nice lad.'

'We need sommat to cheer us up – a bit of fun in our lives, lass. We should go out how we used to. Your Aunt Jean comes around most evenings, don't she?'

'Aye, she and Ma sit nattering while I twiddle me thumbs.'

'Well then, how about we go to the pictures one night? The Royal Pavilion has some good films on.'

'Eeh, Daisy, that'd be grand. Only we mustn't be late getting there, like we were last time. It were that dark, you went and sat on that bloke's knee thinking it an empty seat!'

'Ha, I wouldn't have minded, but he was old and had knobbly knees that stuck in me bum!'

This set them off laughing, making the doom and gloom they'd descended into flit away as if it hadn't happened.

'Poor chap was that shocked he had a coughing fit!'

'Aye, and was shown out as he were making too much noise!'

Hardly able to speak for giggling, Daisy said, 'And I got to pinch his seat and it were nice and warm an' all, and you had to sit in a cold one next to me!'

Their laughter increased and Maddie began to feel better. Daisy could always lift her and it was one of the reasons she loved her.

A week later, a letter arrived for Jimmy from his ma. Maddie was surprised that she'd written a separate one to herself.

What she read conjured up a picture of Hattie just as Jimmy had described her.

Dear Maddie,

Ta for your letter and the kindness you're showing to me Jimmy.

It's hard seeing a kid who thinks he's a man go off to war. I didn't know about him signing up until it was too late and me heart's broken in pieces, I miss him that much.

106

I don't think that Jimmy mentioned that I have someone in me life. He doesn't want to accept it and thinks it's like before when I had to do stuff to keep me kids alive. But it ain't.

Grantham, me man, runs a grocery shop near to me. He was widowed a long time ago, as I was. He can't go to war as he is blind in one eye. We were friends for a long time before we realised that we were in love. We're going to marry and he's taking on me family as his own. Me girls and me youngest son adore him. He understands that what I did, I did for them.

It would be a help to me if you'd settle Jimmy's mind over it all. I know he likes Grantham, he's just afraid for me.

But Jimmy tells me you have a lot on your shoulders and you ain't much older than him!

Maddie had to smile at this as she felt a million years older than Jimmy. But her smile encompassed her relief too, as she had been at her wits' end as to how to help Hattie get out of the hovel she lived in and bring her up to Blackpool.

I was sorry to hear that you have troubles, and hope your mum's health improves. Anyway, keep in touch. Me Jimmy thinks the world of you, and I hope that one day we will meet.

If you were a man, I'd call you a diamond geezer as that sums you up, but as it is, you're an angel, ta for everything.

Love, Hattie x

As she put the letter down, Maddie giggled. She had no idea what a diamond geezer was, but it sounded complimentary. And how glad she was that Hattie was happy and she hoped with all her heart that her troubles were coming to an end.

Putting the letter on the kitchen table, she looked up when the door opened. It was Jimmy. 'Did me mum tell yer she's getting married, Maddie?'

'Aye, she did. What do you think of that, lad?'

The legs of the chair Jimmy pulled out from under the table scraped noisily over the tiled floor. He plonked himself down with a huge sigh that spoke volumes.

'Jimmy, love, I don't knaw your ma, but it sounds to me like she loves this Grantham and has a chance of a better life with him. You wouldn't deny her that, would you?'

'No, but I worry that he's taking advantage of her. He's a nice bloke, but well . . .'

'Jimmy, it's grand how you care for your ma and want her to be happy, and I can understand your concerns, you've all been through a lot because of her . . . well, her way of coping. But it sounds as though she didn't have much choice. But now she's got a chance of happiness, and you should be happy for her and tell her so. She's worried sick about you as it is, going off to war, when you ain't been wearing long-'uns for more than a couple of years.'

'What's long-'uns?'

His expression made Maddie giggle. 'Your trousers, lad! It's a saying we have which means that you've only just matured as a young man. But to your ma, you're still her little boy and it's breaking her heart that you left. So, give her some comfort of knowing you're happy for her, eh?'

'I am. It's . . . well . . .'

'Tell me about Grantham. What kind of fella is he?'

'He's no looker! He's got a funny eye and he's a bit on the fat side, with a shiny red face, and he's always smiling. He jokes a lot, and he's kindly – always giving stuff to them as can't afford to buy it . . . He's an all right bloke, I suppose.'

'Well then, how about you write to your ma and tell her that you think that of Grantham and wish her every happiness, eh?'

'I will. And do you know what? I am glad, as I do think Grantham'll care for her. And I'll take her a present when I go back home. I keep trying to win a brooch on the hoop-a-prize stall on the prom. It's in that arcade place where the slot machines are.'

'Eeh, lad, save your pennies and buy her one. Them things are rigged so you'll never win!'

'Really? Well, that's a bloomin' swizz!'

'It is, but in one way it ain't. It gives the punters enjoyment as they try.'

'Ha, and a lot of junk that they win on the way to keep them hoping for the one thing they want!'

They both laughed. But then Maddie sighed. 'You'll be going on your leave soon, lad, and then'll be posted. I'm going to miss you.'

'And me you, Maddie. Would yer . . . I mean, well, only if yer have time, but I'd love yer to write to me.'

''Course I will, Jimmy, lad. But ain't a handsome fella like you got a girl at home?'

'I have. Her name's Linda.'

'By, you kept her quiet. Is she your lass?'

'D'yer mean me girlfriend? Yer speak another language at times, Maddie.'

They both laughed once more, and Maddie thought that Jimmy was like a ray of sunshine in her life, and it was getting unbearable to think of him going.

'Naw, it's you who speaks funny, not me. You rarely sound your aitches! You say "yer" instead of "you" and you use words that don't sound nice!'

'Like "bleedin'", yer mean? Ha, that's a cockney expression, and anyway, I don't call girls "lasses" and boys "lads".'

This set them off again. Maddie had to wipe tears from her eyes. 'Eeh, lad, there may be differences atween us, but I reckon we're friends for life.'

'You're the best mate I have, Maddie. Me Linda'll love yer, as I do.'

Though a profound statement, Maddie knew what he meant. They'd found something in each other that was special. 'And I love you, lad. Now hop it as I've work to do. Go and enjoy your day off with the others.'

'No, I'll stay and help yer. I told yer, I like cooking and working in the kitchen.'

'Right, get them spuds peeled while I go and check on me ma.'

Running down the stairs, Maddie had a lightness to her step, and yet a heavy heart. But when she entered the living room, she exclaimed, 'Ma! By, Ma, you look grand!'

'Ta, lass, I feel it an' all. Me pain in me side has eased, and I'm more like me old self.'

'Aw, Ma, I'm that glad.'

Maddie was by her ma's side in seconds and hugging her to her as she sat in her chair next to a roaring fire.

'You've even managed to put more coal on, I see.'

'Aye, well, it was getting a bit chilly and there's nowt like crackling flames to bring you comfort.'

'And you're to stay here and enjoy it. Jimmy's helping me.'

'Aw, that's good to hear. He's a lovely lad. And for all we knaw about his ma, she must be a good person at heart. I hope you can sort things for her, lass.'

'I don't have to, Ma.'

Maddie handed her ma the letter telling of the change in fortune that was happening for Hattie.

'Eeh, that's good. I was worried. And that'll teach you an' all, lass. Never make a promise you can't keep.'

Maddie slid down to her knees and put her head on her ma's lap. 'I'm good at that, ain't I, Ma?'

'It's your heart that's good, lass. You want to help and please everyone. I've thought a lot about how things are turning out, and me and your Aunt Jean didn't help things. I'm sorry. Sommat'll happen to put it all right again, you'll see.'

After a moment, Maddie said, 'Ma, I haven't said owt, but I have made another promise and one I want to keep, but only if you're all right with it.'

Ma sighed. 'Aw, me Maddie . . .'

'Naw, it ain't owt drastic like saving the world!'

Ma grinned. 'You'd do that if you could, lass ... Come on then, what's it all about?'

'Daisy's asked me to go with her to the flicks now and again, or to sit in the balcony of the Tower Ballroom and watch the dancers and have a giggle at the eccentric ones.'

'Ooh, like that lady who always dresses up like a fruit bowl, you mean?'

They both laughed. The lady was well known for her elaborate costumes, often worn with a huge hat that had imitation silk fruit sewn onto it, and for her elegant dancing with a gentleman who looked as though he'd stepped out of the last century.

'Yes. There are so many characters who are regulars on the dance floor and lots of young couples to watch an' all as the soldiers flock there and dance with the local girls. But we'll be up in the balcony, just having a laugh at their attempts and at the spectacle of the regulars. It'll be relaxing.'

'And you're worried about leaving me?'

'Yes. You knaw what it's like, there's always someone needs attention during the evening. The bell can ring a dozen times.'

'We should be like Aunt Jean and just put all the lights out in the kitchen and a big notice saying, "No service till breakfast!"'

'Naw, Ma, I couldn't do that. And especially with how young this lot are. They're all missing home, let alone owt else they face. We're like family to them, and family ain't just available at certain times, but when needed.'

'Aw, lass. You're your dad all over. He was a compassion-ate man. He'd put himself out for anyone and everyone ... I do miss him.'

'I love it when you say stuff like that, but you should get out more an' all, you and Aunt Jean. There's things you could join, like the Women's Institute, and there's other things now an' all – knitting and craft groups, and choirs. You both have lovely voices. I knaw me dad would want that for you. He wouldn't want you shut up indoors for weeks on end.'

'You're right. I'll see what Jean says about doing sommat together when I'm fully fit, eh.'

This cheered Maddie. 'Aw, it'll be grand. Me and Daisy can be the ones sitting upstairs in the kitchen, playing cards or whatever, while you two are out, and you can do it while we are.'

'It's a deal, Maddie. Now off you go, or you'll be all in a rush. What's on the menu tonight?'

'Lamb chops and mash, followed by spotted dick!'

Ma burst out laughing, such a lovely sound, because always she found the name of the rolled and steamed suet pudding with currants amusing.

'Thought that would get you going, Ma ... Eeh, you've a dirty mind.'

Maddie was laughing her head off as she went up the stairs. It seemed that all the doom and gloom had been lifted; that there was a lot to look forward to and a life still to be lived. Yes, it would always be marred by her missing Arnie and her problem over Reggie, but they could make the most of their lot. They'd done it before when tragedy had struck, and they could do it again.

With this resolve and feeling much better about her ma, Maddie felt enthused about getting the meal done.

Jimmy greeted her with, 'Been skiving, have yer? I've done the spuds, three each for the lads and two each for you and your mum. Then I looked to see what veg you had and found carrots and peas. I've scraped and cut the carrots and shelled the peas.'

Maddie looked astonished. 'By, I weren't gone that long, lad. You're like flipping lightning!'

'If I knew which meat we were having, I'd have trayed that up, but I found stewing beef and chops on the cold slab.'

'It's the chops tonight. And aye, they need traying up and there's some big jars of me ma's mint sauce that she made during the summer. You can fill one of those little jars for each table and stick a teaspoon in it. Ta, lad. You're a great help.'

'I'll do that for yer, but what's that long sausage thing steaming in the oven then? It smells good.'

Maddie just couldn't tell him its real name; she would have died! Whoever thought to call it that was stupid!

'Suet pud with currants.'

'Oh, spotted dick! I love spotted dick ... What? What you finding so funny, girl?'

This made Maddie laugh even more. Her sides ached.

Jimmy knew very well what she was laughing at and laughed with her. How she loved him. He'd become the light of her life.

When at last she controlled herself and dried her eyes, she told him, 'Get on with them lamb chops, lad, while I make some custard.'

Once the dinner was served and she and Jimmy were washing up, Maddie said, 'You don't go out to the pub much with the other lads, Jimmy. You should go out more, you knaw.'

'I ain't got the money. I wire me allowance to me mum so she can add it to what she gets of me pay.'

'Eeh, lad, why didn't you say?' Maddie reached for her purse. 'Take some off me for all your help and go out and enjoy yourself, Jimmy ... No, please take it. You've a long time to face without having much fun, as I see it, lad. Go on. Catch up with your friends and have a pint and a laugh. It'll do you good.'

Although still hesitant, Jimmy reached out and took the bob she offered him.

'Ta. You're a darlin', Maddie.' And then as if she was his big sister, he hugged her and kissed her cheek.

'Me life's been made better for meeting you, Maddie. I'll never forget yer.'

'You hadn't better do, me lad! Now, go on, or the others'll be drunk before you've had a sup.'

Jimmy laughed, hugged her again and was gone.

Maddie was left thinking how much he'd brought to her life. A young lad with so much love in him. She was sure he took after his ma, as Hattie sounded like a lovely person willing to do anything for her family, even if it meant selling her body. *Poor lass. I hope marrying Grantham changes her life and that of her kids for the better, and she finds the happiness she deserves.*

Maddie had never prayed as much as she did these last weeks, but now she lifted her eyes to heaven. *Please, God, do*

115

your best for us all. Make me ma well, make me problem with Reggie go away, keep all our lads safe, especially Jimmy, and even more especially me lovely Arnie.

To this she added, *And of course, Reggie. Don't let owt happen to him, except . . . well, if you could arrange for him to fall in love with a nice girl, that would be a help.*

As she finished this prayer, Ma opened the door to their flat and said, 'Has Aunt Jean arrived, lass?'

Maddie smiled to herself. No matter what anguish she felt, life went on. Aunt Jean still came around every evening when her work was done, and Ma still looked forward to her doing so. If only everything was as predictable as that.

'She'll be here in a mo, no doubt. Our supper's in the oven. I'll get it out and we can sit together. By, it seems ages since we did.'

'Is everything done then?'

'Aye. As you can see, the kitchen's spick and span and the dining tables are laid for breakfast. The lads have all gone out, so we can enjoy our meal — a tasty one it is an' all. Jimmy's got a special touch when he cooks.'

'Maybe we should employ him for the future when he comes home, eh?'

'A good idea. He loves Blackpool.'

'He's a lovely lad, a credit to his ma.'

With this, Ma tucked into her meal, a sight that warmed Maddie's heart — her ma was well again. Prayers were heard and did get answered.

It was two weeks later that Maddie was on the station platform once more, this time seeing Jimmy and all the lads off.

It surprised her how they had all come to look on her affectionately, and most hugged her and said they would come and see her when they came home. But from Jimmy, there were tears. Hers mingled with his as they hugged.

'Stay safe, lad. No heroics, eh?'

'Write to me, Maddie, that'll mean so much to me ... And if yer can try to get to see me mum and tell me how she's really faring ...'

'You'll knaw later today when you see her, Jimmy. You'll be able to tell if she's happy or not, you're that close to her. So, you write to me afore you leave next week and let me knaw what you're thinking about the situation, eh?'

'I will, I promise.'

'And, lad, with you having written to your ma and told her you're happy for her, I reckon you'll find her the happiest she's ever been. Now, hurry, you're being called into line.'

Jimmy took hold of her again and held her close. She disentangled and told him, 'Go, lovely lad. I love you, and will write.'

And then he was gone.

'Making a habit of this, ain't you, Maddie? By, your dad would turn in his grave.'

Maddie swivelled around. Cyril Grunding, the train guard, who she'd gone to school with, stood looking at her with disgust. 'Never thought you'd be unfaithful to Reggie, and with a kid an' all.'

'Shut your filthy mouth, Cyril. It ain't like that!'

'It looked like it to me. And Reggie not gone these many weeks.'

'Jimmy's just a kid, like you say. I knaw his ma and his family, he's a good friend of me and me ma. You can ask her if you like. What you saw was two friends hugging, that's all. God knaws, we're allowed to do that without you gossiping, ain't we?'

'I'm just saying, you should be more careful. A lot of girls are getting themselves a name in this town. They've gone mad, going with all the different soldiers that are passing through.'

'Well, that ain't me. I'm stuck in me boarding house, and wouldn't do it anyroad. You shouldn't make assumptions.'

'Sorry, lass . . . Only, well, I lost me Penny to one of them soldiers.'

'Naw! You and Penny have been together since . . .' It suddenly hit Maddie hard in the stomach as realisation dawned. It had always been Cyril and Penny – Maddie and Reggie . . .

Oh, God, me and Penny, and many like us, were all drifting into sommat that weren't right for us.

'I – I'm sorry to hear that, Cyril, lad. But . . . well, maybe it were meant. Happen there's someone out there for you. Maybe you and Penny have, well . . . grown out of each other, eh?'

Cyril shrugged. 'Well, I knaw one thing. It's made me mind up. I weren't going to volunteer for this lot. I don't believe in killing folk, I think things should be sorted by talking out your problems, but I'm going to sign up tomorrow. I've nowt here for me now. I may as well go and get meself killed.'

As he walked away, Maddie's whole body shivered.

That's what they're all doing, she thought. The reports were of hundreds having been killed, maybe Reggie … *Oh, no!*

And me Arnie! Will me Arnie ever come back to me? Oh, Arnie, Arnie.

CHAPTER NINE

Daisy looked out of the café window at the cold February morning. Soon they would be into March and Tom had been gone since just after Christmas.

She put her hand inside the bib of her apron and felt his letter pinned there. It told of his love for her and how he thought about her every minute and every waking hour of the day. It thrilled her just to touch it.

'Daisy, lass, get them tables set, will you? It's time to open the doors and we've to be ready as that sergeant was telling us there's a new intake today, and you knaw what that means.'

'Aye, they all flock to the prom before they have to report for duty and they're all starving.'

Daisy rolled her eyes. Her ma always panicked, even when everything was under control. To reassure her she said, 'I'm on with the last table now, Ma, and I've opened the door ready.'

'How you can be so calm, love, I just don't knaw. The thought of not knowing if we'll be snowed under, or quiet, gets me all het up, and what with seeing you staring and dreaming, it worried me more.'

'Ha, a girl's got to have her dreams, Ma. Anyroad, that's the last of the salt and peppers in place. We're all ready for whatever comes through the door.'

It was hours later that they managed to get a breather.

'Eeh, lass, I can't keep this pace up. It's good for the till, but not for me nerves.'

'I'm sure someone will answer our ad in the window for staff soon, Ma. You sit down and have a cuppa. I'll soon get everything shipshape again.'

'Aye, and then it'll all kick off again when it gets to teatime.'

'By, Ma, there's a word for you, love. I learnt it the other day when I was reading and looked it up in that old dictionary you bought me from the jumble that time. It's "pessimistic". It means you see doom and gloom in everything, and not the upside. We have a laugh with the soldiers, don't we? We're making more money than we've ever made, and we get to have fun — you with your mates down the pub and me with Maddie.'

'You're right, lass. I've to try to look on the bright side like you do ... Did you enjoy watching the dancers last night then?'

Just as Daisy was about to answer, a young girl of about the same age as herself came through the door, making them jump as the bell clanged, echoing around the empty café.

'Hello, love, come on in out of the cold and put the wood in the hole.'

The girl's voice quivered as she said, 'I — I ain't getting your meaning.'

'She meant shut the door, lass,' Ma explained.

'Oh.' With the door closed, the girl wiped a tear from her eye as she turned back towards them.

'It's the wind, it . . . it . . .' The girl plonked down on the nearest chair. Her face crumpled; she dropped her head. A sob shook her body as she buried her face in her hands.

Daisy ran to her, and Ma wasn't far behind.

'Eeh, lass. What's the matter?'

The girl's sobs deepened and racked her whole body.

'Get that cuppa for me, lass, and one for this poor girl an' all.'

As Daisy went to do as her ma asked, she heard the girl say, 'I – I ain't got any money, I used it all to get here. I came looking for someone. He'd have helped me . . . but he's gone!'

Always kindly, Ma held the girl to her. 'We'll help you, lass. We've had times when we ain't had two pennies to rub together. So we knaw what that feels like. Now, drink this tea, and tell us all about what's troubling you . . . Daisy, put the catch on, love, we could do with a proper break.'

'Aye, all right, Ma, and I'll hang the "Back in ten minutes" sign.'

After a couple of sips, the girl dropped a bombshell that stunned Daisy and her ma.

'I just don't know what to do. I – I'm pregnant, and – and I came looking for the man who did it . . . though it weren't his fault . . . He . . . he and me, we were kids together, and good mates . . . We were daft one night. He was going to war, you see. He told me it'd be Blackpool first as he was being sent there to train . . . He was excited about it . . . We got drunk and, well, it just happened ... I – I know he'd have looked after me, even married me on one of those special licences. But I spoke to a few army lads when I got here and they told me ... he's already gone to France ... His name is Arnie. Arnie Brown.'

'Good Lord!'

'I'm sorry, I didn't mean to shock you. I just don't know what to do.'

'Are you from Liverpool, lass? You've a slight accent.'

'I am, and me and Arnie were brought up in the same orphanage. I – I've nowhere to go ... I had a job as a live-in maid. The orphanage sent me there. It ... the thing we did, it happened during me leave days. I – I stayed with Arnie, and we were just playing around! ... We were both upset about it the next day and said we would just forget it. But then I started being sick in the mornings, and me mistress said I was to leave ... Me only option is to go to one of them convents for unmarried mothers ... I couldn't stand it ... I couldn't! So, I came looking for Arnie ... Please help me.'

'We will, but on one condition.'

'Daisy! What a thing to say, lass! There'll be naw conditions. If Molly hadn't have helped me when I was in the same position, then you and me wouldn't knaw each other, you'd have been taken from me and adopted. That ain't going to happen to this young lass, and that's that!'

'Ma, me condition is that ... What's your name, lass?'

'Brenda, but everyone calls me Bren.'

Ignoring her ma's look, Daisy said, 'Me condition is this. You never tell anyone about who your babby's da is. Never!'

123

Bren looked afraid.

'I'm sorry to be so harsh, but me best friend fell in love with Arnie and he with her. She's pining for him, and this would devastate her.'

Ma nodded her understanding and her agreement. 'Can you do that, lass?'

'I can, I promise. I'll do it for Arnie, as he's me best friend in all the world, only . . . well, when he comes home, it'll be hard to deceive him . . . Oh, I wish we hadn't acted so daft that night!'

'Well, it's done now, lass. Naw more tears. We'll deal with things as they happen. But Daisy's right. We'll have to have a story of how you came to be here. Daisy's good at that, she'll think of sommat.'

'I have, Ma. We'll tell folk that you're the daughter of an old friend of Ma's, Bren. And that you, Ma, ain't heard from this friend for years. And then out of the blue, Bren came looking for you after her ma died. Her ma had told her all about you, and that she was to come and find you, as she knew you would look after her. Mind, in all of that we'd better say that Bren's man was killed in the first wave of the war, and she's pregnant and all alone, and so we took her in.'

Both Ma and Bren stared at Daisy for a moment, and then her ma said, 'Eeh, you should be a book writer, lass, you can come up with a tale in an instant. But aye, that'll work. We'll sort out the finer details in case some nosy parker or other wants to delve more. But you're safe now, Bren. You can stay here with us, and we'll look after you and your babby when it arrives . . . Mind, you'll have to work. Me and Daisy can't cope, so you could wash pots, and do odd jobs to help us out.'

Bren burst into tears again. Both Daisy and her ma hugged her. Ma said, 'I knaw what you're going through, lass ... Eeh, how it was for me is all coming back to me now, but it turned out all right, and it will for you, love, I promise.' Ma put her hand out and clutched Daisy's.

After a moment, Ma, rallying the strength she'd always shown, spoke in a more determined voice, 'You just do as Daisy says, Bren, and stick to your story, eh?'

Seeing Bren nod didn't altogether quieten the nerves in Daisy's stomach. *I've to do all I can to make sure the truth never gets out; it would break Maddie's heart. But eeh, I've never lied to Maddie afore and now I've to start.*

This last didn't sit well with Daisy, but she knew there was no alternative.

'Right, we're to get on. Have you eaten, Bren?'

'No, I haven't eaten since yesterday, Mrs ...'

'Call me, Sandra, love.'

'Aunt Sandra would be best,' Daisy told them. 'You haven't got a distinct Liverpool accent, Bren, only the odd words. But if folk pick up on it, they're going to want to knaw how ma knew someone from Liverpool. It just gets too complicated. You see, Ma was from Manchester.'

'I can do that, Daisy, and I'd love to. I ain't ever had an aunt. And I promise that I ain't going to be any trouble. I'd never hurt your mate as it would be like hurting Arnie.'

Daisy relaxed. 'Aw, lass, I'm sorry if I came over unfriendly. You gave me a shock and, like you say, me mate mustn't get hurt. She's going through a tough time. I'll tell you later, only we're to open the doors again soon.'

'I'll get you a plate of chips to tide you over, lass.'

'Ta, Aunt Sandra.'

For some reason, this made them giggle and Daisy was glad as she knew she'd created an atmosphere and poor Bren didn't deserve that.

'I'll help out straight away too, if you'll show me where to hang me coat and where the lav is.'

'I'll take you to the lav, Bren. It's outside.'

Once they were in the yard, Daisy asked, 'Ain't you got any clothes with you, love?'

'I've a bag at the station. The porter took pity on me. He asked me where I was staying, and I told him I wasn't sure. He winked and said he'd put it in the office. That there was usually a charge, but if I didn't say anything, he wouldn't. He gave me a ticket.'

'Well, we'll pick it up later. There's the lav. I'll wait by the kitchen door for you.'

'Ta, Daisy.'

Daisy had a lot of questions. She knew she always wanted to know more than anyone else bothered with, but her curiosity didn't rest. She wanted to know how Bren came to be in the orphanage, and where her live-in position was, and where Arnie lived – everything. *Eeh, I'm a nosy parker.*

When Bren came out of the lav, she asked, 'What happened to Aunt Sandra, Daisy?'

This took Daisy aback. She wanted to be the one asking questions, but she told Bren her ma's story.

126

'Her circumstances were similar to yours, Bren. She was brought up in an orphanage and sent to be a maid in a big house. Only it wasn't a friend who made her pregnant, but one of the stable hands raped her. She was put out on the streets to fend for herself. She made it to Manchester and an elderly lady helped her after finding her crying on a bench. She took Ma to her home and looked after her. Her name was Molly. She said me ma was like the daughter she'd never had. Then Ma looked after Molly in turn and Molly became a gran to me. When she died, she left her house to Ma, and that's how we came to buy this business. I was only five at the time. I met me mate, Maddie, the one I told you about, at school. You'll like Maddie.'

'So, you never knew your dad, like me, though I didn't know me mum either. I was left at the gate of the orphanage, so have no knowledge of any relatives. And we didn't go out of the convent much, so I never really picked up the Liverpool accent. Just like you say, the odd few words.'

'What was it like in the orphanage?'

'I don't like to think of it. We had no love. No cuddles. Just care, lessons and severe punishments. We found our own love with each other. Arnie was my most loved friend. I had a few others, girls, but I don't know where they landed up. Me and Arnie kept in touch. Have you someone special, Daisy?'

'Aye . . .'

As they went back inside, Daisy told Bren about Tom. 'He's a friend of Arnie's. They met when they joined up.'

They were finding a pinny for Bren when she asked, 'Are your mate's troubles bad ones?'

'It ain't for me to say, love. She must keep a lot of secrets and I can't break them. But just to say, Arnie brought real love to her life, but upset the apple cart. Mind, I'm glad he did.'

'That's Arnie all over! He always gets himself and others into trouble – or a tangle, rather than trouble.'

'Well, that's exactly what he's done for Maddie. But he brought her happiness too.'

'Oh, he can do that just by smiling at you! He's a great person. I miss him.'

'Are you sure you ain't in love with him?'

'Honestly not. Love him to bits, but he's more like a brother . . . I know, that makes what we did even worse, but we had too much to drink. Arnie bought a bottle of gin. We'd never had a drink together and it was my first. I didn't like the taste, but it went to me head and . . . Well, I lost all sense. So did Arnie.'

Daisy knew how it had happened. It had been like that for her the first time. She hurried the thought of it away. How she could have done that with a stranger, she just didn't know, but she'd had a glass of sherry and lost all reason.

'It's like a bit of an adventure, ain't it?'

'That's just what it was, a silly "shall we try it?" thing. Oh, Daisy, I wish we hadn't.'

'Don't keep saying that, it's not fair on your babby. He or she is there now. And given life by you and your best friend. You've to get on with it . . . I – I don't mean to sound harsh, love, but you can't go around thinking like you do. It won't do you any good.'

'You've a wise head, Daisy. And you're right. I can't believe I've met kindness like you and your mum are showing me. And I'll do me best to repay you.'

'No need. Though we might use you as a slave, lass.'

They both laughed.

'Hey, you two, Bren's chips are ready, and I've opened the café again. Look lively!'

'Coming, Ma.'

The teatime service went much better with having an extra pair of hands. Bren was a marvel and had things done before she was asked to do them, but Daisy was troubled. She had to think of a way that Bren could know Arnie as she thought it would be too difficult for her to pretend that he was a stranger. And what about when he came home? Maybe later Bren could write to him and let him know the situation. She could tell him that she'd met Maddie – as she would have done by then, and explain to him that she wanted to either keep it a secret or for him to be the one to tell Maddie.

It wasn't until they were clearing up and the possibilities had been driving Daisy mad that she suddenly exclaimed, 'I've got it!'

Ma jumped, and Bren giggled, making her face look different now as her swollen eyes were back to normal too. This gave a true picture of Bren as she really was – beautiful. A beauty that shone out and was enhanced by her olive skin, jet-black hair, and eyes like two gleaming coals – lovely expressive eyes.

'You've got what, lass?' Ma asked.

'Let's all sit and have our supper, and I'll tell you about me thoughts.'

'Good idea. Are you all finished, Bren?'

'I think so. I've done what I think needs doing, but if there's anything else?'

'Naw, everywhere is gleaming, ta, love. I'll get that lamb casserole out of the oven, and we'll have chunks of the fresh loaf I've baked to go with it.'

When all was ready and the delicious casserole served, Ma said, 'Right, what amazing idea have you dreamt up now, lass?'

'I've been worrying over how, if Bren stays with us, she can possibly keep up the lie of not knowing Arnie. She's bound to slip up.'

'Are you saying that she can't stay, lass, 'cos that ain't—'

'Naw, Ma. I'm saying we've to have a story that's better than the one we had. Look, there's nowt wrong with Bren knowing Arnie, or even having been brought up with him and them being close friends – what we need to keep secret is that Bren's babby is his.'

'Eeh, lass, you've lost me, I thought we had it all settled.'

'I did an' all, until I began to see all the things that could go wrong, how Bren could be caught out just by being what she is – a very good friend of Arnie's. So, it's only the father of the babby we need to lie about. And your story could be Bren's. Everything about her life can be in the open except what she and Arnie got up to. Bren has to say that she was raped by the stable hand, or the butler, or whoever, and kicked out. Having nowhere to go, she hoped to find Arnie as she knew he would help her.'

Bren was the first to speak. Her face shone with relief. 'Oh, Daisy, ta. That would work much better. I've been worrying about slipping up. And I've been worrying too about when Arnie comes home. I've been thinking that I would have to move away after me babby was born, find somewhere to live and just never get in touch with him . . . and that's still something I might have to do as it will be harder to deny him his child if I saw him often.'

With the anguish in Bren's voice and the sight of the tears in her eyes, Daisy was glad when Ma said, 'Let's deal with the future when it happens, eh? For now, you can stay here, Bren. We've a couple of spare bedrooms and we can gradually get all you need for the babby. I'll knit for the little mite, and I'll pay you a wage, so you can get bits an' all.'

'No, I'll work for me keep, that's all I need, Aunt . . . Oh, what shall I call you now with this new story?'

'Carry on calling me Aunt Sandra, love. We'll get all muddled if we change it now. Besides, it's a tradition around these parts for younger people to use the term and it'll seem natural with you living with us.'

'Thanks. I'm glad you don't mind. I like it. It makes me feel as though I belong to someone.'

'By, I knaw that feeling. Lovely Molly did that for me – Daisy said she'd told you all about me story. Well, it's my turn to do what Molly did for me, and you're to think of us as family, ain't she, Daisy?'

Daisy wasn't sure she was ready to accept Bren in that way yet. She liked her very much and wanted to help her, but family had always been just her and Ma. She didn't express this feeling, though, she just said, 'Aye. It already feels like I've known you all me life, Bren.' Then thinking that sounded a bit cold, she added, 'Working together here in all the hustle and bustle, you have to be family to stand it!'

'Aye, and adding to me family by having you turn up on me doorstep, Bren, was easier than lugging this one around in me belly and pushing her out, I can tell you!'

This from Ma had them all bursting into laughter and Daisy felt better about how her ma had taken to Bren. She told herself she was being silly to feel a bit put out by the affection between them and that it was a natural thing to happen – they'd both been through being brought up in an orphanage, and though the circumstances were different, they'd both found themselves alone, pregnant and put out on the streets with nothing and nobody to turn to.

With these thoughts, Daisy's heart went out to them both and she made her mind up to do as her ma was doing and make Bren feel welcome.

To this end, she said, 'I'm going to see Maddie once I've washed and changed. Would you like to come with me, Bren?'

'I'd like that, Daisy, if you don't think I'd be intruding?'

'Naw. And anyway, with the story we have now, it's the most natural thing to do and it'll have everything . . . well, everything except the truth about the father of your babby out in the open.'

'Yes, and it'll be good to meet the girl Arnie has fallen in love with.'

'You knaw you have to tread carefully there, don't you, Bren?'

132

'Well, I don't know everything, Aunt Sandra, but I do know there's problems with Maddie and Arnie's love for each other, so I'll be guided by Daisy. But I've nothing to change into, Daisy. Me case is still at the station.'

'Eeh, I forgot that.'

'Have a cab to the station, the pair of you. It won't take long, you'll soon be back.'

'We can do that, but you can borrow sommat of mine for now. Then we can pick up your case and take the taxi straight to Maddie's.'

Whilst they chose what would best suit Bren – they decided on a frock that bloused to the hip and then flared out, as it fitted over her small bump, and a thick cardi to keep her extra warm under her coat – the question of where she was to sleep came up.

Ma seemed a bit tentative and as if she'd picked up on Daisy's earlier feelings. She suggested the small box room next to hers. 'I can soon shift the boxes we've dumped on the bed and get it made up while you're out.'

'Naw, she can sleep in here with me. We'll make up Maddie's bed when we get back – we call it that, but Maddie won't be staying over now. She used to quite often in the winter months but there isn't a closed season now, with the soldiers being here.'

Ma looked relieved as she said, 'Eeh, I hope the pair of you don't keep me awake all hours with giggling how you and Maddie used to when she stayed the night . . . Mind, I preferred that to when you went to stay at hers. The place was like a morgue then.'

To further reassure her ma, and make light of everything, Daisy retorted, 'Ha, with the way you worked us today, Ma, we'll both fall asleep before our heads hit the pillow!'

Ma grinned. 'Cheeky devil . . . But I'm glad that's settled. It would've been a bit lonely for Bren on her own. As I remember it, you'd have been sleeping in a room with other maids, lass?'

'Yes, two others. I've never slept in a room on me own. I think I'd find that a bit scary now.'

'Well, if you snore, you'll be kicked out, so you'd better watch it!'

The laughter that followed this helped Daisy. She knew she'd done the right thing. She was to help Bren in every way, not shut her out just because she didn't feel ready to share her ma with anyone. With this thought, Daisy told herself that everything would work out fine. She'd get used to having someone else living with them. It was just that it had all happened so quickly.

CHAPTER TEN

When they arrived at the station and alighted from the taxi, Bren said, 'It's the same porter who helped me this morning. He must have done a long shift.'

'There's only two of them, Cyril and Ray. Cyril hasn't volunteered yet, and Ray – Ray Smith – were in the class above me and Maddie in school. Ray's ma's a friend of my ma. Poor fella's got bad eyesight but the daft a'peth carries his glasses around in his pocket as he don't like wearing them.'

'I thought he squinted when he wrote me ticket out.'

'Aye. He tried to join up but failed the medical because of his eyes. He was mortified to send off his pals and not to be going with them. He's suffering a bit, though, as he gets a few snide remarks for still being around when others have gone – from strangers mostly who alight from the trains, though some locals have called him names.'

'But that's not fair, and if he wore his glasses it wouldn't happen.'

Daisy smiled. She detected a schoolmarm note in Bren's voice and just knew she was going to take Ray to task. The thought amused her, and she hoped she succeeded as Ray did leave himself open to criticism by strangers, and even to having an accident if he tripped over something he'd not seen.

Bren strode rather than walked towards Ray. Daisy had a job to keep up with her.

They were by his side before he saw them.

'I should have said, "Boo!" That would have made you jump!'

'What . . . ?'

Ray peered at Bren. 'Oh, hello again. I didn't recognise you.'

'Put your glasses on and you might!'

Ray looked stunned. 'How did you knaw?' He turned. 'Eeh, Daisy, what're you doing here?'

'Bren's staying with us. She came looking for Arnie. You met him, didn't you, that night in the pub? Though you won't knaw what he looked like proper as you weren't wearing your glasses that night either.'

Ray stepped back. 'What is this? You two look like you're about to lynch me! And how do you knaw Arnie? You ain't Irish.'

'I grew up with him, and . . . well, we were best mates . . . I – I wanted to see him before he left for war.'

Ray hung his head. 'I wish I could go.'

Bren retorted, 'With not being able to see who's who, you'd be shaking hands with the Germans and not know it and would be dead before you'd had a chance to fight!' She softened her voice then. 'I'm sorry, I didn't mean that cruelly, but Daisy tells me you don't like wearing your glasses and that's daft. If you did, you'd have been able to read that medical staff are needed, and they don't have to pass eyesight tests.'

'I do knaw, but I ain't clever enough for that.'

'No, nor rich enough, I suppose. I looked at recruitments to see what part women can play, and it's mainly nurses, but we can't do that unless we're rich as they have to pay for their own passage to France. We can be camp followers. They do the washing and everything they can to help keep the men going, but ... Anyway, something stopped me.'

'I'm guessing it wasn't something nice.' Ray reached into his pocket for his small, wired glasses as he said this, and put them on. His expression was one as if he'd been bowled over. Daisy knew he didn't think before he spoke his next words: 'By, you're beautiful, lass.'

Bren giggled. 'And you're not so bad looking yourself.'

It was Daisy's turn to be surprised. Bren was flirting with Ray Smith, the lad always known as Four Eyes at school.

Suddenly that seemed a very cruel thing for them to have called him, and she realised it had probably contributed to him not wanting to wear his glasses. Shame washed over her. How could she have joined in on such bullying? Maddie never did. Maddie had always championed the underdog.

'Ray ...'

Ray turned his head and looked at her as if seeing her for the first time. And he probably was, she thought, as a grown-up anyway, as she couldn't remember seeing him wear his glasses for a long time.

'I – I ... well, I'm sorry I joined in when we taunted you, lad. I should have known better.'

'Eeh, lass, that's water under the bridge now. Anyroad, I knaw you were just following the others and didn't have real malice in you.'

'Ta, Ray. But, lad, you should wear them, and you knaw what? They suit you ... they do! Your eyes look lovely and bright.'

'So, you'd go on a date with me wearing them, would you, Daisy, lass?'

'If I was free, yes, I would, and be proud to, but I met someone.'

'A soldier, no doubt. By, there'll be naw lassies left for our lads when they come home, and naw doubt a few broken hearts amongst them as they find their lasses have cheated on them.'

'Well, I ain't cheated on anyone and, yes, it is a soldier. You saw me with him in the pub, though I never asked you what you were doing up North Shore.'

'I was sorry I went when I saw Maddie. I never thought it of Maddie to cheat on Reggie.'

'She wasn't! She came with me as me mate and Arnie was with Tom as they are mates. As it happens, Maddie knew them both well as they were stopping at her ma's boarding house, so don't you go spreading rumours or I'll black your eye!'

'Steady on, Daisy. I'm sorry, all right? It just looked bad.'

'That's you making assumptions and why we had to go to a pub where we weren't known by the locals.'

'I said I'm sorry. I shouldn't have said such a thing. I've

had enough stones thrown at me without me throwing them. Anyroad, now I can see and can match the ticket to the right bag, I'll get the one you've come after, lass.'

When he had disappeared through a door, Bren looked over at Daisy. 'I've an idea what Maddie's troubles are now, Daisy. Poor Maddie . . . Though, you have to feel sorry for this Reggie that Ray mentioned.'

'You do. And for all three of them an' all. It ain't straightforward, but now you knaw that, I'll put you in the picture.'

Daisy told how it was that Maddie felt the pressure of her ma's and Aunt Jean's expectations.

By the end of her telling, Daisy could feel the sympathy that Bren felt for them all when she said, 'That's sad. And it could have happened to me and Arnie. But poor Maddie didn't get the chance to do as me and Arnie did. We grew out of being girlfriend and boyfriend, but still love each other as the best of friends.'

When Ray came back, he had a big grin on his face. 'There you go, I kept it safe for you, lass.'

'Well, there ain't much in it to keep safe, but thanks . . . And, Ray, as Daisy said, you do you look more handsome in your glasses as you don't squint.'

'More handsome? So, you reckon I was handsome without them an' all, eh?'

'Don't be getting ideas!'

'Eeh, I've no need to get them, I've had them since this morning when you got off that train, lass. You looked like a lost little kitten, and I wanted to save you.'

Daisy was astonished at this exchange; she'd never seen Ray so confident.

'No one can do that, Ray.'

Daisy turned and looked at Bren. She saw her lip quiver. She opened her mouth to intervene and bring this to an end, but Ray forestalled her as he said in a gentle voice, 'I'd like to try. Troubles are always halved by sharing them ... Look, I finish work in an hour. I could call for you and we could go for a walk or sommat.'

'In this freezing cold!'

Daisy felt like giggling. The exchange between Ray and Bren was something she'd never expected. Bren was proving to be a feisty lass, and Ray seemed to like that.

'Well, I could run to a glass of beer at the pub, if that would suit you better.'

'Now, if you offered a night at the theatre and dinner after with a glass of champagne, that'd be a bit more like it! No, I'm only teasing, but maybe another time, Ray. I've had a tiring day, and me feet are killing me. And besides, well, there's stuff you don't know and if you did, you wouldn't be asking me out.'

Bren's head dropped.

Daisy knew a sadness over Bren's situation, and for Ray too. She'd never seen him take an interest in anyone. He always gave the air that he wasn't worthy. He joked and was everyone's friend, but he was just Ray with the squinty eyes, who they'd all made fun of. Now, she saw him differently as he said, 'Everyone's got a skeleton in the cupboard, lass. Mine was me stupid glasses. I can see yours is deeper than that but it won't matter to me. I knaw I said that about Maddie, but I ain't usually one to judge folk. I've always been on the end of folk judging me as an idiot to poke fun at, and now the visitors to Blackpool and those of the town who don't knaw me are making remarks in me hearing about some men being cowards.'

Bren didn't react to this, and Daisy knew her plight was weighing heavily on her shoulders, so thought to try to lighten the moment. She grinned at Ray. 'Well, I never knew you were that forward, Ray. You've only just met Bren and here you are asking her out! Eeh, you're a different bloke to what I thought. I might be after you meself!'

'Ha! I didn't knaw this Ray meself until I met Bren. She's knocked me off me pins. But I were daft to think someone as beautiful as you are could look at a bloke like me, Bren.'

Bren looked up at this. 'It's not you, Ray, it's me. I've stuff I'm dealing with. I'm sorry . . . I – I'll just take me bag and me and Daisy'll get going now. I'll see you around, eh?'

'Aye. I'm glad you found Daisy and her ma as there's naw better than them. They'll help you, whatever your troubles are.' With this, Ray seemed to finally accept that he'd been rejected as he turned away, put his hand up, and said, 'I'm to get back to work now, there's one more train to come in afore I'm off duty.'

His strides took him away and through the barrier to the platform.

Daisy looked at Bren and sighed. 'Come on, don't let that put a dampener on you, love. Ray ain't one to hold a grudge, and we've to see Maddie yet and it's getting late.'

'It's just that I felt like soiled goods. Like me choices have gone because of one silly mistake. I would have loved to say yes and had a date with Ray. I like him. He's different somehow – like he's had a lot of troubles as I have … but …'

Daisy didn't know what to say. Her heart went out to Bren. Yes, Bren had been foolish, but she wasn't one to talk herself. Shame gave Daisy an uncomfortable feeling as she remembered letting the stranger at the Tower do that thing to her and her stupidity at thinking that if she let Mickey Stanton do it, he'd want her as his girl. But then another thought suddenly struck Daisy. One that hit her in the pit of her stomach! *Why didn't them times result in me having a babby? I never thought about it, and it didn't occur to me when I did it with either of them. But …*

A sense of relief washed over her that she hadn't found herself in the same plight and this prompted her to link Bren's arm as a feeling of wanting to protect her came over her and all trace of holding back a little on her friendship left her.

'It'll turn out all right, love, don't worry.'

'It's a lot better already, Daisy. This morning, I thought me world were at an end. I was that close to throwing meself under one of the trams that rattle by. But then as I looked across the road, I saw you and your ma through the café window. You were chatting, and I don't know why, but I felt drawn to you both.'

'Eeh, I'm glad you did.'

'And I am too.'

'And it ain't just us giving to you, Bren. You're a godsend. Me and Ma have been struggling, and couldn't get help, then you walked through the door. We needed you as much as you needed us, lass.'

The little squeeze that Bren gave to Daisy's arm with her own warmed Daisy's heart.

Maddie was shocked to have Daisy walk into the kitchen with a stranger.

'By, love, you didn't tell me you were bringing someone with you. I've only saved two of me raspberry buns for us to have with our cocoa.'

'I didn't knaw meself, lass. This is Bren. She's going to be living and working with me and Ma now. But eeh, we've a tale to tell you ... She's a friend of Arnie's ...'

Maddie stared at the girl. She hadn't heard Arnie speak of a friend. But then, remembering the flat door was open and Ma and Aunt Jean were down there, she sidestepped around Daisy and closed it.

'Eeh, sorry, lass, I thought your ma was out.'

'They're going out. There's a sing-song on at the church hall ... But you said a friend of Arnie's?'

'Yes, this is Brenda, only she's called Bren for short. She was brought up with Arnie.'

Still feeling as if she'd been shoved sideways, Maddie smiled at Bren.

'Pleased to meet you, Bren. Though I have to say, I'm shocked ... I take it that Daisy has told you about me and Arnie?'

'Yes. And I'm pleased to meet you, Maddie. And you look perfect for my Arnie.'

'Your Arnie?'

'Look, let's sit down and we'll tell you everything.' As she said this, Daisy did her usual pulling of the chair along

143

the tiled floor, but this time the sound grated on Maddie and she wanted to scream, *Lift the bloody thing!* But she swallowed hard as she indicated for Bren to sit down and told her, 'I'm sorry, I should have invited you to sit down as soon as you arrived, but you took the wind out of me sails.'

'I know. I did out of Daisy's and her mum's too. I opened the café door and sank on a seat and burst into tears . . .'

Maddie listened to all that Bren had to say about how she was raped and thrown out, and by the end of her telling she had taken hold of her hand.

'Aw, lass, I'm so sorry. Arnie would have helped you, I knaw he would, and any one of us would an' all. I'm so glad you found Daisy. But you'll be all right, we'll watch out for you.'

'Thanks, Maddie. And I'm glad Arnie fell in love with you. He's lovely, he'll never let you down.'

'Ta, love. But by, I'm sorry for what happened to you. I don't suppose anything happened to the man who did this? He probably kept his job, and it was all put on your shoulders?'

Bren nodded her head.

Thinking that her telling her story was enough for Bren, Maddie didn't delve any further.

But as she got up to make the cocoa, saying they would share the raspberry buns between them, her heart was heavy. She'd so looked forward to having Daisy to herself when her ma and Aunt Jean had gone out. She badly needed to tell her of her own plight and to be held by her and to have her think of a solution.

But was there one? *Oh, God, how could this have happened after just making love the once?*

She hadn't thought anything of it when she'd missed her first monthly, she'd always been irregular. But then she'd missed another, and now she should have come on last week and didn't. Then this morning she was sick!

Maddie shuddered with the fear seeping through her. She could still hear the tone in her ma's voice this morning as she'd called out, 'Maddie, Maddie, are you sickening for sommat, lass?'

She'd said it was just something she'd eaten, and Ma had seemed to accept this.

But I'm not sick. I'm having Arnie's babby!

The thought sent joy through her, but only for a second as the anxiety took over once more.

'You're quiet, lass.'

Daisy made her jump. She hadn't heard her get up and come to stand beside her. For once, she must have lifted her chair.

'Sorry. I was deep in me thoughts. I – I'm nearly done. Get a knife from the table drawer and cut the buns for me, love.'

Daisy's arm came around her and she whispered, 'Are you sure? You look peaky, love.'

'Aye, I'm sure, you daft thing.'

Bren put in then, 'I'm sorry if I was a shock to you, Maddie.'

'Naw, naw, lass. It's lovely to meet you. I want to hear all about Arnie. I didn't have long to find out about his child-hood, and he didn't seem to want to talk about it.'

'No, he wouldn't. But for having each other, we wouldn't have got through it at times. It was a harsh life, one full of severe punishments and no love. It was worse for Arnie as he'd known a family, but for me, I never knew anything different. I thought that was how everyone lived until I went to work with a family and heard the kids laughing and playing with their grandparents and eager to greet their dad when he came home from work. And then I thought, *Why them and why not me?*'

'Aw, I'm sorry. Look, we don't have to talk about it.'

'It's all right. I like talking about Arnie. We became friends soon after he arrived. I found him crying in a corner of the playground. I mothered him, as little as I was, but I remember thinking that he talked funny. Nice funny. And he told me about Ireland and what happened, and I took hold of his hand. He didn't shove me away as most boys would but held on to my hand and that seemed to seal our friendship. We were inseparable after that.' Bren laughed. 'We used to talk about how one day we would marry. But when we reached about thirteen, all of that went out of the window and we knew we were just friends and like brother and sister.'

'I knaw exactly how that feels.'

'I told her about you and Reggie, Maddie. I knaw it weren't my place, but it came up.' Daisy went on to tell her about their conversation with Ray.

Maddie took in a deep breath. 'He won't say owt about seeing me with Arnie, will he?'

'Naw, he's promised not to, but I thought you'd better knaw.'

146

Some relief entered Maddie. 'Well, we didn't see anyone else, so it should be all right. I can't even remember seeing Ray.'

'Naw, 'cos you only had eyes for one person that night, as I did . . . Aw, I miss me Tom.'

'I knaw, Daisy. It's like an aching sore that you can't heal and none of us knaws when it will end.'

After a moment, Maddie knew Daisy was trying to lighten things as she said, 'Anyroad, talking of Ray . . .'

As she told what had happened at the station, they giggled, had moments of sympathy and, for Maddie, moments of being glad she had never made fun of Ray. But then with the final revelations she said, 'By, it sounds as though Ray fancies you rotten, Bren.'

Bren hung her head. 'I like him too, but with me condition . . .'

They were all quiet then. Maddie had the urge to blurt out about her own suspicions, but hearing her ma and Aunt Jean coming up the stairs stopped her.

When the door opened, her ma said, 'Eeh, there's a lot of frivolity going on in here . . . Oh, hello, you're a new one.'

'This is Bren, Ma. She's going to be living with Daisy and her ma, and she knaws Arnie. She came looking for him, hoping to catch him before he was deployed, but missed him. They grew up in the same orphanage.'

'Eeh, lass, you're very welcome. And you're just what Sandra has been looking for, a helping hand at the café. I wish someone like you would turn up at our door! Anyroad, we'll see you later.'

With this, they both kissed them all and left.

When the door closed on them, Bren said, 'I've never met such lovely people as I have in Blackpool. I didn't go into Liverpool much, but when I did, I found whoever I spoke to friendly and kind, but here, they take a stranger into their home and are grateful to you for turning up. It's overwhelming.'

A tear trickled down Bren's cheek, and Maddie almost bumped into Daisy as they both rushed to be by her side. It ended up in a huddle with them all giggling as they almost fell over.

'I'm all right, thanks, girls. Just like I say, overwhelmed and grateful. It ain't everyone who'd take in an unmarried pregnant young woman.'

Maddie's own troubles came to her then and she knew she needed what Bren had found – someone to help her. 'I've sommat to tell you both ... And I'm going to need support an' all.' Before they could ask anything, Maddie blurted out, 'I've missed two monthlies, and this morning I had to run to the bathroom the minute I sat up and was as sick as a dog!'

The silence that followed this deepened Maddie's fear and her dread of telling her ma.

Her cheeks burnt with embarrassment as she said. 'Me and Arnie only did it the once.'

A look passed between Daisy and Bren that Maddie didn't understand but which alarmed her.

'I'm scared, and I've let me ma down. It's what's she's dreaded the most for me ... but, well, she allus warned me not to give in to Reggie if he tried owt. How am I to tell her it's Arnie's?'

Bren stood. 'I – I need the lav . . . I'm going to be sick!'

Already, Bren was retching. Maddie jumped up and grabbed the bucket from under the sink. She only just got it to Bren as her body retched once more and all she'd eaten came out in a torrent. The sight and smell hit Maddie's already churning stomach, and she had to leave Bren to Daisy and turn, only just managing to get to the sink before she brought up her supper.

'Eeh, what a carry-on. If it weren't so tragic for you both, I'd be splitting me sides. Hold the bucket, Bren, I need to get you both some water to stop this.'

When they'd calmed and cleaned up, the tears that flowed down Bren's face affected Maddie. She put her head in her hands and sobbed out her despair.

An arm came around her. Looking up, she saw that a crying Daisy held them both.

It seemed to Maddie that for three young women, they had the troubles of the world on their shoulders. Daisy was without her Tom, Bren had had that terrible thing done to her, had been abandoned and was carrying a child, and her own troubles seemed insurmountable.

It shouldn't be like this, but she couldn't see at this moment how things could come right for them ever again.

CHAPTER ELEVEN

Three weeks later, Ma stood with her arms folded on the other side of the table.

The cleaning up was all done and the soldiers now stopping with them had left to report for duty – a time when peace descended on the house and she and Ma had a nice cuppa and chatted. But instead, Maddie saw a look on her ma's face that she remembered from her childhood. It told of how she knew Maddie had done something bad and it was time for her to be truthful.

'Please tell me that what I'm suspecting ain't true, Maddie.'

The tears that had seemed to be forever waiting to be shed spilt over and down Maddie's cheeks.

Ma was by her side in an instant. 'Please tell me it's Reggie's, not—'

The shrill ringing of the doorbell cut into her words. Maddie's blood ran cold as she instinctively knew the sound held bad news.

'I'll go, you sit down. You look as though you're about to pass out, lass. It'll only be the postie.'

Maddie's dread deepened as through the door that Ma

had left open the words, 'There's an official-looking brown envelope for Maddie', sliced a pain through her heart. She just knew her Arnie had gone for ever.

Opening the envelope confirmed this. The letter, typed on thick, crisp paper, told her that in the event of his death Arnold Brown had requested that Madaline Foster of Fosters House, Albert Street, Blackpool, be treated as his next of kin.

Private Brown was sadly killed during his company's courageous attack on a German stronghold during the battle of Neuve Chapelle, an engagement that destroyed a rail link that was important to the German offensive. May he rest in peace, knowing his bravery may have advanced the victory of the war.

With every part of her shaking, Maddie picked up the sealed envelope that had dropped out onto the table when she'd withdrawn the letter.

Opening it carefully, knowing that Arnie's hands had held it, that he'd written her name and address on it, she took out the single sheet of lined paper.

Me wee darlin' Maddie,

If you are reading this, it is that I have copped it and am on me way to me maker. But Maddie, I leave a piece of me with you — me heart, me soul, and all that makes me a person. Because, me wee love, when I met you, I instantly belonged to you.

All I have been able to think of since leaving you is when

*we joined as one. Never did I feel a complete and worthy
person until that moment.*

*I wish it was that things were different, Maddie. I wish it
was the end of the war, and that I am for tearing this letter up
and holding you in me arms once more.*

*Me love will always be with you, me wee darlin' . . .
always. But be happy. Don't mourn me passing for ever. Fall
in love again, and have a happy life.*

*Me heart will rejoice in your happiness, but me arms will be
around you in the times you fall, ready to lift you and to help you
face life's challenges. Me love and me life are yours, me darling.*

Your Arnie x

Ma's words were full of despair as she sat down. 'And
you're carrying his babby! Oh, Maddie, Maddie . . .
Poor Arnie . . . But Maddie, it can't be, me little lass, it
can't.'

Tears streamed down Ma's face, deepening Maddie's
feeling of desolation. As did the feel of Ma's cold hands as
she held hers even tighter. 'Please, Maddie! Please tell
everyone that the babby's Reggie's. Folk will understand
that – they knew you were going to marry, and even had
the date fixed. Your name'll be mud if they find out you
cheated on him and gave yourself to another man when
Reggie had only just left to go to war.'

Maddie's mind was screaming against her darling Arnie
having gone. She didn't want to talk about having a babby,
but then, she didn't want to deny it was Arnie's.

'But I never did owt with Reggie, Ma . . . We . . . we
nearly did, but Reggie, well . . . he . . .'

152

'Spare me the details, me little lass. No one needs to knaw owt ... Let me think ...'

Maddie couldn't think. She could only see her beautiful Arnie grinning at her, but then that image faded ... 'Don't leave me. Don't go, Arnie, I love you.'

'Maddie, stop this!'

The desperation in Ma's voice brought Maddie back to the conversation she didn't want to have.

'Look, me darling, I knaw I sound harsh, but I'm not. I want you to knaw that me heart is breaking for you and for lovely Arnie, but I'm your ma. Me first duty is to save you from being dragged through the mud, and me little grand-child from having a slight on its name for the rest of his or her life! You don't want your child known as a bastard, do you?'

Maddie, not really knowing what her ma was saying, shook her head.

'Well, it will if it's known as Arnie's. But if thought of as Reggie's and he comes back and marries you, then it will be forgotten and understood how it happened that the child was born out of wedlock ... If he doesn't make it, God forbid, you will also be forgiven as two young people facing being parted, and you'll always have sympathy.'

'But, Ma—'

'Naw, Maddie. If you can't think, or don't care how it will be for you, think of your babby. He or she is innocent. They didn't ask to be born on the wrong side of the blanket. And they don't deserve to carry the consequences of it being known they were born to a fling their ma had while her fiancé was in France risking his life fighting the Germans!'

The starkness of these words got through Maddie's pain, but stung her in a different way. She stood up, could hear her own voice screaming, tasted the salt of her own tears and felt as though she was tearing her heart out as words tumbled from her:

'It wasn't a fling! It wasn't dirty, it was beautiful! It was the man that I love who gave me babby to me. I am not in love with Reggie – that's sommat as you and Aunt Jean put on our shoulders. Nice for you, eh? Best friends' kids marry. But it ain't like that! Ma, it ain't. I love Reggie, but only with a big brother-type love. I am in love with Arnie.' Her voice raised even more as she screamed, 'Arnie ... Arnie ...' It broke then into sobs as she slumped back down. 'And he's gone ... gone ...'

Sobs racked her body, hurting her chest and splintering her heart as she rested her head on her arms.

Her ma's sobs joined hers as she lifted her and held her to her.

'I'm sorry, me lass, I'm sorry. I – I knaw your pain, God knaws I do. But ...'

Feeling beaten as she connected to her ma's own grief and now knew the depth of it, Maddie said, 'I'll go along with you, Ma, love. Don't worry, but me and you'll allus knaw who the real, lovely man is who's the father of me babby.'

Ma sighed a deep sigh. 'We will, me darlin', but naw one else must. Not even Daisy.'

'She already does. We all talked that evening when I first met Bren and you were going out. You see, Bren is preg-nant an' all.'

'What? Sandra never said.'

Through gulps of rebound sobs, Maddie told how it happened that Bren found herself alone and pregnant.

'Poor lass. No wonder Sandra took her in. Aye, I knaw the true story of Daisy's birth. Do you knaw it?'

'I've since been told.'

'And so hearing Bren was having a babby prompted you to tell them? Well, there's nowt like mates; they take your troubles and help you in different ways to what mas do. We think of your future, not the excitement of you having done sommat with your boyfriend. And that's why I'm saying what I am.'

'I knaw, Ma, and Daisy and Bren will go along with it. But Reggie mustn't be told. It won't be fair on him. He'll knaw it ain't his. Imagine the pain that'll give him. And him being away an' all.'

'But Aunt Jean will have to knaw.'

For a moment, Maddie felt the anguish of this, but then knew that there was only one way. 'We must convince her that if she tells him, it will break his heart. We'll say that's because he can't be here. We must, Ma. We can't do this to Reggie ... I mean, I can't. It's all on my shoulders, not yours, or Aunt Jean's. I'm the one who has done it, but I love Reggie enough to want to protect him from hurt. When he's home it will be different. I don't knaw what he will do or how we will all cope then, I just want to protect him now.'

'Eeh, lass, what have me and Aunt Jean done to the pair of you? I can only say we believed you were in love, the kind of love that would lead to marriage.'

155

'I knaw. And that alone put pressure on me as I couldn't bear to hurt all three of you, but now we must think of Reggie. He does things when they pop into his head. Hearing about this could make him desert and end up with him being shot by his own men!'

'Oh, God, I never thought of that, but you're right. And that's how we'll stop Aunt Jean from telling him. We'll warn her that could happen.'

Maddie knew a kind of relief. She hadn't wanted to give Reggie a thought in all of this, but now she had, he added a new complication and one that would hang over her till the end of the war.

But for now, she had greater things taking up the space in her heart. Her Arnie was never coming back!

With this, her whole body collapsed.

Maddie woke to their doctor leaning over her.

'Maddie, open your eyes. That's it. You're all right ... physically, that is. But from what your mother tells me you've been deeply stressed by finding out you are having your boyfriend's baby, when you didn't get the chance to marry him.'

He surprised her then as he said, 'This bloody war has a lot to answer for,' and then almost echoed what her ma had said would happen. 'It's just not fair that young people are having to say goodbye, rather than take the vows they were going to, and then find themselves in the position that you do. It's one you would never have faced if your marriage had gone through, Maddie. And you're not to look on this as bringing shame to your name or your family. Everyone will understand. Your job now is to take care of yourself and give your little Reggie the best chance in life. His father will come home and take care of you both. In the meantime, you have your mother, and Reggie's mother, to support you.'

For some reason, all Maddie could think of was why it was always assumed a new babby was to be a boy. A daft thought at such a moment when she should be feeling that all would be all right. But it wouldn't and it couldn't be because her babby's da was never coming home to take care of them both and she was afraid of how Reggie would be if he did.

'Now, don't cry. I know you have a lot on your plate, but if your baby is to thrive, it needs a happy mother who takes care of herself. You must do that for your child's sake, Maddie. The time will pass, and all will come right.'

His gentle tone made her want to tell him the truth, but she knew she mustn't. The peace of mind of the two women she loved most in all the world, and who stood at the end of her bed quietly shedding tears, was at stake.

Their tears were for different reasons. For poor Ma, it was knowing the truth and having to deceive her best friend, something Maddie had forced on her, knowing how it would hurt as she and Daisy would never do such a thing to each other. And Aunt Jean, whose tears were probably for her son, mixed with her joy of thinking the child her grandchild.

When the doctor left, they were both by her side.

Aunt Jean took her hand. 'I'm sorry me lad did this to you, love. He should have taken care – well, not done it at all, but I knaw the temptation. I'm feeling very cross with him. But I understand you not wanting him to knaw. I knaw you love him with all your heart and are thinking of how he would react. And I knaw you're right. We must all keep him as happy as we can in our letters.'

As she bent to kiss Maddie, Maddie's heart weighed heavy with her guilt and with the tears it held for her Arnie.

'And I'm so sorry to hear about Arnie. He were a lovely lad. He had me and your ma in tucks. Life's unfair. So unfair.'

Ma looked as though she could hardly bear to speak. Maddie understood. The love Ma held for her gave her a share of the pain of loss and deceit.

When Ma kissed her, she said, 'Daisy and Bren are here, love. Sandra has closed the café for the afternoon.'

'How long have I been out for, Ma? I can remember us talking and then nothing.'

'That happened this morning, me darling. The lad who delivers eggs also goes to the café and I asked him to take a message to Daisy, and the doctor came almost immediately as Aunt Jean went to fetch him.'

'Oh, Ma . . . Ma . . .'

'I knaw, love. I knaw. I'll go upstairs with Aunt Jean and send the girls down to you.' Ma patted her hand before she left.

Maddie rested back on her pillow. *Did I only hear this morning that I've lost me Arnie?* This thought stung her, but she couldn't cry. It was as if she'd shut down and it was all happening to someone else.

A few minutes later, Daisy popped her head around the door of Maddie's bedroom. 'Aw, Maddie, me darling, I can't believe it.' Her lips quivered and she burst into tears. 'Poor Arnie! And you ... and ... Oh, how could your ma make you say your babby is Reggie's!'

'You knaw?'

'Aye, she wrote a note to me. She made me promise, for your sake, to go along with it.'

'Eeh, Daisy, I knaw it sounds bad, but she's right, love. Think about it. The truth would hurt Aunt Jean and leave me and me babby open to being outcast by all who knaw me. Me ma couldn't stand that.'

Bren stepped forward. 'I'm so sorry ... I – I ... Oh, Arnie, our Arnie.'

With this, Bren sat on the edge of the bed, bent her head and wept.

Maddie eased herself up till she could reach for Bren. Holding her, she said, 'You've lost someone you knew from being a young 'un, lass. And someone you loved. I'm so sorry. It's like part of us has been taken too.'

'It is. I loved him so much. He always cared for me. And I was so happy for you, and for him when I met you. You would have been perfect for him.'

Maddie's tears broke then and the three of them cried and hugged.

When at last they came to a peaceful place, Bren said, 'I'm thinking of going to mass for Arnie. He loved the Church. I ain't been much for it, as I think God loves some people more than others. I mean, you only have to look around to see he blesses some with everything and others with nothing.'

Maddie had no answer for this, but she did say, 'I'd like to do that an' all. I went with him at Christmas, and I could tell he loved it. I loved the service as well, it was grand.'

'Well, you can count me in,' Daisy said, 'I've never been brought up to go to church, life's too busy, but I do pray and some of me prayers get answered. Though this has brought home to me how sommat can happen to me Tom, and I need to beg of God not to let it.'

They both sat on the bed then and just held Maddie's hand.

There was some comfort in having them, and in knowing Bren was in the same boat.

'We're to think of our babbies now, Bren. Neither will knaw their dad, and in your case, you wouldn't want your babby to, but we can be the best mas to them and make sure they're happy.'

Bren nodded. It seemed she was unable to speak, but Maddie knew she was grieving for a best friend, as she herself would be if it happened to Reggie.

Daisy changed the subject. 'But how will you cope when Reggie comes home, Maddie? You said you never did it with him, so he will knaw it ain't his. He ain't going to take that lightly.'

'I knaw. I dread to think of it. And I don't want to be forced to marry him either. Not that he ain't a good person and I do love him, but . . . Eeh, I don't knaw, it's too much to think about. I just want to think about me Arnie.'

It was a week later, on a sunny spring Sunday in April, when the café closed and breakfasts at the boarding house

160

had all been cleared away, that they went to a midday mass.

Maddie gained some comfort from knowing this was what Arnie would have wanted her to do for him, but the agony deep inside her had to stay there for most of the time without release while she'd listened to her ma counselling her to try to be cheerful and look forward to Reggie coming home. Sometimes it seemed that her lovely ma no longer cared for her, only for her good name and not hurting Aunt Jean, and that left Maddie feeling so alone.

When they came out of the Sacred Heart Church on Talbot Road, the priest stood by the gates saying goodbye to each member of the congregation. When it was their turn he said, 'Nice to see you young ladies join us this morning. Remember, God is always there for you, and so am I. I may not seem like the kind of person you can approach, but I promise I am. I know that many young people are going through a great deal.'

Daisy answered, 'Ta, Father. We came because we lost a dear friend to the war, and me two friends are expecting babbies and ain't married. So, yes, a lot to contend with.'

'And none of it shocks me, young lady, as I am sure you thought it would. It saddens me very much, and makes me want to help. And I will if I can.'

Maddie, cross at Daisy for being so outspoken, said in a tone that suggested the priest was to blame, 'I don't think there's much you can do, Father. We're cared for, and have each other, and we just have to get on with it.'

'Well, I will keep you in my prayers and if coming here gives you comfort, you are always welcome.'

161

Daisy hung her head. 'I'm sorry, Father, I didn't mean to be so blunt. It all hurts, that's all.'

'I know. You're the young lady from the café, aren't you? I've been in there and had your lovely mugs of tea when out on my walks.'

Daisy brightened. 'Well, the next time there'll be naw charge. I'll look out for you.'

The priest laughed. 'So, it wasn't altogether a wasted morning, it got me a promise of a free cuppa and that can't be bad.'

They all laughed then, and it felt to Maddie as if help could come from where you least expect it. From the little she'd had to do with churches, it seemed the rich folk were the ones accepted and chatted to, but this priest was different. He had wanted to speak to them, and he hadn't condemned them after what Daisy had told him. This made her feel that she wasn't the dregs of society, but a person to be valued. Something she hadn't felt since realising she was pregnant.

As she looked around her at the congregation spilling out, there were very few men, and those there were were older ones.

The women smiled, but their smile didn't touch their eyes. These were wives, sisters or mothers of those who had gone to war. Some of the younger ones were probably what were now being called 'war brides' – those who married by special licence days before their men went to war. Did any of them regret their action?

How different things might have been if Reggie hadn't have gone so soon and they had been married as they had planned.

162

Daisy's hand taking hold of hers brought her out of this surmising. They had walked away from the priest as his attention was taken. He'd called after them that he'd meant what he'd said, and they'd smiled and waved.

'I'm sorry for blurting that stuff out, Maddie. I just feel that God is unjust to women. Men can have fun and do stuff and never face the consequences.'

'I don't think many are having fun right now, love, but I knaw what you mean. It does seem an easier world for men at times.'

'What do you want to do now? Have you got to get back?' Daisy asked.

'Naw, I've got a couple of hours.'

'I'd like to pick some of them daffs near the railings over there and put them somewhere for Arnie, so that it feels we've given him a send-off of sorts.' Bren pointed towards the daffodils nodding their heads as the wind bent them this way and that. Her eyes filled with tears.

Maddie looked away before she answered. She didn't want to touch the deep pain within her. Not here in the busy street. 'I'd like that an' all, Bren, and you knaw, it helps having you here as you knew Arnie long before we did and the little bits you tell me piece his life together for me.'

Daisy's arms came around them both. 'I think that's a grand idea. And eeh, how you're both holding up I don't knaw as I feel like breaking me heart. I'll go back to the priest and ask him if it will be all right about the daffs and then we can walk to Layton Cemetery, as that seems the right place to lay flowers.'

* * *

When they arrived at the cemetery, they walked around it, unsure what to do next, when Maddie spotted a gravestone that read, 'In loving memory of Arnold, only son of Mabel and John Potter, 1890–1895, forever in our hearts.'

'I've found somewhere!'

The others came over and were silent as they read the words on the stone.

'Eeh, five years old, and his name was Arnold. I reckon there's naw place better, Maddie. You put yours on first and then Bren and then mine.'

As she bent to put the daffs in the jam jar that was by the grave and had filled with rainwater, Maddie said, 'I hope me Arnie finds you in heaven, lad, and gives you lots of cuddles.'

As she straightened a voice said, 'What do you think you're doing, eh?'

Swivelling round, Maddie saw a woman in her mid-forties carrying a small bunch of pansies and looking cross and afraid.

'That's my son's grave, you have naw right! Who are you?'

'I'm so sorry, we didn't mean to intrude. We ... we lost a dear friend in the war, we had nowhere to put our flowers ... His name was Arnold – Arnie. We meant naw harm. I was just wishing that me Arnie would find yours and look after him, I ...'

'Eeh, I'm sorry for you, lass. And it's all right. Ta for that, it's a nice gesture. We called our lad Arnie ... Me husband, Arnie's da, died not long after – broken heart they said.'

'Aw, sorry to hear that. This is Maddie, I'm Daisy and this is Bren. Maddie's fiancé and my boyfriend have gone to war. We all knew and loved our Arnie. He was a good bloke and a good friend.'

'Aw, bless you all. And I'm sorry I sounded cross. Me name's Mabel, as you've probably gathered. Me lad died from having measles. Anyroad, you two put your daffs on his grave, it's all right and very welcome.'

'After you, Mabel,' Daisy said. 'I'll see if there's another jam jar around somewhere for ours.'

Bren went with Daisy, leaving Maddie with Mabel.

'So, you're Maddie, and you have your man in France. By, it's not easy, is it? Not having them with you. I sit twiddling me thumbs most of the day, and then crying as loneliness makes you think of things you've tried to cope with but haven't really. The daytime hours are long and the night-time hours even longer.'

'I keep busy. Me ma's got a boarding house and we're full of soldiers who've been billeted with us. That's how I met Arnie. And through him Bren, as she grew up with him and came looking for him after he'd been deployed.'

Mabel gave her a funny look which unnerved Maddie. 'So, you ain't known him long then? He must have been a nice bloke to have made such an impression.'

Composing herself, Maddie said, 'He was Irish and you knaw how they can get into your heart, such lovely folk.'

'They are. Well, all those I've met, and yet we've treated them badly an all . . . You say your ma has a boarding house?'

'Aye, on Albert Road.'

'You ain't looking for any staff, are you? Only, I've been thinking of getting a job, more for company than owt, and to fill me days, then I'll only have the nights to contend with.' Mabel bent down and placed her flowers in the jam jar. 'There you go, me lad. Ma's smiling at you. Love you always.' She blew a kiss into the sky, 'And give that to your dad.'

Maddie's heart went out to her. That's all she had to give to her son, and husband, and all Maddie knew she and her child would have to give to Arnie, a kiss to blow heavenward towards him.

After a moment of silence, Maddie said, 'We do need someone as it happens. Call around and see me ma. I just knaw she'll like you. It's general work.' Maddie sorted through her bag for a scrap of paper and a pencil; she always had old shopping lists still stuffed in there. Finding what she needed, she wrote her address down. As she did, she continued, 'Bedrooms, mainly, as Ma likes to do the cooking and I help with that and serve and do the waiting on, but then after we've done the breakfasts, we have to go upstairs and do the beds and the bathroom. It's all too much now as Ma ain't so well.'

'I'm sorry to hear that, but eeh, lass, if she would consider me, I'd be in me element. I love cleaning and washing. I'm a fair cook an' all if you need to call on me. And I can do any hours you need me as I've naw commitments.'

Daisy and Bren returned as Mabel said this. They'd been a little longer than Maddie had thought they would be as the water butt where spare jars were to be found wasn't more than a few steps away. The sight of Bren's eyes showing she'd shed fresh tears gave her the reason. Poor Bren, Daisy would have kept her away until she could compose herself.

Maddie didn't know why but as she surmised this, an unsettling thought popped into her head. Bren was grieving very heavily for a childhood friend and she wondered if she and Arnie were more than that. But then she told herself she was being silly. That she imagined when you've no family your friends become even more dear to you. And that's all it was.

Daisy, who always picked up on Maddie's feelings, came straight to her and hugged her. 'I'm glad we came here, and aye, met you, Mabel. Is it all right if we put our flowers on now?'

'Aye, that'd be lovely, lass. Me lad ain't had so much attention afore and it's warming me heart.'

When Daisy and Bren rose from placing their daffodils, Maddie told them the news.

Daisy's raised eyebrows showed her surprise, but she recovered quickly. 'Eeh, that's grand, Mabel.'

'Ta, love. I only hope Maddie's ma takes to me and sets me on. It sounds just what I need.'

Maddie had a sudden thought. 'Could you come with me now, Mabel? Me ma'll be up from her rest and having a cuppa before we start to prepare the evening meal. I knaw she'd love to meet you, and you can have a natter before we get busy.'

'Aye, I can do that. And be pleased to, as I've only an empty house to return to.'

As they turned to leave the cemetery, Maddie knew a small easing of her troubles as she thought that even on a

167

dark day you can find a little brightness. With meeting Mabel, she felt she had. Mabel would ease the load on Ma's shoulders and maybe then Ma would return to full health as still she had many bad days with her condition, and this frightened Maddie.

CHAPTER TWELVE

It wasn't until they left Daisy and Bren at the café and went on alone that Mabel said, 'Is the young lass pregnant, Maddie? Only I never saw a ring on her finger, though her belly shows her condition.'

'Aye. She were forced ...' Maddie told what she'd been told by Daisy.

'Aw, poor lass.'

Wanting everything out in the open, Maddie blurted out, 'I am an' all, Mabel. I – I ... well, me and me boyfriend were to marry in a few weeks after ... Anyroad, he was deployed early.'

The lie had slipped easily off her tongue.

'Eeh, lass, naw!'

'Are you still all right with coming to work for us, knowing that?'

'Aye, of course I am. I didn't mean that to sound like anything other than me feeling sorry for you. You ain't alone, lass. I was in the same boat, only nowt happened to take me man away. We were married, and everyone just thought I had the babby early.'

Maddie released the breath she'd been holding. 'Ta for that ... I mean, not taking anything away from what happened to you, but for understanding. It's not easy facing folk.'

'I knaw, but most will understand in the circumstances, lass, so don't worry. There ain't many brides who go up the aisle with everything intact, you just didn't get the chance to go up the aisle, love.'

With this, Mabel linked arms with Maddie. 'Whether your ma takes me on or not, Maddie, you can allus come around to mine and find a friend in me.'

Maddie thought it strange for a moment to be told this by an older woman, but as she looked at Mabel's smiling face, it seemed natural. Mabel was looking on her like her ma would, or her Aunt Jean. She wasn't trying to be a friend in the same way as Daisy and Bren were, but another mother figure who would be looking out for her.

'That's nice to knaw, ta, Mabel, and the same goes for me as I knaw it will for me ma. We'll be a friend who's there for you an' all.'

By the time they reached her home, it felt to Maddie as if she'd known Mabel a lot longer than a few minutes. 'Here we are, Mabel. A little earlier than Ma was expecting, but she'll be up and I knaw she'll be glad to meet you.'

'Eeh, it looks nice and welcoming. I like the flower boxes outside.'

'That's me ma's touch. She tends to them as if they were babbies!'

'And it shows. As does how hard you both work. Them windows shine, and your curtains all look fresh. I'm going to love working here as your ma seems to be a woman of me own heart. I hope she takes to me, lass.'

Maddie didn't doubt this as she opened the front door and called out, 'Ma, we have a visitor!'

The kitchen door opened. 'But you knaw we're full, Maddie! Oh, hello, love.'

'Hello, Maddie's ma, pleased to meet you. And I ain't looking for digs, but a job.'

'A job! Eeh, come in, lass, come in. You're a welcome sight to me eyes. Aye, and to me aching body an' all!'

As they all giggled at this Maddie felt the relief of there not being any ice to break. Ma had accepted Mabel on sight.

As they walked through to the kitchen, Ma said, 'I won't shake hands, lass, I'm up to me elbows in flour, but I'm Sally, everyone calls me Sal. Take your coat off and hook it on the back of the door, and you can sit at me table and tell me who you are, how you met me Maddie and what job you'd see yourself doing in a boarding house.'

'Her name's Mabel, Ma, and we met in Layton Cemetery.'

When Maddie told her ma why she went there and how she chose Mabel's little boy's grave, Ma's head went to one side and her look held sadness. 'Aw, I'm sorry you went through that, Mabel, lass. By, five years old? That is sad. And your man gone an all? Well, you've found a place of welcome here and where you're so needed. When can you start, love?'

'Right now, if you like, Sal. I can wash the cooking pots as you finish with them and then as crockery and cutlery come in from the dining room I can wash and dry them. Only, I've nowt but an empty home to go back to.'

'That'd be grand, lass, ta, and I'll sort out a wage to pay you. Me mate next door has staff, and she tells me the going rate is—'

'Eeh, you've naw need to worry about that tonight. Though I wouldn't say naw to a slice of that roast as me payment. I ain't seen the likes of a side of beef in a long time!'

'Aye, it's a rare thing these days, but we get extra rations from the army as the lads have got to be fed well. But, lass, you'd be welcome to stay for supper. You've made it seem as if heaven's come to me door after we've been through hell.'

'I knaw, Maddie told me of her predicament, poor lass. But you're not to worry, folk'll understand. But for a wedding, most of us would be in the same boat. I knaw I would!'

'Aye, but poor Maddie and Reggie had that snatched from them.'

A feeling took Maddie of wanting to scream out the truth, but she clenched her fists as Ma continued, 'Anyroad, I'm glad you knaw, Mabel, and have accepted it in the way you have. And did Maddie tell you about me condition?'

Maddie interrupted. 'I've to pop downstairs and get changed, Ma. I'll bring a clean pinny up with me for Mabel . . . And Mabel, I'm so glad you're going to take the job.'

Ma hardly acknowledged Maddie but carried on with her tale. She didn't mind. It was so nice to hear her ma nattering away to Mabel as if they were old friends.

Once downstairs, Maddie went to her bedroom and sat on her bed. Her whole body felt weary – weighed down by what felt like a rock lying in her chest. She wanted to cry out her pain – to change things and to not have had them happen. Bren was right, God did seem to deal out blows to some and treat others with kid gloves. *Why, why, why?*

Shaking herself out of it, she got off the bed in one determined action. She was to think of her ma and get on with things. Her ma still needed her. The world didn't stop because of one broken heart.

With Mabel's help supper was much earlier than usual and, Maddie discovered, she knew when chatting was acceptable and when not, which was a great blessing, as neither Ma nor herself could take anyone going on about this or that during the very busy hour of dishing up and serving the soldiers.

Those they had billeted with them now were older and much quieter than Jimmy's crowd, who'd seen everything as a prank.

Thinking about them now as Ma and Mabel nattered to each other over their supper, Maddie wondered how they were faring, and more so if Jimmy was coping. She prayed he was all right and longed for his first letter to arrive.

Her wish came true a week later when a thickish envelope plopped onto the doormat – a rag rug that ma had made in one of the quiet winters. It was black, as she'd used an old coat of hers, and into it she'd sewn in the words 'All welcome' in many colours taken from various scraps she'd bought from the market and bits of old frocks. It was lovely and often remarked on. To them, though, it was always known as 'the welcome mat'.

Going back into the kitchen, to the sound coming from upstairs of the carpet sweeper being wielded by Mabel and to where a steaming mug of tea awaited her, Maddie sat down and sliced the envelope open with the paper knife she'd picked up from the dresser as she'd passed it.

Looking at the signature, she exclaimed, 'Oh, it's from Jimmy! I was hoping it would be, Ma.'

'That's good. What does he say?'

'I'd better read it out. It's like a novel.'

Jimmy's vivid descriptions of all he saw and experienced took them into the world of war.

The sight is one of mud, splattered with blood, and trodden by a thousand boots – some that returned to the trench, many that didn't.

The sounds are of ear-splitting gunfire, horses screaming, or breathing loud, heavy breaths as they pound the ground with their hooves and their eyes flare with fear.

The smell is of sulphur – I didn't know that word, but me corporal told me it's in the gunpowder – and of urine and shit and stale, sweaty bodies, as there's no lavs, only dug-out holes, and hardly ever a bowl of water to wash ourselves. But most of all there's the stench of death. A smell like no other and one I wish I didn't have to breathe in, Maddie.

The words, except the one word that she couldn't read out to her ma and had substituted with 'poo', gave a vivid painting of the horror of war, but didn't tell her how Jimmy was, or how he was coping, till they suddenly changed and became him.

Oh, Maddie, I want to come home. I want to be hugged by yer, and to see me ma and me sisters and brother. I want to sleep in me bed, or in the comfy one you and yer ma offered and do the spuds for yer and wash the pots. And I want to hear silence, Maddie. Not like in the dead of night here, when me body breaks out in sweat as I feel the fear of what might happen tomorrow, but the silence of peace. We had that, Maddie. But we didn't know we had.

Suddenly, cheeky Jimmy was there beside her, his need for love and assurance clear.

I miss everything and everyone. I think about you all and the life I had. Sometimes it was a grind and it hurt to know me mum was leaving us alone to get some money to care for us. But it was always just home.

Now, I like to think of me mum happy with Grantham – ha, we kids used to call him Fat Grantham, and now we have to call him Dad!

I know I played up when I heard about him, but he's a diamond geezer really. He often sent more than Mum had put on her shopping list – we know why now, the crafty sod.

175

Didn't mean that nasty, but I keep remembering bits that tell me he's been after me mum for a long time.

He went on like this for another two pages, and by the time she'd read them, Maddie was laughing and crying at the same time, especially as he described how one of the lads who had been with him – Walter – had the nine lives of a cat.

I tell yer, Maddie, he was running back to the trench but doing a dance at the same time as he jumped and hopped this way and that, and then bent and crawled, then belly crawled, as bullets whizzed passed him, but when he stood to get his leg on the ladder me heart sank, as I thought he were bound to cop it. But no, his bleedin' trousers fell down and tripped him and he landed flat on his back in the bottom of the trench!

When we stopped laughing, we found he'd hurt himself, but now the lucky bugger is waiting in the Red Cross tent to be shipped home!

But then his tone changed.

I didn't want to write this next bit, Maddie, but I know you'd want to know. It's about Graham. The quiet one amongst us.

Oh, Maddie, I can't get it out of me head. He had these fits of shivering all over. We tried to help him, but he was scared, Maddie. Then one day, he woke and all his hair – even his eyebrows and that around his private bits – had fallen out!

The medical lot said it was this word beginning with 'a', and it stems from shock. They told him not to worry about it and to trust in their sergeant as he would look after all us lads. But they can't, Maddie, and sometimes they even seem to sacrifice us. Anyway, Graham started wetting his bed. We all tried to help him, but he cried a lot and then ... Oh, Maddie, he wouldn't go over the top one day, but instead, ran along the trench screaming like a baby ... Our sergeant shot him dead!

Ma gasped. 'Eeh, how could they do that to one of our own, Maddie? The lad weren't well.'

'It sounds like hell, Ma. Them poor lads, and Reggie ... It don't bear thinking of.'

For a moment, Maddie's thoughts went to Arnie and for the first time, she felt a small comfort that he was no longer there. But Reggie was, and she didn't want him to be either. She read on:

Oh, Maddie, I can't get the sight out of me head. I'm sorry if me words are smudged but I cry a lot. I'm not a coward. I'll always do me duty. But it's all so scary and I just don't want to be here.

Then there's the other kind of bloke here, them full of themselves, who are lapping it up and sneaking out of camp and going with girls and telling of their conquests. They bring whisky back with them and give it to us to drink. I've come to look forward to it as two glasses of it and I'm out cold and don't know me fear.

177

This worried Maddie as she knew of men who couldn't leave the bottle alone. She decided to tell him to stop this. She'd put it to him that it was like being a coward, relying on the drink to take stuff away from him. She knew this was harsh but thought it might work with Jimmy.

The letter ended with:

But, Maddie, thinking of me ma now happy and me sisters and brother well fed and looked after, and most especially of you and your ma and of Blackpool, is keeping me going. We had some giggles, didn't we? And, well, I felt love from you both. Especially you, Maddie. And I've made me mind up that I'm going to settle in Blackpool when this lot's over. So, I'll need a job. Keep me one, washing pots or something.

I've put this in me letter to Linda, but I've had nothing from her, or me mum or any of you. But no post has been getting through. All the lads are desperate and the sarge said he'd see what he can do. I am longing for news from home.

Sending me love and one of our hugs. Love to your ma.

Jimmy x

'Eeh, you've written him at least three letters. And you get post from Reggie saying he's had your letters. That ain't fair on them young 'uns. It wants sorting out!'

'It does, Ma. The lads must feel that none of us care back here.'

'It all makes you think, don't it? Here we are getting on with our lives, and aye, we knaw there's a war going on, and miss our lads and fear for them, but none of what they are going through touches us and we don't realise how bad it is.'

Maddie was quiet as her mind gave her the different pictures of how it could have happened that Arnie was taken. She didn't want them and tried to bat them away, but Jimmy had brought it all alive for her.

Reggie's letters – she'd had two so far – spoke a different tale, one of things being harsh and uncomfortable, but full of bravado. He even boasted that he'd killed two Germans one day. But she knew Reggie so well and took it all as him trying to make light of it. She hated to think of the reality of it for him. He would hide all of that.

With this, she thought that he didn't deserve what she'd done. And for the first time, she saw wrong in it. No matter that she wasn't in love with Reggie, he didn't know that and she'd promised herself to him.

The familiar feeling of guilt clothed her like a heavy wet coat. She didn't want to feel like this. She needed to make it up to him. Maybe be more loving in her letters. Maybe that would make her feel how she used to for him, and not leave her feeling she was saying things she shouldn't to a brother figure.

His letters were full of his love and how he wished things had been different on the night they nearly made love. She'd looked on this as him thinking of only one thing, but you do when you're in love. She thought often about how it had felt to make love to Arnie.

She should be the same with Reggie. He was out there, in the thick of what Jimmy described, and he didn't deserve any of what had happened.

With this, she said to Ma, 'Are we all done? Jimmy's letter has made me want to write to Reggie, as now I understand what he is in the thick of.'

'I'll see to these cups and say ta-ra to Mabel for you. You go ahead, love.'

As she got up and turned towards their flat door, her ma added, 'And it's nice to hear that you want to write to Reggie, me darling, and not to hear that note of it being a chore you must get done.'

Maddie managed a smile. 'I ain't been meself, Ma, but suddenly I'm thinking of Reggie, not meself. And that makes me feel better. I'll write more of the type of letter he should receive.'

'That's grand, lass. It'll work out, you'll see. Reggie loves you ... Oh, aye, it'll take a bit for him to get used to, but you knaw, I've sommat to tell you an' all. I've been waiting for me moment. Only, I've been to the library, and I got a book on how babbies get inside you ...'

'What? I thought you knew that, Ma!' For the first time in a long time, Maddie's giggle with her ma was deep-seated and heartfelt.

'Ma slapped out with the tea towel she'd picked up. 'I knaw, you daft a'peth, but when we were young lasses, I heard it said that a man doesn't have to do it to make you have a babby. I've laughed at it, but it niggled at me after what you told me happened with you and Reggie ... I knaw you didn't give me details, but what you did say was enough.'

180

'Enough for what, Ma? What's all this about?'

'Well, I searched through books on it, and I found that it is possible for a woman to become pregnant, if ... Look. I borrowed the book. It's in me bedroom in me bedside cupboard. I've left a bit of paper between the pages. You read it for yourself ... But lass, well, you might get a shock as, if you and Reggie nearly did it, it might be possible that your babby is Reggie's.'

Maddie frowned and drew in her chin. This was all ridiculous. What on earth was her ma talking of? Besides, she had a monthly after Reg left.

'Look, Maddie, I ain't saying it is so, but we might have a case to help us convince Reggie that it is.'

Maddie just shook her head in disbelief. 'Ma, I'm grieving the da of me child. You knaw what that feels like. I – I need your love and your support ...' She could hear her own voice rising with the emotions she was unleashing. 'Always I'm thinking of you! Trying to spare you worry, trying to make you feel better about it all. And yet all you can do is work at convincing me me babby don't belong to the man I love and have lost, when you've been through the same loss yourself!'

By the end, she knew she was screaming.

The door opened. 'Eeh, what's to do? ... Aw, Maddie, Maddie ...'

Mabel was by her side, holding her as her body crumbled. Ma sat down heavily on the chair. Her head shook from side to side. Her words were of being sorry, of trying to help the situation, and of how she'd felt she could broach the subject now that Maddie had said she would show love to Reggie.

'Aw, me lasses, what brought this on? Come and sit down, Maddie, and talk to your ma. Whatever it is, you sound to me like you're talking at cross purposes.'

Maddie resisted, but in her broken state, Mabel was too much for her and steered her to a chair.

'Now, if you want me to leave, I will, but promise that whatever it is, you will talk it through and clear the air, eh?'

'You can stay for me, Mabel, but it's up to Maddie.'

Maddie nodded, and as she did, the whole story spilt from her. Including how she felt under pressure to continue a relationship with someone she loved but wasn't in love with and how she fell for Arnie, and it was his babby she was having.

All the while she spoke, Ma was silent. At one point she lowered her head as if feeling shame, but at the end she said, 'If only you had spoken to me, Maddie. Told me how you felt. Aye, I assumed you were in love with Reggie. And was happy as it seemed just perfect for you and for me and Jean, but I would have helped you out of it had I known. I was always telling Aunt Jean that we must prepare ourselves for both, or one of you, growing out of the attachment you had, and Aunt Jean always agreed.'

'Aw, Ma, you never said!'

Mabel butted in. 'Well, it's not my place to say owt, but this is an age-old problem. Mother and daughter not communicating. Or trying not to hurt each other by keeping silent, and making things worse. But if I may speak frankly?'

Ma nodded. And Maddie managed an, 'Aye, it's all right.'

'Well, what must be thought about, Maddie, is what you're to do about it all now. And though I understand how you feel, I'm on your ma's side in this. Your priority now, Maddie, must be to protect your babby. And that means giving him or her respectability. You want everyone to take the news of your pregnancy how I did when you told me, as sommat that could happen to any one of us. You had me sympathy, not me condemnation – and you still do, me lass. But I'm just saying, you want that from everyone, for your babby's sake. You don't want it to be an outcast, and folk can be cruel when it comes to sommat like this.'

'I told her that, Mabel.'

'Well, hearing it from me an' all won't hurt owt, love. And nor will it if you go along with your ma on this, Maddie, as in your heart you'll knaw the truth. But if there's a chance of convincing Reggie that your babby is his, jump at it and stick by it.'

Maddie couldn't answer this. In her mind she could see herself and Arnie in a loving, yearning, longing situation, expressing their love for each other and feeling it. And yet, with Reggie, it had been something he needed to try. He'd got her drunk and had her up against a wall in a back alley. He'd been almost there, when wet sticky stuff had come from him, and he'd moaned his pleasure. She knew now what had happened, as it had happened to her and to Arnie, but they had been joined. Reggie hadn't been able to wait for that ... But then, Ma had said that could still result in pregnancy!

Realisation dawned on her of how Ma and Mabel were right. Of how she could use that one incident and Ma's book to make things right for her child. She didn't want to, but neither did she want the baby Arnie had given her to suffer the slur it would if she didn't.

Looking up, she saw the waiting, expectant expressions on her ma's and Mabel's faces and nodded. 'Aye, there is sommat I could use to convince Reggie.'

Ma let out a huge sigh.

Suddenly, Maddie saw the strain on Ma's face, the dark circles under her eyes, how thin she was. Had all the worry she'd brought down on her beloved ma done this to her?

Getting up, she scooted around the table and into her ma's arms.

'I'm sorry, Ma, I'm sorry. I didn't mean to cause you all this worry. I'll do it, Ma. I'll convince Reggie it's his babby and I'll marry him. I – I knaw he'll be a good da and I do love him dearly. It – it's just that … Oh, Ma. How you felt about me da, that's how I felt about Arnie. He was the other half of me, me missing bit … I can't bear to think I'll never see him again.'

Ma was sobbing with her. Two arms came around them both. 'And this will always be in your heart, Maddie,' Mabel said, 'but you must never let it out. Not if you're to protect your babby and your ma.'

Maddie nodded as best as she could. She would do that. She would keep Arnie deep in her heart and in her memory, but for his child, she would do what others expected of her.

CHAPTER THIRTEEN

The months passed with Maddie finding that most of the time, life went on as normal around her, with her playing her part, and yet not really being a part of anything.

It was as if she had put her emotions into a trunk and closed the lid on them so that nothing could hurt her more than she could cope with.

If others noticed this, they didn't try to cajole her out of it, which sometimes seemed to Maddie as if they'd made a pact to allow her to be how she wanted to be and to carry on around her as if this was the Maddie they'd always known.

Only Daisy made extra effort to help her back to who she had been, and Maddie loved her for it.

Daisy didn't mind when tears flowed. She didn't get cross and tell her to put it all behind her and think of her babby. But she allowed her to be the new person she'd become – a functioning, but not feeling, person, living day by day.

Bren, too, played her part, recognising when Maddie just needed to be with Daisy, and making excuses that she was tired so wouldn't go on a walk with them, or she needed to be alone for a while, leaving them to be together.

Often of late, Maddie had tried harder to include Bren and gradually they were getting to a place where it was the three of them and it felt good. This gave more of a distraction to both herself and Bren, who was troubled as her time to give birth approached and she wondered how she would cope and if she'd be a burden on Daisy's ma and not the help she had been.

Maddie tried to reassure her that Daisy's ma was looking forward to the baby coming as if it was a grandchild she was having. And Ma helped by reassuring Bren that what she was going through was normal.

'Nerves get you all in a whirl, lass,' Ma said as they all sat with her in the yard, catching the intermittent sun in what was a changeable July, often giving them a promise of summer, but being not nearly as nice as June had been. 'You start to question whether you can cope with a babby. Are you a fit person to be a ma? Will your babby love you? It's endless and natural, but aye, what is natural an' all is how all that disappears when you hold your babby for the first time as the love you feel is overwhelming and you knaw then that whatever it takes, you can do.'

'Well, I for one am excited! I can't believe it's happening. I'm envious an' all. Here's Maddie and Bren with their bellies up, but I haven't got mine up!'

'Naw, Daisy. Think yourself lucky, lass. I'm sure both girls would rather be in your shoes.'

Maddie didn't say so, but she wouldn't have swapped. All she had of Arnie was his child, and she would treasure that gift for ever. But she knew Ma was looking at them as just being young women with no men to support them.

As if Maddie had prompted this to come to the fore, Ma said, 'You've never spoken about what happened to you, Bren. We were sorry when we learnt about it, but you're coping so well with it. Though Sandra thinks you've bottled it up and don't talk about it much.'

Maddie was shocked at this. None of them had mentioned the rape that Bren had endured since they first knew about it.

'It – it's something I leave locked away, Mrs Foster. I – I try to pretend it didn't happen.'

'Eeh, lass, I shouldn't have said owt. Forgive me. I don't knaw what I was thinking . . . Only to say, you can allus talk to any of us if you need to. You don't have to keep it to yourself, you didn't do owt wrong – even though it's you that's being punished.'

Daisy saved the day. 'Don't worry, Aunt Sal, Bren talks to me. We sometimes chat well into the night. And we cry together an' all, don't we, Bren?'

Bren looked relieved as she nodded her head. 'Yes, I'm all right. I have me moments, but thanks for thinking of me, Mrs Foster . . . And well, is it all right if I ask you something?'

''Course it is, lass.'

'It's just that me and Daisy are worried about you. You seem to have lost a lot of weight and don't look well. We were talking about it last night, weren't we, Daisy?'

Daisy looked embarrassed but Maddie knew a feeling she'd forgotten – had shut down – a feeling of deep anguish and pain that cut through her as she looked at her ma as if seeing her for the first time. And there, for all the world to see, was a very sick lady.

'Ma, Ma, why didn't you tell me?'

'I'm all right, lass. The doctor says that there's nowt more can be done. I've to watch me diet and try to find what irritates me condition, and aye, of late, I have had more bouts of going to the lav a lot. But you've enough on your plate, Maddie, love, to start worrying over me.'

Getting up as fast as her bulk would let her, Maddie went to her ma and took her in her arms. As she did, she heard a cross whisper from Daisy. 'I told you not to say owt, Bren!'

'It's all right, Daisy. I'm glad sommat was said. Aw, Ma, I've been in me own miserable world and ain't taken care of you. That'll change, I promise.'

'Eeh, lass, if you would start living again – taking notice of life around you, answering your letters to Reggie, Jimmy and Jimmy's ma, and just taking care of yourself – I'd be a lot better, I'm that anxious over you.'

'We all are, Maddie.'

'I'm sorry, Ma . . . Sorry, Daisy. I – I just can't seem to be me any more.'

Ma patted her arm. 'I knaw, lass, I was just the same. But me and Aunt Jean, we told each other that we had our young 'uns to look out for and we were to buck up and get on with it. That was a few months after we lost your da and Uncle Ted. And we started planning for the future and learnt to live with our grief. You've to do that somehow, Maddie, love.'

'I will, Ma. And I can start by shopping for me babby.' Trying to lighten things, Maddie added, 'Mind, I've naw need to buy clothes, you and Aunt Jean have knitted or sewn a mountain of them. We could clothe all the babbies in Blackpool!'

'Ha, we're the same, Maddie! Me, Bren and Ma have been stitching and knitting hell for leather!'

They all giggled at Daisy, and Maddie felt better.

Bren, suddenly leaning forward and moaning, changed their giggles to concern as they all gave their attention to her.

'It's your babby coming, Bren, love. We'd better get you home.'

But as Ma finished saying this, a pool of water formed around Bren's feet.

'Eeh, we've naw time to do that now! Maddie, run and fetch Mabel. She was telling me that her ma was the local midwife and she used to help her. She said she'd help you when the time came. She'll knaw what to do.'

'Really? She's said nowt to me about that!'

'Naw, none of us could chat with you, love. We just had to leave you to come out of your sadness.'

'I'll never do that, Ma.'

'You will, lass, now stop talking and go!'

Maddie was shocked by Ma's urgency. Although what was she thinking of standing and talking, wanting to know stuff she hadn't been told, when poor Bren was sat on a wooden bench about to give birth!

But then, that was how her world had been – everything happening around her and her not taking part. That had to change.

As she went towards the door that led to the sitting room of her and ma's flat, she thought, *Only I can change that, and I will.*

Hours later, and with Daisy having had to leave to be back to help her ma with the evening rush, and Maddie coping in the kitchen of the boarding house, Bren's cries of agony stopped, and the sound of a baby crying took over.

The tension left Maddie's body as the miracle of a new life filled her with excitement. Putting the heavy saucepan of boiling potatoes to the right of the hot plate to keep simmering, she ran towards the flat door and down the stairs.

The sight that met her filled her heart with joy. A smiling, red-faced Bren held a little bundle to her, wrapped in one of the many blankets Ma had knitted.

'It's a girl, Maddie ... A girl!'

Maddie rushed forward, unable to believe how Bren had been through so much pain and yet looked glowing as if she'd been to a party!

'Aw, Bren, she's beautiful ... Did it hurt badly?'

'Ha! I can't remember! It did feel like it was never going to end, but I don't know why now. All I care about is that me baby's safe. She doesn't have anything wrong with her, no bits missing, or damaged, she's just a perfect little human, and I made her!'

'You did, Bren, you did. Can I hold her?'

Feeling tentative at first as she took the baby, Maddie looked down into the bluish-reddish, screwed-up little face and felt a love surge through her. For a moment when the baby opened her eyes, Arnie came to mind, but then she saw his face in everything and everywhere – in the wall outside where the bricks had chipped, in puddings she was mixing, when the dough formed patterns, and in her mind when she lay down to sleep. He was never far away.

Her stomach moved and she laughed. 'Eeh, me little one is kicking you up the bum as if to say that's my ma!'

They all laughed, and Maddie knew it was with relief as much as amusement. She laughed herself as another more determined kick made her jump. 'I'd better give her back. Have you a name for her, Bren?'

'Edna. You see, if I had a girl, I wanted to call her Sandra as without Aunt Sandra, as I call her, I wouldn't be here to see this day. I was very near to taking me own life when I found . . . Anyway, Sandra said she'd get all mixed up with that as if she was talking to herself when she spoke to me little girl!'

There was a giggle from them all, but Maddie knew it held sympathy too for Bren not having any family of her own to call the baby after.

'So, it's Edna, which is Aunt Sandra's second name and was her gran's.'

'It's lovely.'

'Yes, Maddie, I like it and her second name is going to be Daisy.'

'Edna Daisy,' Ma repeated. 'That's lovely. Eeh, lass' – Ma had put her arm around Maddie's waist – 'I wonder what ours will be and what he or she will be called.'

Maddie knew the answer to that. 'If a girl, Rosanne Sally. Don't ask me why Rosanne, I just heard it somewhere'

191

– she didn't tell them it was Arnie's mother's name. 'And if a boy, Frederick after me dad.'

'Well, I didn't even knaw as you'd given thought to it, lass, but it warms me heart that you have. And they're lovely names ... But eeh, we'd better get upstairs and see to dinner!'

'It's all right, Ma. The spuds will be ready to mash soon, then we've only to spoon in the savoury mince and top with mash and pop them into the oven. The bread is baked ready to give them chunks with the cottage pie and there's extra gravy simmering on the stove an' all!'

'By, that's good. And what about the rice pud?'

'That's doing nicely in the oven. There's nowt to worry over. We've another hour yet afore the lads'll be ready for their supper.'

Ma sighed with relief and sat down on the end of Maddie's bed. 'I could get in there with you, Bren, lass.'

'Ha, naw you can't!' Mabel said this in a voice that brooked no argument. 'I've to get the babby onto Bren's breast yet for her first feed. So off you all go. And, Sally, love, go and lie on your own bed. I'll stay later and take care of everything with Maddie. I've done it afore. Me and Maddie make a good team, don't we, me darling?'

'Ha! Not aways, Mabel, love, as you get under me feet and won't stick to your job like me and Ma do but want to do it all! But I forgive you as I love you.'

'Eeh, lass, don't. Me heart's near to breaking as it is. I never thought to bring another babby into the world, I couldn't face helping others after ...'

'Aw, Mabel.' Maddie took Mabel in her arms. It felt good

to be comforting someone else, and to do so knowing their pain as it seemed her sympathy was more meaningful.

'Are you all right, Mabel? It's all right to feel sad.'

'Aye, it never leaves you, but it's sommat you can live with. And really, I'm more all right than I have been in years as I've just done what I love doing best – helping to bring babbies into the world.'

'I couldn't have done it without you, Mabel, thanks. I didn't know how much it would affect you, though. I'm sorry.'

'Naw, lass,' Mabel told Bren, 'it has helped me. I'm going to think about taking some training and doing a bit more of it, as I loved it and feel it's me vocation.'

'Eeh, Mabel, that'll mean we lose you, but if it's what you want, then you must do it. Look, I'll go up and make us all a cuppa. I'm sure you could do with one an' all, Bren?'

'Ooh, I could, thanks, Maddie.'

'And you look in need of one, Ma. Now, do as Mabel told you and go and get into bed for an hour.'

'Ta, love, I do feel whacked out and I've only been watching and helping when asked. How you must feel, Bren, I don't knaw – or I've forgotten!'

'I'm all right, Mrs Foster, I feel full of energy.'

'Good, and naw more Mrs Foster. It sounds daft. Call me Aunt Sal, lass.'

Bren beamed, but then a tear glistened in her eye as she said, 'It's like for the first time in me life I've got a family of me own.' She looked down at little Edna. 'And you, me little love, have topped that as you are real family.'

They all wiped a tear away before Mabel hustled them out of the room and turned to Bren. 'Let's get little one fed, me darling, then you can have that cuppa.'

In the small hallway that connected all the rooms of their flat, Maddie took hold of her ma.

Shock zinged through her at the feel of her ma's bones sticking out, and her ribcage almost bare of flesh. 'Aw, Ma, I'm sorry. I've been in a world of me own and didn't register how ill you were. You're to stay in bed for a few days. Mabel will help me. We'll do everything between us.'

'You can't, Maddie. Not in your condition. You'll do yourself harm.'

'I won't, Ma. I'm strong. Anyroad, I've still a couple of months to go.'

'I've been thinking, lass. We'll need another hand soon, so why don't we put an advert up now, eh?'

'Aye, though I'm sure if you get stronger, you and Mabel could do it between you. Me and you did for a long time. And don't worry about her wanting to train to bring babbies into the world. It might just be a fancy of the moment. I can't see her leaving us in the lurch.'

Ma seemed settled by this. She thought the world of Mabel and it would be a wrench for her to have to manage without seeing her every day.

When Aunt Jean came in later, Maddie didn't just accept her hug, but hugged her properly.

'Eeh, lass, that does me heart good. Are you feeling more able to cope now?'

'I am.' And to make Aunt Jean even happier, Maddie added, 'I'm still missing Reggie with all me heart, but I've been moping around for too long. I got a shock today when Bren asked how Ma was. I – I hadn't even noticed her losing weight and looking so yellow.'

'I knaw, lass, but we understood. Especially me. Where is your ma?'

'She's in bed. She's so weak, Aunt Jean.'

Aunt Jean hugged Maddie once more. 'Eeh, lass, don't be worrying too much, I was with her when she saw the doctor last time and he assured her that this and the bleeding is normal for her condition.'

'Bleeding?'

'Aye, your ma's losing blood from ... well, her backside. But it ain't masses and as I said, the doctor wasn't over-concerned.'

Maddie had a moment of feeling cross at herself. She'd selfishly wallowed in her own self-pity.

'Are you on your own then, lass?'

'Naw, Mabel's been helping me ... Eeh, I haven't told you! We have a new babby in the house!'

'A what?'

'Yes! A babby! Bren was visiting and she went into labour and Mabel delivered her babby in my bed!'

'By, it all happens! How many talents has Mabel got? She kept that one up her sleeve!'

'She'd told Ma about it. Anyroad, the babby's a girl and she's called Edna Daisy.' Maddie explained why.

'Well, well, the goings-on in this house are sommat as you could write a book about! But eeh, it's exciting. We ain't had any new babbies since you and Reggie were born … Ha, history could repeat itself if yours is a boy as they might one day fall in love and marry like you and me Reggie!'

Maddie laughed out loud. And to her surprise, it was real, heartfelt laughter. Something she hadn't done for months. 'You daft a'peth, Aunt Jean. Go on with you. I'll be down in a moment to see if you need owt. But if you knock on me bedroom door, Mabel might let you in to see Bren and her babby. She went down about half an hour ago to wash both the babby and Bren and get them comfortable for the night. I'm going to be sleeping in there in a put-me-up bed that Ma keeps for if we have more guests than beds.'

'That canvas thing? Well, good luck to you, me darling. I can't see you being comfy on it.'

'I knaw it doesn't look like it, but it's comfy to sleep on. I often did if Daisy slept over. I'll be fine.'

Left alone in the kitchen with the door open to let in the cool breeze, Maddie put the kettle on and let out an involuntary sigh. Now she'd had this breakthrough, she needed to work hard at keeping a better frame of mind. Her ma needed her, and she was to be there for her. She was to get herself strong, mentally too. She thought of what her ma had said about how she and Aunt Jean had coped, and told herself, *They did it and so can I.*

With this, she did feel some extra strength come into her and felt better for it. From now on, she would take over the business, do the ordering and the menus and organise which guest should have which room, as now they were given a list of who was being billeted with them.

196

Thinking of this last, she so wished everything could get back to normal. Looking after a sometimes rowdy lot of lads, who walked mud and sand in on their boots without a care, and who did everything in a loud, banging-about way, was wearing. Whereas she and Ma had loved looking after the holidaymakers – listening to their tales of what they had done that day, where they had been and where they planned to go the next day. And to kids boasting about building the biggest sandcastle ever, and eating not one, but two ice creams!

But then, giving the lads a home from home before they went to war was rewarding too, in its own way.

All of it was very hard work, but Maddie felt up to the challenge, and better for facing it.

CHAPTER FOURTEEN

By the time September came around and Maddie's baby was due, she had the boarding house running like clockwork, with a lot less hassle than there used to be.

She'd engaged a part-time waitress, whose duties included cleaning and setting up the dining area and sitting room, and a part-time chambermaid and laundry woman to assist Mabel. Both were worth their weight in gold.

But Maddie had made one rule regarding these staff members and that was that they were to be treated like staff and not family members. This was alien to her, but she'd decided this as it was always more difficult to be a boss to family, and more so with her being so young. As with Mabel, it was more often she ruled the roost, something Maddie didn't mind, but that she didn't want from others.

This rule was working well and made for increased efficiency and less gossiping and involvement, leaving time for herself and her ma to rest.

Ma's health was up and down, with good days and bad, but the new regime helped, as Mabel had more time and could help with the kitchen work, leaving Ma only doing the jobs she could do while sitting down.

It was while Maddie was bending to put a meat pie into the oven that the pain that had been niggling her all day suddenly became intense. She gave an involuntary gasp and hung on to the back of a chair.

'Maddie, love . . . Eeh, Maddie! Is it the babby?'

As if she'd made up her mind that it was, Ma dashed to the kitchen door that led to the hall and in a voice near to panic, shouted, 'Mabel! Mabel, lass, where are you?'

As Maddie clung on to the chair consumed by a pain that grew in strength to nearly take her off her legs, she heard Mabel's footsteps hurrying down the stairs and her shouting to the chambermaid, 'Take over, Rosie! I've nearly done all the beds. Just room four to do.'

And the answering call, 'Aye, Mabel, will do. I've finished my lot now.'

Then Mabel, her lifesaver at this moment, came to her side and gently rubbed her back. 'This is it, lass, you'll soon be meeting your young 'un. By, I can't wait.'

The softness left her voice then as she yelled, 'Sally, I'll get Maddie downstairs. You get hot water as before, lass.'

'Naw. Ma's not to do that, Mabel. Call Aunt Jean. She said she can come at any time to help as she hardly works now, her staff do it all. I want Ma . . . Ooh, God, it hurts!'

Ma was by her side in a flash. 'Ma, I just want you to hold me hand . . .'

'I will, me darling. I'll fetch Aunt Jean first ... Go on, love, go with Mabel. I won't be a mo, and do all Mabel tells you, as in this she's the boss, not you, me lovely lass.'

The tone of this made Maddie realise that she must have seemed bossy of late, but she had a role much bigger than most of her age and had had to make everything work.

She looked at Mabel as her gentle hands steered her towards the door of their flat, and smiled at her. 'I've naw need for me ma to tell me you're the boss in this, Mabel, love. I trust you and am so happy that you're here and on hand. I've allus dreaded sommat might happen in the night when you're at home.'

'That's good to hear, love, as I want you to do all that I tell you, even when it's difficult and you feel like smashing me face in.'

Maddie laughed loudly at this.

'Eeh, you might laugh, but I can tell you, many a lass hit out at me ma! Aye, and she took a lot of abuse an' all. The most she ever had was from a vicar's wife. By, that lass had a mouth fouler than a guzunder when it's had a number two done in it!'

This tickled Maddie so much that she had tears rolling down her face and couldn't move. Though the laughing soon stopped when her pain gripped her once more and brought her to her knees.

'Maddie, Maddie, lass, we must get you downstairs. Please, love, hang on to me and crawl if you have to.'

Somehow, they managed to get to the door, and once there, with the pain subsiding, Maddie was able to get to her room.

'Naw more tales, Mabel. And I hope I don't add to them, but . . . oooooh! Help me, help me!'

Hours later, with her whole body wet with sweat and feeling she couldn't take any more, Maddie screamed out the gasp she'd taken in as a stinging pain between her legs seemed it would split her in two. This was followed by the wail of her newborn baby and her lying back exhausted.

'You did, it, Maddie . . . Eeh, me Maddie . . . I love you, me lovely lass.'

These words of her ma's creased Maddie's face into a wide grin . . . Her babby was born – she had her Arnie back. With this, a huge sob racked her body.

'Naw, Maddie, this is a happy occasion.'

'Don't worry, Sal, it's a natural reaction,' Mabel told Ma. 'All will be right when she holds her babby. I won't be a minute cleaning the little mite up.'

Maddie calmed at this and waited, not thinking to ask what she'd had, but then Mabel turned and in a flamboyant gesture, handed over her baby saying, 'There you go, Maddie, your beautiful son!'

'A – a boy?'

'Aye, and he's a pair of lungs on him – I'd say he's going to be the town crier – and a willy to rival anyone's!'

Ma burst out laughing and this set Maddie off. Aunt Jean, who'd stood by without saying much throughout the birth, joined in with them as she and Ma crowded around to get a glimpse of her little Freddie.

Maddie took in a deep breath of joy. Her son. Her's and her beloved Arnie's son was snuggled in her arms!

A love like she'd never felt for anyone in the world consumed her as she looked into her child's face, and said, 'Hello, Freddie.'

After a moment, her tears of happiness, mingled with those of sorrow, slowed as something of the atmosphere around her, delivered in hushed whispers, penetrated her emotions.

She looked up to see an anxious ma staring down at her, and a fidgety Mabel rolling her bloodstained pinny into a ball, while Aunt Jean seemed as though someone had turned her into a statue.

'What? Is there sommat wrong? ... Oh, God, not with me little Freddie!'

As she began to unwrap her child, Mabel said, 'Wait, love ... let me prepare you ... You see, lass, Freddie has what was allus known as a club foot.'

Maddie stared at Mabel as the shock of the words sank in. She'd heard of the condition, and how those afflicted couldn't walk without a crutch.

A picture of a lad at school came to her. Peter ... She couldn't remember his surname, but he had to use crutches and he went through hell. She got a pasting herself once for trying to protect him. Other kids used to knock his crutches from under his arms and then laugh at him as he struggled on the floor to get up, or they would take his crutches and throw them into the ditch! She didn't want that for her child.

'Naw ... naw ... not me Freddie!'

Mabel nodded, and as she did, tears plopped onto her cheeks. 'Your lad may never walk, or he might with the aid of crutches.' She audibly sobbed as she said, 'His foot is twisted and almost points backwards. I – I tried to straighten it, but that's when he yelled.'

Maddie looked down into her son's beautiful face – smooth and pink, not red and blueish, like Edna had been. Gently, she unwrapped his shawl. This was a moment she'd waited for and had wanted to savour: the first sight of his little arms and body, and his legs. She hadn't imagined anything could spoil this time for her, but now, she dreaded it.

When finally she unwrapped his feet, she flinched at the ugly sight of the wrinkled and swollen foot, which was almost back to front.

Her ma's 'Poor darling' zinged through her, but the impact wasn't as deep as when Freddie gurgled and twisted his head this way and that.

He was her beloved son, and this affliction didn't lessen that. It increased her instinct to protect him and to be there for him through every trial he would face in life. She would make sure he had the same chances as every other child. She'd work her fingers to the bone for him and scrimp and save to get the money together to have everything possible done medically. She wouldn't just be his ma. She would stand in for Arnie and be his da too. And she would make him into a man to be proud of who would make his mark on the world. She loved him . . . Loved him with a love she didn't think possible.

'He'll be all right. There won't be owt "poor" about him, Ma. He has us, and we're a force to be reckoned with.'

Aunt Jean spoke then and shocked them all. 'Eeh, I don't knaw what Reggie will make of this. We ain't ever had anyone crippled in our family.'

'Freddie ain't a cripple, Aunt Jean!' It stuck in her throat to say the next bit, but she forced herself to. 'This is your grandson. Don't think of him as being just his poorly foot!'

'Aw, I'm sorry, lass. Can you forgive me? I was thinking aloud, it's not how I feel. I feel a love for the lad like naw other. Can I hold him?'

'Not till after me, Jean, lass.' With this, Ma bent and, putting Freddie's shawl back over him, lifted him up. Her look that was only for Maddie told of her love and her pride in what Maddie had just said to Jean.

Mabel came over to her then and bent over her. 'You're the bravest lass I've ever met, and I love you, me darling.'

Maddie knew Mabel meant the same as her ma had with her look. She put her arms out and Mabel leant into her. But the hug didn't last long as Aunt Jean, trembling a little and looking like an outcast, ran her fingers through Maddie's hair. 'Naw one loves you as much as I do, love.'

Mabel lifted herself and looked at Jean. 'Eeh, Jean, love, we're none of us in control of what comes out of our mouths when we're in shock. We all knaw you didn't mean it like it sounded. You have a cuddle with Maddie, then I'll have to get on and clean her up. Poor girl's still sitting in the mess the afterbirth made.'

The hug from Aunt Jean, though a familiar occurrence, felt different this time. It was almost as if she felt she wasn't worthy.

'I love you, me lovely Aunt Jean. You've allus been there for me. Giving me sweeties when I was crying because Ma had smacked me bum . . .'

'She didn't! Eeh, Jean, it's a wonder me Maddie ain't a spoilt brat!'

'Naw, it weren't like that. I allus told her that her ma was right, and that she'd done wrong and if she went and said she was sorry, she could have a sweetie, but mind, she had to be truly sorry . . . Eeh, Maddie, you'll get me hung!'

Maddie grinned as Ma handed little Freddie over to Jean, and that deepened as an expression of pure love was directed at her child. But so did her guilt over her deceit of this lovely lady who'd only ever given her love.

When Daisy and Bren came later, Maddie knew they had been told about Freddie's foot. She could see the sympathy on their faces and for some reason it made her angry.

'Don't you dare pity me or me little Freddie! He's perfect. He's mine and I love him!'

'Eeh, Maddie, I'm sorry, love. It – it were more me feeling sorry it had happened. By, naw babby can be anything but perfect. And especially yours, as he will be like me own.'

Maddie reddened with shame. 'It was just your expression, Daisy. I wanted you to come in looking all happy for me.'

'Maddie, it's because we love you. Not because Freddie has the affliction, but because he and you will have to manage it and we didn't want that for you both. You've enough on your plate.'

Bren spoke then. 'I know how you're feeling, love. It's like a happiness mixed with tiredness and sadness because of the situation we both found ourselves in, but us who love you are only trying to support you, Maddie.'

'I'm sorry. Aw, you're me best friends in all the world. Can you forgive me?'

'Nowt to forgive. You had to take it out on someone, and we're the best ones as we don't mind, and we understand . . . Now enough of you, we came to see our darling little lad.'

'Daisy's right, and I brought Edna to see him too. And she's an impatient little girl at the best of times!'

They were laughing now.

Daisy picked Freddie up from his cot. He didn't protest but snuggled into her. 'Aw, you're a good lad, and your Aunt Daisy loves you. I'll be in your corner, as they say. Standing by your mum. Naw harm'll ever come to you. We promise.'

After Bren had passed her little Edna to Maddie and had a cuddle with Freddie, she gave him to Maddie too.

Maddie looked down at the two babies snuggled into her and was struck by how similar they looked.

'By, they could be brother and sister. They have the same nose, and mouth and—'

Bren interrupted her, 'All babies look the same, Maddie!'

But there was something about her haste to say this, and how Daisy jumped in too, saying, 'I can't even tell a boy from a girl, let alone telling them apart at this age', that set up a funny feeling in Maddie. But she dismissed it, as it couldn't possibly be true. Daisy would never lie to her. Not in a million years. She was just being silly.

But then, had she ever thought that her ma would deceive Aunt Jean? After years of the closest relationship ever, Ma was willing to let Aunt Jean think that Freddie was fathered by Reggie.

'Is there sommat you're not telling me? Is – is it true that you were raped, Bren?'

Bren sat down on the end of the bed and buried her head in her hands. The sobs racking her body wrenched at Maddie's heart.

'What is it, Bren? Tell me!'

Daisy's face was awash with tears as she took hold of Maddie's hand . . . 'How will you ever forgive me, Maddie? But I did it because I love you. I – I wanted to save you from hurt.'

Everything became clear to Maddie then. Bren hadn't come looking for Arnie because she'd been raped, and he was the only one she could turn to; she'd come to find him because he was the father of her child!

A moan of pain came from her. She clung on to the babies and sobbed her heart out.

Bren was first to reach her. 'It wasn't like you think . . . Maddie, listen to me!'

But the heartbreak of Arnie's deception was too much for her to bear on top of all she had weighing her soul down.

She felt the babies being taken from her, and then Daisy's arms around her. 'Maddie, please . . . it meant nowt to Bren and Arnie. It was just a silly thing that happened after they'd been apart with Bren working away . . .'

As Bren took up the tale and everything came out, Maddie began to see how it had happened and how devastated Bren must have felt on not finding Arnie and on hearing of his death. 'But you lied to me, Daisy! How could you?'

'Because I love you, Maddie, lass. I didn't want you hurt ... God, Maddie, it would have devastated you – Arnie was away, but you had both committed to each other. You were worried sick about Reggie and how you could break it off when he was away fighting, and about your Aunt Jean ... I couldn't add to that. But it broke me heart to lie to you. And then I was having second thoughts, when Arnie was killed and you found yourself pregnant! How could I add more pain to that? But, Maddie, I'll never do it again. I'll never lie to you, naw matter what, I promise.'

Maddie had never heard her beloved Daisy cry like she was now. Snot ran from her nose and mingled with her tears.

'Forgive me, Maddie, I couldn't bear me life if you didn't.'

But a cold place in Maddie's heart made her scream, 'Just go ... go! I never want to see either of you again!'

And then out of spite, mixed with revenge, she added, 'You have your new friend now, Daisy. One that made you lie to me. I hope you're happy the pair of you!'

Daisy ran out of the door, but Bren held Edna to her and stood staring at Maddie.

'I know you're hurt badly, Maddie. And I wish none of it had happened. No one can wish that more than me. But everything was done to save you pain. It hurt me to have to deny the father of me child, and my pain cut me in two when he, my best friend in all the world, died. Me and Arnie shouldn't have done what we did, we both felt ashamed after, but neither of us knew you existed then, or that you were to become the love of Arnie's life, so we didn't deceive you, or anyone. But though I hadn't met you, I understood why Daisy and Aunt Sandra wanted to keep it from you.'

Some of this penetrated Maddie's anger. And she began to feel remorse for her action towards Daisy.

'How you're feeling now, Maddie, will pass when you realise all of this, but Daisy's hurt won't. She doesn't deserve to be shunned for doing something out of her love of you. And she does love you dearly. This will break her heart and all because she wanted to save you from pain.'

An understanding came into Maddie. It didn't eradicate the pain of the revelation, but it helped her to see that what Daisy had done was an act of love to protect her, just as she and Ma were doing to protect Aunt Jean, and to protect her and Ma's good name, not landing Freddie with the stigma of being known as a bastard.

Folk did it all the time – lie to protect others. That's all Daisy had done, and Bren had gone along with it . . . mostly, Maddie imagined, out of love for her best friend, Arnie. With this realisation came the pain of what she'd done to lovely Daisy.

'I – I want Daisy . . . Bren, please, please fetch Daisy back to me.'

The door opened and Ma stood there. Her eyes showed she'd just woken. Her pink housecoat hung on her thin body, her yellowed skin looked almost orange against it, and Maddie had the feeling that she'd lost, or was about to lose, her whole world.

'What's to do? For God's sake, Maddie, you've only had a babby hours ago! You'll be ill . . . How can you and Daisy have fallen out? That's never happened afore!'

Bren took charge. 'Aunt Sal, you come with me and we'll send Daisy down to Maddie. I'll explain everything . . . Only don't hate me for what I tell you, that would break me heart.'

'Hate you . . . what?' She looked over at Maddie. 'Maddie?'

Between sobs, Maddie said, 'Do as Bren says, Ma. It'll all sort out . . . only . . . well, when you hear of it, remember what we are doing to Aunt Jean, and then, like I have, you'll come to an understanding.'

She spoke to Bren then. 'Bren, none of this is your fault. You didn't knaw who we were from Adam when you set out to find Arnie. All you've done is to try to stop me from feeling the pain of the truth, and you only did that at the bidding of Daisy and her ma, so I've to thank you, not condemn you.'

'Thanks, Maddie. And don't worry, I know everything will be all right with you and Daisy.'

Ma, looking less concerned, went with Bren.

Maddie looked down at her little Freddie lying in the cot, undisturbed by all that had gone on around him, and told him, 'You have a half-sister, me little darling.' But as she said it, she still couldn't believe it. Mostly she wanted the picture of Bren and her beloved Arnie making love to leave her.

She wanted him back to just being hers, and father only to her child!

The door opened very slowly and a red-faced, swollen-eyed Daisy put her head around it. Maddie opened her arms. Daisy ran forward and flung herself on the bed next to Maddie. They didn't speak, just held each other.

And Maddie thought that between such deep and loving friends, no words of sorry were needed. Each knew how the other one felt. Their silence and hug healed quicker than words. Daisy was, and always would be, her best friend.

PART TWO

Rejection
1918–1923

CHAPTER FIFTEEN

The war had been over for months now and had taken a terrible toll, added to by the deadly Spanish flu that had swept the world, taking thousands of lives.

Maddie sat on the hard pew of the front row of the church and pondered on how much her life had changed and how it was set to do so even more with Reggie on his way home.

A couple of times he'd written and said he had leave due to him. She'd dreaded the thought of him coming home but had been ready to introduce Freddie as his son, although she had feared what that would do to him – would he have gone back even? But he'd never made it as his leave was cancelled. On the second occasion there was no time in his four days to get across France and then the Channel to England, and then up to the north to Blackpool and back in time, not to be absent without leave. She hadn't known until afterwards when he'd written saying that he'd been too tired to even try to make the effort and had spent the days resting and exploring France away from the fighting.

With this thought giving Maddie the feeling of relief that Reggie coming home hadn't yet happened, she looked to her right. If she reached out her hand, she could almost touch her beloved ma's coffin, but she wanted to do more than that. She wanted to unscrew the lid, take her ma into her arms, make the flu leave her and breathe life back into her body.

They'd all been taken ill, but Ma, already weak from her condition, hadn't been able to fight off the infection. Maddie had held her in her arms as she'd sighed her last breath, three days ago.

How Maddie was to face the future, she didn't know.

Before Ma had become ill, she'd begged Maddie to go through with marrying Reggie. 'Lass,' she'd said, 'everyone is expecting you to. We've led all our neighbours to believe that Reggie is Freddie's father, but mostly Aunt Jean.'

Maddie had wanted to say that part of her had died with Arnie, even though she was still only going towards her twenty-second birthday at Christmas and for most girls, that was the marrying age.

But she'd been loved and had loved. She'd suffered the loss of that love and been given the gift of her son, who had renewed her happiness as being ma to her darling Freddie, now nearly four years old, had fulfilled her.

As had being surrounded and loved by her 'family' – Ma, Aunt Jean, Daisy, Aunt Sandra, Bren, little Edna and Mabel.

Life had been a mixture of hard work and fun times. But now, she dreaded the future. Not just for herself, but mostly for Freddie.

She would keep her promise to her ma to marry Reggie, but would he accept Freddie as his son? And how would he cope with Freddie's affliction?

Freddie fidgeted on her knee. He didn't really understand what was happening. Maddie held him close, snuggling him to her as if he was a lifeline – he'd been that to her so often in his young life. He'd made her laugh when she'd felt down, he'd shown her what courage was as he'd found his own way of getting around in a kind of crawl that had him almost hopping like a frog at times if he was in a hurry. But lately, he'd been learning to walk with a crutch and had shown his usual cheerfulness and determination, and such pride when he'd managed a few steps.

Edna was by his side whenever she could be, trying to help him, and yes, learning from him, as Freddie was exceptionally clever in other ways. He could read and write, and often sat reading to Edna, who, although older by a few months, couldn't grasp how letters were formed or put together to make words.

Freddie never ridiculed her for this, but patiently tried to teach her the alphabet, making her giggle, and always clapping his hands if she got anything right. Neither knew they were half-brother and sister.

But it didn't matter. Freddie would cope if ever he was told as he had the most adorable character, funny, kind, patient, loving and accepting. Reggie couldn't help but love him, could he?

Although it had wrenched her heart to do so, she had gone along with Ma's suggestion of planting it into

Freddie's head that Reggie was his da. And now, he was excited that his da was on his way, while Maddie dreaded his arrival.

Yes, she still loved Reggie as she always had, as a brother. And she'd missed him, and yes, she'd written of her love and all the things expected of her, without feeling any of them. Now, she wished she'd told him of Freddie, but always she'd held back, afraid. Not of his anger – he'd rarely shown that – but of hurting him so badly that he did something stupid like going AWOL, as a soldier running away was termed – an act that nearly always ended in them being shot, and the family being informed that their son/brother had died a coward.

Maddie shuddered. *I couldn't have been a party to that happening . . . I had to keep Freddie a secret from Reggie . . . But now, I must face him with the lie of him having a son he knew nothing of . . . Will he believe me? Will he swallow the story Ma always drummed into me, that the time we almost did it could have resulted in me becoming pregnant as Reggie had been so near to entering me when it had come to an end?*

Oh, Ma, Ma, I know you were only trying to protect me and Freddie, but now you have left us to face this alone.

Whatever the vicar had been saying came to an end as Maddie thought this, and the echoing footsteps of the pall-bearers took over from the sound of his monotonous voice. How Maddie had wished, from the moment of first meeting the judgemental vicar, that they were all Catholics like Arnie. She'd loved the service in their church and the priest, who hadn't questioned their faith, just welcomed them. The church had felt different to this one too. She couldn't have said why, but maybe it was just to do with it not being so old, draughty and echoey.

The pallbearers surrounded the coffin now. They were going to carry Ma out of the church and put her into that freshly dug hole that had seemed to glare at Maddie as she'd followed the coffin up the path to the church. A path flagged on either side by gravestones declaring the names and ages of those who'd gone before, and just behind the first row of these, the mound of earth waiting beside the hole to be shovelled over her ma and swallow her into oblivion.

Daisy's hand took hold of Maddie's free one. And on her other side, Bren, clutching Edna on her knee, extended her free arm to put it around Maddie's shoulder.

These two were the rocks who she leant on when she needed propping up.

Tears ran down Maddie's cheeks as she threw her handful of dirt onto her ma's coffin, silent tears that drained her heart of her sorrow and gave her the courage to carry on. She had to.

A hand came onto her shoulder. She turned to see Jimmy looking sad and lost. He'd been like that since returning home six months ago with shrapnel in his chest that couldn't be removed, to find his Linda had married someone else and hadn't told him. He'd made his way up to Blackpool as soon as he'd recovered enough, and had lived with her and Ma ever since. He'd become a right-hand man to her and a big brother to Freddie. He, too, was part of her 'family'.

How Reggie would take to him, she didn't know, but maybe as he worked in the kitchen, he'd see him as a soldier needing a job and that would be that.

It pained Maddie to feel this wariness of Reggie. Always, until war had been declared and Reggie had been fired with the notion of marrying her, he'd been such good company and all she'd wanted in her life, but just as that began to change for her, it intensified in Reggie and all he'd seemed to want was to possess her! And this had carried on in his letters.

But then, she thought, his letters had shown his love too. Maybe she could make it work. She'd make a friend of him during the day and submit to him at night. The thought repulsed her. She didn't know why and counselled herself that she could get through it.

The time between burying her beloved ma and now standing on the station on a hot July day seemed to pass without Maddie noticing an hour of it. Except that added to her grief was a dread that weighed heavily on her as she tried to be as excited as Daisy was.

'Eeh, Maddie, I still can't believe me Tom is coming home, let alone on the same train as Reggie! I wonder if they knaw each other?'

Maddie shrugged.

Daisy didn't seem to notice how distracted she was.

'Do you think me Tom will find me the same after four and a half years, Maddie? Have I put weight on? Do I look older?'

'Daisy, love, you haven't put weight on, you can still get into the bridesmaid's frock you had ready for me wedding, and if we marry first, you'll be wearing it as me bridesmaid! And, in any case, you still look like a fresh-faced youngster! You're as pretty and as adorable, and Tom will love you more than he did. He only had six weeks to get to knaw you, now he has a lifetime. I've had that with you, and I love you more than ever.'

'Aw, Maddie. I wish you had this excitement in you for Reggie … But it ain't going to be easy for you. You just have to pull it off somehow, love. Everything hangs on you making Reggie believe it all – Freddie's happiness, Reggie's, his ma's and yours. Everything. Just try to remember how you loved him so much until you met Arnie.'

This shocked Maddie. 'It wasn't Arnie who changed things. It happened before that. I told you … Oh, never mind, what does it matter now? All I can say is that I'll do me best, love. But I'm so happy for you. And I hope, with all the young men returning, that Bren finds a love who will take Edna as his own.'

'She may have done that already!'

'What? Who?'

'Ray!'

'Naw! When? I mean, how? I mean … Ray Smith and Bren!'

'Aye. They hit it off the moment she met him when she first stepped off the train and he took her case for safe keeping till she found digs. Mind, it's taken all this time for their friendship to develop – for Bren, anyroad. Ray was smitten from the beginning.'

'I knew they were friends, but why didn't you tell me it had gone further?'

'Because since it happened, and it has only been weeks since they realised their love, there just hasn't been a good time for anyone, and especially not for you nursing your ma and hurt in body, mind and heart when she died . . . It just didn't seem fair to tell you of Bren's happiness.'

'I can't believe it, but I'm so happy for them. Ray's a good sort.'

'Aye, you allus championed him as you did that lad with a foot like Freddie's. I wonder where he is now? Anyroad, love, you're going to need all of that compassion and strength to get you through what you face, lass.'

'I knaw. All I can do is me best, and I think it's wonderful news about Bren and it would have been a tonic to me. I don't understand why you have all kept it from me!'

'I'm sorry, lass. We were thinking of you. They didn't want their happiness in your face when you were suffering so much. They knew I was going to pick my moment when with you today.'

'Have I been that unapproachable, Daisy?'

'Aye, a bit. But it was understandable to us all. You have the running of the business and coping with the loss of revenue with naw more soldiers and very few visitors. Then the anxiety over Freddie and his future, and your battle over your own, besides nursing, then losing your ma.'

'Eeh, you daft lot, so you thought to keep any happy news from me! But by, it is good news. And they both deserve happiness, as does little Edna, and I knaw Ray will love her. You've cheered me up, lass.'

'Good, and Ray already loves Edna. And she him. We've all been thinking she might give the game away by talking about him . . . But anyroad, if it can happen for Bren, it can happen for you. Reggie will love Freddie. Everyone does.'

Maddie wasn't so sure, but she hoped with all her heart that he would and knew that it all hung on whether she could make him believe he was Freddie's da.

The train puffing into the station in a swirl of thick smoke took this thought into its rhythm as she chanted in her mind, *He-has-to-believe, he-has-to-believe!*

And then he was there as the smoke cleared around him – Reggie, and yet not Reggie. Broader, tanned, and with a smile on his face that didn't light up his eyes as it used to.

'Maddie . . . Aw, me Maddie!'

Something compelled her towards him. And he to her. They collided in a hug and then a kiss that warmed her heart but left a tiny bit of it cold. The bit where Arnie lived.

'I made it, Maddie . . . I made it.' Sobs racked his body.

Maddie clung to him. 'It's all right. It's over, Reggie. It's over.'

As they drew apart and he looked into her face, his gaze became intense. 'You've changed, Maddie.'

'Well, I am nearly five years older, love. And by, you ain't the fresh-faced youngster who waved goodbye, anyroad!'

'Ha! Still me Maddie, feisty and strong. How is everyone? Me ma? Your ma?'

'I've a lot to tell you, Reggie, love. And a lot you won't be expecting in a million years. Come on, let's go to the pub before we go home so that I can prepare you.'

'Eeh, Maddie, you're scaring me.' But though he said this, Reggie went with her.

Glancing back, Maddie saw Daisy in the arms of her Tom, holding each other as if they would never let go. She hoped they never would.

The pub was full, which was unusual for a lunchtime, but the many black demob suits told of most being soldiers just returned home, with wives or girlfriends clinging to their arms.

They found a seat in a corner, on the other side of the dartboard hockey.

Reggie went to the bar to order a drink, a pint for him and a sherry for her. But while he was there, she saw him down a pint before bringing a fresh one with him. Never had she known him drink like that before.

Dismissing it as his first for many a year, she just smiled as he returned to her, saying, 'By, that first pint never touched the sides, lass.'

She could tell he was nervous so she didn't beat around the bush. As soon as she'd sipped her sherry and swallowed the sweet liquid with a hot bite to it, she took the hand he'd lain on the table. 'Reggie, I have sad news and a surprise for you that I hope, though a shock, will be grand news to your ears.'

He didn't speak. Just stared at her, a frightened little boy look on his face.

'There's naw nice way of telling you, but ... me ma ... she passed ...'

'Naw! Naw!' His head shook from side to side, his eyes welled with tears. 'Not me lovely Aunt Sal! Naw ...'

Maddie's lips trembled, but she swallowed hard. She had a mountain to climb yet.

'In the end, it was the flu, but I didn't mention in me letters, and I knaw your ma didn't, that Ma had been ailing for years. She had this condition called colitis. It was a kind of disease of the bowel and laid her low many times. When the flu struck, she was so vulnerable, and couldn't fight it off.'

'Aw, Maddie, I'm sorry, me little lass. I'm heartbroken. I loved me Aunt Sal like me own ma.'

'I knaw, love. I have the same love for your ma.'

'We were all one family, weren't we, Maddie? It was just us ... Well, I mean, you had your Daisy, and I had me pals from school ... They're all gone, Maddie ... all of them ... I saw with me own eyes, their bodies ripped to shreds by bullets, or lying face down in the mud ... Eeh, Maddie, I can't begin to tell you.'

Maddie's heart went out to him, and she had an overwhelming urge to make his world better for him. To love him and to care for him.

She put out her hand and touched his cheek. 'You're home now, lad, and me and you are going to build a better world for ... Aw, Reggie, love, I've saved the good news till now.'

'I need some, lass. And by, with what you've just said – me and you together, building a better world – I feel better already.'

Deciding to be upbeat, Maddie grinned. 'So, how will you feel when I tell you that you started building that world before you left me?'

'You're talking in riddles, Maddie.' He grinned, the lovely grin she remembered. 'Come out with it. How did I build owt before I left?'

'It was that night when we nearly did it . . .'

'Aw, Maddie, I'm sorry about that, and I'll make it up to you, I will.'

'Naw, don't be sorry. And you won't be when I tell you that a miracle happened. You made me pregnant!'

'What? How . . . I didn't . . . I wasn't even going to . . . I was going to take care you didn't get caught, Maddie . . . But it didn't happen! I never did it . . . I can't have made you pregnant!'

'Well, you must have strong tadpoles, lad. That's how me ma explained it, as she read up on it.'

'On what, and what tadpoles? Eeh, Maddie, talk in language I understand.'

'Well, when I found I was pregnant, she wouldn't believe we hadn't done it. She went looking to see if it was possible. Well, it was. And with the knowledge she had that a man only has to . . . well, they call it "ejaculate" near to a woman and . . .'

'I don't understand it, Maddie. It can't be, I wasn't even near yours, anyroad . . . Aw, Maddie, you wouldn't try to pass off a babby onto me, would you? . . . Maddie . . . You haven't? . . . Oh, God! Maddie, naw, naw . . .'

Maddie's guilt burnt into her till she felt her face was engulfed in flames. But she turned that on Reggie. 'How could you think that of me? Me babby is yours, Reggie!'

'Why didn't you tell me? How come you and me ma have kept it from me? I can't believe you'd be so cruel.'

'For this very reason. You don't believe me face to face, nor will you believe the way it happened, so how would you have felt if you'd read it in a letter, eh? Tell me that!'

'Maddie, your voice is rising. Shush, I don't want to be the talk of the town! Though I probably already am, because of you!'

Maddie jumped up, sending her glass flying. The sound of it shattering silenced the pub. Everyone looked their way.

Reggie snarled at them. 'Mind your own bloody business, this is mine!'

Shocked by this Reggie she'd never known, when he turned and said, 'Sit down, you bitch!' Maddie could do no other as fear clutched her stomach muscles.

'Reggie! You've never spoken to me like that before ... Reggie, it's me, Maddie ...'

'Aye, and you've never cheated on me before.'

'And I haven't now. Me lad is yours, you're his da, but at this moment, I wish to God that he wasn't!'

With this, Maddie got up. She was almost screaming now as she told him, 'And I wish you hadn't come home either! Me and your lad have been happy, but with your attitude, I can see that all changing!'

She was at the door when she heard Reggie yell, 'Have any of you who didn't go to war seen Maddie with another fella while I've been gone?'

With her face already burning, this further embarrassment had no effect on Maddie. She knew the answer, as she had never gone anywhere she would be known with Arnie.

It was the landlord who answered, 'Naw, lad, what are you talking about? This is the first time I've seen Maddie, but I've heard how she's been through the mill. How you left her with child, how her ma ain't been well, and how she's run that boarding house almost single-handed, and then losing her ma to the wretched flu . . . You should be ashamed of yourself for even asking!'

Ray came to Maddie's mind. He'd been in the pub up North Shore that night! But he wouldn't say anything, Bren would make sure of that, wouldn't she?

Reggie's chair scraped on the floor as he rose. The sound of his pint jug being slammed on the bar increased the fear Maddie felt. He stormed towards her. 'Some bloody home-coming this is! Well, sod the lot of you. Good lads have died for scum like you.'

Maddie was mortified to see his remarks directed at the older men in the opposite corner of the pub.

Before he reached the door, the landlord called out, 'Reg, we understand, mate. We may have been here and not out there, but most of us have lost someone and are suffering. We're not going to hold this against you, you've a lot to face yet. You'll be welcome back, lad.'

A murmur of approval went around the bar. Reggie, who was now by her side and had caught hold of her arm, looked around the room before nodding his head and pulling her outside.

'You're hurting me, Reg. Let go!'

When he did, Maddie told him, 'I ain't standing for this, and I ain't going to marry you either! I'll make me own way home and see you around.'

'Maddie, Maddie! Naw, I'm sorry. I – I . . . was shocked, that's all. You would be, and the way you say it happened, I ain't never heard of . . . It don't seem possible!'

'Well, it is, and you can read about it in a book me ma got for me. But even if that convinces you, me and you are finished, Reggie. I don't want you to father me lad. And I'm afraid to tell you the full story.'

'Maddie . . . Maddie, me little lass, try to understand . . . I may not be the same lad. I'm damaged by horrors, by death, by seeing kids mangled, and worst of all, having to shoot one meself!'

'What! You shot one of our lads?'

'Aye. The poor kid had done a runner. He were a good kid, Maddie. I – I don't knaw if me bullet were a real one as I was ordered to line up with the others, but our tears were as much as the pee running down the lad's legs . . . I needed to be held by you, to be comforted, to find you as I left you, me sweet, for ever love, me little lass . . .' His voice caught in his throat. 'But I'm faced with sommat I can't comprehend . . . sommat that's shocked me and left me angry and bitter, when it should have been a moment of sheer happiness that wiped out the last five years of mud, blood and tears.'

Maddie saw a broken Reggie standing crying like a baby in front of her and her love for him melted her heart. She'd never heard words like he'd spoken come from deep within him as these had. They helped her to understand.

'I can't imagine the pain of all of that, Reggie, nor can you imagine mine. And none of us can live the other's pain over, as we were torn apart by war. But just as I must understand what you went through and how it changed you, so you must understand what I have been through and how it has changed me.'

Reggie looked deep into her eyes.

'Aye, I had a mate, a good mate. He were training to be a priest before the war, and he told me there'd be a lot of adjusting to do when we got home. That life had gone on and our loved ones would have experienced things without us. And that they would have no knowledge of what it had been like for us. He told me that we weren't to blame them for that. But here I am doing the opposite of what he advised . . . I'm sorry, Maddie. I'm sorry.'

'Aw, Reggie, your homecoming wasn't meant to be like this. I was to meet you and to prepare you for changes that you shouldn't just walk into, and then we have a celebration ready for you. Friends and neighbours, all gathered for a happy occasion, but first you were to meet little Frederick Reginald Baker, your son . . . And, well, I hoped you'd be so happy that me and you could announce a date we would wed.'

'We can still do that, Maddie. Eeh, Maddie, please say you'll still marry me . . . It – it may take me a while to accept stuff, but once I read that book . . .'

'And you'll be nice to little Freddie, won't you? . . . Only, there's sommat I ain't got round to telling you yet.'

'Is it bad? I don't think I can take more bad news . . . I'm still reeling over me Aunt Sal not being there to greet me with one of her hugs.'

'It ain't good. Well, not for little Freddie, but for us as his ma and da, we've to be brave and help him through life with it . . . You see, the poor little mite were born with a club foot and—'

'Naw!'

'Reggie, it ain't his fault . . . He's adorable. I love him with all me heart . . . I want you to an' all. As his da, you should love him like that.'

Maddie couldn't believe how easily the lies rolled off her tongue. She knew that with all Reggie had done and said, she deserved his anger and disbelief. But for everyone's sake and, most of all, Freddie's, she had to carry on living her lies. It was the only way, the only hope she had as a mother, to keep her son from stigma, on top of all else that he suffered.

'I've a lot to take in, Maddie.'

'Aye, and you're the man to do that, Reggie. You're my man. And the da of Freddie.'

A small smile came onto Reggie's desolate face. 'I am, aren't I?'

Maddie laughed. 'Finally, I got through to you, Reggie Baker. A lot may have changed, but me and you have been for ever, and we allus will be.'

'Aw, me little lass. I'm sorry.'

Still oblivious to folk hustling them as they pushed past them to get on their way home from the station, Reggie took her in his arms. When his lips came down on hers, she wasn't repulsed, but relieved.

Some of her hopes had come true. She had a father for her son. On top of everything else he suffered, Freddie would never be known as a bastard.

Now, she hoped he would never suffer the consequences of war – of his ma having brought him into the world through her love of a man killed in battle, and her now giving him the false security of a man who would maybe always doubt that he was his da.

Her new hope as a mother would be that Reggie would love her son as his own and give little Freddie a happy life.

CHAPTER SIXTEEN

Maddie couldn't believe that her wedding day was upon her. And not only hers, but she and Daisy and Bren were having a triple wedding!

'Maddie, yer look like the smasher you are, and I'm proud to be giving you away.'

'Aw, Jimmy, ta, love. We've all had to find someone, as none of us have a da. Daisy has the man who runs the rock stall next to the café – Cyril. He's a nice man and has wanted to be Aunt Sandra's man for as long as I can remember!'

'Well, he'll be close to that, with giving Daisy away. And who did you say is giving Bren away? . . . Yer know, I think Ray and Tom are bleedin' great blokes.'

He didn't say that hers was. Reggie hadn't been kind to him but had snapped at him and made it obvious he didn't like him working in the kitchen with Maddie.

She ignored this and told him, 'You!'

'Me? I'm to give Bren away too? Blimey, you didn't say!'

'Naw, I didn't want you getting even more nervous. You've been worried sick as it is about walking up the aisle with me on your arm, let alone two of us.'

'Ha, you'll both keep me wobbly legs from giving in under me! Well, well! So, when will we see Bren?'

'They'll all be here soon, and so will the horse and carriage to take us to Sacred Heart.'

Just saying this made Maddie happy. She'd gone along to see the lovely Father Matthew, as she'd found out his name was, and had opened up her heart after Ma had died. She'd cried with him and told him how she'd hated her ma's funeral and wished he'd been the one to carry it out. He'd taken her hand and told her that he'd welcome her into his church just as God would. Her baptism and Freddie's had been with just him. She hadn't wanted a fuss. But when she'd told Bren and Daisy, they'd understood. It was then she found out that Bren was a Catholic, and so was Tom, and so her dearest wish to be married by Father Matthew, who she thought of as a friend, was coming true.

When she told Reggie, he didn't mind, though he couldn't understand her and said he would think about it as the priest he'd told her of had made a huge impression on him.

With this happiness completing her day, Maddie laughed at the look on Jimmy's face. He resembled a frightened rabbit.

'It'll be all right, lad. We all love you.'

'Reggie don't. I'm not sure he agreed to this.'

'I'm sorry, love . . . Look, you were out there, you knaw what it was like. You've had time to grow in strength, Reggie hasn't. He had a number of shocks to come home to – Freddie, then finding we'd lost me ma. He loved her so much. Give him time. He'll come round, you'll see.'

As she said this, Maddie's heart weighed heavy, and her usual hopeful self filled with dread.

Reggie had seemed to take to Freddie, but she wasn't sure. He ignored him a lot of the time, but when she pressed the issue and asked him to play with him, he relaxed and made Freddie giggle.

He seemed more taken with Edna, and she with him. And this, Maddie knew, was because there were no ties, no responsibility, nothing to accept with Edna.

With herself, Reggie hadn't been like his old self. Not the self she'd known before war was declared, but demanding, and getting cross because she wouldn't give in to him, telling him she wanted to wait until they were wed. That she wanted it to be a lovely occasion when they came together for the first time – not the hurried, against the wall affair it had been the last time.

His words at this still stung her. 'Aye, you're right. We want naw more kids like Freddie, born of me just being near you and not having you. Look what we've ended up with!'

But his kind moments had helped her. Moments when he'd said he'd work hard. That his ma had made a lot of money with having the soldiers billeted with her, and she'd saved it all for him. 'I'm going to start me own painting and decorating firm, Maddie. We're going to be rich, with you having the boarding house. You will open it up again, won't you?'

'Yes,' she'd told him. 'I only closed it for a couple of weeks to help you to settle back home and to get it ready – I could do with a good painter and decorator!'

They'd laughed, but then Reggie had become serious, and yet made her heart soar, as he'd come back with, 'Well, you'll have one. As soon as we wed, your and me ma's places will be me first job. And then, I'll start to make me fortune, and one day we'll find medical help for Freddie and be able to pay for it . . . He's a good lad, ain't he? He's got a way with him that makes folk laugh with him, but not at him.'

Her heart had warmed at these words, and she made herself remember them because they gave her hope for the future.

A hope that soared as she, Daisy and Bren, with Jimmy and Cyril, arrived at the church, each wearing a cream silk frock of the same style made by Aunt Jean and Aunt Sandra, and as she saw Reg, standing at the altar, turn and wink at her.

But that hope died at the wedding reception held in the church hall afterwards.

Everything had gone well – the service, the food and the speeches – and now, with beer flowing and sherry glasses tinkling, merriment was high, giving a happy feeling, until a drunken Reggie's voice could be heard shouting at Daisy.

A hush descended just as he said, 'Tell me the bloody truth, Daisy! Did me Maddie go with someone else?'

Tom stepped in. 'Reggie, mate, this ain't no way to behave at your own wedding, nor at ours! Think of Maddie. This is her day too. Calm down. Daisy has told you that Maddie was faithful to you the whole time you were away.'

Swaying backwards, Reggie snarled, 'They're all liars! They're sticking together! I ain't never heard of a virgin birth after Jesus's ma had one. Have you, eh?'

A child crying took the attention. Edna had burst into tears. Freddie's voice carried to them all. 'It's all right, Edna. Me da didn't mean it.' But his lip quivered uncontrollably, and a tear plopped onto his cheek.

Red-faced and cut deep with hurt, Maddie joined Bren as they rushed to them.

Holding Freddie to her, she told him, 'Da's not well. And you have to be very understanding, Freddie. As you have a poorly foot, Da has a poorly mind. But with our patience and kindness, he can get better. Can you help Da in that way?'

'Aye, Ma, I will. But what's a virgin?'

A snigger behind her lightened the moment a little. Maddie didn't know who it was but decided that theirs was the best course of action.

She put her head back and laughed out loud, 'That's not sommat for little lads to knaw!'

Tom stepped in. 'No! And while I go to see if your da's all right, you look after Edna, and make her laugh again, like you always do, Freddie.'

Freddie was happy with this. Maddie put him down and turned towards the many faces looking at her with sympathy in their expressions.

Mrs Arkwright was the first to speak. 'Eeh, lass, whatever's got into Reggie?'

'War, bombs, death and fear, Mrs Arkwright. It messes with a man's head. Reggie can't remember much about what happened before he went away, but it's coming back to him.'

'Aye, poor lad. And yet he's a hero to us all. He'll get over it all and you'll be the happy couple you were. Pity your ma ain't here ... Eeh, Maddie lass ...'

This overwhelmed Maddie. She'd tried her hardest to smile through the pain of not having her ma with her today or of having her support with Reggie. She turned and ran to the door leading outside.

Aunt Jean arrived just after her and held out her arms. 'Aw, Maddie, lass, what's happened to our lovely Reggie? Why don't he think that Freddie is his? I don't understand it.'

Maddie went into the cuddle that Aunt Jean offered.

'I don't meself. It were only the once that we ... Anyroad, he didn't ... I – I don't knaw how to explain it ... Me ma has a book; I'll show it you. Reggie has read it, but he still don't believe.'

'But what is the doubt? I'm all at sea with it. So much so that I have to ask, lass, though I don't want to. But did you and Reggie, well, you knaw ...'

Maddie sighed. 'Ma ... Can I call you that now me and Reggie are married, Aunt Jean? I knaw me ma would want me to.'

'Aye, love. But so all knaw who you're talking of, how about Ma Jean?'

'Aye, I like that.'

'And, Maddie, love, I don't care about the outcome of all of this, I'll allus be ma to you. It's a step up from aunt, but one I'm going to love ... Look, lass, you don't have to answer me question. If you say Freddie is me lad's, then he is.'

Maddie curled up inside. *What have I done? I should have told the truth in the beginning, but Ma . . . No, I can't blame Ma. It's all been my doing. Now I'm going to have to live with the consequences.* The thought came to her that there were many consequences of war and all had to be faced with courage.

'I'm tired, Ma Jean. I think a lot of folk have left now. I saw Daisy and Bren chatting and calming the situation.'

'Aye, I'll go in and help them. We all have to behave as if it hasn't happened.'

Somehow, they had managed to wind the reception up on a happy note. Tom had brought Reggie back inside, and he'd gone straight to Maddie and put his arm around her. Still drunk, he'd shouted, 'I give you all me lovely bride, Maddie, who has given me all the happiness I could want and a lovely son an' all. I'm sorry I said what I did, my head gets all messed up at times.'

The guests had surrounded him then, with the men shaking his hand and women crying, saying he was their hero and that they'd heard of how he'd looked after their sons. Uncles and aunts hugged him, and kissed Maddie, telling her they would always be there for her. At this, Maddie had to smile as Aunt Jean, whose relations they were, always said she never saw them from one year to the next. 'Weddings and funerals and then only 'cos they knaw there'll be free booze!'

★   ★   ★

Once back at the boarding house and in her flat that was to be their home, Reggie fell asleep in the chair he'd plonked down into. Freddie sat on the floor at his feet, looking up at him.

Maddie, resigned to this being probably how her wedding night would be, scooped Freddie up. 'You're getting to be a heavy weight, lad. I'll have to feed you less!'

Freddie giggled, then hugged her neck, his usually chatty self subdued.

Once he'd settled into bed he put his hand up and touched her face. The gesture said a lot but she had to kiss his cheek quickly and have a bit of fun with him to cover how she so wanted to sob her heart out.

Upstairs in the kitchen Jimmy greeted her with, 'I've a pot of tea on the go, Maddie. Will Reggie want one?'

'Ta, Jimmy. Naw, not right now, he's sleeping it off.'

Jimmy gave her a sidewards glance, but she ignored it.

They sat down at the table. 'So, you're a married woman now, eh?'

'Aye.' She could have added 'mission accomplished', but she didn't. It felt like that, though.

She'd hoped to feel full of happiness, and that she'd done the right thing, but the dread in her had been fed plenty to make it deepen today.

'Yer should have gone with Daisy and Tom and Bren and Ray to Morecambe, luv. I told yer that I'd have looked after Freddie. Me and him get on like an 'ouse on fire! And I'm used to looking after nippers with the brood me mum had.'

'How is your mum, Jimmy? You haven't said owt much lately.'

As she asked, though she'd never met her, Maddie felt a kinship with Hattie. She'd chosen to save her child by prostituting herself. *Aren't I doing the same?*

'She's doing great. Her letters are full of working in the shop alongside Grantham and 'ow lovely he is. And I saw that with me own eyes. She's a different woman, loved and respected as she should be.'

'That's good to hear.'

'Yes, I'm 'appy for her. And the girls are too. There's always a letter from them in with mum's. They're all working and well fed, and me brother's doing well at school. Grantham 'elps him in the evenings, and he's catching up well.'

'A good outcome for them all. I'm so pleased.'

For some reason, the last word came out on a sob. 'I – I'll be all right, Jimmy ...'

Jimmy had risen and was by her side.

'It was, just ... Eeh, I don't knaw ...'

Jimmy put his arm around her. Always she felt like a big sister to him, and she knew it was in that way that he now comforted her.

'You've 'ad a rough day, Maddie, when it should have been a good one for yer. I'm sorry it went 'ow it did ... Though I understand Reggie. A lot were like him over there in France.' Maddie heard Jimmy swallow hard but let him carry on. 'It's a lot to get over. I ain't over it yet. I hide meself in this kitchen, not taking much notice of life. It's like an angry feeling. I take it out on the dough when I'm making the bread, and I cry a lot when I'm on me own, but Reggie, well, he's one of them blokes that hits out at the world and drowns his sorrows swilling down the ale.'

'Aw, Jimmy, you can allus talk to me, love.'

Though she felt for him, Maddie couldn't stop the tears streaming down her face for her own plight, and for the man she should have married – lovely Arnie.

But she somehow managed to defend Reggie. 'He – he used to be a lovely lad, but I just don't knaw him now.'

The door to the flat crashed open. 'Don't knaw who? And get your filthy hands off me wife, you!' Reggie barged at Jimmy and shoved him so hard he landed heavily against the back door.

'Reggie! Jimmy were only comforting me ... Leave him! If you hit him, I'm walking out and not coming back!'

Reggie stayed the fist he'd raised in the air, but his voice was menacing. 'You mess with me wife and you'll knaw about it!' He turned to Maddie. 'And you! Get downstairs where you belong! Sneaking up here behind me back!'

'It wasn't like that . . .' Maddie sighed. What was the use? She'd not win an argument with a drunk, who probably had a sore head and no reasoning left.

She was halfway down the stairs when she heard a cry, and then a crash. Turning to go back, she was met with Reggie barring her way. His words came out on a snarl, 'That'll teach him! He'll not touch you again!'

'Reggie, what have you done? Is he hurt? Aw, Reggie, what's happened to you?' As she said this, Maddie went up the few steps towards him. 'Let me by, I have to see if Jimmy is all right.'

'Oh naw you don't.'

The shove he gave her sent her backwards. Her back jarred as she landed and slid the rest of the way down the stairs. Catching her breath, Maddie gasped. 'Reggie! You pushed me!'

He was by her side in seconds and roughly pulled her up. Holding her arm in a grip that stung, he dragged her to the bedroom and flung her onto the bed.

'You've hurt me, Maddie!' His face creased with pain. His sob hailed the tears that began to fall down his cheeks. 'You've hurt me so deep, I can't forgive you. You say the crippled kid is mine, but he ain't. I just knaw he ain't. You ain't even mine yet!'

His voice changed then, became menacingly low and gravelly as he spat out, 'But you're going to be ... You're going to be mine in every way!'

Maddie lay quietly sobbing.

It was over – the tearing of her clothes, the slaps, the rough taking of her, leaving her sore, and the names he'd called her. And now Reggie was snoring, and flapping his lips, exhaling stale beer fumes into the air around her, making her feel sick. She asked herself, *What has happened to me lovely Reggie? This wasn't him. Oh, God, how am I to live like this?*

But she knew she must, for her little Freddie's sake. She'd do her best to placate Reggie and try to get him well again. Because he wasn't well. His mind was unbalanced. He'd turned into a monster!

CHAPTER SEVENTEEN

For most of the following week, there was peace between them as Reggie spent his day knocking on doors touting for work, coming home most evenings with the promise of two or three jobs, until, at the end of the week, he announced he had enough booked in to begin his new business.

Evenings had been spent discussing this, and the equipment he would need, with him saying that for now a horse and cart would do him to get him and all he needed to each job.

Their nights had taken on a pattern of Reggie doing what she could only term taking her for his own pleasure, as he pounded her with little thought for her feelings, and without much loving attached to it.

With Freddie, Reggie seemed to be kind on the surface, but Maddie held a fear in her that this wasn't how he really felt. She'd catch him watching Freddie wriggling along the floor with something of a loathing in his eyes and her blood would run cold.

But this morning, a different Reggie woke. He reached out for her. 'I'm getting better, Maddie. I can feel a hope for me future. And I want you to knaw that all the decisions I take are for us, me and you.'

He hadn't said they were for Freddie, but she let this pass and smiled at him. 'I'm glad, love.'

'I'm sorry how I was with you on our wedding day, lass. But it's been all right since, ain't it?'

She wanted to scream, *No! You've made me feel used . . . nothing but an object from which you can take your pleasure!* But instead, she kept her smile on her face and said, 'Aye.'

'I've been thinking. I'll take Freddie with me today. He'll love having a ride in the trap and with his charm he'll get me all the work I need.'

'Oh? I thought you had enough now and were getting on well at your first one?'

'I can't go today as they're having a bit more building work done and it'll be dusty, so I thought I'd try to get more into me book. I'll just go for the morning, but I thought me and Freddie could do with some time on our own. It'll help me and hopefully help us to get along a bit better as me and Freddie become a proper da and son.'

Maddie felt that something wasn't right, but she couldn't think what, so couldn't object. But then it came to her. 'But Daisy and Bren are coming today.'

'They won't come until this afternoon as they've to work in the café. I'll be back by then.'

Maddie felt she'd lost except to say, 'How will Freddie manage in the cart?'

'I've made a seat for him. It was a surprise for you both, only, if today goes well, I'm hoping to take him with me a few times.'

There's was nothing more Maddie could say, but she couldn't dispel the feeling deep in the pit of her stomach that something wasn't right. Freddie could only be a hindrance to Reggie. Why would he want to take him with him like this, out of the blue, as if everything was fine and he'd accepted Freddie as his son? Maddie knew he hadn't and she wondered if he ever would.

A few minutes later, Maddie stood on her doorstep waving off a laughing Freddie. He waved till he was out of sight, his giggling face melting her heart and taking away her worries. Reggie had said they'd be back in an hour. All would be well. *So why do I have this feeling it won't?*

'Eeh, lass, come on in. Freddie'll be all right. It's good that Reggie is trying to form a father and son relationship. Sometimes that's hard to do with a ma present. You mollycoddle Freddie too much. There's a big wide world out there and Freddie's got to make his mark on it.'

'I knaw, Mabel.'

'And when are you going to open these doors to the holidaymakers again, love? I've turned three families away this morning while I was cleaning the sitting room. They all want a holiday with their man now the menfolk are home.'

'I will, Mabel. Just give me a couple more weeks.'

'By, season'll be over soon. And Jimmy has nowt to do all day except cook your meals. The lad worries me. He's lonely . . . He should go out and meet others of his own age.'

For the first time, Maddie felt irritated by Mabel. She knew she was only trying to help, but there were times when she just wanted to be left alone.

Sighing, she went back inside. The feeling in her heart was that something terrible had happened. She'd had it when Arnie was killed and then when Ma died. She couldn't name it, it was just there like a lead weight.

Reggie's taut nerves almost made him give up his idea when he pulled the cart up in the station car park. Freddie's face was full of joy. 'I liked that, Da. Jonas is a good horse.'

The love glowing from the lad's face cut Reggie in two. He wavered for a moment, but then knew he was doing the right thing. Without Freddie to constantly remind him of what he knew Maddie must have done, he could find a way of coping. He'd make Maddie happy. She'd soon forget without her sin to remind her.

Would he, though?

He didn't know, but he knew he'd have more of a chance without Freddie there as a thorn in his side.

He knew exactly where to take him.

Maddie had told him Bren's story. It had intrigued him, especially as this Arnie bloke she'd come looking for happened to be a friend of Tom's and both had stayed with Maddie and her ma. And then to find out he was the father of little Edna! It seemed it all went on while he was in the thick of it! How Ray could stand having a kid that was not his own under his feet, he didn't know. But then, he didn't stand much chance with women, so second-hand goods wouldn't matter to him.

His anger rose. *That's what Maddie is, I'm sure of it!*

This thought strengthened his resolve. 'Let's get you out of the cart, as you ain't going to do it on your own, are you, not with that ugly foot!'

Freddie looked afraid, but then with the same spirit Maddie had, he said, 'Ma says it ain't ugly. It's special as it's mine and naw one else has one like it!'

'Aye, well, your ma says a lot of things, and none of them are true.' Why he did it, Reggie didn't know, but he snatched the lad out of his seat, catching his bent foot in the reins. Freddie screamed with pain.

'I'm sorry. I'm sorry, lad. I – I didn't mean it ... Look, I were just going to show you the trains, but I tell you what, we'll go for a ride on one, how would that be?'

Freddie wiped his eyes and snuggled into Reggie's neck. A warm feeling came over Reggie, but he denied it.

'I'd like that, Da, but make me leg stop hurting.'

'I will once we're sat in a cab. Now be a brave lad, eh?'

By the time they reached Liverpool, having had to change trains at Preston, Freddie was lively once more. His joy in everything he saw through the windows endeared him to Reggie. So much so that when they alighted, he wanted to jump straight back on the train and take Freddie home again with him. But he had to do this. He had to. He'd never be sane again if he didn't.

The taxi dropped them outside the Liverpool Orphan Asylum in Myrtle Street, a huge building with a spire, more windows and chimneys than Reggie had ever seen on one building, and a high wall surrounding it.

Once again, Reggie nearly changed his mind. Everywhere was silent. He'd thought he'd hear loads of children playing.

Carrying Freddie to the gate, he opened it, taking a deep breath at the loud creaking sound of hinges lacking oil.

'Right, Freddie, I'm going to sit you on that bench. Just wait and someone will come for you.'

'I want Ma . . . I don't want to wait. Don't leave me, Da.'

Reggie's heart gave him that same wretched feeling he'd had earlier. Freddie's large blue eyes reminded him of an Irish lad. A lad who'd stood wetting himself and crying while Reggie aimed his gun. Trembles shuddered through him. He looked away. All he had to do was to walk through the gate and keep going. Someone would come for Freddie. He'd be all right. Bren was, wasn't she? And she'd been brought up in this building.

He turned and strode away. Screams of agonising fear tugged at him, but he ignored them and kept walking.

'Maddie, you should be pleased, lass. At least Reggie is making an effort.'

'Oh, Daisy, I just don't knaw. Reggie isn't the same man. I just keep thinking, *What if?*

Daisy hugged Maddie to her. The gesture spilt her tears.

'They've been gone hours! They left at eleven this morning. It's now three in the afternoon!'

Mabel opened the door. 'I've brought tea for you all, love . . . I'm sorry about me interfering ways this morning.'

When she'd put the tray down on the occasional table, Maddie went to her. 'Never mind me, Mabel. I'm like a bear with a sore head these days … But I'm so worried about Freddie at this moment.'

'Aye, I am an' all, lass. It's been four hours now. Has the lad had owt to eat even? … I'm thinking all sorts … Hello, Daisy, love. How are you and how's your Tom, and Bren and Ray? Any sign of any babbies for me to deliver yet?'

This made them all burst out laughing.

'Bren and Ray are busy moving out of his ma's and into a cottage they've rented in Marton. They're so excited. And me and Tom move soon. Tom got that job at the theatre making the stage sets, and the manager told him of a place going cheap down Bispham way. It's a three-bedroomed house and could be ours in a couple of weeks or so.'

'Ah, there you go then. Room for a dozen or more babbies.'

Their laughter filled the room and felt good to Maddie.

'Shall we have our tea outside, Maddie, love? It's a lovely day and probably why Reggie's kept Freddie out for as long as he has. I bet the pair of them are building sandcastles on the beach.'

Maddie felt better for the light-hearted moment that Mabel had created.

'Aye, call Jimmy down an' all. I think we'll make plans for opening up again, eh?'

'That's good to hear, lass.'

No sooner had Mabel gone to the door and shouted Jimmy than he appeared.

'Eeh, he was waiting for the call, Maddie.'

'Ha! I reckon you're right. Come on, let's get outside

and grab the best seats. Them wooden ones are a bit rickety; we'll sit on the bench.'

'You knaw you'll give it to Mabel the minute she comes out you, daft ha'peth!'

They were giggling by the time they went outside. Maddie grabbed a cushion on her way and placed it on the bench. 'There you go, Mabel, love, rest your weary bum!'

'Ta, lass. Now, waste naw time. When are we opening?'

Both Mabel and Jimmy looked expectantly at her.

'All right. Next week. It'll be into August then and we'll have plenty of knockers. And we'll put an advert in the *Manchester Guardian* and see what comes from that. So, we've a week to get ready.'

'By, we're ready, lass.'

'Well, there's food to order.' Maddie wiped a crumb from her lips. As she did, Daisy said, 'By 'eck, Jimmy, lad, these lemon cakes are delicious!'

'Ta, love. I made the recipe up – well, it's a variation on one me mum always made.'

'You could go into business as a baker, love. Me ma would buy from you. We never have time to bake and those we buy in are often doughy.'

'I'd love that. Baking's me first love. I like getting meals and making them look nice on the plate but give me a bowl of flour and an egg and I'm in me element.'

'You should think about that as a sideline, Maddie. You'd do a bomb, and it would get you over the slack periods.'

'Will yer, Maddie? I'd make enough stock to fulfil orders . . . though me dream would be to have a cake shop on the prom.'

'Eeh, I didn't mean you to set up as a rival to me ma, Jimmy. I meant—'

'What's going on here then? Teddy bears' bloody picnic? Well, I want you all to leave. I've sommat to tell me wife.'

'Reggie! You're drunk! Where's Freddie? What have you done with me Freddie?'

'That's it, ain't it? He's your Freddie, not mine. Well, he's none of ours now.'

Mabel stood up. 'Just what have you done, lad?'

'Mind your own business. And sod off. All of you. Sod off!'

Maddie couldn't speak. A lump had formed in her throat that threatened to choke her. Her breath caught in her lungs.

One by one the others left them on their own, but Maddie knew they wouldn't go far.

'Where's me Freddie? . . . Tell me, Reggie! Where's me FREDDIE?' Her scream pierced her own ears. Rushing forward, she beat her fists on his chest. 'Naw, naw, not me Freddie! Ple-e-ase, not me Freddie!'

Reggie grabbed hold of her arms and flung her backwards. The bench dug into her back and her cries of pain set up pandemonium. She couldn't move as she watched Daisy jump on Reggie, Mabel hitting him with the frying pan and Jimmy finally rugby tackling him to the ground.

Stunned from the blow, Reggie went down easily.

'Jimmy, run for the coppers. I saw Tony Fielding go by on his beat before I brought the tea down. He'll be around somewhere, lad.'

'Right. Will yer be all right with this bleeder?'

'If he tries to get up, I'll hit him with me cast-iron pan again. Go on your bike, lad, you'll soon find Tony!'

Maddie wanted to say no. She shook her head from side to side, but no words came out. Her wounded body hurt badly. But it wasn't just to Reggie being arrested she wanted to protest; she wanted the world to know that she didn't want her Freddie to be gone. Her cry came out like a howl.

'Maddie, Maddie, love. Naw ... We'll sort it, we will.' Daisy was by her side in a flash.

Reggie gave a moan and tried to push Mabel off him. Her iron pan came down and Reggie slumped back down. Vomit came from his mouth and snot ran from his nose.

'Mabel, help him. Help him, please, Mabel ... He's going blue!'

Mabel got off Reggie and started to administer to him. Taking off her pinny, she cleared his mouth with it. Then she went to the garden tap and soaked her pinny.

Wiping his face, she looked up. Fear had drained the colour from her cheeks. 'I think I've killed him, Maddie ... Oh, God, I've killed him!'

Maddie knew her mouth was slack. That dribble ran from her down her chin, but she could do nothing. Had no sense of where she was. Only one word went around her head. 'Freddie ... Freddie ... Freddie ...' Before the pain in her back took her into a black world where she couldn't feel anything – no pain, no heartbreak, just a blessed peace.

CHAPTER EIGHTEEN

Maddie opened her eyes.

'Eeh, lass. How are you?'

'Mabel, is . . . me Freddie . . . and – and Reggie?'

'Jean's here, love.'

'Oh, Ma Jean . . . It's . . . it's all gone wrong.'

Ma Jean just stared at her for a moment, and then in a voice that spoke of her anguish, said, 'Me Reggie . . . he's in custody . . . Aw, Maddie, Maddie.'

'He didn't die?'

Mabel answered. 'Naw, but he isn't well. He was here in the Vic like you, but they shifted him to a mental institution in Manchester. The coppers are with him all the time.'

Ma Jean looked distraught as she said, 'I've only seen him once, Maddie . . . They won't let me go again. He were in handcuffs, Maddie . . . He didn't knaw me. He can't remember owt.'

Not taking this in, Maddie asked, 'And Freddie? Have they found me Freddie?'

Mabel shook her head. 'I'm sorry, lass. They found Reggie's horse and cart at the station. Poor thing was thirsty and worn out. It appears that Reggie bought two tickets for Preston and was seen getting on the train there with Freddie in his arms, but his trail runs dry then. The police have naw idea where he went from there as there's a few routes, and Reggie can't remember owt, not even his own name.'

Maddie stared at Mabel.

Ma Jean took her attention. 'Me Reggie's hurt badly ... the blows to his head ... But the police have said he's going to prison. Eeh, Maddie. He's being done for kidnap.'

'Aye, and I'm sorry, Jean, but he should be done for assault an' all, but he's getting away with that because Maddie's his missus. It's wrong how a bloke can hit his missus and other men'll say it's his right 'cos he needs to keep her in check!'

'I knaw, I knaw, but that ain't it, is it, Mabel? Me Reggie's going to prison, and he don't even knaw who he is ...'

'I'm sorry, Jean, I am. It ain't in me nature to hurt folk, rather I'd try to help them get better if they're ailing, but Reggie were like a mad man. I had to save Maddie.'

Maddie didn't want to hear this. She couldn't care about herself being hit, and she could feel nothing for Reggie. No hate, no sympathy. Nothing. Oh, but for her lovely Freddie – for him, her heart was in agony.

'Naw ... they must find him. I want me Freddie. I want him!'

'Shush, Maddie. They'll only come and stick another needle in you and put you to sleep again, love. We want you to come home. You've been in here a month already!'

Maddie couldn't believe this. 'A month?'

'Aye. Your bruised back and ribs are almost healed, but with your mental state they keep sedating you ... And Maddie, they are talking of a mental hospital if they can't get you right ... Aw, Maddie, love, we love you, we want you home. We'll care for you, love.'

This from Mabel penetrated Maddie's anguish. She needed to be at home. She wouldn't be able to bear it in a mental institution! She quietened her moans and put out her hands. 'Hold me ... please hold me ... Please stop me from sinking ...'

Mabel got up and went around the bed and took hold of her hand. Ma Jean took her other hand in hers.

But though this helped, and she loved them both, Maddie had an overwhelming desire to be with Daisy. *God, is me Daisy all right? Was she hurt by Reggie?*

'Daisy?'

Mabel answered. 'Daisy's all right, lass. She was shook up but all right. Like us all, she's devastated about Freddie and worried sick about you. She's been a lot of times to see you, but you've always been sedated.'

'And me Reggie's going to prison ...'

With this statement from Ma Jean confusing everything, Mabel got up and went to her. 'Jean, love, you have to accept that Reggie ain't the lad you had before. He's gone ... It's like the war took him. Me heart bleeds for you, lass.' Mabel turned to Maddie. 'She can't get it out of her head that the copper who was guarding Reggie when she went to see him told her that the next time she'd see him he would be behind bars, and he added, "We don't take kindly to them that hurt kids."'

'He . . . he ain't hurt me Freddie, has he?'

Mabel shook her head. 'I reckon he's left him some-where . . . Eeh, Maddie, I don't knaw, we only knaw what Jean has been told.'

Taking hold of her hand again, Mabel said, 'Look, lass, take hope from what I'm about to say, eh?'

Maddie didn't know what to think, her heart pounded with fear.

'Reggie's being charged with kidnap as naw body has been found and there was nothing about Reggie – no evidence on his clothes – to say that he'd harmed Freddie in any way. So, they are assuming Freddie was taken some-where but they can't get nowt from him as he has naw memory of it . . . or of anything.'

Ma Jean gave a moan.

'Eeh, Jean, lass . . . Try to think that the monster who's come home from war ain't the Reggie that you brought up – your lovely son. He was lost to you and to Maddie when he went to France. It did sommat to him and many others. A lot are calling it shellshock. Reggie was a very brave man by all accounts, but it's all messed him up.'

Ma Jean's sob had Mabel turning to her and putting her arm around her, 'Aw, Jean, it's very sad and I'm sorry. I'm here for you, lass . . . Me and you can still be friends, can't we? I can't lose you an' all . . . I had to do what I did to Reggie . . .'

Maddie knew that Mabel, in saying she couldn't lose Jean as well, was referring to them having lost Ma.

Oh, how she wished her ma was here now. Her mind wanted to scream this out – to scream and scream and scream! But she mustn't. Mabel had said that if she did, she wouldn't go home and she wanted to go home.

The sound of Ma Jean sobbing cut into Maddie. Some compassion came into her. Hadn't Ma Jean lost her son too? Wasn't she suffering the same agony as herself?

With this thought, she put out her hand. Ma Jean took hold of it once more, and that seemed to give them both a small comfort.

Home didn't feel like home any more when Maddie arrived a week later. It was a bare empty shell and held nothing but pain that not even her good memories could penetrate.

Mabel had tried to make it feel less cold. She'd put flowers around the living room, and in the garden the bench had been moved to the other side and a tub of flowers stood next to it. They had told her that Tom had made the trellis that now stood where the bench used to be. He'd made it 'L' shaped so that it hid the back end of the yard and the outside lav when she looked out of her window. Climbing roses were planted at its base.

It all looked beautiful but didn't take away the memory of little Freddie sitting on the floor out there, playing games that had him chatting away to imaginary folk when Edna wasn't with him.

They were all there to help her, Daisy, Tom, Bren, Ray, Mabel, Jimmy and Ma Jean. Little Edna was being looked after by Ray's ma.

'We wanted it to look different for you, to help you, Maddie.'

'Ta, Daisy.' She didn't say that nothing would help.

'Jimmy's bringing tea down. Shall we sit outside, lass?'

'Aye, I'd like that.'

Daisy smiled at her encouragingly, then Tom took her arm. He patted it and said, 'We're all here for you, Maddie. I can make anything you need, as long as it's made out of wood! And you have Jimmy in the building to call on, and Jean just next door and Mabel coming in daily. And Jimmy will fetch any one of us the moment you need us.'

Maddie couldn't speak. She just used her other hand to squeeze Tom's.

Outside, she sat on the newly lacquered bench. Ma Jean sat next to her. She hadn't wanted her to, she'd wanted Daisy. Ma Jean had too much of a connection to the hateful, spiteful Reggie.

But she felt ashamed of this thought when Ma Jean took her hand, seeking comfort that she couldn't give but that she felt Ma Jean needed.

Knowing she had to be told, she made it easier for them. 'How's Reggie?'

'The doctor said he may never get his memory back.' It was Daisy who'd answered and was now on her haunches in front of her. 'Maddie, they are saying that Reggie may never stand trial as he cannot defend himself with not being able to remember, but may . . .' She looked at Ma Jean. 'I'm sorry, Aunt Jean, Maddie has to knaw. And it's best while we are all here to help her.'

Maddie saw Aunt Jean nod.

Bringing her attention back to Maddie, Daisy told her, 'Reggie is most likely to be sectioned and put into a secure hospital for life ... Aunt Jean has been told by the police that this is what is being asked for by the prosecution and the doctors. They will let you knaw the decision now you are out of hospital and are his next of kin.'

Maddie couldn't take this in. But Tom added, 'Try to think of Reggie as a casualty of war. It might help you and Jean to do that. You see, there are many casualties of war that aren't counted as heroes, because they're not dead or don't have missing limbs, but they're forced to live with their memories.'

Maddie asked, 'Do you all suffer?'

Jimmy answered, 'Well, yer know I do, Maddie. I'm angry a lot of the time but manage not to channel that at other people and I don't like leaving the safety of home.'

'Aye, you told me of your bouts, Jimmy, and you rarely go out. But talk to me whenever you need to, lad, I've told you that.'

Jimmy smiled and nodded.

'I do too, Maddie.' This was Tom. 'But I find a peace in making things from wood. I rationalise things in me brain while I plane a log to make it smooth. It's as if I am shedding the horror with the bark and finding a nice peaceful place ... It's those who died at me hands that haunt me. But I have to tell meself that they would have killed me but may not have wanted to. We were all just pawns in a power struggle that wasn't of our doing.'

'Naw, Tom. You were all saving your families and your country and other people in other countries from tyranny. And you did it, mate. You must never forget what life would be like here if you hadn't. I feel guilt an' all. The guilt of not

260

being able to go and help me pals because of me eyesight. Very few of me pals came back, but from what I've heard from those who did, Reggie saved them, not just physically, but he kept their morale up. They tell me it was after he had to shoot a young lad who had deserted and who he'd been trying to help that he changed. It affected him mentally. He was in the execution party. He may not have had a live bullet, but they, and he, don't knaw that.'

This from Ray silenced them all, except Ma Jean, who said, 'Me poor lad.'

After a moment Maddie asked a burning question of Ray. 'Ray, don't you have any idea where Reggie went and took me Freddie to?'

Ray came and squatted beside Daisy. 'I weren't on shift at the station that day, lass. I wish I was. I would have challenged Reggie. But none of the others knew him. All we can tell the police is that he bought a ticket to Preston. And the problem from there is that Preston's such a busy station with so many passengers going to different places that the staff find it impossible to help the police. After all, it's only a bloke with a leather bag and a roll of tickets, love, who would have sold two to Reggie.'

Asking no one in particular, Maddie said, 'Will I ever get me Freddie back?'

There was silence. Both Daisy and Ray squeezed her hands.

Tom was the first to speak. 'If we could find him, or even have an inkling where to look, we would, Maddie. But what we can do is to support you until the day he is found, because we should never give up hope. Freddie is a very intelligent little boy. He can tell people where he came from and your name. He was always reciting his address and tried to teach Edna hers, as he knew that backwards too.'

For the first time, Maddie knew hope to nudge the cold part that told her she may never see her Freddie again. A smile widened her cracked lips. 'Yes, of course. Ta, Tom. Ta ever so much. Freddie could just walk through the door at any moment. He'll tell someone he's lost and where he came from.'

'Eeh, lass. Never give up hope, eh? Me Tom's allus right.' Daisy's smile held pride as she looked up at Tom. 'He knaws a lot of things. He's a smasher.'

Tom grinned at this and held Daisy's eyes. Their love was there for all to see. Maddie knew a longing for her Arnie to be here. None of this would have happened if he'd come home. She'd have found a way to tell Reggie. Somehow, she would have found a way.

But that chance wasn't given to her.

But there was something she could do for Arnie: she could keep faith that their son would return.

Further hope was given to her then as Bren said, 'Couldn't we put something in all the local papers of the places Reggie could have gone? We know that he couldn't have gone far as he was back within the day. We could approach the Manchester papers, and the Liverpool ones . . . Wait a moment. Oh, God! It's just come back to me, Reggie asked about the orphanage, where I was brought up in Liverpool! He said Daisy had told him about me upbringing, he even asked what part of Liverpool it was in.'

There was a collective gasp, and then a silence. Maddie looked around and could see hope in the faces of them all. This further fuelled her own.

'Eeh, lass, you may have sommat there.'

'Yes, Mabel, it's a possibility ... I – I ... well, I hope Freddie wasn't taken there, but then again, I do, as we could find him then! I'll go ... We could, couldn't we, Ray? We could go to the Liverpool orphanage and see for ourselves?'

'Aye. I'll get tickets for us, love.'

Maddie's heart soared with this fresh hope as she asked, 'When? When can you go?'

'I have me day off next week, but I'll try to get a swap and go sooner.'

'Ta, Ray.' It wasn't what she wanted to say. She wanted to say that they'll get a taxi and go now! But the cabs in Blackpool were still horse-drawn and didn't take on long journeys. She'd heard that in the cities they used cars now.

Mabel broke into her thoughts. 'Well, is anyone going to drink this tea that me and Jimmy's made, eh? By, it'll taste good now it's brewed well, and with the fresh hope we've all got.'

To help them all feel that they could say yes, Maddie said, 'I'll have a cuppa, ta, Mabel. The tea at the hospital was like ditchwater!'

When the tea was served, Maddie was surprised how the conversation changed, and Daisy was saying how she was settled in her new home now. 'I can't wait for you to visit, Maddie. Mind, we've only two rooms done. Our bedroom and the kitchen. Tom's done a lovely job of them, but we have to sit in the kitchen as there's naw living room yet.'

'Ah, but it's lovely and cosy, love.'

'Cosy! It's boiling with the fire having to be on to heat the oven and hot plate! We've to have the door open till late.'

'Ha, leave the lad alone, Daisy. Me and Ray are in the same boat, but we have to wait for our landlord to make improvements. You're very lucky owning your own home.'

Maddie surprised herself then, but with her new hope she felt so much better. 'I'll come and see you both, and I'll be doing just that – coming to see you, not your houses. Though I'm curious as to where you both live and want to think of you there when you pop into me thoughts.'

With this the mood lightened and became quite jolly, especially when Jimmy went and came back with a tray of cakes.

They all praised him and the question of him having a baker's shop came up once more and seemed a reality when Tom said, 'I've still got quite a bit of my inheritance left – me granny married a well-to-do widower in her dotage and she left me a good bit, and then I lost me parents, who had a two up, two down house in a row of terraced houses in Liverpool that sold for good money as a developer wanted the land the row stood on. I'd like to invest in you, Jimmy, if Maddie could spare you?'

'I can. And I'd like to chip in an' all, Jimmy. Me ma did well out of the billeted soldiers and it's just lying there in me bank – that's aside from the cash she had squirrelled away under the floorboards. I only found it as I wanted to

mend a squeaky one that was irritating Reg . . . Anyroad,
I'd like to back you, Jimmy, lad.'

Jimmy had a grin on his face wider than one of the fish-
ing boats on the sea. 'Really? Ta for that, both of yer. Can I
look for a suitable place? 'Ow much are yer going to put
in? I mean . . . Sorry, me excitement ran away with me. I've
such ideas . . . but of course, we need to sit down and discuss
it properly.'

'We do, Jimmy. And you're sure you feel you can leave
the house now?'

'For this, yes, Maddie. It's like an incentive, and I'm sorry I
blurted out the question of how much you can back me with.'

'Don't worry. I don't know about Maddie, but your
enthusiasm makes me want to back you even more. You're
going to make us a fortune, I can see it now. And when you
do find a place, I'll fit it all out for you.'

Daisy chipped in: 'Huh, ta, Jimmy, lad, you've just put me
living room back another few weeks!'

They all laughed.

To Maddie, it felt all right to laugh with them. She felt
certain now that it was only a matter of time before they
found her precious Freddie.

But when she woke in the dead of night, the possibility
seemed very remote, if impossible. Good coincidences like
finding Freddie in the orphanage where Arnie and Bren
had been just didn't happen, only bad ones did. And if
Freddie was able to tell folk who he was and where he
lived, why hadn't he been brought home by now?

*   *   *

265

After a restless night, to be faced with Jimmy's eager anticipation wasn't what she needed. But she listened to his plans
as he cooked her breakfast, and nodded in the right places.
He, too, must have been up all night as he had details of
what he thought it would cost almost down to the last
penny.

Maddie's head ached by the time he calmed.

'I'm sorry, Maddie, this is the last thing yer want to talk
about. It's just that I'm all fired up.'

'Naw, I'm pleased for yer, Jimmy. I just wish me own
future was mapped out for me.'

'Yer'll carry on with your plans to open this place, won't
yer, Maddie? You've a gold mine here. It'll be something to
leave to Freddie and will give him a good start in life.'

'Aye. I'll have to do that. I've to make a living.'

'Oh, Maddie, yer not to put a penny into me business if
it might run yer short.'

'Look, lad, money under the floorboards helps naw one.
You can make me a fortune with it.'

'I will, as I'll pay yer back every penny, with good
interest.'

'Let's see what Tom has in mind. I've read things about
sleeping partners . . .'

'Well, I weren't planning on becoming that! I love yer
Maddie, but yer like a sister to me.'

Despite her tiredness, and doubts, Maddie burst out
laughing. It took her a minute to sober and to explain to
the baffled Jimmy what a sleeping partner in business was.

He joined in the laughter then and Maddie began to feel
better.

'So, you and Tom would put money in and be directors?'

'Aye, that's right. And if yer make money, we get a dividend, but I see it more as us reinvesting and you growing. You could take on staff and open more bakeries.'

'Yer think so? Blimey, me mum will be so proud of me! A chain of bakeries. That'd be something to boast about. I'd be bleedin' rich!'

It was good to see Jimmy coming alive again. She loved him and he was easy to love. He made no demands on her, no flirtations that made her feel uncomfortable. He was just Jimmy.

'Right, lad. You start to look around, I'll be fine. If I open me doors, it'll only be for a few weeks now. We're already into September and the season will end by the time it's out.'

'Oh, Maddie, it's good to 'ave yer back. But today, yer sound like the old Maddie, and that's because yer've been given hope. Yer'll see. Our Freddie will be at that door in no time. He won't stay away from you, nor us.'

'That's me hope, Jimmy, lad. That's the hope I hold in me heart, and what's given me the will to carry on.'

'Me mum always said that a mother never gives up hope. If she did, her family would be lost. And that's why she did everything she could – though she didn't 'ave the choices you 'ave.'

'One day I'll meet your mum, Jimmy. And I'll give her a hug. She kept her hope alive through the consequences of becoming a widow, and I ain't going to let mine die through the consequences of war.'

With this, Maddie felt a new strength come into her. She would fight for her Freddie till the day she died, and that meant she couldn't go under, but would take the reins of her life and the business again and build a future for him, something his affliction may deny him doing for himself.

CHAPTER NINETEEN

A week later, Maddie went with Bren and Ray to Liverpool.

As they stood outside the huge, imposing building, Bren visibly shivered. 'I – I don't think I can go in there, Maddie. I'm sorry, love.'

Ray put his arm around her. 'You don't have to, lass. Maddie and I'll go in. You sit on that wall over there, eh?'

'Naw, Ray, you stay with Bren, she needs you. I'll go.'

The inside of the building was as bleak as the outside. Paint flaked off the whitewashed walls, and the dark green doors were scratched and showed signs of having been kicked many times as their bottom halves were chipped and panels were cracked.

The air hung with a morbid sadness. Maddie hated to think of Freddie being here or, before him, his da and Bren.

The voice of the woman who'd let her in and who was taking her to the matron's office echoed around the high-ceilinged hall. 'Matron's very busy, but she can spare you five minutes.'

Maddie didn't have time to answer as the woman stopped and knocked on a door.

At a stern 'Enter', the door squeaked on its hinges as it opened.

Maddie's trepidation heightened as she was beckoned inside.

Matron wore a grey frock buttoned up to her neck. Her large bosom rested on the desk in front of her. Her expression showed her distaste. 'So, you're the mother that allowed the father to dump the cripple on us?'

Annoyance at Freddie being called that and at this false accusation gave Maddie the courage to stand up for herself. 'I didn't allow it.' But then her heart raced as she asked, 'So, you do have him here? This is where me husband left him?'

'We did. But he's gone.'

'Gone where? Why? He must have told you where I lived! Why didn't you—'

'If a child is dumped here, and yours was left on a bench outside and wouldn't have been found if it had been the gardener's day off as the boy couldn't move himself to get help, we assume the parents – usually the mother – have done this to him. We are past trying to give them back when they may face more rejection.'

'But didn't me Freddie tell you that I loved him and cared for him? Couldn't you have contacted the police?'

'All children say that no matter what horrors they have left behind, because they crave that to be the truth, and they are afraid. And as for the police! All they do is prosecute, give a fine, and then return the child to more misery.'

'Freddie wasn't living in misery, nor was he badly treated. His . . . his da is not long home from war. His mind's been affected . . . He – he hadn't met Freddie, then when he did, couldn't take his affliction . . . He kidnapped him . . . He's locked away now . . . I – I want me Freddie back.' This last came out on a sob.

'Well, you can't. I'm sorry for you, in the circumstances, but Freddie has been placed. We had a couple looking to adopt. They wanted a son. The boys always find homes first. Anyway, Freddie was crying and asking if they knew his ma. They took him to their hearts. I am sure they will love and care for him and help him to settle.'

'What? Naw! Who are they? Where do they live? I want him back!'

'I am not allowed by law to tell you who they are or where they live, but I can assure you, they are good candidates. They are wealthy, and the love they had for Freddie became apparent and grew as they made many visits in the two weeks it took to prepare things. You see, they could afford to get the wheels turning a lot quicker than others can. Freddie came to love them too. He began to ask for them, and not you.'

'Naw, naw, naw! It can't be . . . Freddie wouldn't, he loved me, I'm his ma . . . I'll get the police on to you! They'll get me Freddie back. They knaw he was kidnapped.'

'Look, I'm sorry, but neither the police nor anyone can undo what has been done in a court of law. Freddie has been legally adopted – nothing unlawful has been done on our or the adoptive parents' part. We had what we believed was an abandoned child on our hands. We did the best by him that we could possibly do. We did not know he had been unlawfully taken. Every year we get at least twenty babies and children come to us in the way that Freddie did. We do what we can and in Freddie's case, we thought we had done well. Going to the police will accomplish nothing.'

Maddie wanted to claw at the unfeeling, stern face, but she turned and ran, a helpless, disjointed run, that had her opening doors, seeing what looked like hundreds of pale-faced kids, until at last she opened the door that led her to the hall and outside.

Her screams pierced the air and had Bren and Ray running towards her. They caught her as her legs gave way.

'Maddie! Maddie, lass . . . Eeh, what's to do?'

'He – he's gone . . . gone for ever!'

Bren's voice was no more than a whisper. 'Where? . . . No . . . not . . .'

'Someone's taken him . . .'

'Come and sit down, lass, and tell us what you found out.'

Ray steered her across the road to a low wall surrounding a tall building that proclaimed itself a bank. Between sobs that seemed they would expel her heart she told them what had happened.

They held her, they cried with her, they said things they and she knew would be impossible to do, but in the end they all came to a quiet place.

'It's like Tom said, Freddie knows where he came from. He may accept the love offered to him, especially after what he has been through, and he may be happy. But he will never forget you, Maddie, nor us, and especially not Edna. And not his Granny Jean as he looks on her as being, nor Daisy – none of us. Freddie would never forget any of us. And when he's old enough, he'll come looking. I just know he will.'

'Aye, Maddie, Bren's right, lass. So, what you've got to do is to build on what you have so you can stay where Freddie can find you. With the war ending, there's talk of Blackpool growing. I read the other day that bookings are up eighty per cent for next year. You need to grab some of that. Get advertising in Blackburn and places. And aye, Scotland an' all. And if folk land on the station and ask about accommodation, I'll send them to you.'

Some of what Ray said found a home in Maddie and fired her acceptance of it. She didn't know how she would do it, but she would. She had no other choice.

Allowing Ray and Bren to lift her to a standing position and then to support her, one on each side, they walked to the end of the road where Ray hailed a cab.

It took another week of kind attention by Jimmy, Mabel and all her friends to help her and Ma Jean to come to a place where they could move forward physically, if not emotionally.

Maddie kept her tears for the night-time hours when she would weep for her lost son, her ma, and her love, Arnie.

Sleep was fitful, but somehow she managed to function, to get the boarding house open for the last few weeks of the season, and to organise the new bookings coming in for next year.

*   *   *

273

Christmas, with all its reminders of plans made that couldn't be fulfilled, and the feel of it having an empty, hollow heart, came and went.

Some attempts were made to make it a normal, happy, jolly time, but most of it went on around Maddie, and didn't really touch her, as now she had a new fear clogging her mind.

It was on Boxing Day morning that she finally admitted to herself that the worst had happened to her as she bent over the bucket and emptied her stomach of the brown, nasty-tasting liquid for the umpteenth time in the last month. She hadn't seen her monthly since the one a couple of weeks before her wedding. She'd hoped it was the shock of everything, but today, she had the sense that ignoring the symptoms wouldn't make them go away.

Nor did she have any tears to cry over her predicament. They were kept for things much deeper – her losses. Nothing could be as hard to bear as they were. She'd just have to get on with it.

And that would be on her own today, as everyone was having a quiet day after the rowdiness of yesterday. Even Jimmy had decided to go for a long walk – he'd taken to walking on his own lately and he covered miles. He said it put him in touch with nature, like he'd never known in the crowded streets of the East End and even since coming to Blackpool.

Once Maddie had cleaned up and her tummy had settled, not wanting to but forcing herself to, she went outside to go next door to Ma Jean's.

As she opened the gate to Jean's, she took a deep breath and schooled herself to appear happy about the coming baby – Jean's real grandchild. The thought sent her reeling for a moment . . . *Oh, Freddie, Freddie, my new babby won't replace you . . . Nowt can ever do that, me lad.*

She found Jean in floods of tears.

'Eeh, love, what's to do?'

'I – I can't carry on, Maddie. I can't. I've tried, but before Christmas, I had so many threatening letters about the debt I'm in. I – I tried ignoring them, but . . .'

'Oh, love, I've been in such a stupor I'd forgotten about you telling me you were struggling. But how did things get this far?'

'I didn't bank everything, Maddie. I did like your ma, I put a lot of it under the floorboards, then when Reggie came home, I gave it to him. But I'd put too much under, and now all me bills are coming in and I haven't enough in the bank to cover them . . .'

'But what could Reggie have done with it? I knaw he was setting a business up, but he didn't spend a lot on that.'

'Betting . . . He always liked a secret gamble . . .'

'Gambling?'

'Oh, aye, it was that much of a secret that you didn't even knaw of it. But it got worse when he came home – like an addiction . . . He'd lose heavy even in the days when he hadn't got much. I was allus bailing him out, but with all that cash I gave him . . . Oh, Maddie, all me hard-earned takings, gone! I'm going to have to close me doors . . . The bank will take me boarding house off me . . . Where will I go?'

'Nowhere!'

Suddenly, Maddie's own new worry evaporated. Having a child wasn't a worry but a joyous occasion, no matter the father and no matter the horror of its conception. She touched her stomach. *Me and you, little one, are going to face what we have to head on.*

'Move in with me, Ma Jean. I'm going to need a granny. I came to tell you that I'm pregnant!'

'Maddie! Eeh, lass. Really?'

'Aye. The circumstances weren't happy ones, but that doesn't take away from us the gift of having a new babby.'

'When?'

'Well, Reggie came home in July, and I can't remember having a monthly after we married in August, so I reckon I'm four months gone.'

'And . . . I mean, you're happy about it?'

Ma Jean looked incredulous.

'I have to be, Ma, for me little one's sake. Boy or girl, they've done nowt wrong. They didn't ask to be planted in me womb, but by, they deserve to be welcomed and to be loved. Freddie wouldn't expect any less of me.'

With saying this, Maddie felt even more enthused. Everything she did, she would do in the way Freddie would want her to. Ma Jean needed help. Freddie was kind, he'd have said he wanted to look after her. She had the same feeling.

'Anyroad, back to your predicament. There's my old room going spare, you could move in there, love. And we'll go together to see the bank and see what can be done, eh?

I've heard that there's going to be a boom coming to Blackpool, so maybe, with all that's gone on, the manager will give us some leeway.'

'You said "us", Maddie. Well, lass, with what you've just offered me, I can do sommat for you, and me grandchildren. I'll sign me boarding house over to you!'

'What? Eeh, Ma Jean!'

'Aye. It's only bricks and mortar as there's naw business left, but the building is all paid for. We just need to sort the debts out so that there's no hold on it. Do you think we can?'

'That depends on how much you owe and who to, love.'

'I'm ashamed to say that it's in the region of twelve pounds . . . I paid me rates and me gas and coal bills, but that was that. It's all owed to the wholesalers. I used to pay three-monthly, but it's going on for five now. They thought I was good for it . . .'

'Eeh, Ma Jean, you must be worried sick, and on top of everything you've been through. Look, I'll sort it. I can pay it all off, but I've promised Jimmy now, as you knaw, so I'll make arrangements with them you owe money to. But are you sure about what you said? You don't have to sign the whole thing over to me.'

'I want to, love. I'll assist you, but I can't take the responsibility any more.'

Maddie looked around her. Ideas began to form of maybe knocking both buildings into one.

'By, Ma Jean, I came around here to tell you of a new babby, and now I own a new boarding house an' all!'

She took hold of Ma Jean's hands and twirled her around. When they came to a giggling halt, Maddie became serious. 'Bad things have happened to us, Ma Jean. We lost the Reggie we knew and loved and were left with a monster who did heinous things. But if we let those things destroy us, then in a sense we are letting the Germans have victory over us as it was through fighting them that our Reggie's personality was changed. We cannot let them win!'

'You're right, lass. We're strong women and we will fight back. But with me as a support to you. And together, we could take on this boom that's expected and really make sommat of it!'

'We can, Ma Jean. We can.'

Ma Jean gave the first genuine giggle Maddie had heard from her since Reggie's trouble began. Others hadn't touched her eyes, or lit up her face, but this one did. And when she hugged her, Maddie knew the deep love that Ma Jean had always had for her had returned. Gone was the suspicion and doubt that Maddie had felt had niggled Ma Jean that all was not right with what she was being told. And though this prickled Maddie's conscience, she accepted that this was the best way. The truth would destroy Ma Jean.

A firm rattle of the doorknob made them both jump. Maddie knew a sense of doom to take her into its depth.

'Answer it, Maddie . . . I'm afraid to.'

Two dour-looking policemen faced Maddie when she opened the door.

'Are you Mrs Reginald Baker?'

Maddie's 'Aye' held fear.

'A neighbour told us you might be here. This is the house of your mother-in-law, Mrs Baker, isn't it?'

'Aye.'

One officer removed his helmet, and the other followed suit. 'May we come in?'

Maddie, feeling sick again, stepped aside.

As she looked towards the kitchen, she saw Ma Jean standing in the doorway looking as though her world had ended.

A few moments later, the future they'd carved out of bravado crashed around them.

'I'm sorry to inform you, Mrs Baker, but your husband, Reginald Baker, was found hanged in his cell.'

'Cell?'

Why she asked this, Maddie couldn't have said.

'Yes, those detained in Broadmoor are kept in cells.'

A cry behind her and Ma Jean falling to the floor brought Maddie out of her stupor. 'Eeh, Ma Jean! Help me with her, officers.'

Between them the policemen lifted Ma Jean onto a sofa in her guests' sitting room.

Instead of thanking them, Maddie said, 'Reggie's dead?'

'He is ... I – I'm sorry to be so blunt, but there's naw easy way of telling folk such bad news.'

The policeman administering to Ma Jean, who was now sitting and staring into space, asked her, 'Can I get you owt – a cup of tea maybe?'

Ma Jean nodded her head, but then burst into tears. A wailing sound came from her. Her pain awoke Maddie's.

She sat beside Jean and cradled her in her arms. Together they rocked backwards and forwards.

The tea brought Maddie to a calmer place where she could feel the release of being shackled to the being that Reggie had become and focus her thoughts on helping Ma Jean. 'I'm here for you, love, I'll take care of you. We have to let Reggie go. He's naw longer tortured in his mind.'

Looking up at the policemen, she told them, 'The war did this to Reggie. He fought valiantly and helped others, but them as ordered young kids should be shot if they show their fear by running are to blame more than the Germans. It got to Reggie and twisted his mind.'

'Aye, there's a lot of casualties of war, lass. And not just among the men who went. But folk like you and your ma-in-law, and all the women left widowed or with a husband or son who is maimed. It's going to take years to get over.'

The one who hadn't spoken now asked, 'Will you and your ma-in-law be all right for us to give you the details of what you're to do next?'

Maddie nodded and then took the official-looking paper offered without realising it was Reggie's death certificate as she listened to the instructions she had to follow to register the death.

It shocked her to hear that Reggie wouldn't have a church service, but that his body would be disposed of by the hospital. 'You could have a service for him if it will help you both, but some priests and vicars are funny about giving one for a suicide. They reckon that only God can take a life and that it's sinful to kill yourself. I think they're out of touch with the suffering that a person must go through to conclude that they'd be better off dead.'

These words helped Maddie. She'd accepted that Reggie was suffering mentally, but to think he was going through so great an agony to make him not want to live shocked her. And yet it was a revelation that helped her to let a little more understanding of him settle in her mind.

Still Ma Jean hadn't spoken, just cried, although it was a non-cry – the sounds were there, the heaving of her body was too, but no tears.

'I'd get her to the doctor, lass. He might be able to help her, as I'd say this has been too much for her to take. Is there a Mr Baker?'

Maddie told what had happened to her father and the man she called Uncle Ted.

They both shook their head. Then the one who had done most of the talking put his cup down and picked up his helmet. 'Well, we'd better be going. Will you cope, or shall we call in on the doctor and ask him to pop round?'

'We'll be all right, ta.'

When they'd gone, Maddie had a sense of being all alone as Ma Jean didn't seem to be there with her and this made her shudder. *What now? What am I to do? A widow with a child on the way and one taken from me. A ma-in-law to care for. Two boarding houses to run. Jimmy leaving me, and Reggie gone for ever!*

It all felt like a scary place to be, and yet, Maddie could feel an inner strength that gave her the determination to tackle all she had to do.

Holding Ma Jean to her, she told her, 'We'll be all right, love. We'll get through this together.'

There was no response, just the blank stare that made her think that in the second she'd been told that Reggie had gone, Ma Jean had too.

CHAPTER TWENTY

Being held by Daisy a few days later helped Maddie to steady herself.

'Eeh, lass, you're a marvel, but you look whacked out. It's dreadful news over Reggie. When you first told me, I thought it was a good thing, but that's denying the Reggie we all knew and loved as we grew up together. I don't want to do that.'

Daisy patted her as she released her. What she'd said lifted Maddie. She had to hold on to having lost her Reggie the moment war was declared, for it was then he'd begun to change.

'Ta, Daisy. I feel the same. But I've hardly had a chance to absorb it all.'

'Aye, I can understand that. Anyroad, life goes on, and today we must make it a good day for Jimmy. Bless him, he didn't let the grass grow under his feet, did he?'

'Naw. Him getting himself out for walks was a healing process for him. He's ready now to take on his bakery. What does Tom think of the shop Jimmy's going to rent? Can he do it up?'

'He doesn't see a problem and he's pleased with Jimmy's choice. He thinks being on the corner of Coronation Street there'll be trade coming in from the hotels as well as those living local and, in the season, the holidaymakers. He tells me there's already a kitchen that'll easily be converted for Jimmy's needs. Have you seen it yet?'

'Naw, not with all that's been going on . . . So, all Jimmy has to do is sign on the dotted line and order all he'll need. By, it'll be a pretty penny that me and Tom have to invest, but it'll be worth it.'

'I hope it will. How is Aunt Jean?'

Daisy asked this, even though Ma Jean stood next to them ready to go out for the short walk with them to Jimmy's new bakery and then on for a walk to the seafront.

This was a rare January day when the sky was a clear blue and, though cold, it felt good to be out, even though thick coats, woollen hats and scarves were the order of the day.

Tucking Ma Jean's scarf into her coat, Maddie said, 'We're doing all right, aren't we, love, eh?'

There was no reaction. The doctor had said it was shock and would wear off. But to Maddie, it seemed Ma Jean's mind had gone. It was as if she didn't allow herself to feel or to think, but just functioned.

'Anyroad, with all this talk of Jimmy, I haven't told you my news . . . I should have done, but haven't felt up to it . . . I'm—'

'Pregnant. I knaw. I can tell . . . Aw, Maddie, love, I'm sorry . . .'

'Don't be! I don't need or want sympathy. I'm happy to be having another child, Daisy. I want everyone to be happy for me.'

Maddie could see this shocked Daisy.

'It ain't to be looked on with pity, Daisy, but as sommat good, 'cos a new life is coming into being.'

'But . . . well, I thought . . .'

'I knaw, and it's natural that you should. But we don't have to think of how the babby got there, just that it's a babby, and will need love and attention. And I'm going to give it just that.'

'By, Maddie, you're the bravest person I knaw. But you're right. And we'll all welcome the little one, you knaw that. Especially now we knaw you will.'

'We? Does everyone knaw?'

'Aye. Jimmy told us that you keep being sick and we put two and two together. We just . . . Well, we wanted to wait for you to tell us and to see how you felt about it. Especially now with everything you're coping with.'

'I'm all right. I need to make a plan for the season and just get on with it. I have Ma Jean's boarding house to run an' all now.' She didn't say that the boarding house had nearly belonged to her. She'd put that out of her mind and was determined to run it in the best way she could, having sorted payments for the debts that would mean there was very little income from it after paying staff. 'I'm thinking of putting Mabel in charge of Ma Jean's as she hasn't mentioned becoming a full-time midwife again.'

'She's naw need to. The three of us will keep Mabel busy in the line of work that would be her first choice.'

'What? But that's wonderful ... Come here, you dafty! How far along have you both gone? You should have told me!'

'We're both three months, so you have a bit of a head start on us if we're right with our calculations ... Eeh, Maddie, I did want to tell you, but you were suffering so much with everything that has happened to you, it seemed an awful thing to say that mine and Bren's lives were the happiest they'd ever been.'

'Ta, love, for thinking of me. But I've told you before, don't ever not tell me owt. It can have the opposite effect than helping me. It can make me feel left out. As if I ain't part of your life any more.'

Daisy took hold of her and hugged her. 'You're one of the biggest parts of me life, Maddie, and will allus be.'

They hugged for a moment, then Daisy said, 'Well, we'd better get going. Jimmy should be back from the solicitor's with his key now.'

Daisy linked in Ma Jean's other arm and the three of them walked down Albert Road to Coronation Street.

Jimmy was there, looking towards them, his stance showing he was eager for them to come and see the beginning of his dream. His face beamed the biggest smile Maddie had ever seen.

Her happiness for him crowded out all the anxiety she'd held within her.

His arms enclosed her when she reached him. 'Thanks for this, Maddie. Me life changed when I met yer, mate.'

Maddie couldn't help but giggle. 'Well, you changed ours an' all, Jimmy, and we're happy for you, aren't we, Ma Jean?'

Ma Jean didn't react.

This hurt Maddie. She wished she could get just a little sign of a good reaction to anything at all. She had plenty of bad times when she came out with a nasty comment that copied something Reggie had said or told her of. Sighing, she didn't say anything, but hoped that one day she would get her lovely Ma Jean back.

Tom's hug was full of eager anticipation. 'Well, we're in business together now, love!'

'Aye,' Daisy put in. 'And this ain't the only business we're all in together – having a family is another one. Maddie's pregnant an' all!'

'Well . . . So, it's been confirmed then?'

'It has, Tom, and before owt's said, I'm very happy about it and me little one will be welcomed into this world with love and joy.'

'I'm glad to hear it as all babies should have that as a given right. Good for you, Maddie.'

'Ta, Tom.'

'I'm happy for you too, Maddie, luv, if you're sure you are?'

'I am, Jimmy. But by, I'm going to miss your help. Not that I'd stand in your way, so let's see what state this shop is in. It's been empty since before the war, so it's going to need sommat doing to it.'

Inside the shop they were met with a surprisingly neat and tidy room with a counter along one end and plenty of room for customers to queue out of the cold.

Jimmy's enthusiasm as he told them how he visualised it would be, was good to see.

'And then, through here.' They all followed him as he took them behind the counter and through a door. 'This room has been used as the stockroom, but I want to convert it to me bakery with ovens here, and here, a butcher's block in the middle – wooden surfaces are best for kneading bread and rolling out pastry. And over there's a pantry which will be cooled by a ceiling fan.'

'It all sounds wonderful, Jimmy. But will you afford it all on what me and Tom are investing?'

'I will, Maddie. I've been looking out for second-'and stuff and 'ave found most of what I need. I've put deposits on them and can collect on full payment.'

Without warning, Ma Jean glared at Jimmy and growled out, 'You brought trouble to me door.' And then she burst into tears before her legs seemed to give way and she leant even more heavily on Tom.

Jimmy rushed to her side to help Tom support her as Tom told her, 'Everything will be all right, Aunt Jean, we're all here for you. And Jimmy didn't do anything wrong, I promise you. It was all in Reggie's mind.'

Maddie put her arm around Jimmy. 'It ain't what she thinks, lad. It's what she was told by Reggie and didn't believe, but everything Reggie said to her seems to come out of her mouth as the truth now. She even turned on me this morning.'

Maddie had tried to forget the incident, but it came rushing back to her. Ma Jean had looked at her in just the same way as she had Jimmy and growled out, 'You broke me Reggie's heart with your carry-on!'

She'd brushed it off and after getting Ma Jean ready had

been treated to a hug – no words, but the hug had helped to heal the hurt.

Ma Jean put her hand out and placed it on Jimmy's. Jimmy took her fully in his arms. 'Don't worry, Ma Jean. I'd be the same. Yer don't know what to think or believe, and me mum would be like you as well, thinking others had made it happen. But you hold on to what a hero Reggie was, not to what the illness of his mind made him do.'

Ma Jean smiled at Jimmy and nodded. They all hugged her. When it came to Maddie's turn, a tear trickled down Ma Jean's face. 'I'm sorry, lass.'

'Eeh, Ma, you've nowt to be sorry for. I knaw what it is to lose a son. We just want you to get better and to start living again, love.'

Tom put his hand on Ma Jean's shoulder. 'And that goes for us all. Don't it, Daisy?'

'It does, Aunt Jean, but we all understand. You're not well. You've been knocked sideways by everything that's happened. It'll take time, love.'

Ma Jean smiled at them all.

'That's better, love. I want your grandchild ... your second grandchild to knaw the lovely person that you are.'

Ma Jean nodded but looked weary as she once more leant on Tom.

'There's a chair in the little outhouse, I'll fetch that.'

'Good idea, Jimmy.'

With Ma Jean sitting and drinking water from a cup Jimmy had found in one of the cupboards, she looked a lot better.

'You three carry on looking around,' Daisy told them. 'I'll stay with Aunt Jean.'

Grateful for this, Maddie followed Jimmy through the kitchen that was already in situ and Jimmy said it would be where he would store his cooking utensils, do his washing-up and boil his whites in the copper in the corner.

Maddie was feeling excited for him and for herself and Tom, as everything Jimmy said showed he'd thought it through and was determined to succeed.

Upstairs they discovered a good-sized flat. 'I'll not be moving in here yet, Maddie. I ain't ready to leave yer and I can still be of help to yer when I come home as me shop will close at five-ish. But I won't be any use in the mornings as I'll be back here before you come out of the land of nod. I'll have to fire up me ovens by six-thirty every morning.'

'You'll have your work cut out with baking and serving your customers, Jimmy, but I knaw what a worker you are, and I knaw you're not ready to live here on your own yet.'

Tom took their attention. 'In that case, with this having its own entrance, Jimmy, how about we let it out? It'll bring in a good income which will help the business get up and running.'

They all agreed on this.

As the months went by, the shop took shape and became the pride and joy of them all as Jimmy put his heart and soul into it and orders began to flock in.

For herself, Maddie concentrated on getting both boarding houses running efficiently. And as her ma had always said planning was the basis of this, she spent hours sitting at a small table in the corner of the kitchen that served as a desk.

Everything she did – planning how much staff she would need and engaging them, setting out fortnightly meal plans as many were booking two-week holidays with her starting from Easter, and umpteen other things – was done with a heavy heart as she longed for a sign that Freddie was all right, or a letter even. But then, that was silly. Yes, Freddie could write and knew their address, but he couldn't get to a post office and buy a stamp and post it on his own. And the people who had adopted him wouldn't help him to contact her; they'd only think bad things of her as that matron had.

As these thoughts assailed her Maddie knew despair to settle in her and her heart felt like a lead weight. She had to hang on to it being true that Freddie would never forget her and would one day come back to her.

Making herself concentrate on the job in hand and with a full house booked in from this Saturday, in two days' time – Easter Saturday, 4th April – Maddie mentally ticked off what she had in place to make sure it would all run smoothly, as she opened the post, entered more bookings into the diary, and put the letters in a pile to confirm later. Everything was ready. Except herself, that is! Taking a breather for a moment, she clutched her stomach. The signs were all there for this to be the day her baby came into the world. She hadn't felt any kicking inside her stomach for a few days, and the pains in her back had moved around to the front and were intermittent but getting stronger.

Panic set in for a moment, but then she told herself that she'd planned for this too. Extra staff were on hand in both boarding houses, and Mabel was overseeing their work.

Though that wasn't necessary with the lady who came to cook, who was a marvel. Janet had the kitchen running like clockwork, cooked delicious meals, and was a tonic keeping everyone laughing. Already the delicious smell of bacon frying filled the kitchen as she prepared breakfast. One of the best things about her was that although she was a chatterbox normally, she knew when to leave Maddie to her thoughts, or to get on with something she had to concentrate on.

And it helped to know that Ma Jean was going to stay with her sister for a few weeks as though stronger in her body, her mind still wasn't back to normal. It was as if she'd forgotten how to do the simple things that were second nature to everyone – dressing herself properly, brushing her hair, everyday things usually done without thinking.

As if she'd conjured her up, the door to the flat opened and Ma Jean stood there with a huge grin on her face.

Maddie, hardly able to believe her eyes, burst out laughing. Ma Jean looked like the pantomime character Humpty Dumpty with her skirt stuffed into her long-legged silk knickers.

Janet turned around from the stove, a big woman with a jolly face and mousy, greying hair caught up in a hairnet, and gasped. 'Eeh, lass, what the ... ?' Then she burst out laughing.

Ma Jean just stared at them both. Maddie, hardly able to stand for laughing, got up and went to her.

'By, Ma Jean, you should be on the stage. You'd have them laughing in the aisles.'

Still Aunt Jean looked at them as if they'd gone mad.

'Come here, love.'

Maddie took her hand. Turning her, she took her back through the door and down the stairs.

Still giggling, she went down on her haunches and righted Ma Jean's clothes, but as she went to rise again, a pain much stronger than any that had niggled her gripped her stomach. Gasping in air, she bent double.

'Oooh, Ma Jean, fetch Mabel. I think me babby's coming.'

Sinking back to the floor, Maddie prayed that Ma Jean had taken this in and wouldn't be distressed but would just hurry upstairs. It was a relief when she did.

Hours later the air was filled with the cry of Maddie's second son, and she was being held by Mabel and allowed to sob her heart out.

'God knaws, He's given you plenty to cry about, lass.'

Maddie felt Mabel's tears wetting her hair.

'But eeh, we've to get on with things. You knaw that. What're you going to call the little one?'

Maddie calmed a little and dabbed at her eyes. 'I've called him Noah the while he's been inside me . . . It was because it made him real and helped me to love him as him and not think about how he was given to me, and because Noah built an ark, and my Noah will have to build me and Ma Jean back up to what we were.'

'By, lass, that's a bit biblical.'

'I knaw. But it's how I feel. Freddie was baptised in the Catholic Church to honour Arnie, and I want Noah to be an' all.'

Mabel seemed to understand as she hugged her. 'Aw, me Maddie, you've been through a lot. I still love how I met you and how it brings me own little Arnie into our family.'

'We are a family, Mabel. A family of strong women and three lovely men, and . . . Freddie and Noah, with two more expected.'

'We are, lass. I was a lonely woman till I met you. You don't deserve what you go through . . . Still, we can't get sentimental, we need to get babby cleaned up and fed and you an' all.'

'Let me hold him first. We've left the poor mite lying there.'

'Aye, well, you needed more attention than he did, me darling. He was only exercising the new lungs he's been given.'

Maddie had schooled herself to love him, but she'd no need to have done. It happened spontaneously. As she gazed down at him, her heart, soul and whole body filled with a love that was wondrous.

'Me little Noah, me saviour.'

Noah opened his eyes and looked up at her and, at that moment, Maddie knew that this child would be special.

She put her finger into his hand, and he clutched it tightly, sealing the deep bond between them.

★   ★   ★

Life became a hectic whirl after that with both boarding houses full to capacity, and still more people knocking on the door looking for accommodation.

Daisy gave birth to a girl – Lottie – and Bren, a boy – Jack. Edna was as proud as punch of her little brother and loved all the babies, turning into a mother hen and wanting to do everything for them all. In no time she became a dab hand at changing nappies, only she wasn't so keen when Lottie needed changing after filling her nappy. She screwed up her face and said, 'You do it this time, Ma.'

But then she brought the house down as she continued, 'Mind, Lottie is the easiest nappy to change as she doesn't have that willy bit. Eeh, that gets in the way, and I nearly stuck the pin through Jack's!'

When they calmed, she asked if she could change Jack now.

'I'm not so sure I should let you after what you said, Edna!' Bren winked at them as she said this.

'Aw, Ma.'

'All right, but you will watch that pin, won't you?'

'I will, Ma. It was only the once, and I'm careful now.'

But as she removed Jack's nappy and he decided to pee straight up in the air, the roof nearly lifted with their laughter as she jumped back. 'By, he's like a flipping fountain!'

Her next words sobered Maddie and had her clutching her heart as out of the blue Edna said, 'I wish Freddie were here, he'd be able to help me', and then burst into tears.

Maddie hadn't realised the grief of others, especially this adored little girl – Freddie's half-sister. Taking her into her arms, she told her, 'Freddie is thinking of you at this very moment. He'll never forget you or any of us, love.'

'But I want him here. I want to play with him and have him tell me about things I don't understand.'

All Maddie could do was to hold her. Daisy helped by saying, 'Aye, but you've your hands full with these little ones, lass, and you're doing a grand job. We all need your help. And you'll see, the time'll soon pass till Freddie comes knocking on the door.'

Edna cheered up at this and busied herself by making Jack comfortable.

They all allowed her to help, and guided her as she took on the task of putting the now cleaned-up Jack to Bren's breast. It was a lovely sight to see, and Maddie could tell that it was helping Edna to be involved and not to feel pushed out by this influx of little ones.

And it was lovely, too, to see Edna with Ma Jean. She took great care of her, making sure she was comfortable and had all she needed.

Ma Jean was in her element with having little Noah, though she often called him Reggie. Maddie didn't mind this. It made Ma Jean happy and that was all that mattered.

It was as she said goodbye to Bren and Daisy and closed the door to the silence of the midday house, with no guests around, and no sounds of banging or clanging in the kitchen or of carpet sweepers being run up and down, that Maddie sighed. Moments like this were when her torment crowded her as a longing for her Freddie made her want to scream out her agony.

But somehow, she managed to function normally, and as she looked down at Noah snuggled into her arms, she told him, 'And you're a big part of that, me little lad. Your lovely placid nature and ready smile fills most of me heart with joy. Aye, and one day you'll knaw your big brother . . . One day he'll come knocking on that door, and he'll love you as I do . . . I promise you that, me little lad. It will happen. It has to. As it's only holding on to that hope that keeps me going.'

PART THREE

Hearts Mended
1931–1933

CHAPTER TWENTY-ONE

1931

Despite the recession warnings following the collapse of the American economy in '29, bookings for the season of 1930 had been as busy as any other and Maddie was glad to see the back of it. Though through the summer months and the lights season, while she was run off her feet, it was easier to cope mentally with the longings inside her that never lessened – for the doorbell to ring and it to be her little Freddie ringing it.

She smiled to herself at this thought as it wouldn't be the way she'd play-acted the moment out, as she'd always looked down and scooped up a five-year-old. But Freddie would be sixteen now!

She'd missed so much of his life. Would she miss it all? Would he never come back to her?

Telling herself never to give up didn't help the pain this thought gave her, as though she'd tried to keep hope alive, it often abandoned her.

Taking herself back to her own five-year-old self, she

struggled to remember details and wondered if her dream of Freddie never forgetting her was realistic.

Sighing, she put down the tea towel she'd used to dry her, Ma Jean's and Noah's breakfast pots and looked at the clock. She'd have to hurry herself – Noah needed to be ready for school, and Mabel and Janet would be here shortly.

It was as she took off her pinny that Noah's cry alarmed her. 'Ma! Ma! It's Granny, she's fallen . . . Ma, oh, Ma!'

Dashing to the stairs, Maddie didn't register going down them as the sight at the bottom made her heart sink.

Ma Jean lay, unmoving, her unseeing eyes staring up at Maddie.

'Ma, Ma!' But even as she called her name in an anguished cry, Maddie knew Ma Jean had gone.

'Is she . . . ? Has Granny . . . ?'

Maddie put her cheek to Ma Jean's mouth. Nothing. She held her wrist but felt no beating of a pulse.

'I don't want Granny to die, Ma.'

'I knaw, lad.' Maddie lifted herself up and took hold of Noah. His body trembled in her arms.

Despite Aunt Jean's dementia, which had been difficult for Noah to understand at times, he and his granny had been very close. Almost like pals as Ma Jean had become like a youngster in her mind, and Noah had taken care of her. Just an hour ago, he'd fed her porridge and made her giggle as he used the spoon as a train, chuff-chuffing it towards her mouth.

Clinging together, Maddie and her beloved Noah cried over the body of the lady who'd sometimes turned on them, but more often been a gentle soul not sure of the world around her. Who'd often chatted to her Reggie as if he sat beside her.

Noah's body shook with tears as Maddie led him to the sofa.

'Me da will die an' all now, Ma.'

Maddie knew what Noah meant. Ma Jean had made Reggie come alive for him.

'They'll rest in peace together, lad. It's all Granny ever wanted – to go to her Reggie . . . Her and our hero. And I think it's your da's turn to have his ma back with him, don't you?'

Noah nodded and snuggled into her – a rare treat as he'd often shrugged her off as treating him like a babby. Though secretly, she knew he loved a cuddle. Especially at night-time when they were alone, and she said her goodnights and there was no chance of him being seen as a cissy.

The next few weeks were lived partly in a whirl, partly in a new dreamlike state as so much happened around her that Maddie didn't seem part of – an inquest that showed Ma Jean had died of heart failure and dementia, the funeral with a burial in Layton Cemetery, and then before they knew it, Christmas flew by in a flurry of work, and sad and happy times, with more happy than sad as they were surrounded by children.

Bren and Ray's three – Edna, now fifteen and showing signs of being a beautiful young woman, Jack, ten and firm friends with Noah, and Alfred, aged four, a proper cheeky chappie.

Then there was Daisy and Tom's three – Lottie, an assertive ten-year-old, who reminded Maddie so much of Daisy at the same age, Vera, six, as pretty as her mum but a quiet, studious type like her dad, and lastly, Lena, two, who adored everyone and was adored by all.

And now, on a cold January morning, Maddie found herself sitting in front of a solicitor who was telling her that she owned Ma Jean's boarding house.

'But surely it goes to Noah ... and ... Freddie, my older son?'

'No. I have a will here, signed by myself as witness, that everything should go to her son, and in the event of him not surviving you, then to you. It was lodged with me in 1913 and was never changed. Mrs Jean Baker was of sound mind when she wrote it.'

'And even though she wasn't when her grandchildren were born, it makes no difference? Because if she had been, she would have changed it, I'm sure.'

'I can only go on the legal document in front of me. If you want your sons to inherit it eventually, then I suggest you make a will stating that.'

'I'll do that, but not yet. I've to get me head around everything and sort things out. But eeh, this has come out of the blue. I never knew of the existence of a will. Ma Jean, as I called Mrs Baker, did once want to sign her boarding house over to me, but she became ill. She never once mentioned a will.'

'Well, it's here for you to see. You now own all Mrs Jean

Baker had in this world ... So, can I get you to sign the necessary documents?'

Maddie left the office in a daze. She'd long given up the idea of owning both boarding houses and had assumed Freddie and Noah would inherit it.

In a way, this twist eased her conscience and saved her from signing more legal documents that would declare Freddie as Reggie's son. It was time for the truth. She was released from lying to save others hurt – though had it? Had Ma Jean ever really believed her? Maybe not.

A huge sigh left Maddie's body as she walked along Talbot Road towards the town. She only had one hurdle – to tell Noah that Freddie was his half-brother, not his true brother. Freddie would know the truth too, if he ever came back to her. That he had a half-brother, Noah, and that Edna was his half-sister as she and he shared the same da – Arnie.

Still Maddie's heart fluttered and then knew a painful stab at thinking of Arnie. Her beloved. How could that be, she asked herself, after him only being in her life for six short weeks? Weeks that changed everything for her and turned her world upside down.

The promenade was deserted. It was hard to believe that in a few months' time it would be difficult to walk along without being jostled by crowds and having your ears assailed by the shouts of the street vendors and stallholders.

305

Now, all Maddie met were a few workmen doing repairs, and a man walking a dog.

Reaching Daisy's café, she was glad to see it open. Of late, Daisy had closed during the week and only opened at weekends.

When the doorbell clanged a voice shouted, 'Sorry, we ain't open for business.'

'It's me, Daisy, and you have your sign saying "open" in the window.'

Daisy's head appeared. Her hair, limp with sweat, hung in tight curls, some stuck to her red face.

'Eeh, Maddie, lass. By, it's grand as it gives me a chance to stop for a cuppa. Turn the sign to "closed", love. I forgot.'

'What are you up to down there?'

'Cleaning. But while I've been doing it, I've had an idea. And you're just the person to tell it to and give advice.'

When they sat down, Daisy said, 'I've had enough of café life as such. I want a change. I'm thinking of a chippy. Folk can eat in if they like but it won't be no fancy service. They can take their chips wrapped in newspaper to a table and sit and eat them, and if they want a mug of tea, they can wait for that at the counter and take that to their table an' all. I'll just need a table clearer and washer-upper and someone to cook and dish up the chips. I'm going to leave it to them to do the work. I just want to be a mum to me kids and a wife to Tom.'

'Sounds wonderful. Where is Lena? I knaw Lottie and Vera are at school, but it's very quiet. Lena's usually clambering over everything.'

'Ma's taking care of her. So, you like my idea?'

'I do. The holidaymakers love their fish and chips. I wish that I could come up with an easier way of life ... though I do have some plans.'

Daisy looked surprised on hearing what had happened at the solicitor's.

'Like you, love, I thought it would go to the kids and you'd be saddled with running it until they were old enough. So, what plans do you have now?'

'Turn it all into one hotel. It'll be so much easier. Knock it through, the staff can be as one, working around the whole hotel instead of two teams, one in each house.'

'And that will make your life easier?'

'It will. There'll only be one kitchen to order for, and one housekeeper's office with cleaning materials in storage for both hotels. Everything will be reduced by half – linen store, guests' sitting room – though we'll have enough room for a games room an' all. One dining room ... And sommat we're allus being asked for – a downstairs bedroom for those who can't make the stairs. It's going to be miles easier overseeing one of everything.'

'You're building your own little empire, love. Tom's so pleased with how Jimmy's bakery is doing.'

'I know, I'm very proud of him – two shops and both doing well. Particularly his one in Lytham. And he's thinking of a bread round and looking at buying a van. It's partly the income from that that will help me to renovate the hotels. I need to chat to Tom to see if he can do some of the work for me.'

'He'll love that. He loves to be busy, and the theatres aren't keeping him going as there's only repairs to the pantomime sets for him to keep an eye on and they'll soon be over.'

They were quiet for a moment and then Daisy surprised her.

'Hark at us – all we talk about is kids and work. We're turning into two old biddies. I ain't done owt girlish for a long time. How about me, you and Bren have a night at the pub where there's a sing-along, eh?'

'Well, that came out of the blue! But you're right, our lives are a bit humdrum at times … All right, why not? Jimmy'll look after Noah.'

'It's time Jimmy had a girl, you knaw. Is there naw one on the horizon?'

'I don't knaw, I don't think so. He never talks of owt like that.'

'That's because he's allus been sweet on you, Maddie, but you treat him like a kid brother. Open your eyes, he's a young handsome man. Aye, and he's got prospects an' all.'

'What? Jimmy! … Me! You daft ha'peth!' Maddie doubled over with laughter. She'd never heard anything so stupid in all her life!

'Well, he's saving himself for someone.'

'It's not me! And it can never be. I couldn't begin to think of Jimmy like that. He's like a brother to me, and I ain't making that mistake again.'

'Look, if not Jimmy, there must be someone out there for you – for both of you. I hate to think of you on your own, Maddie. It's gone on for years now. You just being a mum and caring for Aunt Jean, God rest her soul. Not to mention working your fingers to the bone keeping two boarding houses going. You must be lonely.'

Maddie couldn't answer. The lump in her throat at the truth of this hurt as she tried to swallow her tears.

'Maddie, love, you've just turned thirty-five. Your life is passing you by.'

There was no answer to this.

'Anyroad, let's start with that visit to the pub and make it a regular girls' night out. We can't be classed as floozies now, not at our age!'

Wanting to cry as she'd faced her loneliness head on, when she'd tried to carry on not thinking about it, Maddie cheered at this. 'Well, I wouldn't mind being a floozie, or anything other than a stale old widow!'

'That's the spirit, lass!'

When Jimmy came in, Maddie felt unsettled. The easy way they'd been together had gone for her with what Daisy had said. But she'd decided to have things in the open.

'Had a good day, love?'

'I did, Maddie. I got another customer. These folk coming in buying up the guest 'ouses don't want the work, but it suits me. The owner of one on the prom at St Anne's came in. "E wants meat pies every Saturday and a mixture of fruit pies and custard pies for every evening.'

'Eeh, they don't knaw they're born ... But, Jimmy ... well, are you happy? ... I mean, you've never met anyone after Linda ...'

'She's back.'

'What? Who?'

'Linda. Look, I ain't said anything. Well, yer had enough on yer plate, but in me ma's last letter she told me Linda's husband had been killed about a year ago. It was a shock to me and opened up feelings that I ain't bothered with.'

'So, Linda has contacted you?'

'Yes. She said she got swept off her feet, but she'd never forgotten what we had. That she'd been happy and was devastated that her man had passed, but then me mum told her that I'd never married, and she wondered if we could be friends again.'

'By, that's a turn-up for the books.' Relief flooded Maddie and came out in a huge grin she couldn't control. 'Eeh, Jimmy, I'm happy for you, lad.'

'Ha, I ain't much of a lad now, Maddie, but never stop calling me that . . . Only, well, I ain't said anything because you've lost so much, I don't want yer to think that I'm abandoning you as well.'

'Naw, I couldn't be happier for you. Me and Daisy have been worried that you'd never met anyone and none of us are getting younger.'

'I never wanted anyone but Linda, and when I thought I couldn't have her, well, as yer know, I went into the doldrums for a while. You and Tom rescued me by giving me a purpose in life, so I filled me time with that . . . But me dream's coming true and me Linda is back!'

'But, well . . . I mean, you don't mind that she went off with someone else?'

'Of course I do. It hurts, but I ain't going to spoil me chance of happiness thinking about it. Linda's me life and she's coming back to me, that's all that matters . . . Oh, and she's bringing a family. A lad and a girl. And I'm going to be a dad to them. By all accounts, Dave, who Linda married, was a good bloke. He worked on the docks before the war and went back to his job when he came home. It was an accident on the docks that killed him.'

Suddenly, Maddie realised the implications of what she was hearing. 'So, I'm going to lose you an' all, Jimmy?'

'What? No! You'll never lose me, Maddie. You're a bigger part of me life than me family is . . . Oh, Maddie, I wish you'd find someone. You're beautiful outside and in and it ain't right that you're cooped up in this place for most of your life.'

As earlier, Maddie felt the truth of this last. Not that she thought of herself as a beauty, but that her life seemed humdrum now . . . and yes, lonely. She'd never moved on, in the hope that one day Freddie would find her here where he'd left her, but that had never happened. And now? Was it too late? Was she destined to be for ever on her own?

Shaking the feeling off, Maddie asked, 'So, when is Linda coming?'

'Next week. I was going to ask if she could stay here . . . She can share me room if you've got bookings . . . I mean . . .'

'Well! You ain't letting the grass grow under your feet, are you, Jimmy, lad!'

Jimmy blushed, but then they both burst out laughing.

''Course she can. No doubt you've pushed the two beds in your room together already!'

They laughed again. Then Maddie asked, 'Are her kids coming?'

'No. They're staying with their gran, Linda's mum. Linda said her mum's that pleased about her getting in touch with me and me wanting to see her that she told her the kids could get in the way of us two getting acquainted again. She said her mum loved Dave and misses him but has told her there's no one will ever take the place I had in her heart.'

'Well, it sounds good all round for you, love.'

'Look, Maddie. I know why you stay here building this business; we all advised that at the time that Freddie was taken. But, well, it's time you had some life before it's too late!'

'Ha, you sound like Daisy. Well, you can help with that, lad. Will you sit with Noah tonight? I'm going out with Daisy and Bren.'

'Gladly. And you have a good time. Let your hair down and make it a regular thing too. It'll be good to see you enjoying life again.'

'Ta, Jimmy . . . And I'm so happy for you, love. Though I've sommat to tell you and it may disrupt you for a while . . .'

After her telling of her plans to make the boarding houses into one building, Jimmy said, 'Well, I'm pleased for you, Maddie. This place will be a gold mine for yer. And yet, I wish yer didn't have it. As it's also a millstone around your neck. But with how yer saying it will run, you'll 'ave more time for yourself. And don't worry about me. I've plans to marry me Linda and get us set up in our own home.'

'You mean, things have gone that far?'

'No, not yet, but I'm not going to hang around. I know me Linda will love Blackpool, and her kids will. And I can make a good life for them. As soon as she comes, if things are how they always were between us, I'll ask her to marry me.'

'Eeh, that's grand. Here's me been worrying about you and you're all settled! I'm so happy for you, Jimmy ... Give me a hug, lad!'

The hug was, as always, a brotherly hug that Maddie felt safe within. She didn't know anyone who had a relationship like hers and Jimmy's and she was so glad it wasn't as Daisy had thought and that Jimmy had been thinking of her differently. She wanted nothing to spoil what she and Jimmy had.

She sighed as she came out of the hug. Somehow, between them Daisy and Jimmy had unsettled her. Her life was slipping away as she lived on hope alone. Maybe she should make changes – sell up and seek something different. With this Maddie had let in the despair that Freddie was never coming back, and somehow, she must move on and leave him behind.

The night out at the pub turned out to be a disaster as drunken men – most, Maddie guessed, were married – crowded them and made their evening a misery.

'Eeh, Daisy, let's go. We're being treated like loose women, and I don't like it.'

'You're right, Maddie. Tom'd be appalled at this.'

'And Ray would too. He didn't really want me to come,' Bren admitted. 'He did understand that we need to get

Maddie out. But there just doesn't seem anywhere that women can go to have a good time without a man to protect her.'

'You're right, but ta, both, for trying. Look, why don't we walk along the prom for a bit, eh? Now I'm out, I don't feel like going back yet.'

Bren and Daisy agreed.

Linking arms, they walked along the dimly lit prom. Maddie looked out at the sea – a glittering lake of stars that splashed gently on the sand as it ebbed backwards and forwards in the light of the moon.

Two figures leant on the railing a little way ahead.

As they approached one turned towards them and Maddie could see it was a man of around her own age.

'Excuse me.' He took off his hat. The light caught his face. He was handsome, lean, and his polite approach didn't cause them alarm. Maddie glanced at his companion and had the impression that he was a younger man.

'I wonder if you ladies know of an Albert Road, or Albert Street? Only we've just come in by train and we asked someone and followed their directions this far and then forgot where to go from here! We should have taken a cab, but wanted to see the sea.' He gave an apologetic laugh. Maddie loved the lilt in his voice and guessed he was from Wales. She'd had many Welsh visitors, as well as folk from all over the British Isles, and prided herself on knowing where they came from by hearing their accents.

'Aye, I live there . . .' Maddie answered.

'Mum? Ma . . . ?'

Maddie swivelled round. The light caught the face of the younger man. Maddie gasped. The young man moved towards her, his gait telling her the truth she already knew.

'Freddie! Me Freddie!'

Then he was in her arms – her son, her beautiful son.

An arm came around them both, a strong arm, and the lovely lilt that sounded like music to her ears soothed her. 'I'm so glad we found you. I'm Idris. This is my son, Freddie ... I mean, your son ... We adopted him ... He never forgot you.'

Maddie swallowed hard. 'Ta for bringing him back to me ... Aw, Freddie, Freddie, me little lad.'

'Did you forget me, Ma?'

'Knaw, never, never! You have been with me every waking hour and in me dreams ... Oh, Freddie, there's so much to tell you ... Have you been happy?'

'I have, Ma. Mum and Dad are ... were ... I mean ...'

'My wife, Blodwen, passed away almost two years ago. She adored Freddie as I do. We gave him a good home full of love and happiness and are very proud of him ... Look, it's cold, can we go to yours? Freddie said he thought you and his granny live in a guest house, but he couldn't be sure. We're going to need rooms.'

'Aye, of course ... Eeh, me Freddie, me Freddie ...'

Daisy stepped forward. 'I'm a bit taken aback and ain't said owt, but I'm your Aunty Daisy, Freddie. You won't remember me.'

'I do, Aunt Daisy, I do. You and Ma look a bit different ...'

Freddie wiped his face, taking his glistening tears away.

'Look, I'm sorry. This is all too much for Freddie and he's very tired after the journey and the walk here from the station.'

'We'll get a cab. They're parked up by the North Pier,' Maddie told him, though how she stopped herself from screaming out her joy, she didn't know.

'Yes, I'll need one an' all, Maddie, to get me back to Bispham,' Daisy chipped in. Then she grinned. 'By, love, what a night. First time you've been out in years, and this happens. I'm that happy for you.'

Daisy held out her arms and Maddie went into them. She felt Daisy's sob but couldn't cry herself. Nothing would sink in. Had she really got her Freddie back?

'The North Pier is that way, isn't it, Maddie? ... May I call you, Maddie?'

'Aye, and yes, just a short walk.'

'I'll go. You stay with Freddie. He can't walk any further. Is it just the two cabs we need?'

'That'll be fine,' Bren told Idris. 'I can be dropped off by Daisy's as it will pass my home.'

Then he was gone, and Freddie was looking at her – her Freddie. He truly was here. Maddie held out her arms, instinctively knowing that Freddie had passed the stage that Noah was at of being embarrassed by a hug. He came willingly into them.

Clinging to him, all Maddie could say was, 'Freddie, my Freddie.'

'I have so many questions, Ma.'

'I knaw, lad. But all that matters right now is that you're here ... You are going to stay, aren't you?' A fear clutched

Maddie's heart as she asked this. She couldn't bear to lose him again.

'I want to, but Dad . . . Well, he made me promise that this would just be a visit and that I wouldn't leave him . . .'

'I understand. He must still be grieving for his wife. Even though it seems a good time to us since she died, it won't to him, so he must feel that he can't lose you an' all. We'll work sommat out, don't worry, lad. But whatever happens, we've found each other now and we'll never lose touch with one another again.'

It was then that Freddie said the words that sealed Maddie's happiness. 'I never lost you, Ma. I loved you always.'

'Oh, me son, me son.'

Freddie came out of her hug quicker than she wanted him to.

'I want to tell you while Dad ain't here, but I knew where you were and wanted to contact you many times, but Mum – me adopted mum – well, she wasn't well . . . in her mind, that is. Me and Dad have cared for her . . . She lived in fear that I would leave and begged me not to contact you. I had to promise her that I wouldn't . . . In the end, she – she took her own life . . . It – it broke Dad's heart and I – I felt responsible.'

'Naw, lad!'

As if she hadn't spoken, Freddie continued. 'He always promised me that one day he would help me to find you. But I know that deep down, like you say, he is afraid he'll lose me. I can't . . . You see, Dad has found some peace now.'

'We'll make sure he gets that, lad. And you're never to forget your mum. She'll allus be that to you, just as I'm your ma.'

They clung together then, with Daisy's and Bren's arms encircling them.

Her lovely Freddie had been through the mill, now it was her turn to be there for him and she would be. She'd fight any battle it took to keep him near to her.

CHAPTER TWENTY-TWO

The conversation in the cab was around what their lives were like now. Maddie learnt that Idris had just retired from his accountancy firm and hadn't thought what he'd do in the future other than be there for Freddie.

Maddie found him so easy to talk to and surprised herself by telling him that she'd reached the stage of needing a change.

'The season is so busy, I hardly sleep, but I've liked it that way as it helped me not to think too much ... I've longed for this moment every waking hour of the last ten years.'

'Do you have any other children?'

Maddie clasped Freddie's hand at this question from Idris. 'Yes. Another son.'

Freddie gasped.

'He knaws about you, Freddie, and loves you. I have a picture that was taken by ... by Reggie. You're sitting on me lap. Noah loves it and has it in his room. He kisses you goodnight, even now that he's ten and doesn't like public hugs from me!'

319

'Was Reggie the one who took me on the train and left me on the bench?'

'Ah, here we are ... Freddie, I have so much to tell you. Let's get inside ... Oh, you'll meet Jimmy when we do. Jimmy's a friend. As I say, I've a lot to tell you, love, as you have me.'

'But maybe tomorrow, Maddie?'

'Naw, Idris, I don't think we should sleep another night without the truth being heard. I can tell you have imagined things, and I don't blame you. You only have what that matron told you to go on and she wouldn't have painted a good picture of me.'

'I've always told Dad, and Mum, that you were the best of mums, and it wasn't until Dad ... Well, I can't remember properly, only odd bits. But suddenly, this man seems to appear. He shouted a lot, and I was afraid of him, and yet I remember having fun with him too ... I'm very confused over it all. And the man in the kitchen, he was nice. Was that Jimmy?'

'It was. He was billeted with us as a soldier and came back after the war. He's to be married soon.'

It helped saying this, even though it wasn't relevant to anything. It somehow said, 'He isn't my live-in lover', to Idris, who, Maddie thought, must be making all sorts of assumptions.

As they got out of the car, Maddie thought how mature Freddie was for a lad of sixteen. She wondered how he'd fared over the years with his affliction and hoped nothing bad had ever happened to him. She sighed. There was an atmosphere, and she didn't want there to be. This was the most precious moment in her life. She wanted nothing to spoil it.

Jimmy greeted them with surprise when they opened the front door. He'd always used the guests' sitting room in the winter, and his own room in the summer, as somewhere to relax. Occasionally, she'd asked him downstairs to listen to music on the wireless, or they'd play the gramophone, but mostly they lived independently, and both liked it that way. Jimmy had a large attic room that over the years he'd converted so it had its own kitchenette with a gas ring to boil a kettle or make porridge on. Always they ate supper together in the kitchen before going to their own little snugs.

Through the window, she'd seen him rise as she turned her key, and he was standing ready to greet her by the time the door opened. 'I've the kettle on, luv ... Freddie? Good God ... Freddie!'

Freddie had followed her in. His gait would have told Jimmy who he was, but now in the light of the hall, Maddie could see her Freddie hadn't changed much at all. His mop of dark hair, his lovely Irish eyes – he was Arnie reborn.

'I don't remember you much, Jimmy, sorry, only a little bit.'

'That's all right, you were only a kid. But 'ow did it 'appen that you're here, mate?'

Maddie introduced Jimmy to Idris. Now, in the light of the hallway, she could see Idris was more than handsome. He had a lovely smiley face that dimpled when he grinned, as he was doing now. It was a grin that showed relief as much as anything, as if seeing Jimmy and how they were together, and having Freddie remember him a little, had put his mind at rest. He must have many thoughts on what kind of a person she was and if he was doing right by bringing Freddie back to her.

'Come on in, everyone. We usually sit in the kitchen as my flat is downstairs. Or we can sit in the guests' sitting room as we have no one lodging at the moment.'

'The kitchen, Ma. I can remember it and how it used to smell when you and Granny were cooking ... Is Granny ...?'

'No, love, Granny and Aunt Jean are gone ... I'm sorry, Freddie.'

'I wanted to see me granny. I can't remember her, only that she loved me. I can't remember Aunt Jean. Who was she, Ma?'

'Reggie's ma ... Eeh, Freddie, lad, I tried to find you ... I went to that place where Reggie took you, but you'd been adopted, and they wouldn't tell me who had taken you ... But you've been here by me side in me thoughts and in me heart.'

'Ma ... Why? Was it me leg?'

Freddie's eyes filled with tears, and something else – an accusation.

Shocked, Maddie shook her head. 'Naw, naw! Eeh, me little lad, I'd have protected you, I love you. I – I thought Reggie was taking you out for the day to have fun together ... He wasn't right after the war, it had messed with his head ... Oh, Freddie ... I – I ...'

'Sit down, everyone, this can't be done like this. I'll see to making us all a cup of tea. Take yer coats off and let's sit around the table ... That is if you'd like me to stay, Maddie?'

'Aye, I would, Jimmy. Ta.'

'Maybe if you show us to our room . . . We'd like to share one if possible, and then we can talk in the morning? It's late and we're all tired.'

This from Idris was said in a kindly voice.

Maddie felt the tears stinging her eyes. He was right, and yet she could feel that Freddie needed to know now, and she needed to tell him – but how would it all sound?

She looked over at her son and felt a gulf between them that hadn't been there. 'Freddie, I can explain. It ain't right what happened. Losing you took a piece of me away.'

'But you had another son.'

This again came out as an accusation.

Maddie sank down into the chair next to her. 'Freddie, I – I didn't have him to replace you. No one can ever do that.'

'Son, I think this is all too much. You're tired. Let's take our hot drink upstairs, eh?'

'No. Dad, I have to know. I – I couldn't sleep.'

Freddie looked strangled by the emotions fighting for prominence inside him. Maddie could feel his turmoil and knew his pain – she shared it. And she knew that she must tell him everything, as sordid as it may all sound, and let her son make up his mind on whether she was as guilty as Reggie – so often she'd felt she was.

'Ma, this Reggie you speak of, is he me dad? The man that took me to the orphanage?'

'He did do that, but . . . Eeh, Freddie, don't judge me . . . Try to understand how it was.'

'Well, if we are going to do this, let's all sit down and allow Maddie to tell the story from the beginning as it's sounding to me like it isn't straightforward.'

'A good idea, Idris. But are you sure, Maddie? That you want to tell everything?'

'I do, Jimmy. It's the only fair way. I've lived a lie for long enough. Now Ma Jean has gone, I want it all out in the open. Freddie deserves the truth.'

Once Maddie started, she found it impossible to control her tears as she told of how she and Reggie grew up together, loved one another, thought it a love to take them through to the end of their lives, and how that was encouraged by their mothers.

'But then the war came, and Reggie chose to go ... he changed ... He wanted ... he wanted more than I wanted to give as I'd changed an' all. I'd grown out of the childhood love we'd had. I still loved him, but not in the way that I should, to become his wife ... I can't explain ...'

Telling of the night they almost made love washed shame over Maddie. How could she make it sound anything but sordid? But for Freddie's sake she did just call it a drunken entanglement.

'We were going to marry. Despite my doubts, I was going to go through with everything. I couldn't break everyone's heart by not doing so ... But then when the soldiers were billeted here ...'

The story unfolded, the truth – the wedding not going ahead, her love for Arnie, his death, her ma forcing her to say that Reggie was Freddie's father.

'But Reggie returned, sick in his mind. He didn't accept you, Freddie. He couldn't believe that what we shared had made a child. He tried, and he did love you, but he couldn't live with you around to remind him of his doubts and suspicions. He became violent. He forced me to ... Well, ours wasn't a good marriage. But then, he seemed to change and try to be a proper da to you. I could see that he did love you and had no idea what he planned to do. I didn't realise that all he was doing was gaining my confidence in him. Making me believe that he wanted to be a proper dad until his moment came to get rid of you ... He made a special seat for you in the cart that was pulled by his horse. It seemed such a kind thing to do. I had no idea ... Then came the day that he took you with him. You were laughing your head off as Reggie drove you away ... That was the last time I saw you ... But I came after you – Bren ... do you remember, Bren and Edna?'

'Yes, I've never forgotten Edna ... Though her ma ... was that her on the prom with Aunt Daisy?'

'It was ... Eeh, Freddie, while I was carrying you, Bren turned up looking for Arnie ... She ... she and Arnie were brought up in the orphanage where Reggie took you ... She'd told us – me and Reggie – about it ... I took a chance and went there after Reggie was arrested and detained, thinking it was possible that ... But you were gone ... Oh, Freddie, there's one more thing ... This is all so much for you to take in and sounds a sordid tale, but ... Bren was looking for Arnie, me lovely Arnie, as he is da to Edna an' all.'

There was a silence. Maddie hung her head as she did, and she saw Freddie was staring ahead. But then, his hand reached out and took her hand.

Maddie hardly dared move.

'So, it's all this Arnie's fault!'

'Naw! Naw, lad, don't think that. Let me explain ...'

At the end of her telling, Freddie looked at her and held her gaze with eyes that were Arnie's eyes. 'So, Bren forgives him?'

'She doesn't think of it like that. She loved him as a brother, but they just got silly one night, things happened. They both felt ashamed. But when me and Arnie ... I loved him, Freddie, I loved him with all my heart. He was the loveliest, funniest man in the world. He looked just like you. If he hadn't been killed, we would have married. We'd have told Reggie once the war was over. If I'd have told him before ... maybe I should have done ... but ... I knew he would do something stupid ... By, lad, I made some wrong decisions on the face of it, but you had to live me life to understand why – the pressure I was under from the expectations of mine and Reggie's mas, and Reggie himself. The war, and how it changed everyone, the sudden deployment that took Reggie away before we could wed – then what he suffered. He was a hero in many ways, helping the other lads through it all. But there was one lad not much older than you and though Reggie tried to help him over his fear, he ran off. When he was captured, Reggie was ordered to be in the shooting party. It turned his mind ...'

After telling of how Reggie finally killed himself, Maddie felt drained. 'I'm sorry ...'

Jimmy went to get up, but Idris beat him to it. His arm came around her. The feeling this gave to her made her feel safe.

'Oh, Maddie, Maddie, you've been through so much. Freddie's back now. I won't take him away from you again.' He reached out with his other arm and enclosed Freddie in his embrace. 'Son, it's been a lot for you to absorb, you'll have a lot of questions, but I think your ma could do with a hug.'

And then they were holding each other, their sobs racking their bodies.

'My Freddie, my Freddie, I want it all not to have happened ... Only, I'll never regret having you and Noah.'

'It's all right, Ma, I'm back ... I love you, Ma.'

Those words penetrated Maddie's sorrow and brought light back into her world. She clung to her son.

Out of the blue, Idris said, 'I don't know about anyone else, but I'm hungry!'

Jimmy, who'd hardly spoken, jumped up. 'Well, that's my forte. I'm a baker and can rustle something up in no time.'

Not realising it before, Maddie too felt her tummy rumbling as Jimmy deftly swirled eggs around in a pan of hot fat.

'You cut some slices off that loaf, Idris, and, Freddie, you see that fork hanging up there? Get it down and stick the slices of bread on it and toast them in front of the fire, eh? Maddie, you lay the table, and we'll be sitting down to a feast in no time.'

Grateful to Jimmy for getting everyone busy, Maddie wiped her face, managed a smile at Freddie and set to.

The door to her flat opened and a sleepy Noah putting his head around it made her hold her breath. Noah's eyes opened in surprise as he looked from one to the other of them.

'You must be Noah!' Freddie jumped up from the stool he'd been sitting on toasting bread, put the fork down on the table and went to Noah. 'I'm your big brother, Freddie.'

Noah grinned. 'When did you come back?'

'While you were asleep. Come and help me toast the bread. This lot's hungry, so we've a mound to do.'

'Have you hurt your leg?'

'It hurts all the time, Noah. I was born with it.'

'Oh? It makes you walk funny.'

Maddie held her breath. She wanted to scream out at Noah not to say any more, but Freddie said, 'Aye, and I'm going to need you, Noah. You're going to have to help me at times. Will you mind doing that?'

'Naw. I'll do owt for you. I've dreamt of you coming home one day. Ma's allus sad, now she'll be happy. But where did you come from and how did you get so big? I thought you were a little boy?'

They chatted away as if they were the only ones in the room. From their conversation, Maddie learned that Freddie had been brought up in Welshpool just over the border of England and Wales. And that he'd suffered at the hands of others, as Noah asked questions that only children would.

'I bet the kids at school called you names. Did that hurt you?'

'They did, and aye, it does, but it's behind me now and I'm going to college, and I hope the kids there will be more understanding.'

'College! That's for clever dicks!'

'Well, I ain't that clever, but Dad says it'll be best for me as I can't do a lot of physical work. Though I'd love to work with animals. I love animals.'

'I do. I want a dog, but Ma says it'd be upset by all the visitors we have. I get fed up with visitors as Ma's allus busy.'

To Maddie, the conversation was a revelation. Her two sons discussing life as they toasted bread and piled it onto a plate – both animal lovers, and Noah hating how he had to live as second fiddle to visitors . . . Something had to change, and it would!

'Maybe not for much longer, Noah. I've been thinking about making changes, not just those you've heard me talk about, but big changes – selling the boarding houses and doing something different.'

Noah's mouth dropped open. 'You mean living somewhere were there's a house to ourselves and not lots of people staying in it?'

'I mean exactly that.'

They were all seated and eating their eggs on toast when the talk turned to this once more. 'Where would you like to live, Maddie? Would it still be in Blackpool?'

'Not in the town, Idris, but in the countryside that surrounds us. It's very beautiful.'

'I wish there was somewhere that people like me could visit and be accepted.'

'What do you mean, Freddie? You are accepted, you shouldn't have to hide away.'

The more Idris spoke, the more Maddie felt drawn to him. He was one of the nicest men she'd met.

'I know, Dad, but sometimes, even if it's just for a two-week holiday, it'd be nice to be somewhere where I was with others who were like me and I could just be the person I am, not me with a club foot that drags behind me and makes me look a fool – someone for others to laugh at.'

This shot a pain through Maddie's heart. She'd never wanted that for her Freddie, but it seemed he'd suffered badly from it.

'Like a holiday place, you mean, run especially for those who have some difficulties?'

'Yes. And when I go to the exercise class Dad set up for me, I see some much worse than me – blind, deaf, twisted bodies. And when we get talking, all suffer the same things. It's not just the bullying . . . It's not being able to fit in . . . I mean, look at this place, Ma. I'll have difficulty getting up and down the stairs. I even struggled getting in the front door with the steps. And I remember you carrying me down the steps to our flat and me crawling up.'

'I had thought of that. Well, when me idea earlier was to knock these two houses into one, I thought to have downstairs bedrooms.' She told them how she now owned the one next door as well. 'But me heart ain't in it now. I want a change and what you're talking about seems just the thing . . . Maybe a farm with barns that could become accommodation?'

Maddie was warming to her theme and didn't notice Noah yawning until Jimmy said, 'All great dreams, Maddie, but I think we can talk about them tomorrow. I'll get Noah back to his bed while you show Idris and Freddie to their room, then I'll clean up this mess.'

330

'You're right, Jimmy. I don't knaw where all that came from, but I'm whacked out now.'

'We can find our room, can't we, Freddie? Just give us the number and point us in its direction.'

Maddie did this, gave Freddie a huge hug and then went with Noah. 'Come on. Good job there's naw school tomorrow, lad.'

With Noah settled, Maddie sat in her living room going over all that had happened. Was Freddie really here? Her Freddie, just standing on the prom as if he'd been there for ever! It all seemed unbelievable now.

Getting up, she went to the window. The moon lit up her small yard, making it dreamlike with the trellis now painted white and glistening with frost. Suddenly, she wanted to be out there.

Grabbing her coat and scarf, Maddie wrapped up against the cold and then picked up a cushion before stepping outside. Her cheeks tingled with the cold air, but she didn't care. She wanted to be free of the building that now felt like a prison to her. She wanted to grab Noah and Freddie and run and run as far away from here as she could. She smiled then at this notion as poor Freddie couldn't run … But should she be thinking on him as 'poor Freddie'? He didn't give the impression that he wanted to be thought of like that. Just that he wanted things so that he could manage them. Be independent. She could come up with something, couldn't she?

Plonking the cushion on the bench, Maddie sat down. Her breath looked like smoke as it plumed out. She shivered. But then a sound caught her attention. It was her door opening. Ready to tell Noah to go back to bed, she was shocked when Idris came through.

'The door from the kitchen wasn't locked, and I figured I had to come down to your flat to get to this outside space. I hope I'm not intruding. I saw you from the bedroom window.' He pointed up at the window above. 'May I join you?'

'Aye, but eeh, you might want to grab a cushion, or your bum will stick to the bench.'

Idris laughed. She liked his laugh as much as his accent.

When he was sat next to her, he said, 'It's not as cold as I thought. You're quite sheltered here.'

'I like it. It's like a small haven. Not that I'm taken with being out here on a freezing night like this, but ... well, me mind won't let me body rest.'

'I know just what you mean ... I – I ... Oh, it doesn't matter. I'm sorry. I'll leave you in peace.'

Maddie caught hold of his arm. 'No, stay. Or we can go inside. It'd be nice to have a chat. Just us. There're things you must want to ask me.'

'Not ask but say. I want to say I'm sorry that I didn't stand up to Blodwen and come and find you before. Or that I didn't come sooner after we lost her, but I didn't know how to. I – I had to recover from losing her a long time before as her mind ... well ...'

'I knaw, Freddie told me when you went for a cab. I'm so sorry, Idris.'

'No, I'm sorry. You and Freddie shouldn't have been apart for this long. I feel very guilty. Your love for him shines from you and we deprived you of his love and him of yours. I shouldn't have carried that on after ...'

332

'Aw, naw. You did what you thought best. Freddie obviously loves you and has been happy. I couldn't ask for more after what Reggie did.'

'He sounds like a rotter. I get the impression you were beaten . . . That hurts me.'

Maddie didn't understand why it should but she felt the need to defend Reggie.

'Reggie was the loveliest man until the war came. It was all a tragedy. I shouldn't have been unfaithful to him, but I found true love with Arnie. Not just friendship, or sisterly love, as I had with Reggie.'

'You're a lovely person, Maddie. I truly am sorry that I added to all you were going through.'

'You did what you thought right, Idris. Please don't have these thoughts. We all do what we think right given the circumstances we're in, and can all say we shouldn't have done this or that. Freddie is home now . . . I mean, well, of course you'll want to take him back with you.'

Maddie's throat tightened at this thought, but she had no tears left in her to shed even though her heart was breaking at possibly having to say goodbye to Freddie again.

Her body shivered involuntarily.

'You're cold. May I hold you, or would you rather go inside?'

Maddie couldn't answer. Suddenly she wanted nothing more in the world than to be held by Idris. She turned and looked into his eyes. They held the gaze for a moment, and then their bodies swayed towards each other. Idris's arms came around her and Maddie had the sensation that she was home. Home after years and years of loneliness.

Idris helped her to her feet. They were so close she could feel the warmth of his breath on her cheek. His face came closer. Maddie opened her lips to accept his and then she was lost. Lost in a whirl of feelings she'd only known once before. Lost in a world that held hope for her – that would take away the sometimes desolate feeling that it was her against the world.

These arms holding her would save her. This mouth kissing hers would bring love to her life, as promised by the crescendo of beautiful feelings rushing through her veins.

When he took his lips from hers, Maddie felt bereft.

'Maddie. Oh, Maddie, I've found you.'

He didn't have to explain. Maddie knew what it was to find someone, even when you weren't looking. She knew that her soulmate was with her and that life would change now. No more humdrum existence. It was time for her to live again.

CHAPTER TWENTY-THREE

Taking her hand, he led her inside.

Once he'd closed the door, Idris took her in his arms again. It was where she belonged.

For a fleeting moment she thought of Arnie. She saw his smiling face, knew he approved, and this completed her. Her Freddie was home, and he'd brought with him someone for her to love and to love her, and Arnie, she knew, was happy for her.

She didn't resist when Idris began to undo her blouse. It felt so right, so what she wanted and needed.

His kisses on her neck and then on her breasts took her breath away. Taking his hand this time, Maddie led him to her room. There they scrambled like desperate animals as they took clothing off each other, caressed, kissed, exclaimed the beauty they perceived in each other.

And then they were naked on the bed, entwined, kissing, wanting that moment and yet delaying it. Speaking of love, of finding themselves and each other. And then it happened. Idris was making her his, his urgent pounding of her giving her feelings she'd forgotten. But had she felt them before?

Had this wondrous giving and taking really happened with Arnie? Now, she wasn't so sure as it was all so new, so beautiful, so fulfilling. She cried out with the joy of it, and gave her all. She thrilled at the joy Idris was expressing, at his kisses and, most of all, at his declaration of his love for her.

When they lay back on the pillows, their hands clenched, Idris said, 'I feel as though I have found myself in you, Maddie. I know we only just met, but I know I love you and want to spend my life with you.'

Maddie turned on her side and gazed at him. She loved his hazel eyes, his greying temples in otherwise dark hair, his straight nose, his perfectly formed lips and his clean-shaven, slightly tanned, soft-to-the-touch skin.

'Aw, Idris, I love you an' all. You've completed me, made me whole.'

'That's a lovely thing to say. I had thought that my life was over years ago. I loved Blodwen, but not in the way I should, not for a long time. She became introverted. She was sick in her mind. I cared for her with compassion and love but wasn't in love with her for a very long time. What I feel for you is being in love.'

'I have only ever known the one love. Arnie. It was for such a short time, and our child was taken from me.'

'But he is back now, and we can help him to adjust to this news of me and you, and to his new life in Blackpool.'

'You're not taking him back to Wales?'

Idris leant over and kissed her nose. 'No, I want to stay here with you. I want to sell up and build something new with you. A place where all Freddies will feel at home and not feel different or be bullied.'

'Has Freddie suffered much bullying?'

'Yes, Maddie. I protected him as much as I could, but I couldn't be with him twenty-four hours a day. Mind, it wasn't as bad as it could have been. Freddie is well loved wherever he goes and so there was always someone willing to stand up for him.'

Maddie shivered.

'You're cold, darling. Let's pull the covers over us . . . I say us, but may I stay with you? I never want to leave you.'

'By, I'd trip you up if you went to leave and pull you along by your leg till you're back with me.'

'Ha! I don't think I'll try it then – the indignity!'

They laughed together as they snuggled under the blankets and entwined their bodies. Maddie couldn't believe that all this was happening after a disastrous night out. But she had no time to ponder it as Idris kissed her lips and once more took her to a place she never wanted to leave as he made love to her again.

'Ma! Eeh, Ma, you've got Idris in your bed!'

Maddie opened her eyes. Her cheeks flamed as she looked up at an indignant Noah.

Idris stirred. His arm came around her. He looked up at Noah. 'You were asleep so I couldn't ask your permission, but I love your ma and wanted to stay with her.'

'Aw, well, if you love her . . . But it don't feel right. Not you being in her bed!'

'Sorry, mate, but you might have to get used to it as I'm going to ask your ma to marry me.'

'Ma!'

Maddie had to giggle. Idris, who she hadn't yet known for twenty-four hours wanted to marry her, and she knew for certain that she wanted to marry him! It was madness.

'It's not sommat to laugh at, Ma.'

'Oh, it is, Noah. It's the happiest day of me life, lad. I knaw it'll take a bit of getting used to, but better you start now as I love Idris, and I am going to marry him.'

Idris bent over her and kissed her lips. It was a quick kiss but the brushing of his naked body against hers thrilled her.

'So, do we have your permission, Noah? We will ask Freddie as well.'

'I suppose so, but I'll still be your best boy, won't I, Ma?'

'Mmm, do you think you could share that title, lad? Only our Freddie's home at last and we need him to feel the love we have for him, don't we?'

'Will Freddie live with us?'

To Maddie's relief, this was said in an eager, anticipated way. 'He will. We're going be a proper family.'

'We are, and if you'll have me, Noah, I'll be your dad too.'

To Maddie, it was such a relief when Noah grinned. Her boys had to absorb so much. Noah was just a ten-year-old who'd never met his half-brother until a few hours ago and now was faced with his mother – the only person he had of his own – getting married and his brother coming to live with him!

'Give us a hug, love.'

Noah grinned again, then bent over her. His 'Ma, you ain't got your nightie on!' made Maddie blush again.

She heard Idris's stifled giggle, which made matters worse. But deciding to make light of it as if it happened every day that her son found her naked in bed with a virtual stranger, who was also naked, she told Noah, 'Well, run along and get dressed and we'll get up and make your breakfast. Not a word of this to anyone, mind. It's our secret till we tell Freddie, then we'll tell the world as a family.'

Getting up and getting dressed wasn't what Idris had in mind. He curled around her, kissing every part of her that he could reach until she almost begged him to take her.

Not wanting to ever part, it took a great effort for Idris to get out of bed. He kept getting so far and then rolling back in and kissing her again. Never had Maddie felt so happy, so loved, so needed.

At last, Idris sat on the side of the bed and pulled on his trousers.

He'd visited the bathroom in the early hours so knew where it was.

'I promise I won't be long and then the bathroom's all yours while I go and get Freddie downstairs. Is it possible to breakfast together in private so we can chat to the boys?'

'Yes, Jimmy will have left for the bakery and there's no staff expected today. They only come in a couple of times a week during the winter. Though one is more than staff and has been with me for many years. You'll love her, she's called Mabel.'

'I'll hear all about her later, darling. Must dash!'

Maddie watched his beautiful body as he sprinted across the bedroom, grabbing his clothes as he went, and couldn't take in that such a wonderful person could love her . . . and after only meeting her a few hours ago. It all beggared belief.

As they sat around the kitchen table, Maddie couldn't take her eyes off Freddie, noticing things she'd missed, like the fluffy growth of hair on his face, not yet ready to be shaved, but nodding to that time when he would be a man.

He looked from one to the other as if someone could make sense of all that was happening.

'I know it's hard to believe, but, son, it's as if me and Maddie – your ma – were always meant to be together. We just sat outside talking, it became too cold, we stood, and then, well, I knew I couldn't leave her.'

'And I knew the same, lad. Eeh, it's like you were taken from me, but now you've come back you've me brought happiness untold with you – having you back and falling in love with your dad.'

'Does it happen that quickly?'

'It does. It's something you know in an instant. You don't always act upon it, but you know it. Me and your ma, well, we're not youngsters any more, and saw no reason to hold back for a second. Do you mind, Freddie?'

'No! I'm like Noah, I just can't fathom it. We come to Blackpool, you meet me ma, we come back here and we're all like strangers, then we go to bed, and I wake up to be told by Noah that you two are naked in bed together!'

'Noah! I told you not to say!'

Noah giggled. 'I had to! I wanted Freddie to wake up so that we could be brothers, and brothers don't have any secrets from each other, Ma.'

Freddie warmed Maddie's heart then as he ruffled Noah's hair, and the pair grinned at each other. But her cheeks glowed with how it all must look to her sons, especially after her revelation yesterday about Freddie's real father. For a moment Maddie felt dirty, as if she was a loose woman who would jump into bed naked with any man, but then Idris took hold of her hand and smiled before turning to the boys and telling them, 'No matter how quickly you fall in love, it's something beautiful to be cherished and with me and your ma falling in love, it makes us a family.'

Both boys grinned at this. It was Noah who asked, 'Will you and Freddie live here with us?'

Even though it had only been mentioned a couple of times, Maddie knew they wouldn't. This place stifled her. The two boarding houses were her ma's and Aunt Jean's dream, not hers, and she'd worked hours and hours to keep it alive for them. Now she wanted her own dream – to move away. To live life at a gentler pace with her family. Where that would be she didn't know but she wanted it to fulfil Freddie's dream of somewhere those afflicted in some way could come and enjoy being with others who understood.

The timing seemed so right too as Jimmy would be moving out and making his own life with his Linda and would no longer be dependent on her for a home or companionship. Everything was slotting into place for her to change her life.

As she thought this, Idris was answering Noah, 'For a while, but not too long. We're all going to find somewhere different to live together. Your ma and me have a lot to discuss. We've only just found each other and all we know is that we want never to part. We haven't had time to plan.'

He looked at her. Maddie's heart fluttered. Had it really happened? The rebound feelings in her told her it had. She'd given herself completely to this man and didn't regret any of it. All she could see was happiness lying ahead for her and her sons and Idris – her family.

'I think the first thing to arrange is a celebration where I can announce to me friends the changes in me life.'

'That sounds wonderful. I'd like to meet your friends. And Freddie can catch up with Edna.'

'Aye, and I'll ask Bren to tell her about her relationship to you, Freddie. Then everything will be out in the open – a good place to start our new life together.'

'I still can't understand it all. I came looking for you, Ma, and I've found a brother and sister I didn't know I had! And I'm nervous as though I knew Edna, and we loved each other as kids, will she still like me now that we're all grown-up?'

'Of course she will. Everyone likes you, Freddie.'

'Ha, you've got to say that, you're me dad!'

They all giggled at that, then Noah said, 'I like you, Freddie, and Edna likes me, so I knaw she'll like you.'

'Well, if you think so, Noah, I'm sure it's so.'

Once more, Freddie ruffed Noah's hair. He blushed and looked adoringly up at Freddie. To Maddie, it was a moment she wanted to remember for ever.

With it being out of season, Maddie was able to gather everyone together for Sunday, one day away.

By the time it arrived, she felt as though she and Idris had lived together for ever. A bed had been brought down to the flat for Freddie, and though not ideal, he managed well going up and down the stairs on his bottom, showing Maddie that he was as resilient as ever.

It was Sunday morning when Mabel met Idris and fell in love with him on first sight, blushing and telling him he was so handsome and how, if she was a few years younger, Maddie wouldn't have stood a chance! Idris had laughed out loud at this and given Mabel the biggest hug.

Freddie took to Mabel as soon as he met her. She told him how she'd brought him into the world. 'You were such a lovely babby and it broke me heart when that Reggie took you away.' Freddie told her that he wished he could remember her.

'Don't worry, lad, bits will come back to you. You've concentrated on remembering your ma, and that's a lot for the little chap you were.'

Mabel went on to tell Freddie how his dad shared a spot with her little Arnie in the cemetery. 'We should go up there one day, Freddie. There's a bus from the end of the road.' She told him too, how they had first met. 'Your ma, Daisy and Bren were putting daffodils on me Arnie's grave. It's been for your da as well as me little Arnie ever since.'

'That's nice, Mabel. We'll take the bus to it one day.'

Mabel grinned as if she'd made a great triumph. To Maddie, it was just so lovely how she'd taken to everyone, and they'd all taken to her. Mabel was such a big part of her life.

When the others arrived, Maddie had a fit of shyness. How was she going to tell them all that had happened? What would they think of her?

But as soon as they'd had a cup of tea, Daisy said, 'There's sommat going on here, love, you can't hide it from me. You and Idris seem very close.'

'Oh, we are, Daisy . . . I'm in love – I mean, we're in love and we're going to marry!'

'Flipping 'eck! Marry! Eeh, Maddie, I didn't expect that, but I'm so glad . . . so very glad. It's grand news, lass.'

Daisy flung her arms around her, and Maddie could feel all the love Daisy had for her in the hug. A love that had lasted over twenty years and had been her saviour.

'Tell me all about it, Maddie . . . every detail . . . Well, you don't have to tell me you've slept together, I can see that. You've a glow about you.'

'I'll tell everyone together, Daisy. Though I was going to tell you that much before I announced it. You're like a sister to me, and I wouldn't want you finding out with everyone else.'

They gave each other another hug. Then as she came out of it, Maddie took a deep breath as she looked around the guests' sitting room. The noise filling it was a happy sound of little ones playing as Daisy's and Bren's broods enjoyed being together, and of the men chatting with Idris, as well as Mabel and Bren in conversation, and Noah, Freddie and Edna chatting and laughing in a corner. Edna had clung on to Freddie, unable to believe he was back and was taller than her, when in her mind he'd always been a five-year-old.

Clapping her hands, Maddie brought the room to silence. Idris left Tom and Ray and rushed to her side.

'Everyone, there's such a lot to tell you. As you know, my Freddie has returned to me.' A loud cheer went up, followed by clapping and everyone patting Freddie on the back, telling him they'd never forgotten him, and were so happy he'd come home. Freddie beamed.

'Now, I don't want to shock you . . . I know I have many times in the past, but the happiness of having me Freddie home is doubled as it has brought me and Idris together and we have fallen in love!'

A silence was followed by Jimmy shouting, 'That makes the very best news even better! About time, Maddie. You deserve all the happiness in the world.'

Everyone got over their shock at this and began to cheer, hug her and Idris, and call for a toast.

'I'll get that sherry we had left over after Christmas, Maddie.'

'Ta, Jimmy.' As she said this, she turned back to the room of faces eagerly looking at her. 'Before the toast, I want to tell you all me plans . . . I'm going to put me two boarding houses up for sale.' Again, there was a silence. This time it held an air of suspense as Daisy said, 'You ain't going to move to Wales, are you, Maddie?'

'Naw, me and Idris are going to look for a farm or such in the Lancashire countryside. We want to set up a holiday retreat for those who are like Freddie, coping with stuff that makes them feel apart from others. It's Freddie's idea. But now the idea is in me, it's sommat I want to do more than owt else.'

345

'More than marrying me?'

Idris's mock hurt made them all laugh and the tension in the room eased. The sherry was served by Jimmy and he gave a toast that moved Maddie to tears.

'As your friends, Maddie, who luv yer, we couldn't be more pleased for yer. We've all worried about you and prayed for the day that Freddie came home, and yer found 'appiness on a personal level. For them both to 'appen together 'as made our day. Welcome, Idris. We're 'appy as Larry to meet you, and thank you for taking care of our Freddie and bringing 'im back to us safely. To Maddie and Idris and to 'aving our Freddie 'ome.'

Everyone raised their glasses. To Maddie, it was as if it was her wedding day. Her happiness was almost complete.

She looked up at Idris with tears of joy clouding her vision. One plopped onto her cheek as he bent and kissed her to the cheers of her friends and the little ones, whose excitement, even though they probably couldn't understand what was going on, filled the air.

Jimmy put the gramophone on then, and they all danced. Even Freddie got up with Edna and, leaning heavily on her, managed a circuit of the room. His old grin was back. The one Maddie had etched in her heart. The grin that everyone knew, but that she had kept precious for the day she saw it again. Today was that day — a day that truly brought Freddie back to her, and a day that marked the beginning of a new life for her — for all her family.

CHAPTER TWENTY-FOUR

1933

Maddie stood with Daisy and Bren and the mums who were staying with her on the farm this week. They were in a field they'd marked out as a football pitch watching Noah kicking a ball about with a lad who had difficulty in learning the simplest things, and two who were physically disabled. They were adorable lads, loving, kind and willing to work on the farm, especially with the horses, sheep and cows.

Daisy and Bren's children, except Edna, had joined in and gave squeals of delight every time they touched the ball. Edna stood next to her dad, linking arms with him. Tall and elegant, and with beautiful Irish eyes, Edna loved Freddie. They were the perfect brother and sister. Caring and loving, and sharing many interests, especially visiting the cinema. They both loved to see the latest films.

Lately they had been talking of their futures. It seemed to Maddie that the sky was the limit for kids who had parents who could pay for their needs – Edna was going to college in Manchester soon. She wanted to be a nurse. And Freddie had found he had a talent for languages – he'd started with French when a master who came to teach at his college turned out to be a Frenchman. Freddie was soon annoying them by asking for everything in French! Now he was learning German too. Maddie's pride in him bubbled over at these thoughts. It seemed he'd been dealt a raw deal with his club foot, but had been gifted with a brain that could soak up knowledge.

And not only that, but he had a lovely way with him that helped him through life. It warmed Maddie's heart to see how all the children and visitors had a special love for Freddie and how the children wanted to please him.

Maddie looked over at him. His grin lit up his face as he called out instructions from where he was propped on his crutch in goal. There were loud protests when he saved a goal with it, as it was longer than an arm.

Idris letting out a laugh brought Maddie's attention to him. He shrugged. 'They're all using what they can to win the game. They can't blame Freddie for using what he has.'

Maddie smiled. She'd never been happier in her life as she was now, married to Idris, and living on the farm they both loved.

They had found and bought it together within weeks of being married.

It stood at the bottom of Highfield Road, in Blackpool's South Shore area.

They'd been lucky to get it open for the back end of their first summer, but it hadn't taken much to adapt the three cottages that stood on their land as accommodation for families. Each had a downstairs bedroom and washroom for easy access for a child with physical difficulties.

A lot of the work had been done by Tom, who oversaw contractors as well as doing so much himself.

Next, they planned to begin work on those barns they didn't need for the animals, to make them into accommodation too. They hoped to eventually be able to open to around five families at a time.

'What are you dreaming about, Maddie? You're supposed to be watching the game, Noah just scored!'

'Ha, I saw it. I'm sure Freddie let the ball pass by him – brotherly favouritism . . . Aw, Daisy, love, I was just thinking what a lovely life I have now, compared to what I did have, and how I love all the children who come to stay and to see the peace of mind on their parents' faces as their child is in a place of acceptance.'

'Aye, and it's good for our kids an' all. They don't see anything wrong with anyone since coming here, they just see other boys and girls.'

'I knaw. They won't be bullies to the less fortunate because of this place and what they are learning.'

Maddie looked over at Noah, almost thirteen years old and born of beatings that had led to the rape of her. He had a lot of the good side of his dad in him and this helped her to remember Reggie as he had been and forgive him for what she now saw as something he couldn't help.

She'd met many women who had been hurt by damaged men, men who'd been used in a bloody war by the powers that be. They'd tasted the mud, trodden over the dead

349

bodies that were sunken into it; they'd shot, or witnessed young boys being shot by order; they'd lost mates and felt the guilt of coming home alive, and in one piece – one piece bodily, that was. Not in mind. Many who hadn't died had been destroyed on the fields of war that were now fields of poppies – blood-red poppies.

In this moment of reflection, Maddie knew she'd long since forgiven her own deceit too, knowing that she'd had no choice. And with this came a sense of being grateful for it all, as everything had led to her meeting her Idris. Her beloved Idris.

Idris's arm came around her and he pulled her close. 'Thank you for giving me this gift of a wonderful family, my darling.'

Maddie looked up at him, saw his love and pride in his eyes.

'By, Idris, it's you that's the gift. You've given me love. You cared for me Freddie, and then you brought him back to me, and now you're a wonderful da to both me sons.'

Idris looked around him. 'No one's looking, darling.' With this, he bent and kissed her lips. Maddie giggled.

'Now you know I have other things up my sleeve for you.'

Her giggle turned to a loud laugh. Idris could be very naughty, but she loved his naughtiness. She loved everything about him. He had given her her life back. Yes, it was hard work at times as they toiled on the farm together, but there was a sense of freedom to what they did – no being at the beck and call of others, no set routines, no drudgery. And she now had what she loved the most – the chance to help others without having to be a slave to them.

The families who came to stay looked after themselves. The children helped with the chores on the farm and loved doing so, and Mabel, who now lived in a little cottage near to the main house, oversaw the part-time staff who did the domestic side of keeping the cottages clean.

Part of the family, Mabel was like a grandmother to Maddie's boys and to all the children. Maddie had never seen her so happy.

Looking over at her now, Maddie knew a love surge through her for all that Mabel had done for her: her support through the birth of her children, and with looking after her ma and Ma Jean, and how she shared her son's little plot in the cemetery so that Maddie had somewhere to honour and remember Arnie.

This morning Mabel had worked hard helping Jimmy, who had a rare day off from his bakery, to put together a huge picnic for after the game.

Jimmy stood with his Linda on the other side of the pitch. They were married now, and Maddie was happy that he was happy, though she didn't quite feel that she and Linda had bonded.

Though she got on like a house on fire with his ma, when they finally met at Jimmy and Linda's wedding. It was as if they'd known each other for ever.

Now, she wondered about Linda. Why had she chosen to stand on the other side of the pitch? It was as if she didn't want to be friends with them.

As if her thoughts had transmitted to Jimmy, he looked up and called, 'Shall we set the picnic up, Maddie?'

'Aye, Jimmy,' she called back over to him. 'They've had

fifteen minutes' play now and we said the winner would be the one who scored the most goals in twenty minutes of play. They'll all be hungry.'

He put up his hand, but then Linda surprised them all by hollering, 'Come on, Bernard! One more goal, mate, and you'll win!' to one of the boys who was physically challenged.

Linda waved frantically at her son, Ian. Ian responded by kicking the ball to Bernard and then taking his hand and running after it with him. When they were near to the goal, Linda shouted, 'Shoot, Bernard.'

The look of determination on Bernard's face had them all holding their breath. Maddie tried to catch Freddie's eye to will him to let the goal go in. When it did, Linda went crazy, jumping up and down with joy. Before shouting, 'Blow the whistle, Maddie, it's time!'

Maddie had never seen this side of her. This caring, and joyous side. She began to feel guilty and wondered if she'd given Linda a proper chance.

Blowing the whistle to signal full time, Maddie ran to Linda who was already cuddling Bernard.

'Eeh, Linda, lass, that were a lovely thing to do.'

Linda turned. 'I love kids, Maddie, and wish I could spend all me time 'ere.'

'You can come as often as you like, love. We're allus grateful for another pair of hands.'

'Thanks, I will. I don't know about the animals, though, they scare me.'

Bernard piped up. 'I'd look after you, Aunty Linda. Especially now you helped me to win.'

His face beamed with a lovely smile. He had no concept that he would be going home with his ma in a few days' time.

'Next time you come, mate, I'll be looking for yer to 'elp me near the animals then, eh?'

Bernard hugged Linda once more.

Maddie had a feeling that she'd taken Linda wrongly and that maybe she'd had a difficult job to try to fit in with her, Daisy and Bren, who were tight-knit friends. Making her mind up to change that, she said, 'Aw, that's a done deal then, Linda, lass. When can you start, so that you're here every time Bernard comes to stay?'

'Right now! And me lads will love it if they can come too . . . By the way, I like to be called Lyn. It's only this dafty' – she nodded her head at Jimmy – 'who still calls me Linda!'

Jimmy grinned.

Maddie linked arms with Linda. 'Come over to where we are, love. You can present the cup to Bernard for me.'

It was Lyn's turn to beam now, and it was a smile that changed her face from an expression that always seemed closed and withdrawn to one of a friendly, kind woman.

With the ceremony of presenting the cup over, Linda suddenly appeared at home with Bren and Daisy as they chatted with Bernard's mum.

'Well done, darling. Linda only needed to feel accepted. And you've made Jimmy's day! As I was helping him bring his feast out, he was like a kid. He said, "Me Linda'll settle 'ere now. She's 'ad a tough time fitting in."'

Maddie laughed at Idris's take on a cockney accent in his Welsh lilt. But she felt her guilt once more at not making more of an effort with Lyn. She caught hold of Jimmy's arm as he went by. 'It looks like a feast set for a king, lad.'

'Well, it's a special celebration. Two-year anniversary of opening the farm to visitors.'

Maddie laughed. 'Eeh, lad, we'd better get everyone eating it, it all looks delicious.'

'Thanks for what you just did, Maddie. Linda's felt as though she hadn't fitted in and many a time wanted to go back to London. I think she'll stay now. I hated it when she just visited.'

'I should have made allowances a long time ago, love. I'm sorry.'

'Well, it hasn't been easy for you, getting this place set up, and settling into married life – I know what that's like. Yer do things your way for years, then yer've this other one to consider.'

'Aye, and for you, taking on kids as well. But Linda's boys are lovely, they seem to have fitted in.'

'They 'ave now. They had a job at first, especially at school. It'll 'elp them coming here with Linda.'

'It's grand here, ain't it, Jimmy?' Daisy had come up to them. Her cheeks were rosy from the sun that was beaming down on them.

'It is, and I reckon everyone's sorted and 'appy now.'

As he went off with his tray of scones, Daisy said, 'Eeh, lass, I don't knaw how you did it, but you broke the layer of ice covering Lyn. She ain't a bad stick after all.'

They looked over to where everyone was eating, chatting and laughing and Maddie felt that everything was right with her world.

As Daisy left her side and went to rescue one of her brood, who was about to take a sip of Bren's sherry, Maddie's heart swelled watching her friends, and the families who'd found a haven with her.

Idris, relaxed and happy-looking, joined her.

'We did it, Maddie, darling. Two years of hard work, and we're now providing a wonderful retreat for children suffering any difficulties.'

'No, you did it, Idris. You brought me happiness enough for me to see a different future and to grasp it. I was realising the dreams of Ma and Ma Jean, whilst not really living. For years, all I had to keep me going was hope. Now I am a mother whose hope has been fulfilled. Ta, love.'

His arms encircled her waist, and she leant against him. Looking up to the sky, she thought she saw her ma smiling down on her and her heart brimmed with joy.

'Hope is a wonderful thing. You restored mine, Maddie. And you made me see that it's all right to love again, whilst never forgetting your first love. I hope that my Blodwen and your Arnie are happy – as happy as we are, my darling.'

'That's a good hope, Idris. It's one that has promise. You made my hope more than that, you made it a reality.'

A short story,
by Maggie Mason

Blackpool, 1940

Twenty-five-year-old Freddie grabbed the wheels of his
wheelchair and drove himself at a pace towards Edna, her
beautiful smile warming the love he had for her, but his
heart heavy as he looked at her uniform.

She truly was going to nurse in the war zones of France.
He prayed she'd be safe.

As he came up to her, she hugged him, leaning over so
that he could hold her.

'I'm so excited, Freddie.'

'And I'm jealous. I feel I'm not doing my bit.'

'But you *are*, Freddie. Your work as an interpreter and
translator at the Foreign Office *is* doing your bit. Anyway,
I'll feel safer with you not out there fighting. And remember, nurses are cared for by all nations. They won't attack
when they see the red cross on our vehicles and uniforms.'

'That's something, at least. But, Edna, you'll write often,
won't you?'

'I will, love.'

'I wish you hadn't chosen a career instead of what girls normally do: get married and have kids!'

'Don't you dare, Freddie! All of that's being challenged; we women can carry our own amongst you men now, whether you like it or not!'

Freddie grinned at her. He loved goading her, and on the subject of women doing men's work it was easy to do.

'I've time for all of that, anyway. You never know, I might meet a handsome doctor who'll sweep me off me feet! And what about you? It's time you were thinking of settling down, not just me!'

'Ha, well, I can't dream like that. No one would take me on – disabled, and a lot of trouble.'

'You can say that last again. But you're wrong, Freddie . . . Look, I'm going to tell you sommat, but you're not to say owt.'

'You always become all Lancashire when you have a secret, it's so funny! Come on then, tell me what it is.'

'Jeannie.'

'Jeannie? She's not a secret!'

Freddie thought about the lovely Jeannie, who always set his heart racing. She was a friend of Edna's; they'd trained together to become nurses. When Jeannie came home with Edna to stay, as she often did, they all got on well, but he'd never shown how much he felt for her.

'No. She's not a secret, but how she feels about you is. She adores you, Freddie, but she's asked me never to say as she doesn't think you would look at her twice because of her glasses.'

'Oh, Edna. I would! I don't see her glasses, only her lovely brown eyes. I – I fell in love with her the first time I met her, but didn't think she'd look at me. A man in a wheelchair isn't much of a prospect.'

'You daft pair! Why didn't you say? It's a bit late as me and Jeannie are about to leave for France!'

'Maybe it's best we didn't.'

'No, it isn't, love. Jeannie's already at the station, and now, Ma and Aunt Maddie and Uncle Idris have arrived, but I'll see you get a moment together before me and Jeannie board the train. Promise me you'll tell her how you feel, Freddie? At least you can write to one another. And it'll give Jeannie sommat to look forward to in the future.'

Not having time to answer, Freddie was suddenly surrounded by his kissing parents and Aunt Bren!

Ray was on duty at the station when they went inside Blackpool North. He greeted them as they walked. He clasped Edna's shoulders and looked lovingly into her face. 'I've been given leave for an hour to wave you off, me little lass … Eeh, I wish you weren't going, but I'm that proud of you.'

'Ta, Dad.' Ray enclosed Edna in a hug.

Freddie swallowed hard. He was going to miss Edna so much. Not that they'd spent a lot of their time together in the last couple of years, with him away in London working in a government office. But he'd always known she was there, either at her workplace in Blackpool Victoria or at home with Aunt Bren and Uncle Ray. And they spent wonderful times together when he came home at weekends, or she came to see him to stay in his flat with him. Now, life would change so much.

Edna would be across the sea and in danger. The war was escalating. There was even talk of evacuation as British and French troops were being pushed back towards Dunkirk. His heart was heavy with fear for his beloved brother Noah, and Jack, Aunt Bren's lad of the same age. They'd gone to France weeks ago to fight – but what he couldn't get his head around was, knowing the dire situation, why the government were allowing these young nurses to go into that same danger. But then, they were needed, and yes, they did have a safety guarantee. Would that mean anything, though, when the fighting intensified?

His heart was heavy with the burden of having to accept that there was nothing he could do. His knowledge was top secret information. But it hurt him to know of it and be so helpless to do anything.

Shaking these thoughts from him, Freddie realised he'd allowed them to overshadow what Edna had just told him: could it be possible that Jeannie could love him? He'd dreamt so often of her; he'd cried tears of frustration thinking that he had no chance of finding love, and especially not with Jeannie.

But then she was there, looking down at him as everyone had to since his foot had worsened, and his ankle had weakened, meaning that now he had to spend his time in a wheelchair.

Her voice was soft as she asked, 'Did you want to see me, Freddie?'

Freddie swallowed hard. His nerves jangled. But there was no time for small talk. If he was going to let Jeannie know his feelings, he just had to say it.

'I – I wanted to tell you that I love you … I'm in love with you, Jeannie.'

In one movement, Jeannie was on her haunches in front of him. Her eyes filled with tears. 'Oh, Freddie, I love you too. And have done from the moment I first set eyes on you.'

He took hold of the hand she'd placed on his chair. 'You're the most beautiful woman I've ever known, Jeannie. I don't want you to go, we've so much to catch up on.'

'If only I'd known earlier, I wouldn't have volunteered, but Freddie, we can write to each other and maybe the war won't last long.'

Freddie looked into her large brown eyes and felt himself being pulled into them. How was it possible he hadn't thought she could love him when it all seemed so natural now?

'I will write, and wait every day for your letters to me … May I kiss you, Jeannie?'

Her face came nearer to him, her sweet breath fanned his cheeks, and then her lips were on his and his world changed from one that held no hope of being loved by Jeannie, to a bright glow of knowing he was.

When they parted, he caught the astonished look on his ma's face and the grin on his dad's and wanted to shout, *Yes! I'm in love!*

But Edna was calling out, 'The train has pulled into the station, Jeannie, we have to hurry. Come on, Freddie, we must get onto the platform!'

Within minutes Jeannie and Edna were being taken away from them, their laughing faces hanging out of the window as they waved their goodbyes.

Freddie's heart lay heavy in his chest as the train disappeared and he lowered his arm.

'Eeh, Freddie, you kept that quiet!'

Freddie didn't trust himself to speak. His ma had an incredulous expression. His dad's arm came around him.

'I'm sorry, you've had to part like that, son. You never said you and Jeannie . . .'

'It only just happened, Dad. We knew but hadn't told each other . . . and now she's gone.'

Ma's hand came into his. No one had words for such a moment. And that's all it had been – a few seconds in his life. But Freddie knew it had changed him for ever.

As Bren turned towards Maddie, Maddie held out her arms. She knew Bren's pain. Now forty-five, their sons – Noah, a strapping lad of just twenty, and Bren's Jack of the same age – had left for France weeks ago, and now Bren was seeing Edna off too. Saying goodbye to your children knowing they were going towards the danger of war wrenched at your heart.

Daisy's arms came around them both. For now, she was lucky as she still had her Lottie at home, though there was talk of all young women playing their part by doing the jobs the men were leaving and that could take her away. But her other two, Vera and Lena, were too young to be considered for any wartime work, as was Bren's Alfred.

'Eeh, me lasses, dry your tears. They'll all be home before we knaw it.'

Daisy's words didn't comfort.

'Let's all go to Jimmy's, eh? They're in the same boat with Linda's two lads gone, and Jimmy's siblings an' all, but they allus manage to cheer everyone up.'

Maddie knew that Daisy loved to go to her old café that she'd long ago sold to Jimmy.

It had surprised them all, though, when Jimmy had taken to running it with Linda, preferring that to baking bread and cakes in his many shops – work now done by employees.

Jimmy had gone up and up in the world and Maddie and Tom had reaped the benefit of their investment in him.

As Idris helped Freddie into the back seat of their car, Maddie was torn by wanting to thank God for making her Freddie as he was, as it meant he wouldn't ever go, and tearing a strip off God for taking Noah, Edna and Jack and all those fighting the horrors of war.

Though it wasn't really God's fault but the horrible Hitler's. With this, Maddie prayed instead, *Please keep them all safe and bring them back to us.*

Twenty-year-old Noah lay in the sand next to Jack, willing it to be their turn to be called to a boat. Bullets whistled above them. Planes dived, spitting shells around them as they inched their way closer to the sea.

Jack whispered, 'By, we're almost there, Noah. I reckon we'll be boarding the next one.'

Noah grinned. 'Aye, soon be in sunny Blackpool, eh?'

But then a pain seared his back. He stared at Jack. 'I've been hit ...'

Blackness enveloped him and then an empty void took him.

★　　★　　★

Edna looked up from where she was administering to a wounded soldier in a tent not far from Dunkirk beach. 'Jack! Oh, God, Jack, is that Noah?'

Jack nodded. Tears spilt from his eyes, making silvery lines in the dirt covering his face.

Rushing to his side, Edna could see that lovely Noah had gone. Her heart split in two. Aunt Maddie's face swam before her. 'Oh, Jack, naw, naw!'

Her anguish went into the sound of marching feet. German soldiers appeared at the door.

'Fall down, Jack, quick!'

As he did, Noah's body landed at Edna's feet.

Her voice shook as she screamed out, 'I need a doctor, quick!'

Pierre came running to her side. Edna indicated Jack on the floor and whispered urgently, 'This is my brother, Jack. He isn't injured, but our friend, who he brought in, is dead. We must save Jack from the Germans!'

'Stretcher!' Pierre's commanding voice summoned two orderlies. 'Get this man into the operating theatre now!'

'Come, Edna, I will need your assistance.'

Edna glanced at the Germans. Had they seen Jack carrying a body in? She prayed they hadn't and watched as they went from bed to bed examining the occupants. One of them, using the butt of his gun, stabbed at a soldier with a wounded arm. 'You, get up. Get up!'

This happened several times. Jeannie challenged them. 'What are you doing? These soldiers are wounded and not fit to travel!'

'Out of my way. We know that you are harbouring soldiers, they are our prisoners of war!'

Edna could not let the despair she felt delay her, she had to save Jack. She hurried after Pierre.

Already, Pierre had Jack on the operating table, unconscious, and was making an incision in his stomach. Edna couldn't believe her eyes, but knew this was the only way to save her beloved brother.

It was midnight when they left the tent. Jack was stitched up but sore, though wasn't complaining as he walked with Edna and Pierre to Pierre's house. The beret, a symbol of a Frenchman that Pierre had lent him, sat at an angle on his head, and a doctor's coat covered his underwear.

'You will stay at my house for now. We will figure out how to get you home, but you must not as much as put your head out of the door but stay in the cellar. It is the only way I can keep you safe.'

'But the boats are still ferrying men off. Couldn't I take my chances and go to the beach? I've seen medical staff tending to the injured at night, I could pretend to be one of them.'

Although Edna didn't want to agree to this, she knew it was a good plan and much safer than staying here in what was surely going to be occupied France.

At home in Blackpool, Maddie stared at the telegram. 'I can't open it, I can't. Naw, naw, not me Noah!'

Strong arms held her. Idris's beloved soft Welsh lilt soothed her. 'I have you, my darling.'

365

The words screamed at her: *Killed in action*. Her body crumpled into Idris. Her heart broke.

A few months later, the sirens pierced Freddie's ears as he wheeled his chair towards the underground station.

'We'll carry yer down, mate, don't worry.'

Two men came up to him, lifted him, and ran down the many steps with him to the sound of screaming aircraft and bombs exploding.

In the dim light he saw the men who had carried him were getting on in years but looked strong. 'Thank you ... I was on my way home ... Blackpool ... my brother ... he was killed.'

Unable to control himself, Freddie burst into tears. Kindly, big-bosomed women hugged him, and someone gave him a cup of tea.

Why he'd said that as if it had just happened, Freddie didn't know as here it was late September and Noah had been killed in May. But it seemed that the hell of London burning had triggered the reality of losing Noah.

When he'd calmed, he pulled Jeannie's letter from his pocket. Full of love. Full of sorrow for Noah's passing and telling him that she and Edna were okay and how pleased Edna was that Jack had made it home. She hoped he looked on his scar as his medal!

How had their lives descended into this hell?

Once in Blackpool and back on the farm, Jack found a different world. It was as if the war had nothing to do with here. Still there was tranquillity, though soldiers were there too, wounded soldiers who needed a sanctuary to help them to recover. They found it on the farm with the kids that still came, and with the animals.

Ma hugged him as if she would never let him go. Dad had tears in his eyes as he said, 'You're safe, my son, you're safe.'

Blackpool, 1946

Safe was how they all felt as they stood together in the hall full of soldiers and their families, almost six years later. They were here to collect Noah's medal from the captain of his regiment.

Ma turned to Jack. 'You go up with Freddie, Jack. You should be the ones to collect Noah's medal, you both did so much to help us to win this war. Noah would be proud of you.'

Freddie looked up at Jeannie. Jeannie nodded and encouraged him forward. Her hand came onto his. The ring he'd bought her glinted on her finger. Soon they were to be married, a double wedding with Edna and Pierre. He liked Pierre very much and was glad that he'd decided to settle in Blackpool with Edna and set up a GP practice once he had his papers in order.

He looked around at his beloved family – not all related, but all loved dearly. Aunty Daisy and Uncle Tom, Aunty Bren with Uncle Ray, and all their children, now growing up fast. Uncle Jimmy and Aunt Linda, and her boys who had come safely home. And his beloved Mabel, who he called Gran.

Each had a smile for him, giving him their approval of Ma sending him with Jack to collect Noah's medal.

How he missed Noah. Kind, gentle Noah. He closed his eyes and saw him as he was when he'd first met him, when he finally came home after being abandoned by Reggie – a lovely, funny ten-year-old. Now he was gone but would never be forgotten.

It was two weeks later and two days until their wedding day that Freddie and Jeannie sat outside looking up at the moon. Freddie took hold of Jeannie's hand. 'I want to call our first son Noah, darling. Is that all right?'

'It is, it's lovely, and he will be so happy to have the name of his courageous uncle . . . Now, what are we going to call the other ten?'

'Ten! Ha, are you after a football team?'

'I am, Freddie. I want eleven children, please.'

'Well, we'd better get started then.'

Jeannie sat on his knee. Their kisses held a promise of a better tomorrow. A tomorrow that would bring them happiness. A tomorrow when they would become one.

Maddie thought her heart would burst with the love she had for her son as he turned his wheelchair and looked towards his bride, the lovely Jeannie.

Willing herself not to let her mind go to places that hurt her heart, she looked up at her adored Idris. Yes, there was pain still. Pain in loss. But the happiness she had won her emotions over at that moment, and she slipped her hand in his.

As she too turned towards Jeannie's approach, she caught sight of Daisy. Daisy gave her a little wave.

They'd come through so much and always Daisy had been by her side. She allowed herself a smile now as she thought of their current crisis – the dreaded change of life! Them and Bren fanning themselves when everyone else shivered around them. Would it ever come to an end? Daisy was at it now, wafting Tom's huge hanky as if it would save her life.

Maddie giggled at her. Daisy pulled a face and dabbed at her cheeks.

Once the beautiful service was over and the hugging and kissing of Freddie and Jeannie was done, Maddie headed for Daisy.

Their lives had changed beyond recognition. Daisy was about to become a granny, as Lottie, who'd married last year, was heavily pregnant, and Maddie was looking forward to the same for her and hoped it wouldn't be too long. The future held such promise.

'Eeh, Daisy, lass, give us a hug.'

'It'll be a Sweaty-Betty one, lass, but come here.'

Laughing, the two women clung together. Theirs had sometimes been a rocky and sad journey, but now it was a happy one and they looked towards a future of many little ones to love and protect from all they themselves had been through.

A LETTER FROM MAGGIE

Dear Reader,

Thank you for choosing my book; I hope you enjoyed it as much as I enjoyed writing it. And as this is a standalone – my first for a long time – I hope the short story at the end gives that satisfaction of knowing what happened next without the need for further books in the series.

I very much want to concentrate on standalone novels now. It almost feels like a new concept to me, however I do love concluding a story instead of leaving threads open for the next book. I may change my mind in the future, but for now, all my novels will by standalone – no more waiting months to find out what happened to this or that character.

I expect you are wondering about the dedication in this book, and Idris – the real man my character is named after.

Well, Idris came into my story after I put a competition on my Facebook page. Those who entered could nominate their father or grandfather to be honoured by having a character named after him and a dedication in the book.

Idris's daughter, Glendys, won the competition and it was lovely to be able to fit my Idris into the story; to have him bring Maddie happiness and peace after all she'd been through, and to think of him having brought up Freddie and given him a happy life too.

Glendys's father, Idris, was born in 1925, the youngest of nine children. He was in the merchant navy during WWII. He met and married his wife Muriel in 1952. Together, they had five children. He worked for Welsh Water as a superintendent until he retired in 1984.

I loved the insight to the man that Glendys gave when she said that although there wasn't a lot of money left over after bills etc., there was always enough for an ice cream on the occasional day out, giving his children happy memories of their childhood. A lovely hard-working man who cared for his family and came to that wonderful time of having grandchildren, it's lovely to know that Idris had a long and happy life as a good family man. I hope you all see that in my Idris, and can think of the lovely man he was named after – Idris Jones – Glendys's dad.

Much love to you all and may I ask that if you enjoyed *A Mother's Hope*, you spare a moment to leave me a review on Amazon, or any of the book platforms you belong to on social media. It would be very much appreciated.

To interact with me personally, why not visit my website where you can go to 'contact' and email me, or follow me on social media platforms:

Website: www.authormarywood.com

Facebook: www.facebook.com/MaryWoodAuthor

Instagram: mary.wood.7796420

TikTok: marywood616

Twitter/X: @Authormarywood

Bluesky: @authormarywood.bsky.social

Much love,
Maggie xxx

ACKNOWLEDGEMENTS

My heartfelt thanks:

To all the team at Sphere, without whose support and encouragement, I would never have got through this novel, though it is dear to my heart.

To my editor throughout the process of writing this book, Rebecca Roy – now no longer at Sphere. It was quite a journey. I wish you so much love and happiness in your future.

To my new and lovely editor, Elisha Lundin, for taking over from Rebecca in such a seamless way and supporting me through the edits and onwards in getting a synopsis ready for my next novel.

To Frances Rooney and her team in the editing department for bringing out the best of my novel with their insightful edits and suggestions.

And special thanks to James, my adored son, who helps me with every stage in the process of writing my books; his love and support is invaluable to me and his talent in spotting proofreading edits makes my work sing off the page. And too for the love, support and encouragement of my beautiful and adored daughters, Julie, Christine and Rachel, and my grandchildren and great grandchildren. Always encouraging me on and showing pride in all I do, you are all a joy to me. I love you all very much.

And as always, my wider family of Olleys and Woods, you all help me to climb my mountains. Thank you.